LESLEY J NICKELL

SONS

— OF —

YORK

The second volume of 'Sprigs of Broom'

LESLEY J NICKELL

SONS
OF
YORK

The second volume of 'Sprigs of Broom'

MEREO
Cirencester

Mereo Books

1A The Wool Market Dyer Street Cirencester Gloucestershire GL7 2PR
An imprint of Memoirs Publishing www.mereobooks.com

SONS of YORK: 978-1-86151-460-8

Copyright ©2015

Cover design - Ray Lipscombe

The address for Memoirs Publishing Group Limited can be found at
www.memoirspublishing.com

The Memoirs Publishing Group Ltd Reg. No. 7834348

The Memoirs Publishing Group supports both The Forest Stewardship Council® (FSC®)
and the PEFC® leading international forest-certification organisations. Our books carrying
both the FSC label and the PEFC® and are printed on FSC®-certified paper. FSC® is the
only forest-certification scheme supported by the leading environmental organisations
including Greenpeace. Our paper procurement policy can be found at
www.memoirspublishing.com/environment

Typeset in 19/13pt Garamond
by Wiltshire Associates Publisher Services Ltd.
Printed and bound in Great Britain by Printondemand-Worldwide, Peterborough PE2 XD

CONTENTS

PROLOGUE - FAMILY

PART 1 – THE KING

PART 2 – DIVIDED LOYALTIES

PART 3 – THE PRINCES

PART 4 – THE PRETENDER

EPILOGUE - FREEDOM

PROLOGUE

FAMILY

The boys were leaping and wriggling about her, like a litter of excited puppies. Even Tom, who was thirteen and almost a married man, had forgotten the dignity of an eldest son and was squealing with the rest.

'Look, Janet, look, there's father!' He pointed with conviction into the milling mass of colour outside the Priory gatehouse.

'I can't see!' wailed Dick. 'Lift me up, Janet, I want to see.' Janet hoisted her little brother into her arms, and he craned his neck to pick out the parents who had said goodbye to him only half an hour before.

Thomas Wrangwysh was not always so popular with his family. But he had just been elected to the exclusive Trinity Guild, and he had been in an unusually good humour since the beginning of the Corpus Christi holiday. And it was Janet's fourteenth birthday. She was touched that they had remembered her, in the pre-dawn bustle of such an important morning.

'We shall make this a feast for you to remember in London, lass,' her father had said, beaming at his firstborn and kissing her heartily.

And now the sun was rising over Holy Trinity Priory and promising perfect weather for the procession. The chaos of clerics and burgesses and grave wives, gesticulating and shouting instructions and discreetly preening themselves, was gradually sorting itself out. Crosses and banners, which had been waving about with daunting abandon, were upraised and formed a vivid pattern. The shifting kaleidoscope of costume shook down into blocks of colour, each livery behind its banner, between the sombre habits of the religious orders. Suddenly everything was quiet, and the chaplains of the Corpus Christi Guild bore the Host from the Priory into its place of honour. At an obscure signal the monks broke raggedly into their chanting, and the procession moved off down Micklegate.

As the Host passed them, enclosed in its precious beryl vase, Janet and the others knelt in the fresh rushes and crossed themselves. All the way down the street the watchers were doing the same; dipping to their knees and then rising to gape and cheer at the secular part of the parade. The pungency of incense, the mingled chanting and cheering, the bright wave sweeping past between the curtseying crowds and decorated houses: the assault on her senses almost lifted Janet off the ground. To keep her balance, she glanced at her companions.

The four elder boys were intent on the spectacle, eyes and mouths wide, quivering in anticipation of their parents' approach. Baby Robert had caught the mood too and was bouncing up and down in Bessie's arms.

The fraternities and mysteries of York unrolled slowly before them, in their best silks and furred gowns. Bessie's father and mother swam by behind the blue-and-silver banner of the Tallow Chandlers Company and were given a special cheer by the Wrangwysh children. Then the Trinity banner swayed into sight and there they were.

Resplendent in an apple-green gown worked by his womenfolk, Thomas drew more eyes than the Master of the Guild. With his bulk and his energy, he dominated all those near him. Borne along on this flood of personality, his small wife had caught some of his vigour. She leant lightly on his arm, and carried her seven months' pregnancy almost with grace. There was for once a healthy flush in her cheeks. They came abreast of the handsome modern house hung with flowers and the best embroidered bed covers, and turned to smile at the group of young people outside. Tom and Will and Dick threw up their caps and yelled, Robert clapped his hands, Bessie sniffed sentimentally. Janet felt the hand of her third brother John grip hers, and they alone stood silent, sharing a pride which did not need to be shouted aloud.

Much to her surprise, Janet was given the seat of honour at the Corpus Christi banquet. She protested faintly when her father gestured her to sit beside him, but even in generosity he was not to be gainsaid.

'By Christmas you'll be a married woman and sitting at the head of your own table,' Thomas said. 'Let us do you honour while you're still a Wrangwysh.' The others were nodding and thumping the table and shouting approval, so she submitted. For the rest of the evening she was toasted, spoiled, and treated like the Mayoress at least.

The place at her father's side was in fact nothing new for Janet. Alison Wrangwysh was not strong enough to shoulder all the responsibility of running a large merchant household, and for several years her only daughter had been much more than a helpmeet. She was capable and efficient and her father trusted her.

That was why, although she had been betrothed from the age of ten, Thomas would not part with her into the care of her future family. He needed her too much. But now Bessie had come to live with them, and when she was Tom's wife she would take Janet's place. Since the spring Janet had been initiating the older girl into the mysteries of housekeeping and incidentally found a firm friend.

Fat Bessie Lylley was simpering across the table at her prospective bridegroom. Though she was only three years older than Tom, with her amply-developed figure she might have belonged to a different generation from the dark lad who sat opposite. 'Greasy Bessie' was her nickname, and not only because of Master Lylley's trade. It was good to have someone as predictable as she was in the explosive atmosphere of Thomas's house.

Today, however, he was neither frightening his sons nor thrashing his apprentices. High spirits could run unchecked. Young Will convulsed them with laughter at his wickedly accurate mimicry of some of the dignitaries in the procession; he was particularly good at hitting off Richard York, prosperous woolman and long-time rival of Master

Wrangwysh. They told jokes and riddles and stories, and played their favourite games.

Long after the midsummer daylight had deepened in the high windows, the hall was loud with merriment. When little Dick was asleep against his mother's chair, and John's eyes were big and dark with the effort of keeping awake, they asked Janet to sing. She fetched her lute and led her family in old catches and ballads, until Thomas called a halt. His wife was wilting, and the boys must be up at five to go back to school.

While Bessie was undressing, a process that took an incredible length of time, Janet sat in the window of their room. It overlooked Micklegate, which was scattered with the debris of two days' celebration, all frozen blue in the radiance of a great white moon. Within the stained glass of the Priory church at the other side of the street, a warmer light glimmered where the brothers were saying their final office of the day.

Bessie's deliberate movements behind her and the faint echo of the monks' plainsong, were part of the silence. It was balm to Janet after the strident junketings which had begun before sunrise, but it brought also a gentle mood of melancholy.

Her last Corpus Christi in York. By next summer she would be the wife of a stranger, in a great strange town where the accents were flat and the people unfriendly and cold. Janet shivered, and her eyes filled with tears. She would never love anywhere as she loved York. Her father had kept his promise. This day would always stand for York, for her home and her family, blazed into her memory by the benevolent sun.

'Mistress Wrangwysh has stood up to it very well,' Bessie was saying, punctuating the words with regular thumps. Janet returned to the present, where her room-mate was setting straight the gaudy coverlet, embroidered with a red dragon by Janet when she was nine. It had hung out of the window all day, the gaping leer of the monster's jaws adding to the festive appearance of the house. Quite how Bessie managed to make so much noise with such a simple task, Janet could not tell.

'I suppose so,' she answered doubtfully. 'She looked sprightly enough this morning, but the day has been very long for her.'

The next baby was due in August, and Alison had only just survived Robert's birth. A miscarriage last year had further weakened her. Often Janet had seen her father's eyes on her, bewildered and helpless, as he never was with anyone else. Thomas Wrangwysh could always arrange everything, and bend anybody to his vigorous and persuasive will. He could not persuade his delicate wife into health.

'Why does he go on giving her babies?' asked Bessie.

Perhaps Janet should have been offended by the other girl's bluntness, but she was not. This evening she was very wise and compassionate.

'Because he loves her. What else could he do?'

'Never mind,' said Bessie comfortably, and the bed groaned as she climbed into it. 'If the summer isn't too hot, she may have an easy lying-in.'

Janet snuffed the candle and climbed in beside her.

PART I
THE KING

CHAPTER ONE

She did not have an easy lying-in. Following the glorious June weather came a heatwave, when the River Ouse ran very low, and the flies swarmed over the dry mud of its banks. People in the hovels by the Foss marshes were dying of fever, and even in the well-to-do areas of York the citizens were suffering from the heat. Business was at a standstill in the middle of the day; meat went bad, milk almost came sour from the cow, and Bessie was so red and sweaty that it was a wonder she did not melt away into a pool of candle-grease.

Alison Wrangwysh lost colour as the heat increased. All the health she had regained in the spring left her. Her time came, and passed, and still she grew, though her face became thinner and thinner. At the end of August, the midwife began dosing her with strange potions to induce the birth. If the child remained in her womb for much longer, it would kill them both.

The children were sent to stay with the Lylleys, and the house was prepared as if for a siege. An idle male in a household of busy women, Thomas could not concentrate. He annoyed a good customer by losing his temper at an unreasonable request; he had the kitchen boy beaten for forgetting to rub down a horse. The house was silent and sweltering, but the midwife would allow no windows open in Alison's chamber, because it would let in bad air. With no energy to talk, and no heart either, the inmates crept about their duties as if she were already dead. Alison lay in her darkened room, in acute pain from the simples administered by the midwife. Bessie and Janet took it in turn to sit with her, to bathe her with water which was warm as soon as it was drawn from the well, and to change her drenched sheets.

After an intolerable wait of two days, the midwife moved in, and the two girls became part of her campaigning army. At the last birth Janet had been sent out at the end, although she could still hear the screams. This time there were no screams. Alison was only strong enough to whimper. Banished from the confinement chamber, Thomas had stopped pacing and stood staring out of the window, seeing nothing. Janet did not know what kept her going. She was cold all over, despite the heat, as if her heart had congealed into sickening ice. Working doggedly to ease her mother's pain, she tried not to think and was glad she could not feel.

There was blood everywhere, and now Alison was quite still, moaning very quietly. A little object was detached from the rest of the blood, and when it was washed it was a baby, a girl, and that too was only stirring slightly. The cook-maid, white and retching, was sent scurrying off for the priest who was waiting below. Unresisting and limp, Alison was washed and laid in clean linen before her husband and the priest were admitted. The baby was baptised with her mother's name, but Thomas did not look at his infant daughter. He could not take his eyes from the shadow of a woman on the bed, a corpse already though still breathing shallowly. As the holy water touched her, the child summoned the energy for a thin wail, then was silent again. Janet led her father away, and he went like a lamb. With the bustle over, Bessie was in noisy tears. There was nothing to do but wait for them to die.

The baby lasted for only a few hours. Alison lingered on to the next day, so that her frightened little boys could file past her bed and kneel for her to flutter her hand in blessing. She was conscious, but too weak to speak or move. In the morning the priest came again and gave her extreme unction, in the presence of Thomas, Janet and an awed Tom, who was trying very hard to swallow his sobs. Her husband had hardly left her side. On rising late from an exhausted night's sleep, Janet found him still by the bed, unshaven and drawn from his vigil. Almost unable to recognise her vital father, Janet tried to persuade him away to eat and sleep. But though he seemed pleased for her to join in his watching, he would not go.

'There will be time for that later,' he said. They sat for hours side by side, never speaking, while Alison held on to life by a frail thread of breath. In the end it was Janet who went for sustenance she did not want, ordered out gently but insistently by Thomas. Her mother died while she was in the kitchen, forcing herself to take some bread and rancid butter.

Mistress Wrangwysh's lying-in was followed by her laying-out. It had to be done quickly because of the fear of decomposition in the heatwave. There was no time to arrange an elaborate funeral, but the Trinity Guild took care of everything. Alison was buried with her small namesake in the Guild chapel of St Crux, and the chaplains sung her requiem. After a night of solitary grief, Thomas took up his work with increased vigour. No one could have guessed, as he briskly knocked down the sellers' prices in the cloth-market, that he had just lost his wife.

A messenger was despatched to London, to the house of Philip Evershed, to announce that the wedding of Janet Wrangwysh to his son Giles would have to be postponed for a few months, in reverence to the memory of her mother.

Life went on very much as before. Janet was mistress of the house, as she had been since she was ten, though now in name as well as fact. Her father relied heavily on her, and she was his housekeeper, hostess, and sometimes his deputy as well, with Bessie as her good-natured second-in-command. At Christmas there was no need for Thomas to invite Janet to sit beside him, it was her accustomed place.

Her marriage had been deferred, by degrees, until it was fixed to coincide with Tom's the following May. By then Tom would be fourteen; they could have a splendid double wedding, and Master Wrangwysh would save some expense into the bargain. Janet wasted no regrets on the delay. She had seen little of her fiancé, and what she had seen had inspired her with no great impatience to be his wife. Of course Giles Evershed was a highly advantageous match, as she had agreed when she signed the contract four years ago. The only child of a prosperous mercer who had started his career from a sheep-farm in Sussex and made good, he would inherit an expanding business and a large house in London. But proud as she was to be carrying the banner of York into the city which was its greatest rival, Janet could not look forward to leaving behind all she knew and loved.

So she made the most of her reprieve, paid particular attention to her father's business methods, and at night continued her education by gossiping with Bessie. Or rather, Bessie gossiped, and she listened. Her friend was one of a teaming crowd of Lylley progeny, chief among whom, in Bessie's eyes at least, was her brother Bart. Bart was an inexhaustible well of unusual information, collected from heaven knew where, and spread and amplified by his many brothers and sisters. His particular strength lay in his detailed knowledge of the intimacies which went on between men and women. All these incredible tales were faithfully relayed by Bessie with many suppressed giggles and snorts, and absorbed by a spellbound Janet. Sometimes, as she pondered on what she had learned, beside her snoring companion, she said a little prayer of thanks to the Blessed Virgin that she was not going into marriage in complete ignorance. It was as well to be forewarned.

In the spring Philip Evershed came to stay in York with his son to conclude the arrangements for the ceremony and the payment of the dowry. He was disgruntled by the postponement, seeing in it more of a slight to him than respect for Janet's mother. Throughout their discussions, he disapproved openly of Janet's presence, and hinted that he had had second thoughts about her worth as the mate of his heir. Janet disliked him, and thought his pallid unhealthy complexion and supercilious manner were slightly repulsive. She told her father so one evening when only Thomas's tact had kept them from a serious breach.

'Don't fret, lass,' he said. 'You're not marrying the father. Giles is biddable, and you're quite strong enough to stand up for your husband's rights as well as your own.' His faith in her was reassuring. Then he frowned, and went on, 'Tom is biddable too. And I can't see Bessie pushing him very far.'

Janet laughed at the idea of Bessie as the driving power behind easy-going Tom. She liked her comfort too well to have much ambition.

'You're here to push him,' she reminded Thomas.

He threw her a comical look.

'Oh, I shall put my shoulder to the cart. But there comes a time when one expects the donkey to take over the haulage himself.'

As for Giles, Janet was quite indifferent to him. An unobtrusive young man of twenty-four, he seemed older than he was, very conscious of the burden of an only son expected to carry on the business. She tried, unsuccessfully, to picture herself married to him, particularly doing the things in bed which Bessie had graphically described to her.

At Crouchmas, three weeks before the wedding-date, the whole project did in fact hang in the balance. Philip Evershed was so enraged by Master Wrangwysh's hard bargaining that he tried to break the contract. When Thomas pointed out to him civilly what he would lose by it, and raised the portion, he was only slightly mollified. A letter from London gave him an excuse to leave suddenly for the south, on very urgent business, of course. He would be back in time for the ceremony, he said. Instead came another letter, in which he pleaded an indisposition, but gave permission for the match to take place. Thomas abandoned the admirable restraint he had shown while Philip was there, and stormed about men who behaved like silly women with their yeas and nays and their vapours. To soothe him, his own silly woman said sensibly that the wedding would be much merrier without him.

The chamber which Janet had been sharing with Bessie for a year was over-flowing with Lylleys. Bessie's large mother and innumerable sisters of all sizes billowed round the two brides, cooing and clucking. As they tied her laces and brushed her hair, Janet could not decide whether they were more like pigeons or hens, and came to the conclusion that there were about half of each. She was quite uninvolved in all the fuss, and simply stood there letting them pat and smooth and tweak her, while she wondered absently how Mistress Lylley told her daughters apart. Fortunately Bessie was showing enough excitement for two, giggling uncontrollably and making jokes about their future bed-fellows. There was plenty of hilarity directed at Janet's bed, where Giles was going to join her tonight, and the family, well-drilled by brother Bart, shrieked gaily in response. Bessie's flaxen hair would not hang straight down her back, but insisted on sticking out in all directions, which was a fresh source of mirth. Greasy Bessie cast an envious glance at the other bride, whose brown hair descended in a think smooth curtain to her waist.

'Well, at least mine won't strangle my goodman in the night,' she observed, and was off again into peals of laughter.

Once more the Trinity Guild took care of the arrangements. Thomas's eldest son and daughter had the privilege of marrying inside St Crux, the largest parish church in York, instead of at the door like lesser folk. Nothing was stinted; weddings were a golden opportunity to demonstrate the affluence of the merchant fraternities of York. But Janet, watching Tom flushed and solemn at the coy Bessie's side, and feeling Giles' hand clasped loosely round her own, could only believe it was a rehearsal for something else. When she had made the responses, and Giles kissed her on the lips, she felt just as unmarried as before. She could not raise any emotion at all. Bessie, however, was weeping, and her new husband trying with some embarrassment to stop her.

The impression of unreality lasted through the day. There was a banquet, of course, and a loud family party to launch the two couples into matrimony on floods of goodwill. All the Wrangwysh cousins were there, though they were easily outnumbered – and outflanked – by the Lylleys. Brother Bart, his polished cherubic face and prim mouth belied by the gleam in his eye, was in top form. Wherever he was, raucous laughter surrounded him. His coarse jests left Janet as unmoved as if they were directed at someone else. She could sense Giles flinching at them beside her, and was rather sorry for him.

He alone had no blood-relations here, and though he tried very hard to enter the spirit of the celebration, he was clearly not used to the familiarity of a clan gathering. Her attempts to draw him into conversation were stilted, and drowned anyway by the stridency around them. She was relieved when he was accosted by a cousin who was a wold farmer, wanting to know about the prices of wool in London, because she could drift away without offending him. There was time enough for overcoming the barrier of shyness later. Gratefully she gravitated towards the only other person, apart from Giles and herself, who looked ill at ease.

As a matter of fact Geoffrey Barton never appeared to be at ease anywhere. Among the domesticated fowls of York, he was a bird of passage in outlandish plumage, poised on his long legs ready to take flight.

'Uncle! I'm so glad that you could come.' Janet greeted him warmly and he embraced her in the quick violent way he had. He was her mother's only surviving brother, and not far from Janet in age; she was very fond of him.

'It's quiet in the south at present,' he said, 'so my lord of Warwick graciously released me for a week or two.' Putting his hands delicately on her shoulders, he swept her with an admiring glance.

'Jesu, Janet, you're as ravishing as spring! How your bridegroom can contain himself I cannot imagine – and his face as long as Lent, too! I hope your father has married you to a man.'

One of the reasons why Janet liked him so much was that, in his elegant and courtly manner, he never failed to shock her a little. He was very different from her paternal relations, and indeed from his gentle sister Alison.

Blushing a little, Janet explained about Philip Evershed's excuse, and suggested that Giles might be more worried about his father's health than doing his duty as a husband. Her tact was wasted on Geoffrey, who merely shrugged cynically and then asked, 'And when do you come to London, Janet? I hope to see more of you in the future – if we don't have to clap our armour on again. Great things are stirring. Queen Margaret and the Duke of York glare at each other like a pair of fighting cocks. Feathers will fly before long.'

'Oh, really?' said Janet indifferently. She was not interested in politics. To deflect her uncle's mind into more entertaining channels, she touched the fine grey silk of his sleeve.

'Is this the way they are dressing at court?' she asked. 'You must be as splendid as the earl himself.'

Geoffrey accepted the compliment gracefully, but began to describe, as she had known he would, how much more splendidly the Earl of Warwick dressed. Though Thomas's shop was stacked with bales of cloth, velvets and satins as well as the more serviceable linens and wools, only with Geoffrey did she allow herself to indulge her love of beautiful materials.

'While the lords war with words in the council chamber,' he was saying, 'the ladies fight it out with longer trains and higher hennins. Though I suspect that behind the scenes the women have as much say in the governing, and the men in the costuming. I was commissioned by my lord to buy a length of material for the countess, to make her an Easter gown: nine ells of scarlet cloth-of-gold! And my lady is no beauty. Then there's poor King Henry in the middle, covering his eyes and muttering a Miserere every time he glimpses an inch of bosom....'

Chattering away with her exuberant young uncle, Janet forgot for a while the strange suspension of her feelings. But she was too well-trained to neglect her duties as a hostess for long. Regretfully she took her leave of Geoffrey and went back into the fray.

Later, taking advantage of an empty wine-jar, she escaped to the kitchen for a brief taste of peace. As she replenished the jar, a small sound of sobbing impinged on her ringing ears. Behind a sack of flour she found John, his face streaked and blubbered with tears. He was seven, and the most reserved of her five brothers. When she peered over the sack, he started guiltily and tried to pretend he had been doing something else. But seeing her was too much for him, and he let out a roar of grief and flung his arms round her neck.

'John, you must not cry,' she admonished him. 'You should be happy for Tom and me, not sad.'

'It's because you're g-going away,' he sobbed, and clung to her.

'Bessie will be here instead of me,' said Janet, touched by this unusual show of affection. 'I shall come back to see you often, and you can visit me in London.'

'When I'm old enough, I shall come and live with you,' John declared when he had overcome his sobs a little. She laughed at him gently, wiped his face and said, 'Now you mustn't cry any more. Father will whip you if he finds out you've been disgracing my wedding. Anyway, I'm not going for another week.' Leaving him to bathe his eyes, she carried the jug back to the hall.

The merrymaking waxed wilder and merrier. It was growing dark outside, the torches were lit, and it could not be long before the guests began clamouring for the bedding ceremonies. All the men were congregating round Tom and Giles, pressing drink and advice upon them to fortify them in their coming ordeal.

Then an incongruous figure shouldered his way through the throng, dusty and tired, in a travelling-cloak, asking for Master Evershed. Extricated from the clutches of his well-wishers, Giles exchanged a few words with the man, and called his father-in-law. The three of them vanished upstairs to the solar. Only temporarily disconcerted, Giles' group of assailants transferred their attentions to Tom. The interruption did not surprise Janet in the least. It was no more credible than anything that had happened today.

'Perhaps Master Philip has changed his mind.' Geoffrey lounged up behind her with a faintly lascivious grin.

'If he has, he's too late,' commented Janet drily. A number of curious relations came to ask her what had happened, and she was busy denying all knowledge when her husband appeared on the gallery and requested her to come up.

In the solar her father was moving restlessly about, rolling and unrolling a parchment. The messenger, collapsed on a stool in the corner, was buried in a tankard of ale. Giles closed the door behind his wife and stood quietly, waiting for Thomas to speak.

'Master Philip is very sick and like to die,' Thomas announced. 'He has asked for his son.'

Janet turned towards Giles with sympathy ready; however unpleasant Philip might be, he was his only kin. But the young man was merely nodding to confirm Thomas's statement, so she murmured, 'That is evil news,' and said no more.

'Of course, Giles must go at once,' continued Thomas briskly. 'The question is whether you should accompany him, or follow later. I say you should go now; a woman's hand is needed in illness. Your husband objected that riding post so far would be too much for you. I told him I doubted it.' He looked quizzically at his daughter.

'I shall do my duty,' said Janet non-committally. The likelihood of rushing off into the night with a man she had only just met, to tend another whom she positively disliked, seemed very remote.

'Well, son Giles, what do you say?' Thomas leaned on the table and fixed his son-in-law with a penetrating glare; Janet looked at him too and the messenger came out of the tankard to watch. This was Thomas Wrangwysh's normal method of reaching a decision, and could be quite terrifying to the weak-willed. But those who survived the baleful stare found him the most generous and just of opponents.

For a long moment Janet thought that Giles had been struck dumb by the treatment. At last he spoke, and had evidently only been considering carefully.

'It is possible,' he said slowly, 'that my father has taken the plague. If he has, I would be loath to expose my wife to the risk of infection so soon after our wedding. There is a housekeeper to nurse my father. It would be best if I went alone. When the danger is over I will send for Janet.'

The interrogator swayed back on his heels, well-satisfied with Giles' reaction.

'Janet?'

She was too familiar with his fierce gaze to be cowed by it, and said levelly, 'I must obey my husband, sir.'

'Good girl. So you must.' Only the gravity of the situation prevented Thomas from beaming at them both. He had been the devil's advocate and was glad of his defeat.

'Now, Giles, you must leave tonight,' he resumed. 'But we cannot deprive our guests of their favourite part of the wedding-day. Let 'em bed you with your bride, to prove your good intentions. Then you can be up and away. If you make Tadcaster by midnight, it will give you a good start.'

So it would be postponed, perhaps for weeks. In her relief Janet felt a positive warming towards her husband.

They put Tom and Bessie to bed first, because Tom was the son and heir. Will and John had been turned out of the chamber shared before by the three elder boys, and now they would have to sleep in an attic. Lying side by side under the gaudy counterpane, the bride and groom were like two life-size dolls with over-red cheeks.

The bawdy ritual was done, the curtains drawn on them, and it was Janet's turn. Undressed clumsily by many eager hands, she could hear the racket of the men outside through the shrillness of the women with her. She was in bed, and told herself that it was the chill of the fresh linen on her naked skin that made her shiver. To a deafening accompaniment Giles slipped in beside her. She did not turn her head. The light grew dim as the curtains closed round them, then dwindled into blackness as the encouraging cries faded out of the room and down the stairs.

The stillness pressed on her. She was holding her breath so she could hear her husband's regular breathing close to her. The rustle of the sheets when he moved was unexpectedly loud; she stiffened. There was a rattle of curtain-rings, and in a spurt of flame as he struck a flint she saw his bowed back, long and dark where he sat on the edge of the bed. Then the candle was lit and he disappeared round to the chest where his clothes were laid out.

Janet breathed again, and her heartbeat thudded in her ears; she was limp with the relaxation of tension, and with a sharp sense of let-down. Geoffrey's words flashed through her mind:

'I hope your father has married you to a man.'

A second later she was ashamed, and thought of Philip Evershed far away in London, in pain and perhaps at the gate of death. Reaching for her bed-gown, she huddled herself into it and rose to aid her husband's dressing. She was in time to help him on with his doublet, in the uncertain light of the candle. As she knelt to pull on his boots, he said to her, smiling rather sadly, 'It will be better later.'

All the guests were gone and the children asleep. Thomas and Janet saw Giles off alone. He saluted his father-in-law and kissed his wife, and they walked by his horse through the arch from the courtyard into Micklegate. In the deserted street the hoof-beats echoed from house to house as he rode away towards the bar, lit fitfully by the lamps hung out by conscientious house-holders. Janet waved her handkerchief until he was swallowed up in the warm blanketing dark. Her father put an arm round her and took her inside.

She had the bedroom to herself for the first time since Bessie came. There was no trace of her husband's brief occupation except a small dent in one of the pillows; it was quite impossible to believe that he had been there with her at all. The lavish ceremony, the clamorous crowd, the quiet husband clattering away up Micklegate, were something she had dreamed about, asleep in this same bed. Yet alone in its unfamiliar wideness, the sense of disappointment came back to her.

She realised that she envied Tom his solemn young manhood and Bessie her new husband. Bessie's stories had been fascinating, but she had never taken more than an academic interest in them. Now, despite her indifference to Giles, she felt that there might be something more to them. Could there be a pleasure in marriage which she did not understand, quite apart from the business contract she had been brought up to believe in? She remembered that her mother had died because Thomas would not sleep apart from her; and fell asleep wondering about it.

CHAPTER TWO

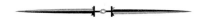

Nothing was changed. Another Corpus Christi day had come, and Thomas walked alone behind the Trinity banner; Janet and Bessie stood outside their house with the boys and cheered. While she awaited her summons from London, Janet continued to rule the household, to untangle Bessie's muddles, to be at her father's elbow and to intercede for her brothers when they were in peril of punishment. Now she was fifteen, and it seemed that fate would not let her leave York. No word came from Giles; only when she talked of him to other people could Janet convince herself that he was not a figment of her imagination. Her wedding ring was small proof that she was a wife.

But Thomas was becoming impatient. June was nearly out, and they did not even know if Giles' father was alive or dead. Though he never said so in so many words, Janet could see that Thomas did not entirely trust Philip Evershed. The illness itself might be a stratagem in dissolving an unwelcome bond; separated from her lawful husband by two hundred miles and five days' hard travelling, Janet could do little to assert her rights. This situation was one her father would not brook for much longer. He was not the man to let a valuable contract slip from his grasp through negligence.

If there was no message by St Peter and Paul's day, he decided, Janet should set out for London. The idea of asking for a deferment did not enter her head. She had been consulted about the date of the deadline, as she had about everything concerning her since she was old enough to think for herself. Thomas played the Roman tyrant with his sons; with his daughter he was a democratic ruler. As a result, Janet was in honour bound to obey him without question whenever she knew he was right. Fate had changed its mind, or revealed its purpose; that was all.

Master and Mistress Lylley were riding to Nottingham in the first week of July; Janet was to go with them. Others in the same party also known to her were travelling all the way to London, so she would be in familiar company. She was taking Nan, the cook-maid, to be her servant and housekeeper; Nan was proud of the promotion, but scared of leaving home.

The Eversheds remained mute, and on the appointed day Janet and Nan joined the southbound caravan as it chattered and ambled past their house towards the Micklegate Bar. There were about fifteen travellers, mostly well-to-do citizens and their apprentices, augmented at present by the friends and relations who were seeing them off. It was traditional for wayfarers to be escorted on the road south as far as Tadcaster Bridge. Thomas and young Tom, as the men of the family, escorted Janet. The others had waved her off from the Bar; because her father was with her Janet did not look back as often as she would have liked. Besides, Nan started snuffling before the walls of York were half a mile behind them, and Thomas was glancing most severely at her. Janet did not dare give way to sentimentality.

There was no opportunity to brood on what she was leaving behind during the nine miles to Tadcaster. As the early heat-haze fled before a climbing sun, Thomas inundated her with advice. How to behave if her father-in-law were still alive; what to do if he were dead; when to insist on her rights and when to give in; how to treat her husband, the London merchants, their wives, the apprentices. She listened and tried to absorb it all: her father never wasted words on trivialities. But it meant they were at Tadcaster too soon. There was an orgy of embracings, hand clapping and kissing and they were on their way, shedding a good half of the company, who stood by the bridge and pursued them with a volley of godspeeds.

Janet turned her face resolutely to the south. What lay in front was quite unknown – she had never been beyond Pomfret – and she was leaving behind far more than her native city. But her father was relying on her and she would not fail him with childish fears. She told Nan sharply to stop snivelling.

All the same, she could not entirely suppress her misgivings about what was to come. Once or twice she found herself dropping to the rear of the column because, quite unconsciously, she had been reining back her mare. She wanted to cling on to every mile which took her further from familiar things, to hold back every minute which took her into the future. It was in order not to give way to her feelings that she refused the invitation from Master Lylley to stay in Nottingham with them. The good chandler did not believe in hurrying anywhere, but Janet would pass no more than two nights in the town beneath its castle rock. The second night was for Nan, who professed herself quite exhausted with travelling so far, but admitted later that she did not fancy going on. Since she was only expressing more honestly what Janet also felt, her mistress poured scorn on her and told her to grow up before they reached London.

Nan had not noticeably matured a week later when they had their first view of the city from Highgate Hill; she had turned from lamenting her lost home to talking fearfully about the terrible folk who lived in the south and would cut your throat as soon as look at you. For the hundredth time on the journey, her mistress bade her be quiet. Her own wary eye had failed to see any great difference between the inhabitants of north and south so far. But here below them lay their destination, sullen in the copper glare of a hot afternoon. Down there, among all the thousands who swarmed unseen about their business, she knew only two people, one of them hostile to her. That was a worse prospect to Janet than an assassin behind every milestone. Taking her last deep breath of freedom, she kicked her horse and plunged down the hill towards the village of Islington.

In the church of St Botolph-without-Aldersgate they gave thanks for a safe journey, and Nan lit a devout candle to the patron saint of travellers. Then they were through Aldersgate and into narrow overcrowded streets which were remarkably like those they had left in York. The same smells, the same houses, the same din; only the accent was different. When she asked the way to Walbrook of a respectable-looking woman, she received a rather suspicious stare before the information was given: it was her own accent that was different. They turned into West Cheap, and her morale sank lower. A broad way, lined with fine mansions and well-stocked shops, displaying gold and silverware, jewellery, luxurious velvets and brocades. Her servant was open-mouthed, and Janet told herself loyally that the goods were almost as splendid as those in York.

On the corner of Walbrook she asked the way again, stopping a stringy apprentice weighed down with a bundle of miscellaneous harness. He looked at her oddly, and she had to repeat her husband's name before he tipped his head to the left and said the house of Master Evershed was opposite the Three Mullets tavern. Janet gave him a halfpenny and went on; she was becoming rather ruffled. After all, she could understand the Londoners without much trouble, although their speech was uncouth. There was no need for them to be quite so offensive.

Some of her irritation evaporated when they found the house opposite the Three Mullets.

'It's a grand house to be mistress of,' said Nan, and cheered up.

It was indeed – nearly as imposing as her home in Micklegate, though not quite so modern. Philip Evershed was right to be careful about who should inherit it. The gate into the courtyard was open, and, confidence bolstered by the thought that this was where she legally belonged, Janet walked her mare smartly inside.

There was none of the commotion going on that always filled the courtyard at home. No sound at all, indeed, and no movement. That was not so surprising, Janet said to Nan. There were no children here, and probably the apprentices were at work. It was a good opportunity to inspect the property. Janet dismounted and tethered her horse next to the drinking-trough. The stable was open too, and empty. Her husband was apparently out, if he kept a horse at all. She peered through an archway into a neat little garden, laid out with beds of herbs and roses and a fig tree against the wall at the end. Drawn by the greenery after the dust of the streets, she wandered into it and sat down on a stone bench in the middle.

The garden was flanked by gabled outbuildings, added very recently, from the whiteness of the stone. On the right, the kitchen, on the left, a storehouse. Above her, the wide mullioned window of an upstairs room looked out across the garden to the trees on the other side of the wall along the Walbrook river. Apart from the muffled roar of the city outside, it was very quiet. She relaxed, and inhaled the faint aroma of rosemary and mint. Her fingers were itching to put the herbs to use in her own kitchen.

Her own house. Whatever opposition her father-in-law might put in her way, she would stay here. It was a surprisingly restful place for the discontented spirit of Philip Evershed to inhabit. The streets and their rude citizens might be hostile, but she liked the house.

She was sunk in the pleasing fatigue of a long journey down when Nan appeared through the arch.

'There's nobody here, mistress.'

Janet noticed that her face and clothes were covered with roadside grime, and wondered if she was as filthy.

'They must be out,' she said vaguely, not wanting anyone to disturb the welcoming hush.

'The doors are all locked,' said Nan.

'Locked?' Janet repeated. Surely London was not wicked enough to dread burglars in daylight?

'And there's dust all over the place.'

In the moment of waking to consciousness a thousand explanations crossed her mind, and none of them satisfied her. She re-entered the courtyard and stood staring about her.

'Go next door and ask if the Eversheds are from home,' she said calmly to Nan. The girl was nervous of venturing outside, but she was becoming even more nervous of the deserted house. Without protest she ran out into the street.

Janet stayed where she was, and the enchanted stillness descended again. Once more the unreal atmosphere of her wedding day swept over her. They were fairy people, the man and his son whom she had married. They had enticed her from her home to this alien city where she was alone, and now she would never see them again. Perhaps Nan had gone for ever too. Well, this was not such a bad place to spend eternity, after all.

But at length Nan came back, looking cross.

'She won't come in, and I can't understand a word she says.'

A very old woman was waiting outside, trembling and mumbling.

'I had to give her a groat to make her come at all,' said Nan, with the generosity of one who is not paying.

Because she had no teeth and was evidently in the grip of terror, Janet could not understand her either. Was she under a spell too? All she could make out was that everyone had gone away – run away – and something about a farthing. But her servant had caught another word. Her eyes popped with fear and, crossing herself repeatedly, she began edging away. She was on the point of full flight when Janet grabbed her by the cloak and asked where she was going.

'Pestilence, mistress, she said pestilence!' Nan gasped, and she was reduced to the same state as the old woman. 'The plague!' The fear brushed Janet's heart and sent it lurching, but she managed to say with passable firmness, 'The old dame doesn't know what she's saying, Nan.' Keeping a hold on Nan's cloak, she turned back to the ancient and tried again. 'What has become of Master Philip Evershed and his son Giles?'

'You'll get nothing out of her, mistress. Old Bridget's not in her right wits.' Stumping up to the tense little group was a squat middle-aged man humping a shopping-basket. With his lank hair and black-beetle eyes he had the look of a foreigner, but though his accent was so strong that Janet could hardly follow him, he was English. His solid figure was so much of this earth that she could have flung her arms round him, basket and all.

'You'll be Mistress Evershed,' he said without surprise. Janet noticed that Nan had stopped straining away from her as soon as the newcomer appeared.

'Yes. I am Janet Evershed,' she answered, and the name sounded strange on her tongue.

'My name is Nicholas Farthing. I was in Master Evershed's service.'

Shooing old Bridget off home with the kind roughness of a shepherd with sheep, he led the way back into the courtyard and up to the kitchen door, which had been unlocked all the time. He dusted off a bench in the kitchen for Janet and her servant, and provided them both with some good cool ale. Then, as he moved unhurriedly around, putting away his purchases, he explained that he had been keeping house since his masters died. The others would not stay, for fear of infection, and they had melted away. He had sent a letter up to York, but the messenger must have run off, or crossed them on the journey.

'It was to tell you to stay in Yorkshire, mistress. With Master Philip and Master Giles dead all of two weeks, the business is well-nigh ruined. There's no family to take it up.

'By the Mass, 'tis an unfortunate name. Since Master Philip turned from farming to trading nothing has gone right. Oh, he was rich enough, else your father would never have made the match, but he had two wives and neither could give him lusty children. Most died at birth, and those who lived a while were none too healthy. They say it was plague carried them off, the masters, but I don't think it was. Just rotten stock, mistress, rotten stock.'

Nicholas Farthing talked about the death of his masters with the philosophical detachment of a farmer who has lost a herd of cattle to disease. After the unreality of her arrival, his plainness was as refreshing as the ale. Janet could summon up no grief at the news he gave her. Gratitude to Giles for not bringing her with him to share his end, but not much more. He had never really existed for her, and so his death did not touch her. She was as alone as if the Eversheds had indeed been fairy people, but with Nicholas Farthing sitting opposite her, stubby hands spread prosaically on his knees, it did not matter. The house was no longer enchanted – just pleasant, and empty .... and very dirty.

'You haven't kept the house very clean, Master Farthing,' she said severely. He excused himself sheepishly.

'Show me the rest, and then we must start putting it to rights. Tomorrow we shall look for an apprentice, since the others have gone.'

For the first time Master Farthing was disconcerted.

'To tell truth, mistress, I have been winding up the business. I was thinking you'd be going home.'

'Going home?' said Janet. 'Certainly not. There's far too much to do.' The tone of her voice was remarkably like her father's.

She was always surprised, afterwards, at how easy it had been to set the business in action again. Her father's training had been sound, and she had his approval and advice behind her in taking over from her dead father-in-law. A number of clients were already lost through the breakdown in trading; several more withdrew their custom because they did not want to deal with a woman. But by the time winter came she had made up for the loss with new customers, and gained a good deal of respect within the Mercers' Company.

Engaging an apprentice during the early days, when she had not proved herself, might have been difficult: fathers were chary of placing their sons where their security was uncertain. Without needing to look far, however, she articled a red-haired lad named Christopher Cely. His father had been under suspicion of Lollardry, and no-one else would take him. The boy was bright, and did not have any obvious heretical leanings; Janet thought it unfair that he should suffer for his father's delinquency. He repaid her by loyalty and quick learning.

Without Nicholas Farthing, of course, she could never have done it. He knew the mercery business inside out, especially since he had run it single-handed during Philip Evershed's frequent illnesses. Once convinced that his young mistress was capable, he was constantly at her elbow, guiding her on the spot as Thomas did from a distance. He was absolutely reliable.

As the evenings drew in, and the frantic rush of the first few months settled into a routine, he became more than an adviser. Though her business contacts were good, Janet had made few friends in London. She had been too busy to cultivate any, and nobody else had made the effort. Widows carrying on their husbands' businesses were not uncommon; such young widows as Janet were. Since she showed no signs of remarrying, and distinct signs of success, the other women despised her as immodest. To the men she was a stranger from their greatest rival city, and though they would work with her they did not care to spend their leisure with her.

After the teeming household and warm friends of York, her isolation hurt Janet a little. She was thrown back on the company of her assistant, and when they were not talking shop, he told her about his youth as a shepherd on the Sussex Downs; she reciprocated by telling him about her family in York. It was a way of keeping them before her, and of passing the long silent evenings. One day in Advent he said to her, 'I'm growing old, and I like to talk about days that have gone. You're too young to be living in the past.'

She protested, and pointed out that all her energies were taken up with planning for the future.

'Ah, you've done wonders, mistress, but you'll want a man in charge when the novelty wears off.'

Her father said the same. It was agreed between them that Janet would put the business into good shape, and then use it as a bargaining point for a far better marriage than her first. Janet did sometimes feel the need for a master; not only when she came up against prejudice among her fellow merchants, but also in the imposing bed which she occupied alone. Her brief marriage, and those fleeting minutes with Giles, had roused something in her that had not died with her husband. But she loved her independence, the sensation of making her own decisions with nobody to answer to, the satisfaction of success when all the credit was hers. That would have to be surrendered to a second husband, who might not even allow her the freedom her father had given her.

When Thomas paid her a visit in early spring, bringing John with him, she prevaricated about the subject of marriage. Though he did his best to find fault, Thomas was clearly delighted with her progress. Noticing some cushions she had worked during the winter, he suggested that she should employ her talent for embroidery as a side-line.

'Then, when you marry again, you can keep control of it in your own hands,' he said. The idea appealed to her, but her father's other suggestion, that he should start negotiating while he was in London, was less attractive.

'Give me time,' she asked him. 'The business is just finding its feet. Give me a full year.'

Because he knew a promising enterprise when he saw one, Thomas acquiesced.

After their departure, the house sank back into quiet industry. Kit Cely the apprentice, who had enjoyed showing off his knowledge before his mistress's solemn little brother, knitted his brows and plunged into the intricacies of accounts and the relative qualities of dowlas and Holland cloth. A gift of embroidered hassocks to her parish church of St Stephen-upon-Walbrook brought Janet several orders for more of her work. But the new green on the trees across the Walbrook brought no more company than Nick Farthing and the garrulous Nan.

Janet had seen her uncle Geoffrey only once since she came to London. As he had predicted on her wedding day, he had soon been back in armour. Only a month after her arrival, he had followed the Earl of Warwick west to the muster of the Duke of York's supporters at Ludlow. Routed by Queen Margaret's forces, the Yorkists had scattered in all directions. Geoffrey fled with his lord to Calais, and there they had stayed, a thorn in the flesh of the royalist navy, for best part of a year.

In London, Janet found, it was impossible to ignore politics. Who controlled London, controlled the country, and the rhythm of trading tended to be regulated by the pendulum of power. The Duke of York had always been popular in the capital. While Margaret of Anjou held sway with her favourites, in the name of the feeble-minded king, the market was depressed. When Warwick came back with York's eldest son the Earl of March, the city rang the bells for his victory at Northampton, and erupted with joy at his entry into London, King Henry shambling in his wake.

After that it was not long before Geoffrey Barton burst into Janet's shop, bubbling with gossip and fingering every bolt of cloth in the place. His year of exile had not weathered him.

'A pirate's life is quite agreeable,' he said, and perched uneasily on a bale of tawny damask, 'Provided that there's a solid fortress at one's back in case of emergency. All the same, I'm not sorry to be sleeping in a feather bed again. Calais is not exactly civilised.'

Surveying his niece with his usual practised eye, he commented that black did not suit her.

'Find yourself a husband, my love. You were not meant for holy orders.'

Leaving a cloud of perfume behind him, he danced away to Westminster Palace.

He came again several times, occasionally bringing companions as gaudy as himself. They bought some of Janet's best material, but she was not sorry to see them go. She indulged Geoffrey because he was different; four Geoffreys at once were rather too different. But London, she had to admit, was much livelier for the advent of the Yorkists. The extra trade kept the merchants happy, the streets were full of liveried soldiers and courtiers, and Nan was in bliss because she had seen the Earl of Warwick 'so close I could have touched his horse!'

Only the weather was in low spirits. It was the rainiest summer people could remember, and the corn-chandlers were husbanding grain against a drowned harvest. The roses in Janet's little garden were ruined. She had pruned them faithfully, under Nick Farthing's direction, but scarcely a flower had opened. One afternoon in August, as murky as a winter dusk, Janet was lamenting over the rotten buds to Nan, while they shovelled the weekly bake out of the ovens.

'And if this goes on, we'll have the Walbrook flooding the privy as well.' There was a thunderous knock at the door from the courtyard, and because Nan was still floury Janet went to answer it.

The rain was sluicing down and making silver pennies among the cobbles in the yard. Crowded under the overhanging eaves, laughing and soaked, were Geoffrey and two noblemen. Behind them, less jolly, dejected in the streaming rain, were a group of retainers and some miserable horses. When the door opened, the three leading men nearly fell into the entrance-hall, so closely had they been sheltering.

Noise invaded the house, chatter, the stamping of feet, the shaking of saturated hats and cloaks, with Geoffrey trying to explain above the din that their lordships had been returning from the Palace to the Tower, and had been caught in a cloudburst. Janet went through the motions of being a well-bred hostess. With the part of her which never lost control, she directed the horses to the stable, the men-at-arms to the hall, her staff to blow up the fire and bring wine and food, while herself conducting her visitors upstairs to the solar.

Soon the two lords were standing steaming with their backs to the fire, tankards of hastily-brewed mulled ale in their hands. Geoffrey darted about as usual, continuing to talk and explain, running his fingers through his wet blonde hair, spilling his ale, trying to put his masters and his niece at ease and yet more nervous than any of them.

Janet's composure, however, was more of a daze than anything else. The sudden invasion of her quiet afternoon by sound and colour and movement had stunned her into a state where nothing was very distinct. Only when her uncle presented her formally to his companions did their identities penetrate. As she rose from a deep reverence she was aware of them individually for the first time. They took shape out of the haze of grandeur which had surrounded them since they entered the house with such informal magnificence.

Two young men, one only just a man, the other crossing the boundary into middle age.

The elder was stocky, his face broad and determined; strong crisp hair cropped unfashionably short: a man who would go his own way and carry others with him. The younger was head and shoulders taller, a graceful giant carrying his inches with almost insolent pride. His wet hair, burnished chestnut, was drying at the ends into fluffy gold, though the dripping fringe tangled with his eyelashes and almost veiled the watchful eyes. He was remarkably good-looking, and the cut of his doublet, broad-shouldered and very short, showed off his well-endowed figure.

The Earl of Warwick and the Earl of March.

She had watched them riding into London a few weeks before, from a distance, between agitated arms and bobbing heads. Caught up in the enthusiasm of the mob she had cheered them too. But, enclosed in their cages of armour, they had been things rather than men: symbols of the firm rule the House of York promised after years of Lancastrian muddle. The Great Earl and the Rose of Rouen. She had heard the crowd call them that. Yet though in one sense she was overwhelmed that such mighty personages should deign to enter her house, in another she was able to assess them as coldly as she would have done a new customer.

It was not difficult to see why Richard Neville inspired such devotion. Energy was in every line of Warwick's body, and there was a recklessness behind the gracious smile in his eyes. The tales Janet had heard of him since her childhood, as he passed with the brightness of a meteor across his Yorkshire estates, took substance and became almost credible. He was a man who would make people believe in his dreams, simply because he believed in them himself.

'It was sheer luck that we came this way,' Geoffrey was saying. 'We would have been washed away if we had had to go further. The Fleet is almost up to the bridge. If this weather continues, we'll be crossing to the Palace by boat!'

They laughed obediently. Geoffrey could be relied on to keep the conversation flowing, and there was plenty to say about the appalling summer and the spoiled crops.

'The victualling companies will suffer badly. You are fortunate to be in the mercery trade, Mistress Evershed.' It was the first remark that the Earl of March had addressed to her. She was surprised that he should have noticed what her business was at all. As she murmured a polite reply, Janet's attention turned from Warwick to March, and was baffled. Warwick's character was written on his face. Young March gave nothing away.

He was leaning his elbow indolently on the mantelshelf, a position only possible to one of his height, and he quietly consumed two tankards of ale while Warwick sipped and Geoffrey slopped their first. As far as the country knew, he was untried as a leader of men. Always he had been in Warwick's shadow, his pupil and follower. But he had seen plenty of action in his eighteen years, and his face, though smooth, was not innocent. There was about him an air of confidence and knowingness which antagonised Janet. She suspected that because he said the less, he saw the more, and once she found him looking at her with an expression which disturbed and annoyed her.

The only thing that was known for sure about Edward of March was that no woman could resist him. It was enough to rouse Janet's sense of independence. She determined to show no interest whatsoever, beyond what courtesy demanded, in the perfect figure before her. The Earl of March might be one of the most powerful men in the kingdom; Janet would not add one jot to his self-esteem.

Nevertheless she was drawn will she nill she into conversation with him. After his opening comment, he began to question her with an interest which, if false, was well-assumed, about her ventures in trading and her upbringing. She explained briefly about her situation.

'But you must have been widowed very young?' said March, and both Geoffrey, who knew all about it, and Warwick, who did not, were nodding sympathetically.

'Last year, my lord,' she answered. 'My husband and his father died of plague. Everything was at sixes and sevens when I arrived, and so I took charge.'

March stirred slightly; now he was watching her closely.

'Your husband had no opportunity to initiate you in the business?'

Janet was so affronted that only strict self-control kept her smiling; her strongest instinct was to slap the bland young face. As surely as if he had asked the question outright, she understood what he wanted to know: was she a virgin? Seething inwardly, fighting down the hot blush that was rising to her cheeks, she replied shortly, 'None, my lord,' and glanced at the other two men. They must have caught the shameless implication. The comfortable politeness of the atmosphere was shattered. If he had stripped her naked to inspect her with those enigmatic eyes she could not have been more exposed.

But the Earl of Warwick was murmuring, 'It was most courageous of you to carry on alone. Your next husband will be a happy man.'

Her uncle chimed in eagerly, 'I'll warrant you, my lord, you'd be hard put to it to find a better head for business in Cheapside.'

CHAPTER TWO

They were completely unconcerned. This was no covering up of an embarrassing moment. March's enquiry had been taken at its surface value. Only she had seen more. Could she have been mistaken? Was her modesty over-sensitive to the Earl's reputation? He had not moved again. The damp golden hair had swung forward across his jaw, concealing his expression. There had been no mistake. Janet was convinced that the question had been asked, and fervently she hoped that she had not given him the answer.

At any rate after that he left her alone. The introduction of hot pasties provided a welcome diversion, at least for the hostess. Fresh from the baking, they were brought in by Nan, who was so overwrought by the honour of waiting on the greatest men in England that she tripped over a stool and nearly threw the whole tray of food in the fire. Scarlet, speechless, and breathing heavily, she was guided out again by her mistress. Warwick ate his pasty still standing, as though expecting a call to arms; one could almost hear the chink of his armour. The younger lord flung himself into the carved chair and Geoffrey, punctiliously awaiting leave to sit, balanced on the edge of a joint-stool.

As they wolfed the next three days' supply of pies, washed down with more ale, even for Janet the tension eased. By mutual consent politics went unmentioned but they talked easily enough of the north, of York and Middleham and Sheriff Hutton. Warwick said he remembered Janet's mother, who had been brought up with Geoffrey at Middleham Castle, and declared with complete falseness that Janet was just like her.

And there was news which for a moment thawed her restraint into genuine pleasure. Her uncle Geoffrey, whom she had thought of as an eternal squire, was to be the Earl of Warwick's chamberlain at Middleham, 'when the present troubles are over,' he added carefully. It was a position carrying great responsibility, especially as the earl proposed to establish his wife and two small daughters there. The air of the Dales would be more bracing for them than the low-lying Avon valley round Warwick Castle. With great affability the earl invited Janet to visit his household when she was next in Yorkshire, in memory of her mother. She accepted gratefully, because the castle in Wensleydale reminded her of childhood excursions with her parents to Christmas festivals and summer hunts.

There was a cry from the oriel window, whence Geoffrey, never still for long, had wandered. The rain had stopped, and for the first time in weeks a watery beam of sun struck feebly through the coloured glass, making faint pastel pools among the rushes.

'Perhaps we ought to release a dove,' drawled the Earl of March, and in spite of herself Janet was amused. To find wit in such an arrogant character was unexpected, and somewhat galling.

A tart reply, 'I doubt if it would bring back an olive branch,' rose to her lips, but she did not think it would be well received. Women were not expected to make clever remarks, especially when they concerned the exclusively male territory of politics. It was a pity. She badly wanted to pay him back.

But now that the weather had improved, and the visitors had dried off, there was nothing further to keep them there. March remained lounging in his chair, but Warwick was fidgeting, as eager to be off as a warhorse scenting battle, and Geoffrey was quivering in sympathy. It was easy to see why the Great Earl imposed such trust in his followers: they were out of the same mould. While she organised the departure, Janet wondered which mould had produced the Earl of March. He was totally unlike his father; by reputation the Duke of York was a conscientious plodder, and in appearance square and plain. Probably life had not yet formed him, she thought loftily, ignoring the good two years by which he was her senior.

He was the last to assume his cloak, and downstairs he was last, by precedence, to take leave of her. Warwick's dry peck was all that civility required, Geoffrey's vigorous and cousinly. When the tall young earl placed his hands on her shoulders, she was trembling. The lips that met hers briefly were as cool and impersonal as his manner had been throughout, and she felt almost sick with shame that she should expect anything more from him. To him she was nothing more than the hostess of an hour, owner of a convenient roof, a dispenser of food and drink. Only her imagination had seen further.

CHAPTER TWO

With her customary calm, she extended the hospitality of her house if they passed by in the future and graciously the lords thanked her. A vague mist rose from the wet cobbles and, accompanied by a hollow clattering of hoofs, they swung into their saddles and turned for the gateway. Geoffrey blew her a kiss just before he went out of sight. The earls did not look back.

Nan had changed her allegiance. On recovering from the momentous visit, she declared that the Rose of Rouen was the most beautiful lord in the world, and beside him the Earl of Warwick a mere soldier. St Edward became her favourite saint, and she spent hours loitering at the corner of Budge Row, on the off-chance that the earl would ride by. Although Janet usually bore with her servant's fancies, on this occasion she took her to task for wasting so much time in foolishness. Her irritation with Nan sprang from her own inability to put Edward of March out of her mind. He haunted her like a question mark, and she was forever puzzling over what the question was.

CHAPTER THREE

Her uncle was back, two weeks later, asking her to do him a favour.

'I am in great need,' he said dramatically, 'and without your help I shall be in disgrace.'

Prepared to lend him money, Janet put herself at his disposal. But what he wanted was really too much, even for Uncle Geoffrey.

'Your partner? At a royal reception? I'm flattered that you thought of me – but I'm not a lady, uncle. You must be joking.'

'Not at all. You're too pretty to be wasted on ells of cloth. And your mother's blood is gentle, if you insist upon a pedigree.'

'My manners would be boorish in noble company.'

'Your manners were good enough for Middleham Castle not many years back. You smiled and danced with me then to the manner born. Now no more arguments, niece. If I go alone I shall be mocked from the court. You shall come.'

Weakly she yielded. Her curiosity to see court life from within overcame her scruples.

Nevertheless, she would not pretend above her order. Let them look down on her if they wished; she would go as a respectable merchant's widow. There were three gowns hanging in her chamber, gifts from her father to a new wife. They had never been worn, and would hang there until another husband took possession of her. Until then, she was sentenced to black. Sometimes she had taken them out and gazed at them wistfully, but she took a perverse pleasure in the simplicity of her gown for the reception. Black taffety trimmed with black fur, and no ornament but her wedding ring. Geoffrey obligingly clothed himself in white and black, and Janet hoped that in such sober garb they would not be conspicuous among the popinjays of the court.

The opulence of the assembly in Westminster Palace was beyond anything she had expected. There would not be much difficulty, she thought, in losing herself among this brilliant throng. Compared with this spectacle, the ceremony and finery of the city festivals were homespun efforts. By the light of hundreds of flambeaus and perfumed wax candles she moved through a garden overgrown with exotic blooms. Hennins and butterfly headdresses sprouted everywhere, with veils floating almost to the knees of the ladies who wore them. Heavy velvet and brocade gowns weighed them down, and brought out perspiration in the damp heat of the evening. The gentlemen were as flamboyant, with absurd padded doublets and hose to lend them broad shoulders and virility, jewelled collars and belts and rings, sweeping sleeves and long-toed shoes. After the long winter of Lancastrian austerity, summer was coming.

When Janet was presented to Geoffrey's friends, she caught a sneer in the eyes of some. It did not worry her. Self-possessed amid the splendour, impressed but by no means dazzled, she was at least as contemptuous of them. Fluttering eyelashes and high shining foreheads, false codpieces and false courtesy. No doubt these fine ladies and gentlemen hated each other beneath the show. Sustained by the conservative pride of her class, Janet was superior to them all.

She felt more of an affinity with King Henry, who was exhibited for a moment as nominal host of the reception. Staring about him anxiously, his hair unkempt, in rough gown and rustic boots, he was as out of place as she. The innocent ageless face and the long fingers clutching a well-worn rosary belonged in a cloister. He had only appeared for form's sake, and clearly he was glad to go, shepherded by the attendants-cum-guards and the quiet doctor.

An accident of birth had given to Henry VI a sceptre which he was too good a man to bear. Since babyhood others more or less capable had borne it for him, and the country had suffered. The bored hush which had fallen at the king's entrance rose again into refined hubbub, and the courtiers gravitated towards the new rulers of England.

Janet had determined that she would not look for him but there was no way of avoiding him. The Earl of March was the most striking man in the hall. Richard Neville behaved like a king, and holding court in an alcove he received the homage due to one. But his young cousin was mixing with the guests, flattering them with his easy courtesy, outshining them with his height and magnificent costume. From a distance, as Geoffrey assiduously escorted her among his friends, she watched his charm at work.

Still as relaxed as he had been in her own house, he had shed his aloofness, and appeared to be delighted with everyone who was presented to him. He paid particular attention to the ladies, yet never to the exclusion of their partners. All the women were quite obviously smitten with him, and Janet observed with amused disdain the manoeuvres initiated by some in order to be in his way.

'If he proves as successful on the battlefield, my lord of Warwick will have to look to his laurels.' Geoffrey had followed her eyes, and was now looking slyly at his niece.

'Please God he have no need to,' she retorted piously. Because she was gazing haughtily ahead of her, she missed her uncle's second sidelong glance, and was unaware that he had misread her meaning.

The musicians had taken their place in the gallery, and dancing was about to begin. Geoffrey was an excellent dancer, and wanted to dance with Janet. Pleading lack of skill, she asked him to find her a place to sit, and then choose a better partner. With alacrity he obliged, and left her beside a dowager of his acquaintance, who was amicable, but deaf.

In a shadowy corner behind a pillar Janet was at ease, an observer merely, absorbing the music and the dancing. She had never heard such lovely music. The full richness of the shawms and rebecs was a far cry from the amateurish tabor and pipe she had danced to in the streets of York. And she was lulled into a dream of beauty by the slow patterns of the dancers; rising and falling, circles and chains, weaving and breaking and forming.

Someone took her hand, and she turned to find the Earl of March smiling before her.

'Mistress Evershed, will you dance with me?'

A shock ran through her as if she had been touched with a red-hot iron. It was the last thing she was expecting; surely it was a figment of her imagination. Surely the earl was in the thick of the dancing, shaming the rest with his grace and poise, gazing down into the eyes of his partner and pretending he was in love with her. But no, he had disappeared, and it was she he was gazing at, with the intentness which made her feel she was the only woman in the room. Once more she was angry with him for taking her at a disadvantage. She could not conceive how he had found her out, among so many and such beautiful ladies.

Swallowing her chagrin as best she could, she rose and allowed the earl to lead her on to the floor. At first she was terrified of putting a foot wrong, and displaying to the court at large her clumsiness in the subtle mysteries of the basse dance. But the strong clasp of his hand, the intimate smile he gave her whenever he caught her eye, dispelled her uncertainty and filled her unwillingly with confidence. She could not suppress a small glimmer of triumph as she sank into the final courtesy.

He had not spoken another word to her, and after he returned her to her obscure corner there was no further sign of recognition. As soon as etiquette allowed, she asked her uncle to take her home. Geoffrey was disappointed, but too well-bred to make any demur. In Walbrook, Kit and Nan had waited up to hear about their mistress's evening of honour, yet she could find little to tell them; she did not mention her dance with the Earl of March. Her first taste of court life had not elated her at all. It had left her tired and vaguely dissatisfied. She supposed it was the artificiality of the atmosphere which was oppressing her.

There was another invitation to court from Geoffrey, and her immediate inclination was to refuse him. Then he mentioned to her casually that a certain knight he knew slightly was looking for someone to embroider a christening robe for his baby daughter. Janet took the bait. To a young merchant eager for expansion, the prospect of court patronage was irresistible. She was aware from the talk of her colleagues that business contacts with the palace were not always reliable: payment was often reluctant. But the prestige was invaluable. So she went to a tournament in Smithfield, met the knight, and opened negotiations. Other commissions would follow, Geoffrey assured her, and in this hope she ventured several more times into the strange overblown milieu where he was at home. Once or twice the Earl of March graciously acknowledged her, but never embarrassed her by singling her out for special attention.

Towards the end of the summer, however, she was petrified by the appearance on her doorstep of a messenger wearing the Plantagenet coat of arms. He carried a summons from the Lord Earl of March to a certain house in Southwark.

'What can he want with me?' she muttered distractedly.

Nick, who happened to be with her, said 'My lord's mother the Duchess of York is lodging in Southwark, with her youngest children. They say he goes there every day. Perhaps the earl has a commission for you, mistress.'

The house belonged to a family of East Anglian landowners, but none of the Pastons were in evidence when Janet was admitted to their solar next day. Modest hangings and comfortable furnishings; a prosperous but unpretentious room. In a heavy oak chair a tall woman was sewing, middle-aged but still with a fine-drawn beauty. At her feet a girl sat on an orange cushion, stabbing her needle through a piece of linen, her sandy brows puckered with concentration. She looked up with sharp black eyes as Janet came in, and did not go back to her embroidery. The Earl of March was leaning on the table, pointing out something in a book to the two boys sitting there. There was no doubt as to the kinship between March and the elder boy: the same golden hair, the same perfect features, and an even bolder stare. The youngest was the odd one out amongst this assertively handsome family, small, sallow, and self-effacing.

It was a surprisingly domestic scene, and Janet stood hesitating on the threshold with a feeling of intrusion. But as soon as the earl saw her he strode towards her and greeted her like an old friend.

'It was good of you to come. Madame, may I present Mistress Evershed to you. She is an ambitious mercer with very skilful hands.'

Janet made a deep reverence to the Duchess of York, and kissed the tapering fingers which were held out to her.

'You are very young,' remarked the duchess with a faint smile. Before she could make any reply, March interposed and answered for her.

'Never was older head found on younger shoulders.' She was not sure whether to be grateful or offended, but with a remote kindliness the duchess bade her rise, and the earl was already gesturing towards the boys at the table.

'I was helping my brothers to parse their Latin, but I'll swear I'm as glad of the interruption as they are. These are your clients, mistress, if you will undertake some work for us. Lord George, Lord Richard, and Lady Margaret on the cushion, who dislikes her embroidery as much as George dislikes his Latin.' The three children acknowledged Janet's courtesy, and young Lord Richard fetched her a stool.

'I should be honoured to serve you, my lord,' she murmured. She was trying hard to accommodate herself to this different Earl of March, voluble, active, teasing his family before her with open affection. This Earl of March did not antagonise her as the others had. On the contrary, she sensed a certain complicity with him, as if it was important to him that she should make a good impression.

'They have been under duress for some time,' March went on. 'I think they deserve some recompense for the hardships they have suffered.'

Rumour had it that after the fiasco at Ludlow, the Duke of York and his elder sons had fled leaving the duchess and children to the doubtful mercy of Queen Margaret. Duchess Cecily had met the Lancastrian victors proudly on the steps of the market cross, the children and townsfolk grouped round her for protection. Seeing the pale lovely matriarch in person, Janet could well believe the tale. She would be a moral match for the Amazonian queen any day.

The earl wanted Janet to supply and embroider a gown for each of the three children. There was a lively discussion between them about the materials and the devices to be used, in which Lord George's voice rang out the loudest. He demanded leopards and lilies sewn all over his costume, and was most put out when his mother vetoed the idea. It would be tactless, she pointed out firmly, to wear the royal arms without a difference at such a time. With a bad grace the lad had second thoughts. His sister was less blatant, but just as decided about her choice: black velvet with white and gold marguerites. The younger boy waited to be consulted, and then asked quietly if he might choose a chalice, the device of St Richard of Chichester, patron saint of himself and his father the Duke of York. The rest he would leave to Mistress Evershed. Janet thought that the two elder children looked rather scornfully at him for throwing away a chance to adorn himself, but the earl commended his selection warmly, and Lord Richard glowed.

Janet was given leave to come again to Southwark for any necessary fittings, and promised a generous fee.

'It is part of my father the duke's policy,' said March as she left, 'to encourage commerce. The welfare of England depends on it. That is why I called for you rather than some foreign master from France or Italy.'

The explanation satisfied her until she was half way across London Bridge. Then, as she stared at a barge shooting the rapids, it occurred to her that during the earls' visit to her house, embroidery had not been mentioned. The tentative improvement in her opinion of Edward of March evaporated abruptly. He knew a good deal too much about her for comfort. And though she should have been delighted with the tremendous fillip this commission would give her business, she was conscious instead of a vague dread as to what such a mark of favour might mean.

When she returned to the Pastons' house, the children were alone. The duchess had gone to meet her husband, who was returning from Ireland to settle the makeshift situation in London. Lord George was of the outspoken opinion that the Duke of York should make himself king as soon as possible; his sister Margaret cast a cautious eye at Janet, and told him to be more discreet. She was only a couple of years younger than Janet, and very much on her dignity. But the long haughty lines of her face broke into delight at the half-finished garment Janet produced for her inspection. The black velvet flowed over her hands, its deep pile brushed with a silvery sheen.

As she draped and pinned the rich material with the aid of an unobtrusive lady attendant, Janet took stock of the young Plantagenets and decided they were not really very different from any other children. When Lord George was not being fitted, he was sprawling on the floor and idly teasing a greyhound puppy with his foot; she had seen her brother Will do the same when their father was not around. Richard, small and silent, sat and watched. There was an earnest concentration about his game which reminded Janet of John.

Before the fitting was over, the reserve between the merchant's daughter and the Duke of York's children had melted. George, Margaret and Richard had spent most of their lives at Fotheringhay Castle, insulated from contact with people of Janet's estate. Her direct approach was new to them, and they responded to it well.

By her third visit the gowns were nearly made up, and she found herself speaking quite freely about her brothers. She made them laugh with an anecdote about Will, who had once pulled off Lucifer's tail while playing a devil in the Corpus Christi play of the Last Judgment. As she knelt at Richard's feet, turning up the hem of his gown, she told them about John. He was of an age with my lord Richard, she said, and very like him. The small boy was looking at her intently, his brown eyes on a level with hers; he was a moorland foal beside his thoroughbred brother and sister. As she carried on with her tales, it was to him she was talking.

She did not hear the door open, and only when Richard glanced over her head, his sallow face kindling, did she turn to find the earl standing in the doorway. She caught a hint of something in his expression she had never seen before, serious and deep. Then it was masked by his bland smile, and the children were shouting their greetings, and the familiar unease took control of her. As soon as she could she made her escape – thanking heaven she would not have to go back until the embroidery was all done and the garments ready.

The Duke of York arrived in London to a hero's welcome. But his faithful Londoners were in for a bitter disillusionment. Instead of the saviour they were expecting, York played the conqueror. Uncharacteristically, and against the advice of Warwick and his eldest son, he rode roughshod over the constitution and demanded the crown. The delinquent duke was hastily brought to order by his anxious followers, and a patch-up compromise was devised. Henry VI should reign for his lifetime; after his death the Prince of Wales would be set aside and his protector Richard of York should ascend the throne. The settlement was sworn to by the Duke of York and his elder sons before Parliament, but few believed it and it satisfied no-one. The delicate poise of power maintained through the summer was fatally upset; before autumn was far advanced the armies were mustering again.

Janet sat and embroidered. News of political upheavals only made her needle work faster. She had not yet been paid and was not inclined to put her trust in princes or the fortunes of war either. If she did not deliver the goods before the glowering opponents came to blows, the Yorkist children might be prisoners again, and her grand commission so many extravagant curiosities. Apart from a sneaking interest as to how the Earl of March would have handled things, given his head, she was unmoved by it all.

The Lady Margaret's flowers were finished, and gleamed in gold and silver thread on their dark background. Her youngest brother's little blue gown lay beside them, and only George's was not quite complete, because he was the most particular of the three. Janet was pleased with them; she had put all her artistry into them and decided, quite independently of Kit's praise and Nick's approval, that they were fit for the highest in the land. It was getting cold in her workshop with only a brazier to warm it, and Janet called for Kit one frosty morning to move the precious garments up to the solar, where a fire had been lighted. The lad did not come at once, and she was beginning to complain when he appeared at the door, his face nearly as fiery as his hair.

'My lord earl is here, mistress. Asking for you.'

She had felt quite safe from him here; he was too busy deciding the future of England to bother about a merchant's widow in Walbrook. Yet here he was.

'Take him up to the solar,' she said, trying not to sound breathless, 'and the gentlemen with him.'

'He only has a page who is holding his horse ...' Kit broke off and gaped. The earl had followed him and, steering him gently out of the way, he came into the workshop.

'No ceremony, please, Mistress Evershed. I am in haste. This will do very well.' He sent the apprentice off with a shilling, and plunged straight into business without even sitting down. The delivery of the garments and the question of payment were dealt with swiftly.

'We shall be leaving London very soon,' he said. 'The queen is snarling for revenge on the traitors who have dispossessed her whelp. She has an army on the Scottish border. God knows when I shall return. But whatever happens you shall have your due.'

Almost afraid to detain this efficient and martial young lord, Janet said diffidently that the work was here, if he wished to look at it. Not only did he look; he inspected each gown with the eye of a connoisseur, turning the embroidery to the light and running his fingers over the texture of the cloth. When he had done he glanced at Janet in pure admiration.

'It is beautiful,' he said simply. 'I was right to choose you.' Before she could give him godspeed, or do more than sketch a courtesy, he was gone.

She did not know what to make of him. Languid womaniser, courtier, good brother, business man; she had seen them all in turn and still she could not tell who Edward of March really was. At least his approbation had been sincere, and she was honest enough to admit that that meant a great deal to her. They had met, this time, on equal terms; he had not been trying to provoke her, and she had not been fighting him. Janet went back to the children's clothes and touched them as he had. He must care very much about his sister and brothers, she thought, to take such personal trouble over their gifts.

The armies had marched; north with York and the Earl of Salisbury; west with March. London seemed empty without the swaggering liveries. As soon as her commission was despatched, Janet had intended to go home for Christmas; her father wanted to present her with a possible marriage contract. But Queen Margaret and her half-French troops were wreaking havoc in the borderlands, and Thomas wrote to his daughter to stay where she was. It was no safe time for travelling.

As the cold weather closed its grip on the capital, so did ignorance and fear. Tidings were garbled and contradictory, but behind them all was the threat of the Lancastrian army. The Londoners hated the queen – 'French wolf-bitch!' they muttered between their teeth – and now she hated them too for the injury done to the Prince of Wales. There were street-fights between opposing factions; Lancastrian sympathisers were baited. Trading dropped off; prudent men buried their valuables; idle apprentices rioted and attacked the property of Jews and Lombards and other minorities. Almost daily there were scares of an advancing host, and citizens stood to arms. It was like the days of Jack Cade's rebellion all over again, they said to each other.

Janet had other worries too. With her father likely to be among the levies from York, he might be at war now; being so near the troubled area, her whole family could be in danger. She prayed for them every day, and for Geoffrey who was riding gaily with his earl in the midlands. And she thought, increasingly, of Edward. Although she had done her best to avoid him when he was in London, now she wished that he was there to avoid. He would never return, she was convinced, and repented of her hostility to a man who had been so good to her.

January was two days old when terror came to the city with news from the north. The Duke of York had been killed at the gates of his own castle of Sandal near Wakefield. Salisbury had fallen with him, the duke's second son cut down in flight, and the army wiped out. The road to London was open to the hordes of the avenging queen and they were coming, looting, burning, raping as they came like foreign conquerors. After the first messenger others came, fugitives from the battle and from the villages and towns in the path of the Lancastrians, with worse and worse tales of their atrocities. London was filling with refugees, and the city fathers held frantic councils of war while the citizens panicked. To open the gates and risk the fate of the north, or to close the gates and face a long winter siege? When the menace was only a few days off, they closed the gates.

The choice was made; Warwick was called upon to direct preparations for a siege. Young George and Richard of York were packed off to the friendly shores of Flanders, but the citizens were more confident now that the Great Earl was in charge. In mid-February he ventured out to confront Queen Margaret, bearing the unresisting King Henry with him as a talisman.

Once more London was thrown into confusion by a thunderbolt of unexpected disaster. Not only had Warwick lost the king, but his forces had been routed at St Albans. Gathering what men he could salvage, the defeated earl was in full retreat westwards. The recapture of Henry VI had stripped from the Yorkists their thin rag of legality, and triumphantly the queen crouched to descend on London and take the last prize.

A thin ray of light was all that alleviated the gloom of the beleaguered capital. Somewhere in the Welsh Marches, the new Duke of York, inexperienced as he was, remained undefeated. For Janet, anxiety for her family had sunk beneath the weight of dread she felt for him. She could not concentrate on her work, and she woke at night sweating with fear. Hourly she expected a messenger to ride through the western gates, crying that Edward of York had died in a skirmish. Nick could not understand the distraction of his normally placid mistress, and gave her the lugubrious comfort that the French queen might be able to keep her soldiers from actually slaughtering the women.

PART I: THE KING

When news did come, it was glorious. Edward of York had won a battle at Mortimer's Cross, put the Earl of Pembroke to flight, joined with Warwick, and was marching with all speed on London. It was his first independent battle, a brilliant victory, appropriately at a place named after his own ancestors. On the morning of the fight, a strange sight had appeared in the sky – three suns which slowly merged into one – and Edward had taken it as an omen of success. So it had proved, and Janet was overflowing with pride as he rode into London, taking precedence even over the Earl of Warwick.

It was a hasty triumph; the Lancastrians had turned north again before the combined forces of Warwick and York, and they must be pursued and destroyed. Men flocked to the Yorkist standards. Queen Margaret's barbarous behaviour had thoroughly alienated the populace, and it was a truly popular army which left shortly afterwards to put an end to fear.

She was brought to bay south of York, and there on the plain of Towton, in a driving blizzard, the bloodiest battle in English memory was waged. Thomas Wrangwysh was one of the Yorkists who fought with shadows, killing wraiths in a white world, who fell away and were replaced by others – friend or foe, real or imaginary. Only when there was nothing in front, when the shadows had whirled away with the snow, did they know that they had won.

Janet awoke one morning to spring and bells clashing wildly from every steeple in London. Without asking she knew what had happened. The people were out in their best clothes in the cold sunny morning. Delivered from the threat of anarchy, everyone was congratulating everyone else, and Janet was kissed by all the acquaintances she met, and by at least three complete strangers. Yorkist devices were flaunted everywhere, and the Lancastrian sympathisers changed their allegiance, or slipped quietly into sanctuary.

He came as king, triumphal and shining-fair in the sunshine, his great banner of the Sun in Splendour taking fire and throwing it back joyfully at its original. His brothers were at his side, back from exile, blonde George and dark Richard, and the Earl of Warwick came behind, yielding place of honour to his protégé. London roared and worshipped; no dissenting voice was heard against the events which had deposed mad King Henry and placed this young golden god in his seat. But Janet was speechless in the crowd, wanting only in her relief to fall on her knees and thank God and all His Saints for preserving him to such a wonderful destiny.

CHAPTER FOUR

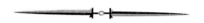

S oon after his coronation King Edward gave a small reception at Westminster for some of the leading city merchants, to thank them for their support and assure them of his. Quite unfairly, Janet was invited, presumably through the influence of her uncle, who had reappeared limping jauntily from an arrow-wound at Towton. It would be the last invitation to court; Geoffrey was due to take up his position as Chamberlain at Middleham now that peace was restored.

She went with none of her former reluctance, braving the raised eyebrows of the merchant princes who had never heard of her. This was to be her farewell to the gorgeous world where she was only an interloper, and to the man who was its axis. Deliberately she stored up images in her memory, so she could tell her grandchildren about the afternoon she had spent as the guest of King Edward IV. Outside the trees were glittering after a summer shower; beneath the painted ceiling the sober affluence of the burgesses mingled with the jewelled nobility. Yet these were only impressions on the borders of her vision, unimportant embellishments, because all the time she could not take her eyes off him.

Except for a thinning of the face which matured him, and an aura of majesty now acknowledged, he was unchanged. Still he moved among his guests, as easy with the commons and their wives as with the highest in the land. And her only desire was that he should look at her. Modest and unnoticed she stood at the side of the hall, remembering the time when she had tried to hide, and he had asked her to dance. Her legs felt weak as she thought of how he had taken her hand, and she was close to weeping at the opportunity she had wasted.

It was Richard who brought them together. He was the smallest person there, apparently in imminent danger of being trampled unawares by some substantial citizen. Seeing Janet alone he came towards her, very nervous and frail, wearing the blue gown she had made for him. He thanked her politely and then faltered to a stop, staring at her appealingly. Janet realised that he had sought her out as a familiar face among a sea of strange ones, and that now he had found an island he did not want to leave it.

So she asked him gently about his stay in Flanders, drawing him out in the natural way she had with small boys. Before long he was talking quite fluently, though she had seldom heard him string more than half a dozen words together. In the autumn he was going up to Middleham, to be trained as a knight in the Earl of Warwick's household. He enquired shyly if she had ever been there, since he knew she came from Yorkshire, and she told him that her mother's family had lived in Wensleydale, and had served the Nevilles for generations. Rapidly gaining confidence, he explained what kind of things he would have to learn.

Suddenly Edward was there too, tenderly regarding his brother in earnest conversation with the grave girl beside him. His eyes met Janet's over the brown head, in perfect understanding. She sank into a reverence, and he raised her firmly, his other hand on Richard's shoulder. Beyond the circle of their silence, Janet sensed dimly the stir of indignation among the burgesses that the king should deign to look in such a humble direction. Their annoyance was complete when George, freshly created Duke of Clarence, bounced into the royal group. He had grown during his winter abroad, and the set of his handsome head was more assured than ever. With an air of condescension he praised Janet's embroidery and said he had decided to continue his patronage.

'Now that I am heir presumptive to the throne, I must keep up my state. The second gentleman in England should have all the best craftsmen at his disposal. I am staying at court, of course. I don't have to go back to school like Dickon'. He related with distaste that they had had to continue their lessons all the time they were in Flanders, and that Richard had apparently enjoyed them.

'He didn't mind that we were poor and treated without respect. The Duke of Burgundy wouldn't receive us until our royal brother was victorious. Then he was quick enough to send for us.' His blue eyes flashed contemptuously at the time-serving of Philippe of Burgundy. The king was listening to him with an indulgent smile, his hand still resting on the younger child's shoulder. Richard looked from one to the other, utterly content simply to be with the two splendid brothers he idolised.

Their lofty rank did not matter; they were brothers, bound together by blood and affection. For that moment, drawn into their closeness by her love for her own family, Janet ceased to be an outsider, and became part of them. As Edward turned away to attend to a large fishmonger, he gave her a friendly half-smile which made her heart bound. She no longer cared about the envious and frankly venomous glances directed at her by less favoured guests; his smile was warm against her heart, and it was proof against envy and against time.

That was the end of it, she thought. For a few brief months, the remote magnificent figure in the processions had been a real person to her, and had acknowledged her existence with kindness. Now he would retreat again into the middle distance, leaving her to hug her memories.

So absolute was her conviction that it was all over, that she did not believe Nick's laconic announcement three days later that the king had come to see her. She still did not believe it when her servant showed him into the solar and shut the door behind him. Edward said nothing; he crossed the room to where she stood irresolute, took her into his arms and kissed her. There was no time for her to resist. She was nothing and nowhere; everything was swept away but his lips and his body and his hard warm hands.

Bewildered and overwhelmed by him, she could not comprehend the words he was whispering close to her ear.

'Lie with me, Janet. Come back to Westminster and I will give you everything.'

Then she was aware of where his hands were, and what it was he was asking. The hot blood racing through her head cooled abruptly. She stiffened in his embrace, and at once he relaxed his grip.

But he still held her by the elbows and said 'Come with me. I want you.' His expression was strangely impersonal, his grasp possessive but controlled.

'No, your grace.' Though she was still weak from his touch, she could answer him quite firmly.

'If you prefer, I'll send someone back for you later on this evening.'

Janet shook her head, and repeated, more emphatically, 'No, your grace.'

The king smiled faintly.

'I can't make love to you here. I have two gentlemen waiting outside.'

Something about his manner was fast restoring to her the faculties he had scattered. She dared to look into his eyes, and hold his gaze.

'Do you understand what I am offering? To make you my mistress.'

'I understand. But I have said no, sire.'

He dropped a light kiss on her mouth.

'You're very convincing,' he said teasingly. 'If I didn't know better, I might take you seriously.'

'Then I beg you to take me seriously.'

Edward sighed in mock despair. 'Mistress Evershed! I would have thought you a woman who made up her mind and held to it. But, then, you are a woman.' His assured tone, the growing condescension he was using towards her, was arousing in her quite a different emotion from before.

'If I have ever given you cause to think … You have mistaken me, your grace.'

'What! When your uncle has been telling me for months that you were mad for me?'

'My uncle?' Janet was flabbergasted.

'Of course. And like a good uncle he has done his best to prefer you to me.'

Her rising temper boiled over in fury at Geoffrey's duplicity.

'Then he is nothing but a pandar!' Only her innate discipline prevented her from flinging the king's hands from her arms. But the mockery had gone from his face, and he was looking straight at her again.

'You didn't know,' he said quite soberly.

'That my own uncle was busy selling my honour behind my back? No, I didn't know.' Geoffrey's treachery was like being stung by a butterfly. How she hated men! Lords of creation who respected their women less than their horses. She was disgusted with herself for surrendering to one of them, even for a moment.

'Poor Janet,' the king said softly. 'You have been mightily abused.' With two fingers he brushed her temple, and let her go. Deprived of his support, she had to readjust her balance. The wave of anger was subsiding, leaving her with a sense of remote desperation.

'But you know now,' he added. 'Don't waste his labour ... and mine. Come with me, and I'll make you forget your uncle.'

She shook her head again, dumbly. Edward shrugged his shoulders; he seemed to be neither disappointed nor insulted by her refusal.

'Very well.' Turning to go, he said casually, 'When I was in York after the fight at Towton I met your father. We have arranged for your brother John to share Lord Richard's training at Middleham.' Unhurriedly he departed.

She sat on into the luminous twilight, trying to anchor her fragmentary thoughts into some kind of perspective. One thing was definite: she would never give Geoffrey Barton her confidence again. He had forfeited all claims to her friendship by his behaviour. Beyond that, everything was dim, clothed in the same unreality which had surrounded her marriage and the deserted house she had found in London two years ago.

A king, newly crowned, the idol of his country, young, handsome, victorious, coming into her solar and asking her to be his mistress. It was incredible. And she had turned him down. Why had she done it? Were her moral scruples really as strong as all that? Ever since she was deprived of Giles she had half-consciously hankered after the dominance of a man – and what a man! Not only was he magnetically attractive; he was generous too. He had arranged for John's advancement without making any bargain with her, and she knew he would not go back on his decision out of pique. She recognised with awe that she was rejecting what many women in London would have risked damnation for.

It must have been his certainty that she would fall, that masculine arrogance which had annoyed her at their first meeting. She would not give him the satisfaction of raising his eyebrows in the infuriating way he had, and thinking smugly that she was just like all the others. Her flourishing sense of independence revolted against that. It would be hard enough to be subject to a husband; she would be no man's plaything. A mistress for a day or two, perhaps on and off for a few months; then he would load her with gifts and forget her, and she would be the laughing-stock of London. The proud female merchant who had thought herself a match for the entire Mercers' Guild, sunk to being the king's occasional whore. Janet blushed with shame into the dusk, and resolved to hold out against him. She was wise enough now to guess that, despite his apparent indifference, the king would not give her up so lightly.

But it was far from easy to keep to her resolution. At night, and in sleep, her senses revolted against her will. Dreaming, she succumbed to the pleasure she would not contemplate when awake. Then she was furious with herself, and went to confession with fanatical frequency, and did twice the set penance. She threw herself frantically into work, but whenever her mind was unoccupied it was trapped again into its obsession, reliving that one giddy kiss, tormenting her with curiosity about what would have followed, choking with righteous indignation at the king's effrontery, fearing bleakly that now it was too late, he would not try again, and she had lost her only chance of an extraordinary lover. Caught unawares, she would turn faint at the memory of his arms around her; she jumped nervously at each knock at the door, terrified that he would come again and she would not be able to resist. It was like a nightmare in which she was running very fast, but getting nowhere, while the thing behind her, a thing of exquisite terror, was gradually overhauling her. Pointlessly she longed for the days of quiet composure before she set eyes on him, when everything was energetic, and useful, and unemotional.

A summons from the palace sent her into a panic which mystified her household, and was only partly allayed by the information that it came from his grace of Clarence. Her heart in her mouth, Janet waited on the duke, Nick close behind with two bales of fine woollen cloth. Clarence received her with lordly patronage, but showed a decided interest in the stuff she had brought. While he was inspecting it, the king came in, and Janet's suspicions about the interview were confirmed. Whatever the king's brother might suppose, Edward had engineered it. As George was giving his specifications to Master Farthing, Edward asked to look at the cloth. Under cover of a technical question, he enquired if she had changed her mind. Forced to remain unconcerned because of the others in the room, Janet fought down her acute embarrassment. He offered to let her stay the night, and assured her that he would arrange everything.

'Oh yes, he could arrange everything!' she raged silently, with a sudden conviction that every encounter between them had been connived at by this unscrupulous king and her shameless uncle. She knew she was covering up very badly, and Edward knew it too. When she could give him no answer, his manner changed, and softened, and he began talking about the quality of the cloth. He had allowed the line she was struggling on to go slack once more, and she was obscurely grateful to him – far more than she should have been. Perhaps it was because, if he had pressed any harder, she might have consented. In her relief, she thoughtlessly promised to bring the Duke of Clarence's order in person to his apartments.

At home, the full realisation of her plight struck her. She was cornered and sooner or later the king would make his kill. The pen unsteady in her hand, she wrote to her father. In York, Edward would not be able to reach her, and when she was married, or betrothed, surely not even he would carry on the pursuit. But she could not hope for a reply before the middle of August; after two years of prevarication she could not abruptly demand a husband without arousing her father's suspicions. Somehow she was sure he would not be sympathetic to her predicament. Wishing that the messenger could fly, she waited on tenterhooks for permission to escape.

Too quickly, the cloth Clarence had ordered arrived from the warehouse. Unable to delay its delivery any longer, she made her unwilling way back to Westminster alone. Nick her chaperon was down with a summer ague, Kit was visiting his father, and she had to leave Nan in charge of the shop. Before she reached the duke's suite she was waylaid by a straight-faced page, who announced that his grace the king wished to speak to her briefly. With leaden feet she followed him, and made a hasty application for St Agnes to protect her chastity.

He was waiting in a tiny luxurious antechamber, so she was almost on top of him as soon as she entered.

'How long will you keep me waiting? Have pity on my sleepless nights, Janet.' There was no trace of the arrogant male in his attitude. But she was becoming accustomed to his chameleon moods, and was as wary of this approach as of his aggressiveness before.

'I have given you my decision, sire, and I meant what I said.' It was easier, face to face, to keep her voice steady than she had anticipated. Forewarned, she said to herself, was forearmed.

'I hoped that time might soften your heart ....when you realised that you were no mere passing fancy. If it's the loss of honour which holds you back, don't forget that there's no disgrace in being the mistress of a king. Any other woman would jump at what I'm offering you.'

'But I'm not any other woman, your grace. Can't you take one who is willing, and let me be?'

'Don't be such a hypocrite, Janet. You have been in love with me ever since my crowning – and probably before. It didn't take your uncle to tell me that.'

His cool reason cut the ground from under her feet. It was something she had not even admitted to herself, and yet he knew. Had she been so transparent? Trying to regain her equanimity, she said lamely, 'My feelings have nothing to do with it. My conscience – '

'Your life is your own. You would be betraying no-one.'

Except myself, she thought, but she said 'There is my good name. In my profession reputation is everything.'

'Nobody shall know,' he promised her quickly. 'I can be very discreet. You must have noticed that? If I can see a woman is ready to fall, I assure you I don't normally go to these lengths. I simply send for her, quite openly.' There it was again; the assumption that he was irresistible.

'Yes, you are the king.' She could not keep the annoyance out of her voice. 'You may do as you please with me or any of your subjects. But it's unjust of you to take advantage of my duty to force me –'

'I am not forcing you. And I've taken no advantage – except perhaps in stealing some of my brother's time for myself.' It was true. The magnet by which he drew her towards him had nothing to do with his rank. But with words she could keep him at bay. There they were on fairly equal terms.

'But why me, your grace? I'm not well-born or beautiful, and really not worth your trouble.'

'Oh yes, you are.' He stepped nearer to her and she braced herself to resist his demands. Yet though his closeness stopped her breath, he did not touch her. 'Beauty and high blood are round me every day. I have my fill of them. Sometimes their falseness chokes me. Not one of the noble ladies who grace my court would speak to me as you have done, honestly and without guile. I want your sincerity, and your warmth, and your love.'

'I can't, sire.' His appeal had distressed her as the expected embrace could not have done. She wanted to explain that she lived in a different world where his kind of love had no place, only business negotiations and marriage contracts, but he would not understand. All she could do was to refuse him, with that blunt inadequate phrase.

'Well, well, I've been containing myself for a long time. I daresay I can wait a little longer. It's lucky that my lord of Warwick is such a hard worker. The time I've spent on you should have been used elsewhere. But, remember, my patience is not inexhaustible.' The moment of gravity had passed, and he was talking with his usual lightness. Nevertheless, he clearly meant what he said, and her throat tightened again.

'Now you must go, or George will suspect. Though in some ways he's as dense as mud, he can scent intrigue from a mile off.' He had so aptly summed up the odd mixture of precocity and immaturity that was the Duke of Clarence that she could not help joining in his laugh. Suddenly, from the laugh, he leant over her and kissed her gently. Then he spread his hands and said, 'You see how restrained I am?' Without calling the page, who had tactfully absented himself, the king opened the door and directed her to Clarence's apartments.

At least she knew where she stood. He had made his intentions quite plain, and now it was up to her. But the king had also revealed to her how precariously thin were her defences against him. The conventional moral code of her order meant very little to him, and in the face of his persistence it was beginning to lose its meaning for her too. Honour, reputation, chastity were words which merely sounded pretentious when she used them in argument against him. His only motive was lust, she insisted to herself every hour; all he wanted was the sinful gratification of the flesh, and that was the only temptation which drew her towards him. Mortify the flesh, said the priest that she consulted; follow the example of the blessed St Benedict and punish the body you have inherited from Eve.

But that was not all. The severest penance she inflicted on herself could not eradicate the flash of pity she had felt when he asked her for her love. It was foolish pity, because he had everything he could want at his call, but it was eating away at her resolution. There was in her a generous desire to give which had never been satisfied, and this was the hardest thing to fight.

The king was going to the Welsh Marches, to mop up some stubborn resistance to his rule. Making the most of the respite Janet left before him, to meet a cargo from Cyprus at Southampton. The ship was late, and when she returned to London a letter from her father was awaiting her. Bessie's second child, he wrote, was due sometime in September. It would be best if Janet delayed her visit until October, when the fuss would be over; she could attend the christening and they could give their whole attention to her marriage. He had several promising contenders, said Thomas encouragingly. If only I had not delayed so long, Janet thought, and counted the days.

Edward had come back. Three days before she was due to leave she received a summons to Windsor, to join a royal hawking party. A groom would be sent to escort her, ran the message ominously. She did not refuse; she was at the end of her resistance.

There were some twenty ladies and gentlemen idling their horses round the bailey of Windsor Castle, casual and light-hearted in their sporting costumes. Janet, who rode astride like most of her peers, stationed herself diffidently between the wall and a large nobleman and tried to work out how the ladies perched on their elegant side-saddles kept their seat at a trot. Her attentive groom presented her with a merlin, and her attention was diverted to quieting the bird's bad temper. She had not handled a hawk since flying them in Wensleydale with Geoffrey as a child, but this one seemed to be a particularly wild little bird. Sure she was being regarded with derision, and cursing the king for so embarrassing her, she tried to quieten its fierce bating.

By the time she had won temporary mastery the king had arrived, with his close friend Lord Hastings, and the company was preparing to ride. Tucking herself away at the rear, Janet followed them down the hill towards the eaves of the forest.

To compensate for the ruined harvest of the previous year, summer was spreading its warmth into late October. For several weeks the glorious weather had continued, and ungrateful people complained about the heat. The sun was sifting down like powdered gold, and coating the castle and the treetops with its radiance. Parched of its seasonable rain, the countryside was kindling. As yet the oak trees had only turned brown at the edges, but the hedgerows along the road to Windsor had been smouldering; the chestnuts burned with a clear yellow flame, and here and there a dogwood bush had burst into a crown of crimson fire.

Before they entered the trees the party was already stringing out. Dawdling at the end of the line, Janet slowly lost her self-consciousness and gave herself wholeheartedly to the beauty of the day. The groom, unobtrusive at her stirrup, pointed out the busy flight of a pigeon not far away across the meadow, and she unhooded her merlin and tossed it into the air. Business-like and swift, the hawk intercepted its quarry and stooped to the kill. When they came up with it standing over the dead pigeon, its mad bright eyes were defiant. It gave vent to an indignant squawk when the groom took possession of its prey, and was reluctant to return to Janet's wrist.

As the man strung the prize to his saddle Janet saw that the others were far ahead, turning from gold to dark green as they rode between the outlying trees into the forest. She was relieved. Edward had been at the head of the column, talking incessantly to Lord Hastings, a portly merry gentleman with a reputation for knowing how to live. In his congenial company there would be no room for thoughts of her. Probably he had invited her on a whim and forgotten all about it. Lulled by the soporific mildness of the air, the last of her anxiety dropped away and she forgot him too.

A duck flew across the pale patch of sky overhead and she loosed the merlin. Locked together, the two birds plummeted out of sight, away to the right of the track. Janet and her groom urged their horses in the direction of the kill, but the bracken, brown and brittle, was still thick off the path and the going was slow. Though her companion seemed sure enough of the way, Janet's urban senses were soon confused. The groom was calling and swinging the lure round his head, but there was no response. It had been unwise of them, Janet suggested tentatively, to fly the merlin in such a thick patch of woodland. He shrugged and said that it was a temperamental bird, and since it had not taken to Janet it would be difficult to retrieve it. Rather cowed by her own incompetence in winning the merlin's confidence, she agreed meekly to his proposal that they should separate and circle the area. Since the hawk was obviously not coming back, they must find it with its quarry.

She rode deeper into the trees drowsing in the dreamlike stillness of noon. The dead bracken rustled round the horse's knees and brushed her ankles. With the town-dweller's awareness, she drank in the silence. Reaching a glade dappled with sunshine she searched for the birds, but there was no sign of them on the rich green turf or in the undergrowth around. She tried to take her bearings by the sun, and went on into the shade again. As she left the sun and ducked to avoid a low-sweeping beech bough she thought she heard the thudding of hooves behind. Imagining that the groom had found the merlin, she stopped and turned.

Edward was reining in at the edge of the sunlight, very tall on his tall horse, the large emerald in his cap flashing rays of brilliance. He was smiling at her. Her heart leaped, then sank with dull dread. How he had managed it this time she could only guess – the groom must have been given careful instructions, the recalcitrant merlin chosen deliberately. The fact remained. He had caught her.

Without a word she slipped from the saddle into the deep bracken, and stood passively awaiting him. He picked her up and carried her to a small circle of grass amid the undergrowth, and though it was quite dry he spread his cloak there for her. She lay staring upwards through the thinning leaves of a chestnut to the sky, the pungency of the bracken pricking her nostrils. The king took off his jerkin and knelt at her side. His eyes were shining with a preoccupied excitement, as they had the first time he kissed her. As his hands slid over her body, doing all the things she had dreamed they would do, her mind was quite cold. There was none of the incandescent fever which had carried her away before. She knew what he was doing, and that she was letting him, and it meant nothing.

A leaf detached itself from the twig above her, and she watched its leisurely progress, rocking and tumbling in slow motion, to the ground. Occasionally his face blotted out the sky, and she had difficulty in breathing because he was heavy. But there was very little pain, and not long after that he rolled off her and lay on his back beside her, panting a little and gazing at the sky. Presently he said, 'Your husband didn't take you.'

Since it was not a question she did not bother to answer; he had known that a year ago. He turned his head on the grass.

'Did I hurt you?'

She said no in a rather muffled voice. His enquiry was as detached as her mind. There was nothing left of the current of attraction which had flowed between them since the rainy day in Walbrook. He propped himself on one elbow and looked at her, frowning slightly.

'It was my fault; I should have waited for you. I'm not usually so churlish, but I had been patient for too long. It will be better next time.' The words rang vaguely familiar. Then she remembered Giles, the long brown back in the fitful candlelight. That had woken more in her than any of this. She was surprised that Edward should talk about a next time. As he spoke he had reached out to touch her neck; but involuntarily she recoiled.

At once his languor disappeared. Sitting up, he straightened his clothing and then hers, and gave her his hand.

'Up, sweet heart!' he said briskly, and held on to her while she brushed the dead leaves from her kirtle. 'Don't worry, it will pass,' he assured her, and she wondered how he could know that her depression was close to tears. He smiled at her again, friendly and kind, not at all as he had smiled when he caught her, and went to fetch their horses.

They rode on together through the forest.

'We're hunting tomorrow,' he said, 'Over towards Ascot. Will you stay the night at the castle and come with us?'

She explained that she was leaving for Yorkshire the day after tomorrow, and must be back in London tonight. The king pondered this for a moment, then said with a laugh, 'You were trying to run away, weren't you?'

'I suppose so.' His glance took in her bleak expression sympathetically, and he changed the subject.

'While you're in the north you must pay a visit to my brother Dickon. He's very eager to begin his knightly training, but he'll be new and strange at Middleham for a time. I'd like someone to keep an eye on him.'

Janet said that she would, noticing his metamorphosis back into the good elder brother she had met in Southwark. He began to talk about his own upbringing, with his dead brother Edmund, at Ludlow under the Great Earl.

'My lord of Warwick gave me everything I have,' he remarked, 'Including my crown. If I'm a successful soldier, it's due to what I learnt from his example. If I'm a king, it's because he made me one. He's the best master I could wish for Dickon.' This amiable young man, chatting about his admired mentor, was impossible to reconcile with the alien creature who had so recently been striving for his satisfaction above her. Oddly enough, Janet found herself responding to the platonic companion, as she had been unable to do to the lover.

On the main track Janet's groom was waiting, expressionless, the merlin quiet on his wrist. A mallard hung from his saddle, its iridescent head lolling. Edward made no comment, and as the man fell in behind them, he went on in the same easy fashion about his return to Ludlow during the Welsh campaign.

'It's one of the finest fortresses in the land,' he declared. 'I shall send my son there for his education, as my father sent me.'

She ventured to ask if this meant that Wales was subdued.

'For the present. But in those mountains they never stay peaceful for long. There's nothing for them to do except fight – if not the English, then one another. And unfortunately, that trouble maker Jasper Tydder escaped me at Mortimer's Cross, and may well have been behind this latest effort. He's as slippery as an eel. I preferred his father, even though we had to behead him after the battle. He had some panache. I can't imaging Jasper winning any queen's heart.' Janet recalled the story of Owen Tydder, the Welsh adventurer who had followed Henry V into Katherine of France's bed.

'That was a romantic tale,' she suggested.

'Or sordid. According to how you look at it. Although King Harry can't have been a comfortable husband.'

That set her thinking that soon Edward would be seeking a wife, and she wondered if he would let Warwick do that for him too. It was an unlikely prospect. But in a year's time they would probably both be married and absorbed, happily or not, in their own lives. Their paths would not run parallel for long.

Through the smooth grey pillars of the beech trunks flashes of colour appeared, and snatches of light voices, and they came upon the rest of their company. The royal party was resting in a clearing beside a bow-shaped lake, inky-black with centuries of drowned leaf-mould. On a tawny carpet of beech-leaves the ladies were seated, their wide skirts spread round them. The gentlemen reclined at their sides, or leaned against the trees, their booted legs crossed elegantly. Pages plied between them with flasks of ale and venison pasties, and the ladies fed tit-bits to the supercilious hawks on their gloves. In the place of honour an untidy pile of feathers, brown, grey and white, was being counted over by the falconers.

No-one manifested the least surprise when the king rode into the clearing, though Janet could have sworn that Lord Hastings, glancing up as she went past, winked at her. If she had been alone she would have died of shame; this worldly unconcern was worse than open scorn. But despite what Edward had done to her, his protection was round her like a cloak, and the shame barely reached her. It was he who helped her to dismount; it was he who found her a cushion to sit on and a page to supply her with refreshments. Even when he left her, with the same courtesy, she felt immune to knowing eyes.

Dusty shafts of light struck low across the lake, midges and motes dancing down them. The October day was passing, and the party prepared lazily to ride back to the castle. When they emerged into the water-meadows near the Thames, mist was already rising from the river; the willows and grazing cows were wading in it. The indefinable tang of autumn was in the air.

Janet parted from the others at a postern gate, and on the way to

Datchet she looked back at the castle. The sun had gone, and the massive battlements were dark against a dull pink sky. All she wanted to do was to go home.

CHAPTER FIVE

A s soon as she left London she was free. Two summers before, she had come to the capital expecting to be imprisoned, but the snare waiting for her had turned out to be quite undomestic. Since Windsor she had been in a kind of stupor, brooding over why she had given in, and why she felt so unchanged. Though she had committed mortal sin and lost her maidenhead, there was no sense of wickedness; though she had wanted it for weeks, there was no fulfilment. Her act of contrition was as meaningless as the deed for which she was atoning. But as London dropped behind her, so did her troubles.

Brooding would have been difficult in the raucous company of her fellow-travellers. Apart from a group of dyers going to Tadcaster, there were three palmers, two brothers and a wife, bound for the shrine of St Cuthbert at Durham. They were seasoned pilgrims, full of wayfarers' yarns and jokes, and they kept the conversation bubbling as they journeyed north along the well-worn rutted road which the Romans had built. The cockleshells in their hats, said the elder brother, were no fairings; they had bought them in Compostella, after paying their respects to St James, and what was more they had seen King Henry of Castile pass through the town while they were there. Rome, of course, they had visited more than once, but they had not quite made Jerusalem. An epidemic had been raging, and they were turned back at Jaffa. After that, the other brother put in off-handedly, their ship had nearly been taken by a Venetian galley, and only escaped because the wind changed.

With very little prompting the pilgrims displayed the relics they had collected, which made a sizeable bundle, and included a splinter of the wheel on which St Catherine was martyred, and a scrap of the sail of St Peter's fishing boat. The three of them depended on the charity of the rest of the party for their food and lodgings. It was given unstintingly; the merchants were well-off, and were pleased to pay for such good entertainment by the way.

And day after day, as the country changed, the sun remained, bathing the land in a honeyed mist which softened every outline. The inns were comfortable, the company congenial, and they met no hazards.

Now and again, however, they came across burnt-out villages, uninhabited except by stray dogs, and razed woods and fields with a scattering of new growth over blackened soil. There were beggars too, sometimes whole families, whining for alms, made destitute by the ravaging march of Queen Margaret and her horde after Wakefield. Strangers to wanton destruction, the travellers were appalled by the healing scars, but the palmers were unmoved. On the continent, they said with a shrug, they had seen whole provinces with no signs of life, laid waste by mercenaries. England was lucky.

The rolling hills of south Yorkshire were around them, and their last night's stop was at Pomfret. Approaching Tadcaster the following day they passed the upland, now lying fallow and quiet, where the Battle of Towton had been fought in the spring. Janet recalled her father's description, the driving snow, the whiteness flecked with blood all the way to York, and marvelled that nature could recover so quickly.

At Tadcaster the party broke up. The pilgrims had secured an overnight roof from one of the dyers, but Janet decided to press on the last few miles and reach York by nightfall. Only a taciturn farmer from the Vale of Pickering accompanied her. Leaving the noise of Tadcaster, the gaiety of the pilgrims, and the comfortable gossip of the merchants, she went on in silence.

The sinking sun threw an elongated shadow on the road before her; no birds were singing, except the sudden liquid music of a robin. There was only the soft scuffing of the horses' hooves, and a singing warmth in her heart. She strained her eyes for the first sight of the Minster, and there it was, a misty blue shape over the fields to the left. It was soon hidden again, but already Janet could feel the teeming bustle of the streets as she remembered them, in the hour before curfew and the closing of the bars. When she reached the gentle slope that led up to Micklegate Bar, dusk had fallen and she could just make out the watch moving along the battlements to hand out the lanterns. The farmer turned off, pulling his forelock but saying nothing, and Janet persuaded her tired mount into a trot. Through the dark barbican and into the city, past the Priory, and there beside little St Gregory's was her home.

As she rode into the courtyard there was an eruption. Someone had seen her from a window, and the boys rushed out, Will, Dick, and Robert first, Tom behind them, much taller than she remembered him, with his good-natured beam, and at the door under the lamp Bessie with a baby in her arms and Thomas, black eyes snapping with pleasure. Her brothers almost pulled her off her horse, chattering at the tops of their voices, even little Rob with his stammer:

'Father says I can go to Nottingham with him!'

'Look how tall I am, Janet!'

'We have a whole side of venison, just like Christmas!'

Her eyes shining with tears which they could not see in the gathering gloom, she clasped all the excited young creatures to her, and slowly propelled them towards the house. Her father's arms were open; she ran into his bear-hug just as she always had, and she was a little girl again, her nose buried in the sweaty leathery smell of his chest.

Only John was lacking from a perfect homecoming. He had been up at Middleham for two months, but he would be home for Christmas, by dispensation of Warwick's Master of Henchmen. Though Janet missed her favourite brother, there were plenty of other Wrangwyshes to fill the gap, including the two small ones that she had not seen before. The new baby was a girl, named for her mother, a tiny replica of Bessie even to the fluffy flaxen hair sticking out of her swaddling clothes. Young Tom, the firstborn, was fourteen months old, and staggered about on legs like pillars of butter. They were not peaceful children by any means, and their shrill din augmented the usual cacophony of Thomas Wrangwysh's household.

Janet sank thankfully back into the rowdy familiarity of her home, so different from the empty rooms of her London house; in the streets she was hailed with rough delight by people she had known since childhood. Here she was not Widow Evershed the mercer, but just Master Wrangwysh's girl Janet. If her brothers had not grown so much, the clock might have stood still for two years.

There was not much chance to see York in the sunshine. Almost as soon as she arrived, the weather broke. Rain fell steadily, and then sleet, and with December came snow. On the first Sunday the boys were out in the courtyard at dawn, throwing snowballs at the apprentices, sliding and building snowmen, their clear voices carrying crisply in the frozen air. Janet helped with the snowman, and was pelted by Will for her trouble. She shook the melting snow out of the folds of her hood and laughed at Will's red grinning face above his muffler. Last night he had gone to bed furious, because he had been beaten at school for insolence, and at home for complaining about it; she was glad that he was not sulking.

Ten-year-old Will was causing his father much more trouble than his elder brother Tom ever had. He was rebellious, and defiant, and loathed going to school. But Janet guessed that Thomas was in fact much prouder of his wilful second son than he was of his compliant eldest. From hints let slip in expansive moods, she had gathered that as a boy he had been just as difficult as Will.

He wasted no time in getting down to business with her. As he had requested, she brought with her a full account of the assets and prospects of her business, and in return he had two handsome matches under negotiation. One was a merchant of the Staple, recently

64

widowed, influential, not much above thirty, and a Yorkshireman born and bred. The other was rather older, with a teenage son and two cotton-mills in Lancashire. Meetings were arranged, and she travelled over to Beverley to see one, and to Manchester to see the other.

But her enthusiasm was gone. When it came to an issue, the frantic desire for a husband had left her. It had merely been a refuge that she thought she needed from pursuit. Now Edward had caught her, and left her, to hide from him was pointless.

On the way back from Manchester, Thomas said to her 'Your heart's not in it, is it, lass?'

She admitted that she did not care for the mill-owner.

'It's hard to give up the reins once you've held them for a while. I understand.' Giving her a shrewd glance, he added, 'Happen if Giles had not gone so soon, you'd be more eager to be a wife again.'

Janet smiled wryly, and said nothing.

'Well, I won't rush you. I've always taken account of your wishes. But you'd be well-advised to take one or the other. You can't stay widow Evershed for ever, you know!' They let the matter rest until after Christmas.

On St Lucy's Day, Tom and Bessie's daughter was christened Elizabeth Lucy in St Crux, and Janet stood godmother. The baby was very placid, and only smiled when the holy water splashed on her. Bessie, as usual, cried.

The snow stopped falling, and the main roads were cleared, but Yorkshire lay under a thick white blanket. There was some relief in Micklegate when the clouds lifted, because any more snow would have meant no visit from John. But the day after St Thomas Apostle, Janet and her father set out early for Middleham, to pay her promised visit and fetch John.

As they passed through the still flat Vale of York and began to climb up into the West Riding, Thomas told her about the aftermath of Wakefield and Towton, the terror in the north, as in the south, at Margaret's army, and the joyous reception of Edward and Warwick. A number of citizens, including Thomas and the Lord Mayor, had discussed a protest about the bad taste of setting the Duke of York's head on Micklegate Bar, but they had decided on a prudent silence. The paper crown Margaret had mocked him with, however, did not survive long.

'There will be little sympathy in York for the House of Lancaster now,' Thomas remarked. 'And the new king took all hearts when he came. If he is as wise as he is comely, England is a lucky country. But I hear he wastes his time on harlotry and lets Warwick rule?'

Janet said something non-committal; she did not want to talk about Edward. Her father had no such inhibitions. To him the king was a generous patron, both to Janet and to himself.

'He knows how to reward, though. For John to be trained at Middleham is a very great honour, especially as the king's brother is there now, besides the countess and her daughters. I didn't think my small service at Towton was worth so much – though I suppose your uncle Geoffrey put in a word for us.'

If her cheeks had not been so fiery with the keen wind, Janet's blush would have been uncomfortably evident. It was not so much her own guilt that troubled her – she still felt very little – as the reminder of Geoffrey's betrayal. She would meet him at Middleham for the first time since she had found out, and she was not quite confident of being civil towards him.

They crossed the frozen River Ure at Boroughbridge, and stopped to offer a prayer to St Wilfred in Ripon Abbey. Then they were up into the foothills of the Pennines, the cottages and farms embedded in the snow further apart, the country wilder. The road, barely passable, wound sometimes between head-high banks of snow which buried dry-stone walls. Pheasants ploughed through the virgin whiteness and whirred over their heads; the horizon, humpy and hillocky, blended with the leaden sky. As they passed Jervaulx Abbey, the tolling of the bell calling the monks to their office came like crystal through the sharp air.

The hills began to widen out into Wensleydale, and with the arrested grey glitter of the Ure on their right they set their horses at the slippery sloping road up to Middleham. Under the sheer walls of the castle the cottages clustered as if for warmth, their little white caps pulled low over their ears. Some townsfolk were returning home with a cartload of logs; they were having to push the cart far harder than the small reluctant mule was pulling it. Nevertheless, they pressed into the snowy bank willingly to let pass the burgess and his daughter wrapped in their thick furs. Janet called out to thank them and they grinned, touching their hoods, their breath steaming round their heads.

The gates of the castle were open for them, and as they crossed the drawbridge the guard on duty, chafing his frostbitten fingers, greeted Thomas by name. Thomas had done all his courting at Middleham, and was almost as well-known here as his wife had been. They were met by the porter, who took them up to the gatehouse to warm themselves while Master Barton was informed. Standing in the snug cell, her numbed fingers tingling back to life round a goblet of spiced ale, Janet was gradually folded into the security of the ancient stronghold. A peaceful castle it had always been, tucked below the hill crowned with even older earthworks, sheltered by clumps of trees from the nakedness of the open dales. Middleham had none of the imposing starkness of Lord Scrope's castle Bolton further up the dale; it was a family place, long favoured by the Nevilles, with no bloody sieges or tragic prisoners to darken its past. Not as comfortable as Thomas's modern town house, of course, but thick glass and tapestries and braziers kept out most of the chill damp.

There was a light step on the stairs, and Janet drew herself up to face her uncle. He was smiling and elegant as usual, in coat and cap of coney fur, and brought to Janet a faint breath of courtly society, the courtesy and corruption of Westminster. But it was a very long way away, and seemed petty and unimportant from this northern valley. She called a silent truce between them, and let him kiss her.

Geoffrey led them down into the bitter cold of the courtyard, and up the long flight of stairs into the keep. In the stone passages it was draughty and the darkness was scarcely relieved by the guttering torches on the walls. Then Geoffrey held a leather curtain aside for them, and they were in the great hall.

A log fire blazed in the centre, and the smoke wandered aimlessly upwards, drifting around the rafters and filling the chamber with its stuffy warmth. Here the cressets flared steadily, eking out the wintry light which filtered through the tall windows. Tapestries were deep on the walls, rushes deep on the floor, and all round the hall dogs and children were sprawled. Two boys were playing chess; another was squatting cross-legged, plucking at a lute; one was asleep, full-length in the rushes; and near the fire a knot of three children, intent on the doings of a fourth. There were two girls wearing grey tunics over red woollen kirtles, the elder slim with loose blonde hair under her cap, the younger even thinner with waist-length fair plaits. Lord Richard stood with them, an absorbed frown on his sallow face, and at their feet was John, his hair ruffled, long legs folded under him like a colt, chipping away with his dagger at a block of wood which was already recognisable as a doll.

Spellbound by the spectacle, Janet and her father watched them, while Geoffrey explained in an undertone that the tiltyard was dangerously frozen, and that after a furious morning hunt, the Master of Henchmen had given them the afternoon off. The smaller girl was the first to notice the visitors, and she immediately hid behind her sister. Then John looked up, and sprang to his feet with a glad shout. He flung himself at his sister, and she narrowly escaped his dagger in her back as she embraced him. The other children in his group were hanging back awkwardly, awed by the imposing bulk of Master Wrangwysh. John's good manners, temporarily submerged, reasserted themselves and he presented his father and sister to his companions with punctilious ceremony.

'My lord Duke of Gloucester' received the homage of Thomas Wrangwysh a little nervously, but he favoured Janet with a shy smile, reminding her of their alliance at the merchant's reception. She had forgotten that, some weeks ago, King Edward had raised his other brother to a dukedom. A resounding title for an undergrown nine-year-old.

The little girls were the Earl of Warwick's daughters, Isabel and Anne, and though the elder managed a few gracious words, Anne merely gulped, the blood coming and going under her transparent skin.

Richard drew her aside and, borrowing the half-finished doll from John, thrust it gently into her arms. Her hands closed tightly on the puppet, and she let Richard lead her back to the fire.

After that the rest of Warwick's henchmen were introduced, including Francis Lovel with his lute, and Robert Percy yawning from sleep; none of the lads was as self-conscious as the three small aristocrats. Then the visitors were taken into the presence chamber to meet the countess. She was a worried lady of indeterminate age, with the kind of face which is difficult to call to mind afterwards. Her daughters were evidently all Beauchamp, with none of their father's assurance. The countess said she had had excellent reports of Master John's progress, and cordially invited Thomas and Janet to stay the night.

An evening at Middleham Castle was far removed from the formality of court life in London. There was a certain air of improvisation to the ceremony of eating and entertainment which appealed to Janet. The children were learning to be courtiers, but they had only just begun. Francis Lovel slopped the soup on the table as he was serving the countess, and the Duke of Gloucester fell over his feet when he was partnering Lady Isabel in an estampie. Not even the formidable Master of Henchmen was very hard on their mistakes; that would come later. For all their faults, the fledgling knights took their behaviour very seriously. There was nothing of the flippancy of London; here, the 'chevalier sans peur et sans rapproche' was still a possibility. And John was indeed shaping well. He performed his duties with gangling grace, and Thomas's critical eye could see little to distinguish the scions of nobility from the merchant's son.

At a respectably early hour, the countess and her daughters retired. Thomas and Janet were lighted to the chilly cubicles of their sleeping quarters, which made them regret accepting the countess's invitation. An inn in the town would have been far warmer. The lads rolled themselves in blankets to sleep by the fire in the great hall; the king had not sent his brother to a soft life up in the Yorkshire dales.

Before dawn Thomas and his children set out for home. There was a dampness in the atmosphere which penetrated more cruelly than the frost of the previous day. When the feeble daylight crawled into the sky, the snow on the hedges was opaque at the edges, and icicles were lengthening on the eaves of the cottages. A thaw was setting in.

Christmas came; a mad, hectic, joyous festival, with waits and mummers, High Mass at midnight in the echoing nave of the Minster, bob-apple and hoodman-blind. Will was chosen Lord of Misrule, and the twelve days of his reign were the funniest, and the most irreverent, that the Wrangwyshes could remember. There was much visiting and entertaining, to exchange gifts and greetings, and to eat and drink enough to fortify the spirit against the miserable winter ahead. One of the guests in Micklegate was Katherine Barker, aged ten, destined to be Will's wife. Her father was a clothier from Petergate across the Ouse, and she was a pretty child with dark eyes. But Will was still too much of a boy to take any interest. He was more concerned with the possibility of mating his greyhound with the Barker's bitch.

Soon after Epiphany Thomas returned John to the earl's household, which was established for the season at the Augustinian Priory in Lendal. Janet saw him go with mixed feelings. For herself she was sorry that their reunion had been so brief; but John had changed a great deal from the little boy who wept at her wedding. He had matured since leaving home, and the withdrawn temperament was blossoming in his new surroundings. His eagerness to be back with his fellows far outweighed the regret at leaving his family. He had entrusted her one day with his secret ambition.

'I'm going to be my lord of Gloucester's squire,' he said, 'and ride into battle at his stirrup.'

'Battle, John? I pray there'll be no need to fight one.'

His face fell, but after a moment's consideration he said hopefully, 'There's always the Scots.'

Janet agreed that the Scots were always with them, and drew forth an even greater confidence.

'When my lord of Gloucester is a man, he will be the greatest knight in the land, and the best champion of his brother the king. He told me so.' Richard of Gloucester was such a puny child, a poor scrap beside the lusty strength of his elder brothers. The loftiness of his ideal would have been ludicrous if it had not been so touching. Janet saw the sombre light burning in John's eyes and knew who had kindled it. She did not laugh.

With John's departure the shadow of leaving began to spread over her happiness. She had dreaded going before, ignorant of what the future held. Now she knew that it held nothing. Existence in London stretched before her, blank and colourless, and she acknowledged that it was because of Edward. While she was in York she had been able to keep him out of her mind, but that would be impossible in London. In her lonely house, he would be omnipresent. His name and doings would be on everyone's tongue; she would see him riding through the city on state business; and it would be agony.

Her emotions were no longer confused by the urgency of desire. The seduction had been a failure, he had lost interest in her, and her physical longing was quite destroyed. But in a curious way she was purified by the experience which had deflowered her. There was no doubt left in her mind; she loved him. She wanted nothing from him, and she would get nothing, but it was a single-minded passion and she did not even wish for time to blunt it. It might be foolish, it might be fruitless, but she could not believe that it was wrong.

The stapler of Beverley had died suddenly from an excess of Yuletide cheer, and since Janet had expressed her distaste for the mill-owner, both the intended alliances had fallen through. Thomas had no immediate alternatives to offer, and he told his daughter that she would have to start negotiating in London. To tell the truth, he was rather hurt at Janet's cool reception of his efforts. London and independence had evidently corroded the perfect obedience she had invariably shown him before. She had always been far too intelligent for her own good. The sooner she was safely married the better. So he suggested she should leave on St Anthony's Day with the promise, or threat, that he would be down in the spring to see what progress she had made.

Her father and Tom rode with her to Tadcaster, through a land iron-bound by a black frost. There were no jolly pilgrims to shorten the road; her travelling companions were a smallholder and a couple of monks under a vow of silence.

It was warmer in the south. In the mists and rain of February, the glow of her holiday soon died. Despite Nick's competent administration, there was a backlog of business which only she could deal with, and it took several weeks to clear. She was as industrious as ever, driving her staff no harder than she did herself. But it did not absorb all her energies any more, nor bring her the fulfilment it once had. There was still time for her to hear, in the clothmarket, at guild meetings, in the street, about how the king was transforming the court. Westminster would soon rival the palaces of Burgundy, they said, in its magnificence and accomplishments. Moreover, the city merchants were most gratified by the amount of trade King Edward was bringing them. He was buying and selling on his own account in a small way, and ever increasing his spending in the London markets.

'And it's not only money he's spending.' Janet's informant dropped his voice to a meaning undertone. With many nods and winks, he related how merchants' wives were said to be receiving the king's favours as well. Janet raised her eyebrows disapprovingly and moved on, but her spirits sank. Probably Edward had only been after a discount on her embroidery too. She went home and wrote gloomily to an eligible acquaintance of hers in the Broiderers' Guild.

On a stormy evening at the end of the month, she sat up late to balance her accounts. Wind and rain rattled against the closed shutters of the solar and blew the smoke back down the chimney. Because of the din outside, Janet ignored the first knock at the door, assuming it to be part of the storm. When it came again, unmistakably, she was half inclined to go on ignoring it. The household were all abed, and she did not fancy opening the door herself on a wild night like this. But Kit had heard it too, from his winter quarters in the hall, and he came up to her, knuckling the sleep out of his eyes and saying it was a gentleman to see her. Alarmed by the unexpected call, Janet took up the candle and, keeping the boy with her, went downstairs.

CHAPTER FIVE

The flame dipped and swayed, streaming away from the gale which blew through the open door. All the tapestries were flapping and clattering, and the stone flags inside the porch were wet. It was a tall man swathed in a hooded cloak, and behind him in the yard another man stood hunched in the darkness, holding a spare horse. She could not see who it was, but as soon as he spoke she recognised him with the old shock.

'It's a foul night, mistress. May I come inside?'

In a flurry she asked him in, and the servant, and was about to send Kit running for Nan when he stopped her.

'Don't trouble anyone,' he said. 'My man is going, and he'll be back at Westminster within the half hour. As for me, you can fend for me. Send the boy to bed.' She did as she was told and took him upstairs.

And once again he was shaking his cloak and his head, laughing as showers of raindrops fell all round him. But this time there was nobody else here, and as the atmosphere of cold and wet he brought with him faded away, the bad weather and the rest of the house and the world were shut out. They were alone in the close little chamber, with the one flickering candle and the dark panelling and the dying fire. Some of her papers had blown to the floor in the draught, and he helped her to pick them up, complimenting her on her handwriting as he did so.

'Are you hungry, your grace?' she asked him when the table was neat again. 'There's some beef broth I could heat for you.'

He declined, asking only for a mug of sack and sugar.

When she came back from the pantry he was installed in the chair he had sat in before, looking as though he belonged there. Not knowing what to say, Janet gave him his drink and knelt to make up the fire. She could feel him watching her, but he said nothing either. It was not an uncomfortable silence. Janet would willingly have stayed there for ever, shut away from the storm, companionably mute. He sat on one side of the hearth, and she opposite him, looking at each other without words like a long-married couple who needed none.

Yet when they did start talking, they could not stop. She could never remember afterwards what it was they said, but it seemed to be everything, her life and his, unburdened without shame or reserve. As they talked, they reached deeper and deeper into the heart and mind of the other, and the greater the depth, the closer they became. They only awoke to the time when the candle guttered and went out. The conversation died, and they were left in the glow of the fire, his hair and relaxed fingers on the arm of the chair touched with amber. He held out his hand.

'Come here.'

And she went, on to his lap, into his arms, and it was as easy as everything in that enchanted night. The barriers between them were quite broken down, and gladly and willingly she trusted herself to him. At length he made a move to take her into the bedchamber.

'The warming-pan will be cold,' said Janet with a little spurt of laughter. 'It was brought up hours ago.'

'We don't need a warming-pan. When I'm not here, I'll give you leave to use one. When I am, I shall perform that office myself.' And he swung her up into his arms.

So at last the big bed which she had occupied alone for nearly three years was filled with warmth and love. She was very drowsy, and he aroused no passion in her, but he was more than repaid by her grateful wonder at his gentleness. The best part of it for her was afterwards; his arms round her, the long firm body lying close against her, the quiet breathing beside her on the pillow. She slept.

Before sunrise he was away. Janet half-woke to his quietly moving about the room, collecting his clothes from where he had flung them. He kissed her and went, and she sank back into sleep. She knew he would come again.

And he did. Sometimes only once a month, seldom more than once a week, and he could not always stay the night with her, but it was enough. He did not give her notice; he simply appeared, accompanied by the same servant, taking her as he found her. The lack of ceremony helped to preserve the secrecy of the affair outside the house. Naturally her staff had to know, but Kit, putting two and two together after the first visit, had already decided to hold his tongue; Nick was equally discreet. Nan was shocked into dumbfounded silence by a personal appeal from the king, and thereafter told only her most trustworthy friends.

Janet's being was transformed. She realised that she had never been happy before. Until this miraculous spring and summer she had been dreaming, and all her petty little joys were only a foretaste of the reality to which Edward had awoken her. The odd detachment of her mind from her feelings which had dogged her so often disappeared. Every minute with Edward was life full and complete, and when he was away she sometimes wept with sheer exultation at her memories. Having thrown away her reserve, she responded to his lovemaking with an ardour that astonished and delighted him.

Yet it did not distract her from work. To be in love, according to the ballads, was to sit in a shadow and sigh the world away; it had quite the opposite effect on Janet. There was an added sparkle in her eyes, but it was, as rivals discovered to their cost, the light of battle. In high good humour she outbid the other dealers for a bale of violet damask, and sold it at a large profit to a Dutch alderman. She sang at her embroidery, and completed commissions well ahead of schedule. The conviction that Edward wanted her gave her the confidence to accept any challenge.

What had begun for him as a casual fancy turned to respect and, beneath the physical fascination, a growing affection. He found himself visiting Walbrook, not just for a tumble with a desirable partner, but to be peaceful and to talk. Her sound common sense was a refreshing change from the obliqueness of statecraft, and he genuinely needed her advice on his tentative ventures into the wool trade. Since she would take none of the rewards he normally gave to his mistresses, he tried to help her by putting business her way, though even that had to be done with tact. Edward had not encountered before a woman who wanted so little and gave so much.

Only one thing marred her happiness. Her father must be told. Civic affairs had kept him in York, where he was now an alderman, throughout the spring, and fresh rumblings of discontent on the Scottish border made him loath to leave home when summer came. Janet had continued to fob off his efforts with various excuses, but she could tell by the tone of his letters that he was becoming suspicious. She disliked deceiving him.

Edward could not understand it.

'I expect he'll be overjoyed at your good fortune,' he said.

'Oh no, not my father. He'll be furious.' The king looked disbelieving.

'Then don't tell him,' he suggested, 'not until it becomes necessary.'

She had shown no signs of pregnancy yet, but she said that that would merely be prolonging the dishonesty.

'I can't go on refusing the husbands he offers me,' she explained. 'It's unnatural for a woman in my position to stay a widow.'

Edward had a quick answer for her.

'Let me find you a husband. It's been done before – a gentleman in search of advancement who will give you his name and not interfere. You could live at the palace and be near me.'

'I couldn't do that.' Her vehemence surprised him. 'It would make our sin unforgivable.'

The king shrugged and said she was as proud as a countess, but he let her be.

Even so, she could not pluck up the courage to write to Thomas until November, when Edward took a force to the north to Warwick's aid. His great lieutenant had been up there for some time, besieging three castles which had once more declared for Lancaster. Now Margaret of Anjou, quick to scent mischief, was back in Northumberland and extra measures were needed.

Without the hope of a visit from Edward to sustain her, Janet waited in trepidation for her personal storm to break. Her anxiety doubled with the tidings that the king had fallen ill at Durham. At first it was said to be smallpox, but the dreadful sentence was later commuted to measles. Though his recovery brought some relief, a lonely Christmas came and went without any reaction to her letter. She assumed that Thomas was under arms again; the end of the disturbances was unlikely to bring peace to Walbrook.

CHAPTER FIVE

The Londoners had celebrated the rebels' expulsion several weeks since when she came back from the clothmarket to find Thomas pacing in the hall. She dismissed Nick, who went with a condoling glance at his mistress; he had accepted the liaison with Edward as he accepted everything she did. Then she closed the door and faced her father.

He was still fully-clad in his outdoor clothes, mired to the waist with winter travelling, and his face was set with fatigue and rage. Janet had been expecting something like this, but she could tell the depth of his anger by the fact that he had come, and come so fast. There were no preliminaries. Pinned to the door like a target, she was subjected to a hail of abuse, disappointment, and reproach. She was very frightened, because she had never been the butt of her father's temper before, and its power was devastating.

But beneath the fear an aching sadness was growing which made her want to cry. Whenever Thomas stopped for breath, she had to fight a strong desire to throw herself at him and beg him to forgive her and not be unkind to her any more. She pressed her back against the door and waited for him to exhaust his pent-up fury. Then, as if she had prepared the speech, she spoke formally into the shattered air.

'I am not ashamed, father. I know that what I'm doing is sin. But I can't break with the king. He has some use for me, and as long as he needs me I will not deny him. I am sorry that I've been an undutiful daughter to you; perhaps one day you'll understand and forgive me.'

He had not been listening to her. Deaf with chagrin at the fall from grace of his only and much-cherished daughter, he advanced on her gripping his riding whip.

'Don't bandy words with me, girl. No clever argument can change what you are – the king's whore!'

Her self-control was swallowed up in panic; she fumbled for the latch to get out and run away. But her hands were too clumsy and he seized her arm and thrashed her.

Not since she was a child had he raised his hand to her, and he had never used a whip. Time and again she had consoled her brothers, weeping or angry at a whipping; there was nobody to do the same for her. Thomas let her fall onto the rushes and stood over her. The passion had gone from his face; it was drained and slack.

'When you have given up your association with the king,' he said in a dead voice, 'I will receive you again as my daughter. Until then, I forbid you to communicate with me or with any of my family.'

When he had gone Nan crept in, and dropping sympathetic tears all over her, gave her mistress what little comfort she could. As she helped Janet to her feet she could hear her moaning Edward's name, over and over under her breath.

CHAPTER SIX

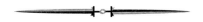

She resolved to tell Edward nothing of the breach with her father unless he asked. Her sense of isolation eased as soon as he returned to London, bringing with him the Duke of Gloucester and, presumably, Janet's brother. There was no hope of a visit from John; instead there was the uncertain joy of waiting for the king. Within a week he was there, and though she had not heard a word from him during his absence, she knew immediately that he wanted her as much as ever. The humiliation and pain her father had inflicted did not matter; they were a small price to pay for her love.

But as Edward undressed her, he discovered the weals of Thomas's whip across her shoulders. His fingers paused and tightened on the healing ridges, and he said quietly, 'Who did this?'

Carried away by his caresses, she had forgotten about the marks. 'My father,' she said guiltily, thinking that he was angry with her.

'How dare he?' He stood up and strode away from her. 'Does he set himself up as a judge over me? How dare he lay hands on my woman! I'll have him thrown out of office!' Even in her state of mild shock at his outburst, Janet could not help noticing that he had rather missed the point.

'My lord, that would be most unjust. It is I he was judging. He has a perfect right to beat me. I'm everything he said I was – a fornicator, a lost woman......the king's whore.'

Edward came back and stared at her in bewilderment, quite put out by her reasonable tone.

'Did he ask you to give me up?'

'Yes, and I said I wouldn't until you wished me to. He has disowned me.'

The king started to mutter something about forcing Thomas Wrangwysh to recognise her, but Janet gently cut him short.

'No, Edward. It's my choice. It would be covetous to want my father as well as you, and I've chosen you. If it means cutting myself off from my family, so be it. He'll forgive me in the end. He's a proud and upright man, but I think he loves me. He'll relent in time.'

Edward sat beside her and put his arm round her. Beneath the bravery of her words he could hear the crack in her voice.

'Let the devil fly away with your father,' he said, 'And come to Westminster. I would see that you lacked for nothing.'

'I lack for nothing now. Thank God, I can support myself and my household. I will be no man's pensioner, whether my father's or yours. However much I love him.'

He laughed at her in perplexity, and began to caress her again.

The next day John came hotfoot into her workshop. Thomas's letter banning any contact with his sister had just caught up with him. Before she could open her mouth he was crying passionately that Janet could do no wrong, and since he was no longer subject to his father he was going to ignore his command. Janet corrected him sharply.

'Hold your peace, John. However upset you are, there's no excuse for speaking like that. It's our father who is in the right, not I. You're only a child, and you owe him duty until you are a man with a family of your own.'

Her brother gulped and hung his head at the rebuff, so she went on with less severity, 'You've always been taught obedience, John. Both at home and now in my lord's service. To disobey just because it's against your heart would make a mockery of all your schooling. If you defy our father now, who knows whom you will defy in the future?'

He looked at her with wide grey eyes of betrayal, which suddenly spilled over with tears. And though he was nearly as tall as she, Janet found herself mothering him as she had when he was much younger. But he was ashamed of his lapse and soon mastered himself. Then she made him sit down and fed him dried figs while he told her what he had done since they last met. His conversation was full of the Duke of Gloucester, and it was clear that in the year since she had gone to Middleham they had become fast friends. She was reassured by the knowledge. With the duke to follow he would not really miss her at all. John had grown out of women, and he would not need them again until he began to look for a wife.

The parting was less final than John had feared. Somewhat exasperated by this ridiculous family feud, the king ordered a truce between Janet and her brother as long as the latter was in London. It was a good excuse to invite his mistress to a few of the court functions in the Duke of Gloucester's honour, though he had the delicacy to leave her with John and not show her overt favour.

It was on these occasions that Janet realised how she missed the company of her contemporaries. She was not yet nineteen, but in the hard mercantile world she had to act with the forcefulness of a much older woman, in order to compete with the seasoned campaigners who were her rivals. Apart from Kit, who was her employee, and Nan, who did not count, she never met people of her own age at all. Only with Edward was she free to feel young; under his admiring hands and eyes she could believe that she was some pagan goddess of youth.

The lads who surrounded Richard of Gloucester, and the young men who attended the king and the Duke of Clarence, radiated life and optimism. Sweetened by her love, Janet could regard the court without the acidity of unsatisfied desire. Although she was still more of an onlooker than a participant, she saw what the king was trying to create around him. A place of beauty and laughter, of courtesy and refinement, where lovers wrote lyrics to their ladies and sang them too; a court with the elegance of Burgundy but without its stifling protocol;

a country where the knightly games of chivalry would replace civil strife and let the people prosper in peace. A second Camelot. Janet's eyes returned to Edward, as they always did, handsome and charming among his satellites. He could do it, if God gave him the time. Everything else he had already.

Like Guenevere and her knights, they rode out maying in the woods near Shene on May Day. It was a select gathering, just the king and his brothers and their intimates. The boys raced each other through the thickets, weaving dangerously among the trees and flattening themselves to their horses' necks to escape overhanging branches. Richard of Gloucester outstripped the rest, handling his big mount with the confidence of one twice his size. The sun vanished and, to the great merriment of all, a shower drenched their colourful spring costumes.

Lord Hastings, who had been missing for some time, reappeared with the sun, triumphantly brandishing a handful of green and gold spikes. With elaborate ceremony he presented a spray to the king and his two brothers, and implored them to wear it for his sake.

'Three sprigs of broom for three noble sprigs of the Plantagenet family tree. And may there soon be new buds sprouting on the old branches.'

Edward bowed, and said solemnly that he would wear the hereditary badge of his family with pride. Then he thrust it through the brooch on his cap, so it stuck out like some unruly feather. George and Richard followed suit, and everyone applauded the three sons of York, their soft suede gloves pattering together like the recent rain on the leaves. On the way back, laden with sharp-scented hawthorn, they sang rounds of French carols to the coming of spring.

That night, Edward came to Janet at Walbrook. It was as if King Arthur had come to her bed.

Though England was quiet under King Edward's rule, there were, as John had said, always the Scots. Before summer was out the court had broken up; the men had gone back to campaigning, and the Duke of Gloucester to his studies. Janet was left with her cloth and her embroidery, haggling with other traders at the cloth-market, haggling with customers in her shop. The men who tried to cheat her because she was a woman usually found themselves outmanoeuvred. Her sex debarred her from joining the Mercers' Guild itself, but she was a respected member of their social fraternity. One of her colleagues who was well-disposed towards her suggested that, with her increasing turnover, she should rent a warehouse in Calais.

To this end she left her native shores for the first time in the autumn, accompanied by the reluctant Nick Farthing. Never in his life, he announced, had he found the need to trust himself to thieving seamen and foreigners. It was only because King Edward prudently held Calais for its rightful owners that he would consent to go. The seamen did not steal anything, but the sea was unpredictable and Janet did not enjoy the heaving boards and creaking rigging at all. Her only consolation for being seasick was that Nick was far worse.

She thought Calais an odd town, defiantly English despite the cosmopolitan accents in its streets, embattled against the encircling foreigners. It was as busy as London, though the activity was crammed into a smaller space, and there were soldiers everywhere. During their stay Nick swore proudly that he had never slept for more than a few hours at a time, but had stayed awake to guard his mistress (and himself) from the depredations of the French. He was convinced that, but for his vigil, King Louis would have crept into Calais and murdered them both in their beds – 'His kind of warfare, mistress, they say.'

King Louis' murderous schemes must have been directed elsewhere, because they succeeded in leaving the town with their transaction duly completed and their health unimpaired. Their health, however, was not proof against a Channel crossing in November, and they were again very ill. On staggering ashore at Sandwich, Janet resolved to leave the adventurous part of her business to deputies in the future.

The Scots had been brought to a truce. Though with ex-Queen Margaret lurking within their borders it was unlikely to last, serious trouble seemed very remote in prosperous London. The people imposed complete trust in the infallible combination of King Edward and the Earl of Warwick.

But Janet was aware that Edward was chafing more and more at the earl's dominance. When the novelty of reigning over an adoring people had passed, the young king had wanted more outlet for his talents than an endless round of progresses, balls, and hunting parties. An idle king, on the other hand, suited Warwick very well, and he had no wish to see the grateful apprentice turn master. In an effort to assert his authority, he had begun negotiations for a marriage between Edward and the French king's sister-in-law. The Lady Bona was not renowned for beauty or wit, and there were other considerations against her. Though Edward had never discussed his inevitable marriage with Janet, she knew that it was Warwick, not he, who favoured a French alliance.

'It is Burgundy we must look to for allies,' he had said. 'England's wealth in the future depends on trade with the Low Countries. And the English will not stomach licking King Louis' dirty boots – not so soon after Margaret's ruffians have been loose.'

At this time he was far from London, and Janet had no idea whether he was happy about the negotiations or merely acquiescing in his mentor's scheme. Throughout the winter and spring he was quiet on the matter, and the traffic of gifts and embassies across the Channel continued.

Once more Janet was cut off from those she loved. The only letters she received were business letters, except for an occasional note under the seal of the Duke of Gloucester. Richard had thoughtfully undertaken to provide a slender link between her and her estranged family by sending Christmas greetings from York and news of Bessie's latest addition to the nursery. This child, another son, had been born not long after Janet's repudiation, and named Edward. Evidently Thomas bore no grudge against the king. Yet though it hurt her to be excluded from a share in a family event, it was Edward she missed most. When he returned in March, she spent her days in a state of happy restlessness, sure that the next evening would bring him and an end to her loneliness.

He left within the month, and she had not heard from him. For the first time a shadow of doubt crossed her mind. It was not his habit to keep in touch with her while he was away, but always before he had contacted her, with a message or a small present or a visit soon after he reached the capital. Janet told herself unconvincingly that he was extremely busy; that a king's time was too precious to be squandered on dalliance; and that when full peace was restored he would have leisure for her again. Nevertheless her heart sank as he went, cheered away by the London mob.

Disapproval of the French match rose to a crescendo as the indefatigable Margaret of Anjou once more led her tattered followers on to English soil. They were defeated in two pitched battles and put to flight, and great was the jubilation of the citizens.

But that was as nothing to the news that ran from Reading in September and spread over the city like fire in a dry summer. Men and women shocked, excited, condemning, excusing, crowded the streets, heads together, discussing the open secret in loud whispers. The king was married.

'Married to an English woman – not the French – '

'A Lancastrian's widow, forsooth!'

' – married her on May Day – very romantic!'

'She wouldn't yield her virtue, so he had to wed her – '

'They say she's a witch, a golden witch, with an ugly old hag witch for a mother, and they put the king under a spell – '

'No, no, he held a knife to her throat to make her give him her body, but she wouldn't and he married her in admiration.'

'But nobody saw them married, except her mother. Who's to know it's a true marriage?'

'Of course it is! It has been accepted by the Great Earl himself, though with a bad grace.'

'And no wonder! Warwick won't take this lying down.'

'Serves him right for meddling with the French. At least we have an English queen, and we'll have English heirs, true-born, like our own Harry V, not half-French madmen like his son.

'There'll be trouble, mark me there will – '

Janet listened, offering no comment, not daring to assess what she felt. It did not surprise her, and it was clear now why he had not come to her in March: he was planning his marriage. As the days passed, her dread grew. Whether or not he had done it to defy Warwick, one thing was inescapable. It was a love-match. If Edward had a wife he loved, who could give him the companionship and comfort Janet had provided as well as the physical satisfaction, it was the end for her.

The king-pin of her life was crumbling away. She had said many times that she did not want to hold him against his will, that she expected nothing of him. But it had been the generosity of a woman in possession. There was no jealousy of his other mistresses; she knew that she meant as much to him as any of them, and more than most. A beloved wife, to share the weight of kingship, to be the mother of his children – that was something she could not fight. Had it happened earlier she might have been able to face it with equanimity. But after two years he was too deeply rooted in her heart. The faint hope of reconciliation with her family was no consolation. She was plunged into despair. Why could he not have married the Lady Bona? The only thing she could pray for was that Dame Elizabeth Grey should be worthy of him.

The crowds that gathered to welcome back the king with his new queen were agog. Although if anything Edward's reputation was enhanced by his romantic defiance of royal conventions, they would judge the queen as they found her. Hostility to her politics, disapproval of her undistinguished origins, envy of her sudden raising, mingled with rumours that she was beautiful and virtuous, and had two helpless little sons. As if she were attending her own requiem, Janet went to watch the cavalcade.

They rode side by side, and every now and then Edward turned lovingly to his wife and placed his hand on her bridle or her glove, speaking to her intimately with the charm that Janet knew so well. And Elizabeth Grey was beautiful. Straight, shining blonde hair glinting through her gauze caul, a high forehead, a gracious smile; slim and graceful, looking much younger than her reputed thirty years – 'Which proves she's a witch,' hissed one plump citizen's wife to another. Very beautiful, and yet – Janet put it down to her jealousy – and yet condescending. She should have been humbler, as humble as the king himself, grateful for the acclamation rather than expecting it. For some reason Janet was slightly reassured.

All the same the following months were dark ones for her. To lose a lover like Edward was infinitely worse than never having known him. Her eyes were opened and she could not shut them again. The anguish of a vanished happiness was hard to bear.

At court all was well. The Great Earl had apparently swallowed his humiliation and was reconciled to the king; the court was growing more lavish every week: the Christmas celebrations at Eltham were said to be the most extravagant ever. But there was a new set of courtiers, the Woodvilles, the queen's multifarious brothers and sisters. Rumours began to circulate that they were climbing high and that the queen was surrounding herself with ceremonial quite foreign to the king's easy nature.

To see anything ominous in this was pure envy, Janet decided, and went to Dover. She had a warehouse there too, and a chartered barge which ran cargoes of cloth from the weaving centres of Flanders. Among the great bales stacked in the shadowy barn, stamped with her mark of the small horse, the jennet, which was a pun on her name, breathing in their familiar smell she was secure. She made many trips to the coast at that time, undertaking the work that Nick usually did, to keep away from London.

Another spring flowered, a year since the king's marriage, two years since they had gone maying at Shene. She came back to London along roads already dusty. The city streets were beginning to stink with their summer foulness.

The stench of the kennels did not penetrate to her garden. As she tended her herbs, the air was lightly spiced with the scent of bruised rosemary and marjoram. The sun had set; the sky was washed pale green. Janet was down on her knees, a bucket beside her, with her kirtle hitched into the waistband of her apron and a linen scarf tied over her hair. It was June, and she was just twenty-one.

She heard a step on the flags behind her, and thinking it was Kit she stood up unhurriedly and turned, a root of thyme in her hand, almost into Edward's arms. They stared at each other for a moment, unsmiling.

'I have come back,' he said.

She took a few paces backwards, away from him, shaking her head slowly.

He followed, and said 'I haven't come lightly, Janet. Do you still love me?'

'Yes ...' she would have said more, but he stopped her.

'Then please hear me.'

In a confusion of fear and hope she consented, and he drew her down on to the stone bench.

'I've fought for weeks – no, for months – with the desire to come and see you. I guessed the reception you'd give me – and that I deserve. But you accepted me long ago for what I was, a man who cannot make do with one woman. Whether she be his wife or not.'

'You have been married scarcely a year,' protested Janet in a stifled voice. Her heart was beating painfully.

'It doesn't take a year to discover that one has made a mistake.' His admission came with difficulty. It was something he had not acknowledged to anyone else. 'And don't preach at me, Janet. I know well enough that, having made my mistake, I should abide by it. I have tried. But I can't. It's not in my nature. Perhaps I could never have been faithful to any woman. Certainly I can't be to Elizabeth. She is – '

Janet interrupted wildly. 'I want to hear nothing of the queen's defects. You were right to hesitate to come. Yes, I suspected that she wouldn't always content you, however much you loved her. But why so soon, and why does it have to be me? I willingly cut myself off from Holy Church, and from my family, for you, only because I believed, deep in myself, that I was not doing wrong. But to take you from your wife – and a wife freely chosen, not foisted on you as a political match – that is evil. To be your mistress again, or even your companion, it would endanger my soul and destroy my self-respect. You must find your consolation elsewhere, sire!' Contempt, and disappointment, and grief for what she was throwing away choked her.

Edward touched her arm, but she twisted away. 'Please go away, my lord! I was learning to do without you.'

'But you don't understand. You haven't listened to me.'

She rose and tried to get away into the house.

'Stay here!' A sudden royal command arrested her flight. 'Now be silent, woman. I will have no more words from you until I've said my say.'

Taken aback by this manifestation of his authority, she subsided on to the bench. She very much wanted to be convinced.

'First of all, contrary to general opinion, I didn't take Elizabeth from sheer lust. True, she held out against me until I was crazy with desire for her, but there were other reasons. I didn't plunge into wedding her without considering first – I had already known her for three years.

'To show Warwick who was master; to put paid to an alliance with France which would be unpopular and unprofitable; to get sons quickly for England, from a woman who has proved twice that she can bear them – unlike the wilting French virgin, who sounds unable to bear the weight of a man, let alone a child. All this was in my mind. And her own adamance, and her mother's urging on top. Inclination and policy were running together. So I yielded. It was a legal marriage, Janet.' An anxious note had entered his voice, as if she had expressed disbelief.

'I never doubted that,' she said, puzzled, and then went on with a touch of bitterness, 'but what difference does it make to us, what you thought last May? You seem to have succeeded in several of your aims. The earl is to heel, from what I hear, France is discomfited, and you have a new clique of courtiers who owe all their advancement to you. That doesn't justify you. If your wife is inadequate in bed, it merely means your judgement of women is not as good as you thought it was.'

'Oh, she pleases me well enough in bed.' Because he was so eager to press his point, he did not notice her rudeness. 'She knows how to give pleasure – and takes her own, in her way. But there is nothing there.' Janet looked at him blankly. He was staring at the ground and talking almost to himself. 'She was so beautiful, so unapproachable.

Like a rich fortress that has never been taken. I was burning to penetrate it, to capture it, because when I did I was sure I'd find gems of great price. But when I took it there was no treasure. Only another wall, still inviting, still promising. And every time I thought I had reached the heart of the mystery, it withdrew before me, and I was left unsatisfied. Elizabeth's citadel is unconquered. I think it's not there at all.' In the darkening garden, Edward dropped his head on to his hand. She had never seen him so upset. His distress was dulling her indignation and making her feel protective.

She found herself close to him, taking the other hand which lay limply on his knee. Trying to sound casual, though her voice was unsteady, she said 'It must take time, Edward. Perhaps she doesn't love you yet as she should.'

He shook his head.

'She's incapable of love in the way you mean it. Her passion is for possession. When she holds me in her arms, there is no … exchange. It's as though she is drawing me into her, and giving nothing in return. In all the months of our marriage, I have never found a spark of warmth in her. Sometimes I believe that I may grow cold also.'

'You could never be that!'

'No, not with your help.' Edward seized both her hands and turned to her, his eyes gleaming faintly in the twilight. There might have been tears in them. 'That's why I came to you Janet. You have everything she has not. With us, making love has always been the natural outcome of drawing together. Between Elizabeth and me it seems to drive us further apart. If you refuse me, I shall find warmth elsewhere, wherever I can, but it will only be a substitute for what I would find with you.' He tried to see her face, but it was averted. 'Do you refuse me?'

Heavily she raised her gaze until it was level with his.

'How can I?' She sounded defeated. His mouth met her half-parted lips, and very softly he touched her tongue with his own. Then, slowly but inevitably, they moved into each other's arms, pressing closer and closer as if to keep out the cold of a winter's night.

PART 2
DIVIDED LOYALTIES

CHAPTER ONE

'The king has been taken! Warwick's brother the archbishop found him alone at Olney. All his friends have fled and no one knows if he is alive or dead.'

It was the Nevilles' most drastic move yet in a struggle that had been going on for years. London was divided on the seriousness of such a step. The tidings were the only topic of conversation in the nave of Paul's Cathedral after morning Mass that August day.

'Peace for five years, and now Warwick does this. After all, he's Great Chamberlain of England and God knows what else besides. What more can he want?' asked a fishmonger. 'Biting the hand that feeds him, I call it.'

'Biting the hand that feeds the Woodvilles, more like,' said a vintner tartly.

'That's true,' another chimed in. 'The king has given too much power to the queen's kindred. A bunch of grasping nobodies. The Great Earl put King Edward on the throne. He has reason to feel hard done by.'

'Not enough cause for treason.'

Only Edward's diplomacy had kept the two factions from each other's throats thus long. Lately, however, the discontented Warwick had found an ally in the equally discontented Duke of Clarence. A clandestine marriage in Calais last month between George and Lady Isabel Neville had committed Clarence to Warwick's cause – or Warwick to his, as George preferred to think.

Of course, the earl denied any treasonable intent in taking possession of the king. He was only protecting him from evil counsellors, he announced. But there was another king in England receiving protection from evil counsellors – mad Henry VI, who had been captured wandering in Lancashire, and kept in the Tower ever since. No one minded much about him, except the exiled Queen Margaret. Edward of York in captivity was a different matter.

Confident that the populace would rise for him, Warwick summarily beheaded the queen's father and one of her brothers, kept Edward in ward and waited for supporters to flock to his side. But England loved their young king more than they hated the Woodvilles. The people sat tight in their houses and on their estates, and waited too. Instead of being borne to supreme power on a wave of popular sympathy, Warwick was forced to move Edward by night marches, further and further away from London, where the mob was on the brink of rioting in the king's favour. There were reports that he had reached Middleham.

Somehow, the thought of Edward in Wensleydale reassured Janet. She did not believe, for one thing, that the Great Earl would actually harm the king. His ambition was boundless, but he followed a certain code of honour even if he did make his own rules for it; he was no secret assassin. For another thing, Geoffrey Barton was still chamberlain of Middleham Castle. And it was within a day's ride of York. Breaking the silence of six years, she wrote to her father, begging him to assist the king in any way he could.

There were other friends of King Edward who needed no urging. While Warwick delayed, puzzled by his misreading of the English temper, they were industriously doing what he could not – raising men.

CHAPTER ONE

Events in the north, as usual, reached London distorted by distance and hearsay, but apparently the king had been seen in public, at York and then at Pomfret. The first definite news was somewhat startling. He was on his way south, escorted by the Duke of Gloucester and Lord Hastings, by all accounts in perfect freedom. Two months after he had been taken prisoner, King Edward entered his capital, smiling blandly, to a civic reception. The Earl of Warwick was not there, and neither was the Duke of Clarence.

Not three days later the king strode into Janet's kitchen, vital with high spirits. With a hearty slap on the buttocks, he despatched the giggling Nan and seized Janet round the waist and lifted her into the air.

'Sweet heart, your family is magnificent!' he cried, while she shrieked and scolded him delightedly for interrupting her ironing.

'Then wear a crumpled coif tomorrow. I prefer you without, anyway,' said Edward, and plucked off her headdress.

When the horseplay was over, she asked what he had meant about her family.

'Did you see them? Are they well?'

'All flourishing. And but for Wrangwysh resourcefulness, I might not be here today.'

'Did they help you, Edward? No one in London knows how you escaped from my lord of Warwick. The wildest stories are flying about. What happened?'

'It was just a question of patience. Of biding my time until his moment was past and mine had come. I knew Dickon and Will Hastings were rallying their men -- that's why I made them leave me in Olney. At Middleham I established contact with them – your uncle kindly turning a blind eye – and when they were close enough I told Warwick to escort me to York. The people cheered me, I took more liberties, and finally announced that I was going to London. He couldn't stop me. He had no army, and I had two.'

Edward had defeated the earl by sheer intelligence. Bending before an adverse wind, it had passed over him harmlessly. Unlike Warwick he had read the situation correctly and regained the upper hand without spilling a drop of unnecessary blood.

'That's all,' said the king, and shrugged.

'It is you who are magnificent, not my family,' said Janet, almost shyly. It was at times like this that she was most conscious of her lover's greatness, and her own insignificance.

'No, no. I couldn't have outwitted Warwick without loyal servants. Your father was my surest channel of communication, and your brothers acted as go-betweens – even the little clerk with a stammer who's taking holy orders – '

'That must be Robert.' Her youngest brother had been five when she last saw him. She suppressed a pang at learning from an outsider that he was going to be a priest.

'Yes, they called him Rob. Master Wrangwysh deployed his forces with the skill of a general. He'll be Lord Mayor one day, if York has any sense.' Janet bit her lip. 'You are your father's daughter, Janet, though he is fool enough to deny you.

'But I'd rather bed with you than with him,' he added, and made her laugh. Suddenly he frowned and said, 'When I left, you thought you were with child. Are you?'

'I was. It's gone.'

'Oh, my dear.' Edward was all concern. 'How long was it?'

'Only two months. I lost it in August. Forgive me, Edward.'

'There's nothing to forgive. Were you ill?'

'Not really. I hardly noticed it. It was like the other time.'

'Don't fret, sweet heart. We shall make another.'

'Perhaps......' She sighed, sad at having marred his triumphant homecoming with her small failure.

'What will you do with my lord earl?' she asked, changing the subject.

'Demand his submission to my grace, and pardon him. The queen would have his blood in payment for her father's and brother's, but that's no way to rule. I owe Warwick a great debt, and he has his grievances. He could yet be valuable to me.'

'And.....the duke?'

Edward glanced at her sharply, and she thought she had asked too much.

'George is easily led,' he said shortly. 'Warwick has dazzled him with too many promises. I can handle him.'

For once he was overconfident. Warwick and Clarence made their submission, but their reformed behaviour scarcely outlasted the year. Before the winter was over they were stirring mischief and inciting rebellion as busily as ever. There were mutterings of a plot to dethrone the king, and they were traced unmistakably to the two rebellious noblemen. Edward realised that his clemency had failed. Further tolerance would only lead to a renewal of full-scale civil war. In March he issued a proclamation charging them both with treason. Pursued by the royal army, the earl and the duke collected their womenfolk from Warwick Castle and fled for the coast. The governor of Calais refused them permission to land, so they went on to Honfleur, and as soon as they were ashore Warwick set off to pour his troubles into the sympathetic ear of the King of France.

They were still in Normandy when Edward asked Janet for her help. He had been unusually taciturn that evening, and eventually he said 'Do something for me, Janet.'

'If I can. What is it?'

'Bring my brother back to the fold.'

At first she was utterly incredulous. He was prepared to entrust to her the delicate mission of persuading the Duke of Clarence to desert Warwick and return to the family allegiance. But Edward brushed aside her protests.

'You're capable and trustworthy, and he would listen to you. He likes women, and he would recognise you as my personal emissary.'

'Then why not send one of your.....ladies from court?'

'I shall be sending several messengers to him, on various pretexts. You'll have an excellent one. As a merchant, you can cross the channel without attracting the attention of Warwick's spies, and you are well-known to my brother's household; they would let you in without question if you take a bolt of silk with you. When you're with him, you can offer him the silk, if you like, together with various concessions and pledges from me.'

'But he's in Normandy.....it would be dangerous.'

'Not as dangerous for you as it would be for some accredited diplomat. English traders have free passage through France, and you won't have to contend with the Earl of Warwick. He's hobnobbing with his friend King Louis.'

'Surely my lord duke has gone to the king with him.'

'He did go, but now he's been told to run off and play while men's business is discussed. It won't be a difficult task, Janet. I think George is beginning to discover that Warwick is not omnipotent.' There was an edge to Edward's voice which suggested that he had not quite come to terms with the discovery himself. 'He's sure to come back to us in the end. Such an unnatural division between brothers can't last.'

The king fell silent, and Janet knew why the mission was so distasteful to her. It was not the daunting journey through a foreign land, nor distrust of her own powers of persuasion.

'His wife is Warwick's daughter.'

'Yes.' Edward moved uneasily in his chair.

'What will the Lady Isabel do?'

'That's not for you to question.' His tone softened. 'Will you do this for me, sweet heart?'

'If you command me, Edward.'

'No. I shan't command you. I ask you. For the sake of England's peace, and for my family's unity.' In giving her the choice, he bound her to accept. She had learned nine years ago that she could not deny him anything he really wanted.

Nevertheless, her spirits were low as she set out a few days later for Dover. She did not have the solid comfort of Nick's company, because he had flatly refused to cross the sea again. Young Kit, who was rising twenty, had a good head for business but was more of an employee than a friend. The crossing was smooth, and only made her slightly queasy, which was fortunate, because there was no time for recuperating at Calais. Edward had chosen the shortest sea passage, as the least likely to attract attention; that meant travelling the breadth of northern France, to reach Clarence before his father-in-law returned.

CHAPTER ONE

From the time they left the sheltering walls of the English fortress, Janet hated every mile of the way. Grinding poverty was everywhere. The ragged peasants stared at her from the stony fields with the suspicion of hereditary enemies. Their twittering speech was as unintelligible to her as the careful French she had repeated with her brothers' tutor was to them. And more than the natives she feared the apparition of soldiers wearing the bear and ragged staff badge of Warwick. She kept her nervousness from Kit, who regarded everything with lofty disdain, but she was glad of a stalwart male at her side. They were riding post, and after two nights of insufficient sleep there was the extra unpleasantness of fatigue and stiffness. That, thought Janet crossly, was something that a soldier like Edward would not even consider. Apart from an altercation in Rouen over a broken-winded horse, however, it was the worst they had to face.

As the king had predicted, Janet gained easy admittance to Clarence's lodgings. She had brought a length of saffron kersey with her, smooth and closely-woven, and the servant who opened the door happened to be a man she had dealt with before. He came back within ten minutes and said his grace would see her. Doubting if her jaded appearance and heavy eyelids would have the effect that Edward had wanted, she took the material from Kit and followed him.

From a distance she could hear a raised voice, harsh and querulous. By the time she was shown into the duke's presence it had stopped, but its echo still hung on the air. Clarence stood scowling into the fireplace, his thumbs hooked aggressively into his jewelled belt. Behind him the three ladies were huddled like a group of disconsolate hens, meekly bearing the wrath of the rooster.

Duchess Isabel lay on a couch, still feeble from the ordeal of giving birth to a dead child at sea, when the governor of Calais would not let them land. Her sister Anne sat beside her, scarcely matured from the slip of a girl Janet had seen at Middleham, though she was turned fourteen. The Countess of Warwick was staring ahead of her, her blurred features composed into a mask of patience. No doubt being the wife of the Great Earl had instilled stoicism at an early age.

The duke greeted Janet with exaggerated courtesy, but his eyes were cold.

'It's good to see someone I can trust,' he said pointedly. 'I hope England is prepared for invasion. We do intend to invade, you know, if my good father-in-law can spare the time from revelling with the French king.' He waved an elegant hand at the quiet women, and tapped his foot impatiently as they left the room, the duchess carried by a manservant. Then he said more amiably 'Well, mistress, I suppose you've brought a letter from my brother.'

'No letter, your grace. His loving concern for your welfare.'

'He should have thought of that before,' grumbled Clarence, 'While he was lavishing attention and offices on those upstart Woodvilles. He didn't start concerning himself with my welfare until it threatened his.'

'My lord the king deeply regrets that you felt yourself neglected. If he has offended you, he is prepared to make due reparation.'

'What kind of reparation? The disgrace of being declared a traitor is not wiped out by some trivial olive branch, mistress.'

'A free pardon, full reinstatement, and confirmation as heir-presumptive to the throne.'

The heir-presumptive snorted.

'That clause is not worth a straw. I hear Dame Elizabeth is breeding again.'

'She has not produced a son yet.' Repeating the king's words, Janet found them sticking in her throat. 'Daughters, but no son.'

'No, but she will.' Suddenly the duke abandoned his sulky aloofness and flung off down the room. 'Why does everyone spurn me? Edward has always preferred others before me. Warwick, the Woodvilles, Richard.....I stand nearest to the throne. I should be first in his heart. Yet he drove me out of the kingdom. I thought Warwick knew my value. Now he's going to give Anne to Queen Margaret's brat.'

Involuntarily Janet gasped. She had been prepared for a catalogue of complaints, but not this.

'Oh yes, that's what he's brewing. An alliance with Lancaster. He's set on making one of his daughters queen of England. First he toyed with me as his puppet king, but now I've been cast aside. The bastard

Edward of Lancaster will marry Anne Neville, and together Warwick and Margaret and Louis will dethrone my brother and crown them instead. That's why I'm kicking my heels here. They've finished with me. And I'm left with a plain woman who can't bear live children.' He subsided into a chair and sank into gloom.

Despite her impatience at his self-pity, Janet was touched by the desolation of this blonde Lucifer, unable to support the blow to his pride. She began to see why Edward was so slow to blame him. His beauty deserved to be pampered, like a tame leopard, but he was not content merely to be decorative. He wanted to do, as well as to be. Then she thought of what he had said about his wife, and her sympathy fled. Isabel was already the victim of her father's ambition, and was likely to become the victim of her husband's.

'My lord, will you come back?' Janet could not summon up any more diplomatic phrases.

'What will the king ask of me if I do?'

'Nothing except your loyalty.'

'No forfeits or humiliations?'

'No, your grace.'

'Do I have his royal word that I shall be given my proper place of honour?'

'Yes, your grace.'

'Then … I shall consider my brother's proposition,' said Clarence off-handedly.

'May I carry a message back to him?' she asked, a little desperately, though Edward had warned her that she might not receive a straight answer.

'Tell him I shall join him when the time is ripe.' He sounded bored, and Janet saw she would have to be satisfied with that.

Presenting the kersey as a pledge from the king, she left him thankfully. She was too tired and too depressed to want to tell Kit about the interview. Fortunately she had been given an apartment for the night, and dismissing her apprentice to do as he wished she retreated to her bed.

She overslept the following morning and, since she had to go to

Barfleur and bespeak a passage home, she made haste to leave. Her room was nowhere near the Countess of Warwick's suite, so she was surprised to encounter her younger daughter in the corridor close to her door. Janet curtseyed and would have passed on, but the Lady Anne wanted to speak to her.

'Will you be seeing the Duke of Gloucester, Mistress Evershed?' she whispered. There was no attendant with her; the future bride of Prince Edward would not normally be allowed to run around on her own.

'I don't know, madame,' Janet answered in the same tone.

'You must have some way of reaching him – through your brother, perhaps?' Her eyes were pleading so hard that Janet did not demur. 'There is something I must return to him – if you would take it for me. There's no one else I can ask.'

'I'll take it for you, my lady.'

She produced a pendant on a fine chain, and pressed it quickly into Janet's hands.

'Just give it to him – he will understand,' she said, and picking up her skirts, she fled away down the passage.

When she had gone, Janet went back to her room to put the pendant in a safe place. Wrapping it carefully in a clean kerchief she marvelled at its exquisite working. It was enamelled in blue and gold with a tiny device of St Anne on St Anthony's tau cross, and encircled with small pink and white stones. A childhood gift, perhaps, which the Lady Anne thought it wise to restore now that their families were divided. But as she helped Kit to load their horses, another explanation occurred to her. The Duke of Gloucester had taken St Anthony's boar as his personal badge. There might have been a secret hope given with that token which would die with Anne's betrothal.

Feeling more and more guilty of treachery, Janet made her farewells and rode for Barfleur.

Her head still ringing with lack of rest and the motion of travel, she presented herself to the king at Westminster. He was alone except for the Duke of Gloucester, and together they were poring over a map of northern England. Edward looked up as she was shown in and said

CHAPTER ONE

with a smile, indicating the map, 'More trouble, Janet. Can't you keep these fellow-countrymen of yours in order?'

'Not from Normandy, your grace. And I'm sure the trouble comes from the other side of the Pennines.' Rising from her reverence she met Richard's eyes, and he was nodding in grave agreement with her. He was eighteen, brown and slight, and did not reach to Edward's shoulder.

'Don't encourage her, Dickon,' said the king, and made her sit down. 'I can't knock Yorkshire out of her heart even after eleven years in London. Now, sweet heart. What news from the court of King Warwick?'

She delivered her inconclusive report. Though Edward shrugged and said he had expected no more, she could tell that he was disappointed. Gloucester made no comment, except for a faint sigh. He did not break his silence when she handed over the Lady Anne's pendant, yet from the closing in of his face Janet suspected that she had guessed right.

'This monstrous alliance with Lancaster is true, then?' asked his brother, and she confirmed the stories that had preceded her across the channel.

'I didn't think he would go so far,' said Edward quietly. 'He must be a very desperate man.' It was Warwick he was speaking of. Janet wondered if he did not, in his heart of hearts, think with her that he was worth two of the Duke of Clarence.

He managed to find a few hours that evening to thank her more personally. A reward for such a mission was suspiciously like blood-money, but Edward insisted on her taking it. And when she handled the carved box which opened into a green velvet pincushion, she could not resist it. Their lovemaking went very sleepily for Janet, and she was almost relieved that he could not stay. Though later on, lying wakeful in spite of everything, she wished he was there to tease her guilt away. She could not rid herself of the conviction that she was presiding over the sundering of two families entwined by loyalties, love, and kinship.

In late summer the royal army was ready to march north again.

Confidently and casually Edward said goodbye to Janet before riding off at the head of his troops, Richard of Gloucester beside him. For the second time his optimism was misplaced. By October Warwick's invasion force had landed, and it was King Edward who was fleeing for his life. With one or two companions, including Gloucester and Hastings, he managed to reach Lynn; after a hazardous voyage he was received, with no notable enthusiasm, by the governor of Holland at Alkmaar. He had only a gown lined with marten fur to pay his fare.

Knowing only that their king had been chased out of his kingdom, the Londoners found their city occupied by the Earl of Warwick. Passively, they allowed him to take over the government, and there was little open protest when he announced that Edward Plantagenet was merely the Duke of York and Henry of Lancaster was true king of England. Fetched away from his books of devotion in the Tower, the old man was paraded through the streets in an ancient patched mantle. He blinked with vacant eyes at the crowds which turned out to line the route, as bewildered as they at his change of fortune. The people were too hushed with pity and contempt to cheer. That was left to Warwick's men-at-arms, planted here and there in the throng, and those immediately near them who were persuaded to enthusiasm by strategic displays of sharp daggers. Janet stayed at home.

The hybrid regime established itself with a crop of executions and the issuing of attainders on Edward of York, his brother Richard, and anyone else who would not admit that they had been wrong for nine years. As usual, only the nobility really suffered, and the citizens philosophically resumed their work. There was, however, a little discreet rejoicing at Soulmass, when Edward's wife, in sanctuary at Westminster, at last gave birth to a son. Some bold spirits were heard to refer to the child quite openly as the Prince of Wales.

The Duke of Clarence sent for Janet after Christmas. He told her conspiratorially that he was 'biding his time'. Since the marriage between Anne Neville and Edward of Lancaster had been solemnized, he considered all obligations to his father-in-law null and void. But nobody, he explained with the air of a reasonable man, could expect him to stand out alone for his brother.

CHAPTER ONE

'When he returns, as soon as I can be of use to him, I shall join him.' In other words, as soon as Edward turned from hare to hound, Clarence would turn his coat. Janet wondered in disgust why he had bothered to tell her. Perhaps because he owed her money.

One of the men brought to London by the new situation was Geoffrey Barton. Janet found him in her solar, urbane and restless as ever. She had never been easy with him since he had deceived her, and now there was a more serious difference between them. But her uncle showed no consciousness of it, and paid her the usual extravagant compliments.

'And since I'm back in London, you can come to court again with me.'

He was most surprised when she refused point-blank.

'Why ever not?' he asked. 'Very few people know of your association with Edward, and anyway my lord of Warwick would bear no grudge against you. It's as well to make friends in all quarters, Janet.'

'You forget, uncle,' Janet answered shortly, 'I'm not a courtier. I have no need of that kind of friend.'

'Yet I notice that you still supply the Duke of Clarence with mercery,' said Geoffrey slyly.

'That's business. I have a contract with him. But I will not flaunt my disloyalty to the king. And what became of your oath of obedience to King Edward? You helped him the year before last at Middleham. But at the next crisis you prove to be as much of a fair-weather friend as Clarence.'

Unperturbed, Geoffrey lifted his shoulders.

'Think what you please, niece. I serve the Earl of Warwick. I always have and always shall. Whoever is his king is my king too.'

It was impossible to argue with him. He was not the kind of man to lose any sleep over questions of conscience. Yet there was none of Clarence's calculating ambition about him. Geoffrey Barton simply did as he was told.

Dropping the vexed question of politics, Janet asked him for news of home. There was much to tell. Will was married, and his wife

Katherine, the small girl whom she had seen during her last Christmas in York, was with child; Bessie had three more children, and Dick was betrothed to a girl nine years his senior. The familiar names, attached to people who had by now grown beyond recognition, never failed to move Janet. With a relish for gossip nearly as great as Bessie's, her uncle painted a detailed portrait of the family she was forgetting.

As usual at times of conflict, Janet feared for her father. He had declared his allegiance to Edward in no uncertain terms, and he would not be a weather-cock. If Warwick chose to persecute Yorkist supporters, Thomas would be a clear target.

But, with the Yorkist cause in eclipse, Janet also had other absent loved ones to pray for. The deposed King Edward was wintering in Flanders, working ceaselessly to raise an army, and with him was his brother the Duke of Gloucester and her own brother John. She did not know whether to ask God to keep them safe and far away from herself and England, or to bring them success in returning with a large force when all their lives would be at risk.

She found it difficult to follow the fortunes of their enterprise, with scarce Yorkist news necessarily vague and brief and Lancastrian news often more false than true. But by concentrating on every morsel thrown to her, almost like a diviner gazing into a crystal, she could imagine their progress as if she were there with them.

Edward's sister Margaret of York had recently married young Duke Charles of Burgundy and he did not scruple to use family pressures to obtain the support he needed. With the first hint of spring he was ready to embark at Flushing in Holland with a small but well-appointed force.

It was a gamble; Warwick knew it, England knew it, even Edward with his unquenchable optimism must have known it. The earl had mobilised all his supporters, and their troops were patrolling the whole country; the Nevilles held London and the channel, and Margaret of Anjou was expected to land at any time in the West Country with another huge host financed by King Louis.

And at the outset the expedition almost met disaster. Edward's ships were beaten off Cromer, and storms scattered his fleet as it sailed on north to the favourable shores of Yorkshire. Thanks to the presence of mind of Richard of Gloucester, the invading band met up safely near Ravenspur. They marched to York, which nervously closed its gates against them. With adroit modesty, Edward declared that he came only as Duke of York. That night he and his captains slept in feather beds within the city. Men with long memories scoffed at his stratagem. Henry Bolingbroke had landed at Ravenspur too, and claimed only the dukedom of Lancaster - until Richard II fell into his hands.

But York was an island in a sea of danger. Between the northern capital and the supreme goal, London, were at least four armies waiting to nip the enterprise in the bloom. The Earl of Northumberland and Warwick's brother the Marquis of Montagu were manoeuvring in the north; Warwick and Clarence hovered in the midlands. Edward had always won through before with a combination of luck and skill. He would need an extraordinary helping of both to succeed this time.

Incredibly, his luck held. Somehow he slipped between Northumberland and Montagu and with a growing following made swiftly south. Those who knew the straightforward brother of Warwick wondered if Montagu had tried very hard to catch him. The anti-Yorkist element in London, who until now had been very loud, suddenly shut their mouths. All the armed men were gone from the city. The two principals were facing each other near Coventry. Edward threw away subterfuge and proclaimed himself king.

Everything hung in the balance. A first sign of the way things would go came with Clarence's movement. The cat jumped again, and was received with elaborate affection by his long-suffering brothers. He must have been very sure that Edward would succeed.

There was a race for London. It had happened so often before: the trained bands keeping their bows and staves within reach, the citizens half-heartedly carrying on their business, starting at every sound, naked to the forces that were bearing down on them. But Janet's anxiety was lifting. Edward was coming home. His lightning marches were legendary. No one had ever beaten him in a race.

And of course he won. Following the harbingers and unofficial messengers, he entered London on Maundy Thursday at the head of an army tired but in splendid spirits. As in the old days, he was flanked by his two brothers: George handsome and assured, Richard now grown to his full height and weathered by the hard winter. The family of York was complete again. The Neville supporters and diehard Lancastrians had disappeared; it seemed that the entire population of the capital was there to acclaim King Edward and help him on his way to offer thanksgiving at St Paul's.

As soon as his respects to God were paid, Edward hurried to Westminster to greet his wife and his son. Nan described to Janet, sniffing sentimentally, how tenderly the king had embraced the queen and cradled the infant prince. Janet did not want to listen. Elizabeth had given Edward the healthy heir he had married her for, and he had rushed to her with gratitude. All Janet had achieved for him were two miscarriages. For the first time in years she was jealous.

There was little time for domestic celebration. Warwick, joined now by his brother Montagu, was hot on the king's heels. On Easter Eve Edward led his men out of London's north gate for the final confrontation. He would force a fight, and the issue would decide once for all who ruled England. Somewhere, not far away, the two great men would meet in a fratricidal battle which few of their followers would have sought: Richard, brought up in the shadow of Warwick's glory, who had learned his chivalry in the Great Earl's school; Montagu, who had served Edward faithfully for ten years but at the final choice had sided with his kindred; George, Warwick's son-in-law, his ally and protégé, until it suited his ends to desert him. Behind them were the lesser men, like John Wrangwysh and Geoffrey Barton, comrades in former days, now fighting on opposite sides. With what reluctance would such men raise their swords, fearing to find beneath the blade a friend or brother? Or did considerations like that disappear in the heat of conflict? Did the grief come afterwards?

As the brave column tramped into the distance, the elation of the city went with it. Many Londoners were with the armies, as volunteers or conscripts, most with the king, some with Warwick. The majority would probably come through safely. This was a battle of great men, and the great would bear the brunt. But London had worshipped the Great Earl as well as King Edward. It was hard that England could not contain both. The city waited.

With nightfall came fog. The cold clinging blanket made the hours until news came interminable. Theories ran round the wakeful town: the armies had missed each other in the fog; Warwick had refused the challenge and retreated to join forces with the expected Lancastrians. When the first trickle of fugitives came in, it only added to the mystery. They had never reached the battle site, but slipped away in the darkness and concocted stories of disaster for the king to cover their desertion. A damp dawn filtered through the mist and soon real fugitives appeared, often unhurt, but frightened and exhausted. The king was almost surrounded, they said; the royal left wing had broken and the Earl of Oxford was forging through to the centre where Edward was making a last stand by the Barnet road.

They had met only a few miles north of London. Straining one's ears through the fog, it should almost have been possible to hear the grind and clash of weapons. The last stand of King Edward. It must have been true that the left had collapsed; so many brought the same information. But the morning wore on, and there was nothing decisive. All pretence at normal life had stopped. The priests went about their religious duties distractedly; not many minds were on the Elevation of the Host at the first Mass of Easter. Men stood idle in the streets, talking little, looking ever towards the north, for one more stumbling figure to materialise out of the mist and give them one more scrap of news as likely to be false as true. Tidings that the king and his brothers were dead, his army in flight, alternated wildly with tales that Warwick had been cut down personally by Edward, who was pursuing the leaderless rebels with great slaughter.

Nan brought each rumour breathlessly home as it arrived, sometimes spread at fourth or fifth hand from its unreliable source. While the fog crept through the closed windows in insidious wreaths, Janet sat before a sulky fire and tried to pray. The men she cared for most in the world were facing death not ten miles away. If her father and any of her brothers were fighting under the banner of York, at least they would not be in the worst of it. It was Edward, swinging his battle-axe at the head of his men, and John guarding Gloucester's flank in the van of the right wing, who were exposed to the most acute danger. She had learned to live with her fear for Edward, but this was her brother's first battle, and that doubled her dread.

When official news came, it brought no spontaneous rejoicing. A royal herald with a token from the king himself rode through the streets, holding it aloft and shouting his message as he made for the Lord Mayor's house.

'The king has won a great victory. Warwick and Montagu are slain!'

The Londoners stared after him. So that was the end of it. Edward's luck had not run out; Warwick's had.

By mid-morning a pale disc of sun had swum through the fog, and at noon powdery blue sky was appearing overhead. The mist had evaporated completely when the advance guard of the royal army came into sight. Soon the northern road was thronging with soldiers, and spring sunshine glinted on pikes and helmets from distant Highgate Hill. Once more London greeted a victorious King Edward, but there was sadness beneath the applause. Not many bothered to laugh much at Henry of Lancaster, who meek and shadowy as he had always been, was led along behind his supplanter. They were looking at the carts full of wounded, torn remnants of yesterday's orderly ranks, searching for faces they knew.

Janet could not see John among Gloucester's train. Instead her unwilling eyes fell on the bloody bodies of Warwick and his brother, stripped of their armour and carried along under guard, as proof that the Great Earl had taken his last gamble. A few ruffians in the crowd threw handfuls of refuse, but she could not be glad.

Sick with anxiety for John, she went home. She had no means of finding what had happened to him. The king and his brothers would be meeting now, preparing to repulse the Lancastrian army which was the last threat to Edward's supremacy. Janet would not push herself into the urgent councils of the great for private satisfaction. So she relieved her feelings by complaining about the untidy state of the house, and cooking an Easter repast she did not want to eat.

But that evening a man-at-arms came, in the White Boar livery of the Duke of Gloucester. She was to go at once to Baynard's Castle, where the duke was lodging with his mother. The soldier's only answer to her questions was that it concerned Master Wrangwysh.

Baynard's Castle was swarming with men, mostly soldiers, on a thousand errands. The man-at-arms shouldered his way through the press to a small ante-room, just as crowded but quieter, with waiting soldiers and courtiers. Janet was left there, blushing under their glances, until her guide returned and led her into another chamber which was empty.

After a moment Richard entered through another door connecting with the council chamber. He was out of armour and had put on a clean gown, but he still wore the sweat-drenched hose in which he had fought at Barnet. There were grey circles under his eyes. In the months since Janet had given him Anne's token, he had gained an air of decisiveness. His eyes had lost their puzzled look, and his mouth had hardened. He greeted her warmly, unsmiling.

'It is your brother, Mistress Evershed. He was wounded at my side during our advance up the hill. A battle-axe glanced off his helm. We have brought him back and he is in my apartments. The surgeon will attend him. If you wish to stay and nurse him, arrangements will be made.'

Janet tried to say several things at once, to thank him, to praise his heroic part in the king's victory, but she only blurted out, 'Will he live?'

Gloucester shook his head.

'I don't know.' He said no more, but she could read sympathy and a hope that he would.

'Now you must excuse me, mistress. We have pressing matters to attend to. My man will escort you.' Swiftly he left her.

Between gratitude at his kindness and terror for John, she followed the man-at-arms. In a large tapestried room a number of wounded were laid out on make-shift couches; as she found later, they were members of Richard's household. There was a smell of blood and decay, groans and murmurs. One or two people were moving about, bathing and salving and bandaging.

John was in a corner watched over by a small page, who disappeared as soon as Janet approached. He was still, white and unconscious. His wound had been washed and the hair shaved away above the left temple. There was not much to see. The skin was slightly discoloured and broken only a little. Janet felt his pulse, which was faint but steady, and then stood gazing down at him, uncertain what to do next. She had never dealt with anything but childish ailments on her own before. Memories of singing her sick brothers to sleep, and binding their bruises after squabbles at school came unhelpfully into her mind. John was a grown man now and this battle had been in earnest. He needed more than a soothing hand.

A soft-spoken old man, who turned out to be the duke's own doctor, came in and gave her the instructions she sought, negative though they were.

'He has been bled, mistress. You can do nothing more but wait.'

So she waited, heavy-hearted, making sure now and again that he was still breathing. The obliging man-at-arms sent a message home for her, asking Nan to bring the necessary supplies for her stay at the castle. Meanwhile she helped with the other patients, exchanging little more than essential words with the attendants and the women who arrived, like her, to nurse their menfolk. At midnight, unable to keep her eyes open after the previous sleepless night, she retired to a specially-prepared pallet in a room close by.

It was the first of many weary days. John revived occasionally, enough to take milk or broth, but he relapsed quickly into the same torpor, with only sighs and a faint flutter of the eyelids to show there was life in him. Richard called in twice a day, sparing a word for each of the wounded and the nurses. Once the king accompanied him and gave Janet the intimate smile which made her sluggish spirits leap up in answer.

They were both very busy, for news of Margaret of Anjou's landing at Weymouth had reached London only two days after the Battle of Barnet. Edward was not going to be caught napping again. And though he was pardoning the majority of the defeated army, he could not afford to be lenient with its dead leaders. He had tried in vain to save Warwick's life when the battle was lost, but the corpse must be used as an example to other would-be rebels. Nan, who visited Baynard's Castle regularly, told her mistress with relish that the Great Earl and his brother Montagu were exposed to public view in Paul's Cathedral, lying in open coffins with only a loin-cloth to cover their nakedness. There had been a time when Nan would have given her virtue to touch Warwick's horse. Janet gritted her teeth and tried not to show her revulsion.

She spent much of her time in the sick-room fighting down nausea. The rotten odour grew no sweeter; she could hardly bring herself to return each morning from the untainted air of her bedchamber. Two of the men died, very noisily, and she was called upon several times to assist with messy operations. In one such operation she held the iron to cauterize a weeping leg-wound which threatened to turn gangrenous. Afterwards she was sitting by John's pallet, faint from the stench of burning flesh, when the Duchess of York came in. The old lady did not flinch even slightly at the atmosphere. Her face had the sweeping lines of an alabaster effigy, framed by the nun-like coif of her widow's mourning. She had witnessed too many scenes of carnage to be shocked by this minor incident. With remote composure she spoke to the whimpering patient, and then made a progress round the room. Recalling that this was her house, Janet thanked her for her hospitality. The duchess's keen glance flickered over her and with an acknowledgement she passed on. Janet wondered guiltily if she knew she was honouring her son's mistress.

On St George's Day, while Janet and Nan took it in turns to sit with John, the king set out for the west. Immured in the infirmary, Janet heard the bells ringing and the people going wild in the streets over the total defeat of their ancient enemy Queen Margaret at Tewkesbury. A week later she listened in alarm to the guns thumping across the river as Warwick's cousin Fauconberg sailed up the Thames and attempted to take the city. He was beaten off, and Janet was still there when the king returned as the undisputed master, at last, of all England. She was grateful then for the excuse not to watch the triumphal procession. Margaret would be dragged through the streets in a rough chariot, subject to the howls and jeers of execration that the Londoners reserved for fallen tyrants. With her, perhaps, in her humiliation would be Warwick's countess and younger daughter, both widowed in a month, for Lady Anne's husband had been cut down in flight in the Bloody Meadow by Tewkesbury. The thought of those two gentlewomen, bereaved and dispossessed with a mob yelling at them, was unbearable.

And the following day the third of the conquered women was a widow. Henry VI was dead – of pure grief, men said with heavy irony – in his Tower prison. That it was judicial murder was common knowledge, and nobody cared very much. The Lancastrians, of course, were mute; there was no outcry. So ended the ill-sorted alliance of the Nevilles and the House of Lancaster, in death and destitution for both innocent and guilty.

The other wounded men had all gone from Baynard's Castle, dead, recovered, or removed. Because the doctor said that a sudden jolt in his present condition could be fatal, John remained, suspended in a half-world between waking and oblivion. Sitting alone beside him, Janet was plunged into deep depression. Edward had not come near her, and she was thankful. The measures he had taken were necessary, but that did not reconcile her to them. She loved the man with all her heart; the king she could not but hate.

CHAPTER TWO

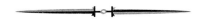

pring was turning to summer. So long had John lain there, chalk-white, that his sister had ceased to expect any change. She had embroidered two pillow-cases and a doublet, and Nick had taken to coming to Baynard's Castle for his orders. It was almost like taking up permanent residence there. The servants passed the time of day with her as if she were an old acquaintance.

Then one morning, as she sat at her desk writing a letter in laborious French to a noble Burgundian client, she glanced from habit at John's pallet. His eyes were open, and intelligent. They moved dully over the unremembered plaster ceiling, and rested in vague perplexity on the face which now hung over him in sudden hope. He tried to speak, failed, and closed his eyes again wearily. Janet ran for the watered wine she kept constantly beside her and, propping his head up, she fed it to him. Eyes still closed, he drank instinctively; shortly afterwards he sank into a natural sleep. Colour was coming back into his cheeks, but when he woke he did not know her, and when he could speak he remembered nothing. The doctor advised her to tell him everything she could: some detail might bring his memory back. John was taking nourishment and regaining strength hourly, and her despondency of weeks began to lift.

Though weak and sleeping a great deal, he mended rapidly. At first he could not even recall his own name, but with Janet's help he reconstructed his life up to the night before the battle. That and the day of Barnet remained shrouded in the mists of his unconsciousness. Soon it would be time for her to go home and leave his convalescence for others to tend. Mindful of their father's veto, she would make no effort to keep in contact with her brother after the necessity was past.

The evening before her departure, the Duke of Gloucester came to see her. He had been away in Kent for a month, chasing off the remnants of Fauconberg's fleet. During the barren hours of her vigil, many topics had meandered through her mind, and one of them was whether Richard still had any interest in the Lady Anne. She and her mother had not been brought to London with the discredited queen. The Countess of Warwick was confined by armed guards in Beaulieu Sanctuary, and Anne had been placed in the care of her sister the Duchess of Clarence. They were nothing now; heiresses to an attainted traitor. Anne Neville would be a sorry prospect for the third gentleman in the land. But whatever Richard might do, Janet decided, it would not be to please himself.

She was sewing in the big empty chamber while her brother slept. Richard came in quietly, and motioned for her not to disturb herself. Having inspected John, he sat down on a chest by the wall.

'He has regained consciousness?'

'Several days ago, my lord. He'll soon be well.'

'Good.' The duke smiled, a rare smile which transformed his sallow face. 'I've missed him with me, the last two campaigns. When I go north, I hope he'll be one of my company again.'

'He talks of little else. But I'm afraid he remembers nothing about the battle.' She explained about his illness.

'A pity. His part in it won't be forgotten by the rest of us. We had to keep our line against the enemy, you see, until the king could force his way through to us. John's kind of courage was just what we needed then – not reckless, you understand. But thoroughly reliable. It was the same escaping to Flanders last autumn. He never wavered.' He stopped, and looked at Janet.

'You're very like him,' he said, faintly surprised. 'You both know how to listen.'

She found herself blushing. From him, it was a great compliment. He asked her whether she had managed to carry on her business from John's bedside, then he spoke abruptly.

'I have asked the king's permission to marry the Lady Anne.'

Janet was taken aback by the unexpected confidence, but she said with impulsive pleasure 'I'm very glad. She has lost so much.'

'Everything. But she shall lose no more.'

Soon after that he left her.

The Duke of Gloucester was a reserved young man who would not give his trust lightly. Janet was moved that he should have spoken to her of his long-cherished wish to make Anne his wife – a wish born many years ago between a frail boy and a frailer girl in the faraway sanctuary of Middleham Castle. Not since they left it had they experienced much peace. They deserved it now.

He did not win his lady so easily. By the time he left for the north, with a shaky but happy John Wrangwysh in his train, it was an open secret that he had made his suit to the Lady Anne. It was also an open secret that George of Clarence had objected strongly. No-one was sure of the details, but there was certainly bad blood between the brothers so lately reconciled.

Due to Richard's confiding in her, Janet felt an almost proprietary interest in the affair. She resolved to ask Edward what he was going to do about it. The king had started to visit her again, and although the subject of Henry VI and his wife was never raised between them, they resumed their old intimate terms. It would have jarred their concord to mention it, so tacitly they let it lie. Janet had accepted that if she was to love a man who was also a king, there were many things she would have to condone.

But one night after they had made love she ventured to question him about his brothers.

'Is it true that the Duke of Clarence is trying to prevent the match?'

Edward leaned across her to trim a smoky candle.

'Yes. By every means in his power. He has no right to do so, but

115

he does possess Anne at the moment. It was a mistake, I suppose, to give her into his keeping, because I knew what was in Dickon's heart, and how jealous of him George has become. But,' he shrugged his shoulders, 'I had much on my mind. Perhaps I didn't believe George would go so far to stop their marrying.'

'How far can he go?' said Janet in dismay. 'Surely your command can overbear his will – and you do want my lord of Gloucester to marry Lady Anne?'

'Of course I do,' Edward said warmly. 'Dickon is very dear to me, and he and Anne are made for each other. I gave my consent at once. But George has stooped to using very ignoble weapons, and I want no scandal. There has been enough involving George and me already.'

'What has he done?'

'I'm not sure. Dickon keeps his own counsel. I think he has threatened harm to Anne if Richard persists in courting her. He would already have seized the Countess of Warwick too if I hadn't kept her safely penned up at Beaulieu.'

By the next day every urchin knew that the Duke of Clarence and the Duke of Gloucester had quarrelled. Though opinions varied as to the bone of contention, the little that the servants had overheard of their meeting was quite enough to start rumours flying round London. Edward tried to get at the truth, but Richard was reticent, and George was truculent. He attempted to patch things up, hoping that when his younger brother returned from his northern mission, his other brother would have relented. Ashamed of his conduct, Richard was ready to hold out his hand; George agreed to take it with surprising readiness. Differences between brothers, he said loftily, were unnatural and displeasing to God.

So in the days that followed the three brothers appeared in public together, apparently the best of friends. Richard, who had the least talent for dissembling, was incapable of bearing a grudge against George for long. It was true that Anne was still living under Clarence's roof, but that golden tongue assured him that she was really perfectly happy. They could come to some arrangement in the end. Won round by his plausible charm, Richard began to believe it.

CHAPTER TWO

While he was away Edward promised to do all that he could to smooth his way with Clarence. Janet, however, was becoming rather impatient with the indulgence shown towards the Duke of Clarence. She did not see the king very often, but whenever she did she plied him with questions about his progress. At last her importunity exasperated him.

'Fond as I am of Dickon,' he said, 'and sorry as I am for Anne, this is a business matter. You're being very sentimental about it. Negotiations are bound to take time. They're not a couple of peasants who can decide to wed and rush off to the nearest priest the same day.'

Janet restrained herself from pointing out that Edward's marriage had been contracted in a similar way.

'Leave it, Janet, and don't dabble in things that don't concern you.'

She was hurt. In all the years of being Edward's mistress, she had never before interfered in politics; and she was only interested in his brother's welfare. For a moment the old domineering, masculine Edward reared his image, and when he went to caress her she could not respond.

He made no further advances, and when he left there was a distinct coolness between them. A feeling of impotence gripped her. He was right. State affairs were nothing to do with her. But in her mind, small and sharp, was the picture of two children bending over a wooden doll in a winter castle, and they seemed to have nothing to do with state affairs either.

She did not ask any more questions. As summer deepened Richard came back and was given the Neville estates in Yorkshire, including Middleham Castle. Though Janet was pleased that he had won his way back to Wensleydale, she could find out no more about his matrimonial plans. For once, she kept her ears wide open to gossip; Nan was cross-examined after each shopping expedition. But as far as popular knowledge was concerned, the Duke of Gloucester had apparently submitted to his brother's whim and given up his suit.

The misty mornings were beginning to announce autumn, and still there were no developments. Janet was serving in the shop one day, and had just finished dealing with a fussy customer – a gentleman in the Marquis of Dorset's train – when she noticed that John was waiting quietly to see her. She gave him a startled glance, called her new girl apprentice to take over, and led him through into the workshop. A wild hope had sprung up that he brought their father's pardon, but his earnest expression did not hold that kind of news. He refused refreshment and plunged into his purpose.

'I have disobeyed on my lord duke's account, Janet, not mine. He needs help.'

'From me?' asked Janet doubtfully.

'Perhaps. The Lady Anne has disappeared.'

'Disappeared? How do you know? The Duke of Clarence would never dare to……' Fear struck at her and she did not go on.

'I went with my lord to his brother's house, soon after we returned from the Border. The Duke of Clarence kept us waiting a long time. When he did receive us he was … not very civil.'

Janet nodded. She was familiar with George's talent for incivility. Apparently, Richard had told him directly that he had the king's authority to remove the Lady Anne from his custody. At that Clarence had looked very unconcerned and said that he was welcome to take Anne – if he could find her. This nonchalant attitude had ruffled Richard and he had bidden his brother speak out in plain words. The Lady Anne, Clarence had said deliberately, was no longer in his household, nor any concern of his.

'She wasn't there. My lord insisted on searching and his brother made no objection.' John had finished, and stood frowning at his sister.

'Why should he show such malice?' she muttered under her breath, though she knew the answer. Only one person mattered to George Plantagenet, and that was the Duke of Clarence. If there was a chance of adding to the greater glory of the Duke of Clarence, nothing would stand in his way.

Nothing? Her fear increased.

'Do you think – does my lord of Gloucester believe that she has come to harm?'

'No. He wouldn't do anything as drastic as that. He has hidden her.....somewhere.'

CHAPTER TWO

'Where? And why?'

'I can't tell. The division of her parents' lands is still in question – though it seems a poor motive for such an action.'

Not to George, thought Janet.

'As to where she may be – that's why I came to you. My lord suspects that she is somewhere in the city – perhaps because he doesn't want to think of her being further away. And you're closer to the city than we at court. If you should hear anything – '

'John, did the duke send you?'

'Not exactly,' he prevaricated. 'He wouldn't ask me to break father's rule. But he mentioned you the other day.' The young man met her gaze defiantly. 'And he is my lord, Janet.' Understanding, she sighed.

'Yes, John. I too would give a great deal to help the Duke of Gloucester to Lady Anne. The king has virtually forbidden me to interfere, but I can't close my eyes and ears. In any case,' she added, almost to herself, 'If the king's brother can stoop to such chicanery, it ceases to be a matter of high state.'

John was ready to go. Even in Richard's service he would not trespass longer than necessary. She put her hand on his arm.

'It's a forlorn hope, my dear. There are thousands living in the city, and I only know a fraction of them. If she's here at all, the Duke of Clarence will not have hidden her carelessly.'

Her brother kissed her swiftly on the cheek, and went.

For a moment she stood staring at nothing, her hands playing idly with the bunch of keys at her waist. If only she could! A wave of energy drove away her helplessness of the past few months. This surely was a task for a woman, for quiet questioning and listening, a task for her. Emerging from her reverie she hurried back to the shop, revolving a hundred fragmentary schemes for discovering the whereabouts of Anne Neville.

But her words to John about a forlorn hope were nearer the mark. She listened for titbits of news about mysterious lady lodgers and unexplained country cousins, in vain. Janet was not a woman who habitually gossiped; it would be out of character and arouse too much interest if she began now. Had she possessed more female friends, wives or daughters of her fellow merchants, it would have been easier to glean information. Almost all her associates, however, were men; their womenfolk persisted in regarding her either as odd and unfeminine or, if they knew about the king's visits, as a loose woman. Either way, she was not popular.

She took Nick into her confidence; both discreet and shrewd, he moved in slightly lower circles than she did herself, and was used to collecting news in the way of business. He cared little for the Duke of Gloucester, or for the plight of Anne Neville, but he would have gone stolidly through fire for his mistress, and he did his best to help. To no avail. Not caring to trust Nan, or the apprentices, with any secret she did not wish spread from Ludgate to the Tower within the day, she could not employ them. Anne was little-known as a public figure in London. She was unlikely to be recognised, except by those like Janet who knew her personally. No doubt Clarence had counted on that.

Days passed, the leaves fell, and it was a wet foggy November. Still Anne's hiding-place was an enigma. Edward came to Janet infrequently, and she did not dare to mention Richard or George to him. She was sure that he would have told her had anything definite happened. George, it appeared, had won. Trying to read his self-centred mind, Janet guessed that when the fuss had died away he would quietly force his sister-in-law into taking orders in some remote convent, so that his claim to the property would be undisputed. Perhaps he had already done it. The possibility instilled a sense of urgency into her flagging efforts. If Anne became a nun, Richard would lose her forever, and without a vocation the wretched girl would eat her heart out. The idea that Anne might not want to marry him never occurred to her. She had always been convinced that they were right for each other.

But it took time to become a fully-consecrated nun, and late in November Janet resolved on a last measure. Her outright defiance of Edward would be justified by success; otherwise, she intended to keep it to herself. She would try a personal investigation in Clarence's house. An outsider might learn something by judicious questioning. Her pretext was ready made: she had to deliver the winter liveries she had embroidered for the duke's bodyguard. With no clear plan in mind, she muffled herself well against a murky day and set off with Nick and two full saddlebags.

The duke was away, but that was the only piece of luck she had. She was interviewed by his comptroller, an unsociable man of few words who was difficult to draw into casual conversation. More taciturn than ever, he paid her there and then for the consignment – bribery, she suspected, to make her leave quickly – and escorted her all the way to the door. It shut firmly behind her. She was out in the courtyard, with no possible excuse to get inside again.

With a bitter feeling of anti-climax, she leant against the warmth of her tethered mare, who turned her head and snorted sympathetically. What she had expected to achieve she could not now imagine. She had little hope that Nick would do any better in the humbler parts of the house. Sunk in gloomy contemplation of her failure, she waited for him to appear.

Presently a fluttering from a low doorway aroused her. A woman was waving a kerchief at her, trying to attract her attention. There was something furtive about her action that made Janet catch her breath. She left the horse and sauntered across the courtyard. Her sleeve was grabbed and she was pulled inside the door. The woman asked her breathlessly to follow and Janet did so, through deserted kitchen passages to a storeroom next to the linen press. Inside was the Duchess of Clarence, flushed and overwrought, twisting her hands together nervously. Janet's guide closed the door on them, presumably to keep watch. Before Janet could curtsey the duchess was talking quickly, stammering.

'Forgive me, Mistress Evershed, for this secrecy. I saw you from this window and took the liberty of sending Ankarette to fetch you. Someone must help. I can't bear to keep the secret any longer. My conscience torments me more every day. You are our friend. Please help my sister!' Isabel was pleading, almost desperately, with Janet to do exactly what she had been trying to do for weeks.

'Of course I will, your grace.' In her rising hope and pity for the duchess she nearly seized her trembling hands. But she contained herself and said calmly 'Where is she, madame?'

'My husband bound me with a sacred oath not to speak of it, but she may be ill. They may be treating her badly. I will confess it tonight.' Now it was she who clutched Janet's arm. 'But don't tell him – don't tell anyone – that I told you. He will ... I don't know what he'll do if he finds out, but he mustn't.'

Patting her hand gently, Janet said, 'I swear I shall not tell a soul. Now, if you please, madame, where is she?'

Isabel gulped and recovered a little of her composure.

'Ankarette's brother is a grocer in the Vintry. Anne is in his house, near St James de Garlickhithe. They have disguised her as a servant.' Her voice cracked with misery. 'We are all sworn to secrecy. Ankarette wouldn't dare to break the oath, because my husband threatened her with the Fleet – or worse. So it was I who had to tell you. Please go quickly. She has been there for months. The disgrace of it! If my father had lived.....But this would never have happened if he had lived.....' Janet interrupted her, speaking softly, trying not to show her impatience. If she were caught communicating with the duchess it would not be good for either of them.

'Ankarette's brother – what is his name?'

'Francis – Francis Twynyho.' Before she could begin to lament again, Janet went on.

'Don't upset yourself any more, my lady. I shall go straight to the Duke of Gloucester.'

'But you won't tell him....?'

'I shall make up a story about how I found out. Now I must go.'

Convinced of Janet's good will and capability, Isabel became tearfully grateful. Attempting to be respectful and yet to detach herself as rapidly as possible, Janet firmly took her leave. There was no time to spare pity for the Duchess of Clarence. With a quick reverence, she slipped out of the door. Telling the lurking Ankarette, who was nearly as upset as the duchess, to go to her mistress, she sped back the way she had come.

She only slowed down when she reached the courtyard. Nick was moving uneasily beside their horses, stamping and blowing on his fingers. Though acting as naturally as she could, her heart was thumping with excitement. As they mounted, she said in a low voice, 'I have found where she is. We must go at once to my lord of Gloucester.'

Trotting down the muddy streets, almost dark already though it was only just past noon, she related to Nick what she had discovered, omitting mention of the duchess.

'We must have a tale ready to account for our knowledge.' They decided on a likely lie.

At the Duke of Gloucester's residence there was a check. She asked for Master Wrangwysh, who was not there. Neither was the duke; he was at a council meeting in the Tower. Slightly dampened, Janet made for the Tower. The haste which had possessed her since last night persisted although a destination was in sight; it was mixed now with incredulity at George's treatment of his sister-in-law, and with new anxiety for her well-being. The daughter of the Great Earl, a gently-bred girl in weak health – disguised as a servant! It was unheard of! Inconsequentially, Janet remembered the story of Sir Gareth – 'Beaumains' – and his humiliation in the kitchens of King Arthur. But this was hard reality, not romance, and the Lady Anne's knight had not yet rescued her.

'Mistress!' Nick's voice penetrated her thoughts. 'You're riding too fast.' She drew in the reins. The houses climbing up to Tower Hill were ahead, and a practical problem presented itself to her. How was she to obtain an audience with the duke?

The sentries at the Lion Gate would not let her in. For once she wished her influence were greater. She tried straightforwardness and then pleading, but the king and all his council were within, and no strangers were allowed. She could not find out if her brother was there, nor would anyone carry a message for her, despite the money she displayed. The guards, with drops of moisture at the tips of their red noses, were not in a helpful mood. All she could achieve with the Duke of Clarence's marks was admission as far as the Coldharbour Gate. There, all she could do was to wait. The dim daylight began to drain away into the thickening fog. She sent Nick home, ignoring his protests, and strove to keep warm between two buttresses.

Torches were fixed in cressets on the gatehouse; the guard changed. With night, the fog froze. The fresh guard took pity on her and let her sit inside the gatehouse beside his little brazier. Even so the icy moisture was stealing into her very bones.

When she thought she would rust up like an old suit of armour and never be able to move again, there was activity. Grooms were leading horses across the inner bailey, gentlemen emerged from the White Tower, wrapping themselves closely in their cloaks and complaining against the cold. There were clouds of breath, voices and bustle, all black and yellow in the flare of the torches. The greater noblemen gathered men to themselves like sheep to shepherds, and moved off towards the gate. Two groups, the largest, were still waiting, for the king and the Duke of Gloucester.

Last of all, they appeared together, deep in conversation, lighted by two pages. Edward's arm was round Richard's shoulders, his cloak flung back oblivious of the cold; he seemed to extinguish his slight brother. Janet had a word with the sentry who had been kind to her, and some more of the livery payment changed hands. Pushing his way through the gathering crowd of retainers, he crossed the respectful space left around the princes. In the lurid torchlight, Edward noticed the man saluting before him, and bent smiling to hear his message. He and Richard both alerted; he questioned the sentry, and nodded.

As the sentry threaded his way back to her, Janet was shivering with combined cold and relief. His manner changed from familiarity to deference, he said that the king would see her. Then she in her turn was before the royal brothers, curtseying as best she could with her stiff aching limbs, marvelling again at the way Edward's blaze of personality threw Richard into shadow. She was unable to believe that Edward was the man who had so often shared her bed. In public, even at night, his royalty was almost tangible.

The king's hand stretched out and gripped her arm. His warm strength came through his gauntlets and her woollen sleeves, and their intimacy was suddenly real again. His face was concerned.

'God's wounds, Janet, you're frozen. How long have you been waiting here? You should have come inside.' Not bothering to explain the obstacles facing a commoner entering the Tower, she answered, 'I've been here a long time, your grace, because I have important tidings for my lord of Gloucester.'

'Dickon?' Edward grinned down at his silent brother. 'Have you been hunting unlawfully in the king's forest?' Richard drew himself up a little primly; Janet had long suspected that his regard for her was in spite of her liaison with the king. 'Do you wish me to withdraw, Mistress Evershed?' went on Edward gaily.

Her teeth were beginning to chatter. She was too chilly and weary for jests.

'No, sire.' Then she said bluntly to the duke 'My lord, I have found where the Lady Anne is hidden.'

Animation sprang into Richard's eyes; the withdrawn personality was abruptly in command. When there was something to do, the usually-hidden likeness to Edward revealed itself. The king dropped his arm and gracefully resigned the stage to him.

'Is she safe?' Gloucester asked quickly.

'As far as I can tell. She's in the house of the grocer, Francis Twynyho, next to St James de Garlickhithe in the Vintry. She was disguised as a servant and they may not know her true identity.'

His expression dimmed for an instant at this new evidence of his brother's treachery; then he turned to his gentlemen and said decisively, 'Bring my horse. Frank, and Robert, you will accompany me. The rest are dismissed.' The two men and the groom leapt to obey; the others gladly began to disperse. As Richard mounted he flung over his shoulder to his chosen companions, 'We ride to the Vintry.' He twisted in his saddle to bow to the king, who strode forward to his stirrup and said in a low voice, 'Is it wise to proceed so openly, Dickon?'

Richard's face was set, but his eyes were alight with a kind of grim elation. 'The time for caution is past. I can wait no longer.'

Edward nodded slowly and stepped back. With a touch of his heel Richard brought his horse sidling towards Janet where she stood outside the circle of torchlight, and gave her his hand. As she bent to kiss it he clasped hers so tightly that it hurt. Then he was away. The straight boyish figure leading his gentlemen, the flurry of hooves was swallowed up in the murky darkness. Janet found she was crying. Probably from the cold.

A little light-headed from the long wait, though well content with the outcome, she turned to go. But she was seized from behind and enveloped in a bear-hug by arms she knew. Gratefully she relaxed against the king's chest.

'You'll not slink off into the night without even a farewell,' he commanded.

Struggling to stand upright again, she said, 'I must go home. They'll be anxious about me.'

'Haven't you a horse?'

'Oh, yes,' she recalled vaguely.

'Come back to Westminster with me,' suggested Edward, and she realised that he was offering her his bed as a reward for helping his brother. 'I want to hear how you ferreted out George's secret.'

'No, my lord.' She refused regretfully, but even in her fatigue, to commit adultery with his wife under the same roof was unthinkable. 'If you would spare me a groom to accompany me home, that's all I need.'

Familiar of old with Janet's determination, Edward shrugged and released her.

'As you will,' he said with humorous resignation. 'Nobody seems disposed to take my advice tonight. Still, defiant as you are, you and Dickon are worth twenty others. Bless you, sweet heart.' A snap of his fingers brought a page running, and soon Janet was being lifted into her saddle behind a broad-backed groom.

With a wave of the hand the king sent them off into the gloom, and called for his own mount. His freezing entourage, left outside and ignorant of the drama that had held them up, thankfully made tracks for Westminster Palace, wishing that the king and the duke would conduct their private business in more comfortable surroundings.

Janet was deposited at her door by the royal groom. A twittering Nan put her straight to bed and dosed her with a hot posset. Lapped in unaccustomed cosseting, she reflected drowsily that she would have been little use to Edward if she had gone with him. As she dropped into sleep in the warmed bed, her thoughts turned back to Richard. She doubted if the concocted story would be needed. Having no interest in intrigue, he was unlikely to ask for details. The recovery of Anne would be enough for him. Always supposing that he did recover her. But in his mood of determination, and if his brother had no more cards up his sleeve, the young man would not be gainsaid.

The next day, she collapsed on her way to the clothmarket. She was carried home and returned to bed, where she remained for a week with a severe chill. By the time she had recovered enough to take notice of outside affairs, everyone in London knew that Richard Duke of Gloucester had rescued the Lady Anne Neville from the kitchens of a London grocer, taken her to sanctuary in the College of St Martin-le-Grand and was asserting his right to marry her.

CHAPTER THREE

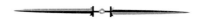

Over the Christmas season, Janet was convalescing. Her illness had deprived her of much of her normal energy, and she kept mainly indoors. Leaving the mercery side to Nick, she intended to catch up with her embroidery schedule, but found it difficult to concentrate. Frequently she would abandon her work and wander restlessly round the workshop, finding fault with young Agnes's apprentice stitches and doing none of her own.

A handsome gift of Rhenish wine from the Duke of Gloucester arrived. Had it not been for this, she would have begun to suspect that the secret meetings and frozen vigils, court intrigue and danger, were a figment of her fevered imagination during her sickness. Nan's gossip from the market, which Janet again reluctantly listened to, kept her in touch with the progress of the Duke's suit, but only as a story told about strangers.

Despite the waits and travelling mummers, Yuletide fell rather flat in Walbrook. It was especially at Christmas that Janet missed her family. A visit from the king, very merry and expansive, was therefore doubly welcome. Usually, Edward avoided all talk about court matters and Janet was very content to do the same; but because of her willing help for his younger brother, he was happy to expand on the dramatic royal quarrel.

He told her how Richard's manner of rescuing Anne had been unsubtle in the extreme, marching into Master Twynyho's house, demanding to see the lady whom the Duke of Clarence had brought to him, then finding her disguised as a kitchen maid and riding off with her like a knight of the Round Table. How Anne had been very ill but was recuperating well in the tranquillity of sanctuary at St Martin-le-Grand. How his royal brothers' wrangling was now out in the open. How, when the Dukes appeared before the Council to plead their respective cases, Richard's cogency was a match for George's eloquence.

'I think Richard will win without any interference from me. In fact, I know he will'. Edward had exhausted his interest in matters of family and state and so had Janet. They could now concentrate on their own festive celebrations.

In February, Nan returned with more bustle than usual from her shopping duties and announced, as if she were the town crier herself, that Richard Duke of Gloucester was to marry the Lady Anne Neville in the Chapel of St Stephen at Westminster Palace.

Shortly after their marriage, the duke and duchess sent for Janet. Their chamber presented a domestic scene already – a bright room jewelled with tapestries; dogs sprawling before the fire; Frank Lovel playing softly on his lute while John Wrangwysh and a page hummed the tune; and Richard balanced on the arm of his wife's chair, examining an illuminated Book of Hours sent as a wedding present by the monks of Coverham Abbey. The duke and duchess greeted Janet kindly and she presented to them the gifts she had hopefully worked during her convalescence. For Richard, there was a dark green velvet cap, embroidered with a white boar in seed-pearls. Anne's slippers were in matching materials but her device was the bear and ragged staff of Warwick. Genuinely delighted, they tried them on at once. Then the duchess gave Janet something too – a miniature pair of scissors on a silver chain, with carved ivory handles. Through the formality of the exchange, Janet felt herself drawn into this close circle of friends. When she was pressed to visit them in Yorkshire, she was sure it was no empty politeness and she determined to herself that she would do so at the first opportunity

They did not talk about the past. It was the future that possessed the young couple, the bright prospect of bringing order and prosperity and security to the north of England which Edward had entrusted to them. Richard was in a fever to be off, out of London and up to Yorkshire, where he could install himself and his wife in the castle at Middleham that they both regarded as home. Anne, restored by three months of peace, was also eager to go, in spite of the long journey. She proudly insisted that she would ride, though her husband quietly mentioned to Janet that he had added a chariot to his cavalcade in case she grew tired.

While speaking of his plans, there was more vivacity in Richard than Janet had ever seen before, but she also saw that Richard was not quite at ease. He could not be content in the intriguing air of the court. He wanted a horse under him, and hills, and Anne to himself, not cushions and Burgundian dances. Anne, it was clear, wanted what her husband wanted. She was still transparently thin, but her smile was freer than it had been in Normandy, and her eyes clung to Richard all the time.

When Janet left, she was accompanied by John as far as the gates of the palace. He was as anxious as his master to go home to Yorkshire, but felt temporarily downcast because the separation from his sister would be almost permanent. He tried to delay her departure and their illicit meeting by engaging her in conversation about the excitement of the courtship. The marriage settlement, it was said, had left Clarence considerably the richer and Gloucester with little more than his new wife and what the king had already granted him. But that, he declared proudly, was enough for his master. John had attended the Duke when he went quietly to the sanctuary and escorted out his bride, and all the way to the door of the chapel where only the king and close family attended the wedding. But although Janet loved to hear her brother's enthusiasm and loyalty, she could not share his involvement. It was his world now, but not hers.

The mood of sadness at the parting remained with Janet as she returned to the city. She should have been gratified with her part in bringing Richard and Anne together, but the happy outcome of their trials left her with a sense of her own aimlessness.

CHAPTER THREE

In the months that followed, this feeling grew upon her. The business flourished, Edward loved her, yet there was something missing. She began to fear the future. Her twenty-eighth birthday was approaching; soon she would be middle-aged. What would happen when she was too old to attract the king? It was unlikely that her conversation alone would hold him. Worse, what would she do if he died? She had nobody else to care for. The knowledge that the Duke and Duchess of Gloucester had settled down at Middleham added selfishly to her depression; before long, no doubt, they would have a child to complete their happiness.

That was the root of the trouble. Since her second miscarriage three years ago, she had not conceived again. She craved a child before it was too late.

She was talking to Edward one day in early autumn about her plans to open a branch in Flanders. Intelligently he discussed it with her, for he had become a merchant almost as experienced as she was herself.

'I shall ask my sister to sponsor you,' he suggested. 'The patronage of the Duchess of Burgundy should be of some benefit.'

Janet protested, as she always did when he offered to help her. But he over-bore her and picked up a piece of her embroidery which lay on the table.

'This is good enough for any duchess, my love. Your work has satisfied George for years. I'm sure Margaret will be keen to follow the example of her favourite brother. It's a fine business you've built up with your own hands, Janet.'

'And no one to leave it to,' she said suddenly in a low voice, leaving his side and going to the window. The king was silent, watching her. She went on, speaking to herself. 'Nick told me, the first day I arrived here, that the Eversheds were a barren stock. I may only be an Evershed in name, but I've fulfilled the destiny of the family.'

'Nonsense, woman.' Edward crossed to her and swung her to face him, shaking her gently. 'It's not too late. We've simply been unlucky.'

'Eleven years, Edward, and no children,' she cried, 'and all your other mistresses and your wife drop them like rabbits.'

He raised his eyebrows and suppressed a smile at the incongruous comparison of the glacial Queen Elizabeth to a rabbit.

'You lost two,' he corrected her, 'and there may be others which you could bring to their full time. You're strong, healthy, and still young enough. And you're built for bearing children.' He ran his hands appreciatively over her wide hips.

'Don't mock me. I can't stand it!' Pulling away from him, she burst into tears. An emotional outburst was very rare for her, and although in other women Edward was irritated by tears, he felt only concern for Janet. Patiently he pursued her and brought her into his arms, wiping her cheeks with his doublet sleeve.

'But think of the shame of it!' he said, tenderly teasing. 'The widow Evershed in her black weeds, who thought herself a match for all the mercers in London, growing large with a bastard!'

The idea had not occurred to her, and through her tears she let out a surprised snort of laughter.

'Could you stand that?' he went on in the same bantering tone. 'Because to my way of thinking it will be easier for you to bear the child than the shame, you stiff-necked woman.'

Swallowing her sobs, Janet tried to answer in the same vein, though her voice trembled.

'The king's bastard, Edward. That always makes a difference, even to merchants – except for my father,' she added in an undertone. To the objection that Edward had raised was joined the foreboding that to have a child, visible proof of adultery, would alienate her father for ever.

Yet paradoxically, as the king had known it would, the obstacles chased away her mood of self-pity. She faced him quite calmly.

'But I'm not with child, by you or anyone else.'

'Well,' said Edward lightly, 'we're not solving that problem by talking about it, are we?' and he unfastened her coif to release her long hair in a flood down her back. As he smiled into her eyes the familiar weak delight rose in her. Then Edward continued, again serious. 'You've never let me give you anything, except what gave me pleasure too. The gift of a child would be little trouble to me either – at least at its making. But if I can't do this, I count myself a scurvy lover.'

Wishing, apparently, could sometimes work miracles. They made love that evening with a fervour which amazed them both, which they had not reached since the first summer of their love. When Edward left, just before midnight, he swore laughing that he scarcely had the strength to mount his horse. A few weeks later Janet began to suspect that she was pregnant.

As soon as the possibility arose she was frightened. The surer she was, the more frightened she became, and when the stage of her other miscarriages approached she hardly dared stir from her bed in the mornings. Nan, her only confidante, urged her to stay abed until the danger was past, but fearing also to tempt providence, Janet continued to go about her business. Her one concession to her condition was to resign to Nick a journey to Nottingham she had planned for November. Doing her best to concentrate on external matters and keep herself from constant introspection, she worked herself into a nervous state. She had heard nothing from Edward, and cried into her pillow that he did not care at all and his solicitude for her was just disguised lust. Then she cried again because she was being unfair to him and tried to assure herself that he was merely being tactful.

Tediously crawling by, the weeks lengthened into months, and there was no sign of the baby's aborting. But with the dangerous time receding into the past, as her fear lessened her discomfort increased. She was sick every morning, and sometimes all day, though she insisted on staggering into the shop, grey-faced and retching, to serve the customers. The winter was severe and, shivering and wretchedly crouched over a fire which left her back exposed to the icy draughts, she wished she were back in last winter. Then she had been lonely and frustrated. Now mere depression seemed infinitely preferable to such physical misery.

Her spirits were raised by the first visit of her lover, who took one look at her haggard face and clasped her in his arms with a sympathetic bellow. Thereafter he came or sent a message every week, and she found herself longing for his attentions as never before. He was always assuring her cheerfully that the discomfort would pass and she would come to enjoy her pregnancy.

For a couple of months he proved right, and in the dreary tail-end of winter she resumed a more active life. News came from the north that Anne of Gloucester had been delivered of a son in January, named for the king; but Edward confided to Janet that he was a tiny, ailing child and had he been bigger the birth would probably have killed the mother. So Janet's joy for the new parents was mixed with pity, and a memory of her own mother, whom the love of her father had eventually driven to the grave. Though she was far stronger than either Anne or Alison Wrangwysh had ever been, it added to her misgivings.

And then the consideration which Edward had warned her of began to worry her. The voluminous gowns of the day might have been designed specifically for a race of women constantly pregnant or recovering from pregnancy; until well into the sixth month few people noticed. But it was a large, lively baby, and before the coming of spring her condition was very evident. Prepared for whispers and nudges, Janet was ready to take them in her stride, refusing Nan's and Edward's advice to give up working until the child was born. She was not ashamed, she declared, so why should she hide herself? Yet she found that although the men quickly accepted the situation, the women became intensely hostile. They could wink at her liaison with the king, pretend it was not happening at all, but a member of their own respectable class expecting the king's bastard – that was unpardonable. It was, of course, partly jealousy. Edward was always charming to the merchants' wives, and they admired and coveted him from afar, envying the chosen few of their number who occasionally enjoyed more intimate favours. But a woman who continued to run her own business, who had never had the decency to secure a complaisant husband as a cloak for her misdeeds, and who now flaunted the fruits of sin in broad daylight, was as untouchable as a leper.

Even the distant politeness of the city wives was completely withdrawn from her. Janet was ignored in public, cut in private. Again, as in the early days of her pregnancy, she wept at night, her hands clasped tightly over the growing belly of her cumbersome body, and wished she had never conceived. Though for a long time past she had hardened herself to being never quite accepted in any circle of society, this coldness hurt her more than she would have believed possible. She told herself it was because of her condition, but that did not help. And there was none of the happiness in carrying Edward's baby that she had obscurely looked forward to. Her back ached, mild spring weather made her sweat, her lumbering bulk grew short of breath and tired in an amazingly short time. To other women, beginning in adolescence and bearing a child virtually every year, it was a matter of course, unpleasant but a fact of life. Edward's wife, for instance, was undergoing her seventh pregnancy with magnificent queenly unconcern. To Janet, going through the ordeal for the first time at the age of twenty-eight, it was new and terrifying.

Only Edward brought any real comfort. When he was with her, showing openly his pride in fatherhood, despite the countless other children, legitimate and illegitimate, he had scattered over England, she could rejoice with him and relax in the warmth of his affection. After he had gone the fears returned, her feeling of incapacity, the certainty that she would never give birth safely, or that if she did the child would be deformed or dead. She knew instinctively that this was her last chance. So many things could go wrong. The midwife gave her vile-tasting simples to ease the backache, and muttered charms over her that neither of them believed. She was unsympathetic; she had attended far too many women in trouble and pain from the same cause.

Janet longed to go to Confession, to receive absolution and to hear Mass, but she dared not go inside a church. Her prayers, offered privately, seemed to fall on deaf ears. There was no reason why God should protect her since she had so often and so blatantly broken His seventh Commandment. Even the Blessed Virgin, who had gone through motherhood's pangs herself to such a holy purpose, frowned on her from the niche above the church door.

At last she succumbed to the combined pleas of her household, and to the dreadful sense of nakedness which assailed her whenever she went abroad, and took to her room. Wallowing in sloth, chafing to be out in the shouting beauty of the new summer, she prowled round her shut-up room. Against all advice she opened the windows to draw fresh air into her lungs and look at the trees in riotous leaf along the Walbrook. The baby was heavy; every time she settled down to read the books Edward had given her or to tackle her correspondence, it kicked her and brought back her worries.

Her time was in June. Agnes was already briefed to call the midwife; but beyond knowing that the birth would be heralded by pains, Janet was quite ignorant of what she had to do. Nan was no help. Being too comfortable as she was, she had never bothered to marry: all she had to contribute were terrifying tales culled from her many gossips. The midwife told her to stop fussing; everything would happen quite naturally, if it pleased God. There was no-one else Janet could go to. For the first time since her marriage she felt the lack of a mother to confide in, an experienced female to rely on, a matronly bosom to rest on. But Bessie Lylley was not there, and even Edward was in the midlands.

It was at the end of the month, in the hour before dawn, that the pains began. The girl was sent to the midwife; Dame Coton, grumbling and out of breath, arrived a good few hours later, complaining that she was having so many calls she did not know which way to turn. By the time she came, Janet was already in a bad way. Her world was narrowing down to the dragging, rending pangs, and the suspended interval between them which was almost worse. The midwife and her assistants invaded her tidy chamber and cluttered it with preparations and mysterious instruments. An old nightmare came back to Janet: her mother white and limp against the stained sheets. After all the waiting, the culmination was beyond her fears.

Everything was dissolving except the pains and the attendant women, an existence of pain thrusting with ever-increasing frequency and cruelty. The day, she vaguely recognised, was passing away. As the clear sky deepened to velvet blue, it was shut out by thick curtains and candles were lighted. So was the fire, though it had been a hot day. Endless day was followed by endless night. Trying through a tired haze to follow the midwife's instructions, she still had enough intellect to wonder how women could go through this regularly, and yet survive. And always the pain increased. The women in the room faded until they were nothing but a support to grip when the agony ripped through her, tearing her wide open, and then subsiding only to return redoubled. Daylight had come and gone again, and then from a distance the confused merrymaking as London kept the Marching Watch on the vigil of St Peter and Paul. But there was no longer any time for Janet. Her life had always been this, and it would go on for ever.

By the dawn of St Peter's Day, she was too exhausted to know that the curtains had been flung back on another perfect day, by bleary-eyed attendants who had slept for a few hours while others watched. All Janet knew was that she was drowning, that she was being sucked down into the depths of a sea where there was only anguish and torture and sharp knives. Someone far away was screaming, continuously and hideously, and she was unaware that it was herself. At last the pain reached a frenzied climax, a pitch she had never dreamed possible, and through it she heard dimly an insistent command, 'Push! Push!' It was involuntary, instinctive, she was striving to rid herself of the centre of her agony, trying vainly to escape from the weight which was drowning her.

With a last searing thrust, she was free. A moment of calm, floating in the sea that had turned red, balanced in the still centre of the vortex, a distant choking baby's cry; then a century later something was placed in her arms, wriggling slightly in tight white wrappings, but she could not see what it was, or anything else. Even as her arms felt the contact, sense left her and the whirlpool swept her away, down into the depths again.

In her dream there were places dissolved in the sea, trees, castles, houses, all familiar, all drowned, and faces too, disembodied, which swam close to her, hovered over her and floated away into the green gloom. Her mother was there, and Bessie, and then Edward came, a welcoming smile and warm eyes. But the eyes turned black, and they were sparkling with anger, and it was her father, his mouth taut with rage. Though she could hear nothing except a high singing note of pain she knew that he was abusing her, hurting her, adding to her torment. She tried to turn away but she could not move, her eyes would not close, or perhaps he was inside her eyes, wounding her with his anger. She wanted to cry out, to struggle, anything to send him away.

The billows returned, eddying and flowing around her in oily darkness, but this time there was a distant light somewhere miles above her head. She was drifting upwards, the light was growing, and one face faded in and out of her vision. Her lungs would burst before she reached the surface; she made an effort to strike out and help herself upwards, and her limbs responded a little.

Light broke, blindingly. She was gasping and spent and soaking wet. The face was still there, steady now above her against an aura of brightness. She could not see who it was. It spoke, and this time she could hear its voice.

'Lie still. You're safe now.' Just as when she had once had a bad dream, and he had come in answer to her terror, when she was a very little girl. He had held her in his arms then until she fell asleep again. And still he held her. Her eyelids could not support the weight of their own weariness.

'Father,' she murmured, and burrowing down into the surrounding warmth she slid into sleep.

Despite constant twinges of misgiving, Thomas Wrangwysh had been determined never to forgive his daughter. High in the civic service of York, a rich and influential Merchant Adventurer twice master of his guild, his pride could not entertain the notion of his beloved daughter as the king's paramour in London. So in the company of his sons' wives and his growing brood of grandchildren, he tried to forget his firstborn, and ignored the appeals to reinstate her. Not from Janet herself – not for years – but from John, occasionally from Bessie and from Robert who, as a novice priest, conceived it as his spiritual duty to reconcile his divided family. Hardest to resist were requests from the Duke of Gloucester and his gentle wife, both now good friends of his, and once, a long time ago, from the king himself. But he would not yield. Let London folk condone immorality as they would – let the merchants of the capital loose their wives and daughters to the lechery of the corrupt court – he would have no part of it.

Thus he was resolved and nothing, he swore, would shake him. But his resolve was shaken when a weary traveller fell from the back of his foundering horse in the courtyard of the Wrangwysh house one evening in early July. Thomas remembered him vaguely – he had a good memory for faces – as a member of the Evershed household. But though he intended to deal with him coldly, the intention vanished the moment the visitor explained his errand. It was Nick Farthing, who had left London as soon as Janet went into labour and the midwife said it would be touch and go. He had ridden night and day to reach York. The poor man was incoherent and half-dead with fatigue, but he would have been prepared to continue his breakneck journey and return to London straight away had Thomas not prevented him.

There were few arrangements to make. Will was fully competent to deputise for his father in all matters and before three hours were past Thomas was a-horse and clattering through Micklegate Barbican. He had not thought about it at all. In his mind the picture of Janet suffering in childbirth had fused with that of his wife, slipping quietly and relentlessly away from him fifteen years ago.

By the time Thomas arrived in London, in the early hours of the fifth of July, Janet's son was six days old, roaring lustily and drinking dry the wetnurse brought in to feed him. Janet was in a raging fever and her life hung in the balance. There was little hope, ventured the obsequious doctor, awed by the authoritative and dusty burgess who had just irrupted into the whispering female stronghold. The birth had been long and difficult because the child was enormous and upside down in the womb; and then the mother had succumbed to childbed fever. Only a mighty fight would save her.

'She will fight,' said Thomas curtly, brushing the man aside to go to his daughter. He had had no faith in medical men or women since the death of his wife.

Besides, he was in no state to be civil. Ten years he had been alienated from her, and only now, at her bedside, as she tossed and raved, her long dark hair tangled about her, her face drawn and marked by her sickness, did he let himself acknowledge how much he had missed her. With the reserve appropriate to his dignity, he had never shown his love for his sons. Only to Alison and to Janet had he allowed himself any tenderness. Alison was long gone and yet he had cut himself off from Janet in his pride, refusing obstinately to replace either of the women in his bed or in his affections. So sweeping all the ministering females out of the stuffy chamber, Alderman Thomas Wrangwysh Member of Parliament knelt by his daughter's side and wept.

For the next two days he stayed with her almost constantly, as he knew she had done with his son John when he was similarly at death's door. All his vigorous will was bent towards saving her, and because she was in many ways so like him, something of it seemed to penetrate her delirium. Nan always said afterwards in hushed tones that her mistress's colour improved the moment her father entered the house, but since she had been asleep at the time and she only had it from the wetnurse who heard it from someone who was there, that might not have been strictly accurate. Certain it was, however, that on the day Thomas arrived Janet, who had been sinking, began at last to rally. After her brief period of consciousness she slept well, and the doctor, visiting on Thomas's sufferance and petrified by him, declared the corner turned.

When she returned to full awareness, and was able to take in the fact that she had not only a son but a father restored, her happiness was almost boundless. For once in her life she submitted to somebody else's dominance, meekly doing whatever she was told, and not fretting to get up and take charge again. Nick had come home only a day and a half after Thomas, and he also submitted, though not with such a good grace, to being bullied by Master Wrangwysh.

The only way in which Janet asserted herself was to insist, as soon as she had the strength to do so, on taking over the breast-feeding of the baby. There was shocked protest, especially from the wetnurse who was being well-paid for her services, and from the midwife who said it was not the custom. But surprisingly enough her father supported her and so, every few hours, Peter was brought to her bed and fastened himself greedily on to her nipple. Like a great pink leech, she thought with fond amusement. He was very large, and very noisy, and she could not believe that he was hers. Though big, he was not at all fat, but firm and glowing, and his hair, spun gold, was Edward's colour. Having gone through such danger for him, having craved him for so long, Janet's love for her son was well-nigh unbearable. She hated his being taken away; she wanted to unwrap his swaddling-clothes and make sure that his body was whole and healthy beneath them. This again the midwife disapproved, warning that his limbs would grow crooked, so she did it secretly.

He had been named Peter by someone because he had been born on the Festival of St Peter, and since Janet would have liked to call him both Edward and Thomas, she accepted the name as a solution, without comment. Maybe, since St Peter had brought her safely through childbirth, he would also take her son under his protection.

Whenever Thomas was not driving Nick and Kit mad, delving into all the business for the last ten years, trying in vain to find fault with it, or firmly directing future negotiations, he sat with Janet. They talked endlessly, filling in the ten-year gap which stretched between them. She had more nephews and nieces than she had ever imagined. Bessie and Tom had five sons and two daughters and were expecting their eighth child. Will was a widower with twin daughters, and Dick had been married three years to a girl nine years older than himself from the Yorkshire Moors. Thomas was not happy about the match.

'No sign of children yet.' He shook his head. 'And I don't care for Mistress Bridget. She tries to boss Bessie, and often succeeds, though you can see she's very jealous of Tom and Bessie's fine litter. But now they're in a house of their own, we'll see less of them. At any rate, she'll stir Dick into being a first-rate woolman. All he needs is scold.'

Janet, who remembered most of her brothers as little boys, exerted herself to imagine them as grown up and married, but it was difficult.

'You must come home, Janet, soon,' her father said to her, and her throat tightened; home, to her as well as to him, was the house in Micklegate.

They never spoke of the king, though Janet could tell that Thomas had accepted the situation and would not ask her to break off the liaison. Time had proved that it was no youthful flirtation, and having been himself a man who gave his heart once and then no more, that heart condoned something that his self-respect and morality abhorred.

By the end of July, Janet was out of bed and taking gentle exercise. Thomas forbade her to do any work, but since she knew more about the business than anyone else their conversation turned to the subject with increasing frequency. Her staff, unaccustomed to a male hand controlling them, was not altogether pleased with Thomas's methods. Before long he realised it, and was generous enough not to take it amiss. Gradually Janet began to take command again. A stream of letters was arriving from York for her father, and as she regained her energy she began urging him to go home. She needed solitude to digest her happiness, and she wanted her son to herself. So in August he left, making her promise to follow him in the spring. The house seemed much emptier without him, though not quieter because of Peter.

The king was still away in the midlands, and when Peter was nearly two months old he became a father again. Elizabeth bore him a second son. This time Janet was not jealous; she was happier than ever before, joyfully anticipating Edward's return so she could tell him her two pieces of good news. Throwing herself into work again, she spent all her spare time with her baby, or writing screeds to the relatives she had not heard from for so long. The hostility of the city women no longer bothered her.

Edward came home with the autumn, and the next day he was with his mistress in Walbrook. His delight in Peter, who Janet was convinced grew more like him every day, was very gratifying; he was as proud as if he had been his first son.

'Very different from my other little mite,' said Edward, as the baby clung possessively to his father's forefinger. 'He's tiny and swarthy, though he's strong, thank God. We've called him Richard, because he's more like our changeling Richards – my father and Dickon – than the run-of-the-mill golden Plantagenets.'

'But, Janet.' A thought struck him and he turned to the glowing mother in the oriel window. 'Why Peter?'

'Are you offended, Edward?'

'Since I'm sure you have a good reason for his name, no,' he smiled.

'He was born on St Peter's Day,' she began, and paused. Seeing that she wanted to say more, Edward waited. 'Though he is your son, I never wish him to exploit his name,' she said in a rush, defensively. 'There can be no more children. He is Peter Evershed, and he will inherit all that I die possessed of.'

'I understand,' Edward said, but he wondered if his son would.

He was less sympathetically delighted about Janet's reconciliation with her father. His patience with Thomas Wrangwysh's obstinacy had run out long ago, but for her sake he pretended to be glad. Never having known a stable home like herself, he could not quite comprehend the closely-knit Wrangwysh family's need for each other.

Another event that year added to Janet's contentment. John was married at Lammas to one of the Duchess of Gloucester's ladies, and from his letter it was clear that it was a love-match. He eagerly repeated their father's invitation and included another from the duke.

And a further piece of news convinced Janet that she had truly been accepted back into the family. Bessie's latest child was to be christened Janet.

CHAPTER FOUR

Although she had fully recovered her health, Thomas insisted that Janet should not set out until the weather was warm enough. Spring came early, and she took the road through the burgeoning countryside with Peter and Nan, and a company of nuns returning to their Yorkshire convent from Canterbury. The land was flourishing; the scars of warfare had long since been covered by green, and by the first shoots of the new year's crops.

She reached York on Palm Sunday, when the bells were tolling for Vespers. The family were all at church, and she was welcomed by Thomas's journeyman, Robert Hikton, whom she had not met before. He was rather taken aback by her arrival, because she was not expected until the next day, but his manners were good and Janet liked him. Peter needed a meal; he had been crying all the way from Tadcaster, and he was scarlet and exhausted. Deafened by his din, Janet asked to be taken somewhere where she could feed him, and the young man led her, with many apologies, to her old room overlooking the street. The usual occupants had been moved out and she had it to herself, with a truckle-bed for Nan and a wooden cradle for Peter. It was all just as she remembered it, except for the absence of the red and green dragon coverlet, which now adorned her bed in London.

CHAPTER FOUR

Saying that she would stay alone until her family came back, she dismissed Nan and the attentive journeyman, and proceeded to feed the baby. His sobs subsided into a greedy contented sucking, and at last he fell asleep at her breast. Gently she detached him and tucked him up in the cradle, rose-pink against the fresh white linen. Stroking the fair curls which clustered into his neck, she left him and went over to the window. Sitting as she used to as a girl, she watched the twilight settle like dust over the street, deserted because of the services in all the churches of the city. Over the way the monks of Holy Trinity Priory were intoning Vespers. Among them was her youngest brother Robert, whom she had last seen as a nervous little boy of five. Already she was surrounded again by the long-lost affection of her family. Turning back into the darkening room, she could hear Peter's even breathing, and with this tangible proof of Edward's love also, her heart was full.

All over York the services ended, and the churches disgorged their congregations. Suddenly Micklegate was thronged with citizens homeward bound from their parish churches, St Gregory's, St Martin's, St John's, All Saints'. Her heart racing foolishly, Janet patted her coif, creased a little from packing, and smoothed the new kersey gown she had made for her homecoming. There was a thundering outside, as many feet rushed up the shallow wooden staircase, and a beating at the door. Peter woke up with a start, opened his eyes and mouth to yell, then gazed in astonishment at all the people that were pouring into the room. Janet was almost submerged by them: the tall men who had been little boys, Bessie plumper and greasier than ever, and a host of children of assorted sizes, to whom Janet was quite strange, but who were taking advantage of the glad atmosphere to let off steam.

At last, when she had been borne downstairs to the hall, some order was imposed on the chaos – not by the parents of most of the crowd, but by Thomas. He dealt out a few cuffs, raised his voice, and the children subsided. Janet was enthroned in state, and the family presented to her formally. John was there; he had been granted special leave from Middleham to welcome his sister; Will, growing towards stoutness, with two engaging little girls peeping from behind him, his twin daughters Katherine and Isobel; Tom, flustered, balding, and amiable.

'I've sent for Dick and his wife,' explained Thomas. 'Though we weren't expecting you today, I think we'll manage a respectable banquet for you, and the family must be together. Robert will come over later, with the Prior's permission.

'Now, come forward, young Thomas, and announce your brothers and sisters.'

Thomas, the fat toddler of twelve years ago, had black sparkling eyes like his grandfather, and his voice had broken. Taking his duty seriously he shepherded the children before Janet and they made their courtesy to her, Bess, Ned, Alison, Bart and Wat. Will's three-year-olds joined the queue, wobbling solemnly into their curtseys, and rushing back to their father as soon as they had performed them. Finally her namesake, roused from her crib and grizzling drowsily, was carried in and duly admired and kissed by her aunt. Privately, Janet thought that Peter was a far more beautiful baby.

The rest of the evening dissolved into a whirl of greetings and reminiscences and family chat at the top of everyone's voices. Dick arrived with his bony wife Bridget, Robert was fetched from his meditations, and á magnificent meal was conjured up from nowhere despite the requisite Lenten lack of meat. Afterwards there was singing and dancing and more talk, and when Janet retired to bed her head was singing with excitement and tiredness, and she slept as soon as she lay down.

On the following morning, John was gone before anyone else rose. Bessie whispered loudly to Janet that he was so smitten with Mistress Margaret his wife that two nights together without lying with her were more than he could endure. In fact, said Will, who happened to be passing, he had orders to ride up to Richmond with the duke. Janet detected a note of sourness in his voice. As she helped her sister-in-law with the starching and ironing Bessie explained with her old volubility and relish that Will was not quite reconciled to his own wife's death, and tended to frown on uxorious husbands at present.

From Bessie she learned all the gossip of the Wrangwyshes and the

Lylleys, and practically the whole of York, in the course of the morning. Despite her vast waistline, her big family and responsibilities, Bessie had not changed a jot from the flaxen giggling sixteen-year-old who had slept with Janet in the year her mother died. With all the changes she saw about her which had altered her home, it was good to find one stolid piece of the past she recognised.

They made her very welcome. The children, and especially Will's twins, were fascinated by the new aunt who had suddenly descended into their world. Once Thomas came back from a council meeting to find five small ones in an awed circle around his daughter, who was peacefully suckling her child. But Janet did not sit back and do nothing. It was pleasant to be looked after, but work was such a habit to her that, before Holy Week was through, she had set talks in motion with one of her father's fellow aldermen on supplying some of her embroidery in exchange for low-priced Yorkshire cloth.

There was a little sadness when the family left her behind to go to High Mass on Easter Day in the Minster. Not being able to face the reaction when she did not receive the Host, she pleaded indisposition and stayed with Peter, following her father in her mind as he processed in state up the great nave behind the mayor in his new scarlet robes. But she did see the parades through the streets, and forgot her feeling of separation in the feast provided by Thomas Wrangwysh for his entire family, his apprentices and servants, to celebrate the ending of the drab Lenten season. Only John and Margaret, over at Skipton with their duke, were absent.

In her own house Janet had always provided for her household every Christmas and Easter and Midsummer, but it had never had the wholeheartedness of this gathering. In London, she was mistress, no one else was her equal. Though from the head of the table she talked affably with Nick and whoever else was honoured by sitting next to her, there was something rather well-behaved about the occasions. The men usually waited until afterwards to go to an alehouse and get drunk.

There was no politeness in Micklegate. Red laughing faces, spilled food and drink, coarse jokes and good fellowship above and below the salt. One of Will's hounds disgraced himself by putting his paws on the table and stealing a capon, but he was spared a whipping because of the season. Thomas commented on the comparative sizes of Janet and Bessie, both of whom where tucking away the victuals at a great rate, and Tom remarked good-humouredly that his wife began with an advantage. In the ensuing roar of laughter, Janet caught a sneering phrase from Bridget, who sat near her, about respectable women who did their duty, but she took no notice. A run of wine sent by the mayor was broached and lasted a very short time; an exquisite confection of York Minster, complete with the tower which was in fact still in scaffolding, was demolished rapidly by hordes of small sticky hands. Only afterwards, in a semi-maudlin state induced by too much good fare, did Janet reflect that never would her house be filled with such merriment.

The day before Low Sunday a messenger came from Middleham, with an invitation to Mistress Evershed to spend a few days with the Duke and Duchess of Gloucester. As long before, when John had just entered Warwick's services, Janet left before dawn for the uphill road to Wensleydale, with Peter and Nan. Spring was late in coming to the uplands of Yorkshire; the fields and wayside grasses were white with rime in the clear early light. But the sun climbed into a cloudless sky and the day gentled. The shadows of trees and walls lay patterned in silver on the new green of the meadows. When the moors rose on the skyline, the nip in the air had gone, and the still brown twigs were almost visibly unfolding their leaves.

She was received by Lord Francis Lovel, who offered a personal apology that the duke was not there to greet his guest. He and his entourage were expected back from Skipton, where he was settling a property dispute, during the afternoon. After the visitors had eaten, Janet was taken to the duchess.

Anne was sewing in her chamber, lit by a shaft of brilliant sunshine from the high window in the south wall, beside her mother the widowed Countess of Warwick. The duke had secured her release into his custody from her long confinement at Beaulieu, and he and his wife had made a home for her at Middleham. She did not change; kindness and security had as little outward effect on her as danger and adversity. But her daughter was thriving in the northern air. With a new serenity Anne gave her hand to Janet, and as soon as the formalities were over a conspiratorial gleam, quite foreign to the frightened girl in Normandy, came into her eyes. She bade Janet fetch her son, and sent one of her ladies to the nearby nursery.

Blinking and warm from sleep, Peter sat on his mother's lap and regarded his cousin owlishly. Edward of Middleham was a tiny baby, thin as an unfledged bird, only half the size of Peter who was five months younger. He needed support to sit up, and when the nurse let him go he toppled slowly sideways, smiling sweetly. But although Anne admired Peter politely, she was not really interested in him. Her delicate son was her one concern. He was very advanced in his talking, she told Janet eagerly, and little Edward obliged by running through all his phrases. Peter's answer was to stand up, clutching at Janet's coif for support, and out-shout the princeling with effortless gibberish.

The duchess's devotion to her baby was uncommon among an order which habitually passed on its children to wet-nurses, then foster-parents, then tutors in other people's houses, until they were old enough to marry and set up their own establishments. King Edward's elder son had gone to Ludlow when he was only three to be trained as Prince of Wales. Yet in her own love for Peter, a fierce possessive passion for her long-awaited only offspring, Janet understood and felt for Anne of Gloucester.

There was a pounding of feet on the wooden bridge outside which led to the keep, and a page, breathless with running up and down stairs, entered with the minimum of ceremony.

'My lord is home, madame. He's riding up the hill!'

At once there was a flurry of activity as the ladies prepared for the return of their menfolk. Anne was the first out of the door, quite forgetting her guest. With a tolerant smile Janet picked up her son, who was looking cross at not being the centre of attention, and firmly took away the rushes he was cramming into his mouth. She took him back to their chamber and gave him to Nan.

By the time she emerged from the dark keep on to the steps which led into the afternoon brightness of the courtyard, the duke and his party were crossing the drawbridge. They had been away for less than a week, yet Janet suspected that, but for her breeding, Duchess Anne would have been jumping up and down in her excitement. Richard reined in his grey beside her, and leaped from his saddle to kiss her forehead. Other gentlemen were fanning themselves with their bonnets, exclaiming at the heat of the sun, swinging down from their mounts to greet their wives, chatting or calling to the grooms. There was an attractive air of relaxation about the assembly.

John came towards her with arms outstretched and she was caught against his tall lanky body, while he cried happily, 'It's good to meet you without feeling guilty.' Then he produced from behind him a diminutive round girl in travelling clothes, whose wide smile filled a vivacious freckled face.

'My wife Margaret,' John said proudly, and when the girl had performed the correct courtesy she too embraced Janet.

'But where have you been hiding her?' laughed Janet. 'She was not with the duchess.'

'No, I've been to Skipton with John,' explained her sister-in-law. 'My estates lie in Airedale.'

'It is difficult to separate them for more than a day.' A grave voice entered the conversation, and the Duke of Gloucester was beside them, smiling his rare smile. Janet kissed his hand and he welcomed her easily.

'I am sorry your father didn't come with you,' he said. 'I haven't yet congratulated him on regaining a daughter.' Then with his wife on his arm he led the way up to the great hall.

After the homecoming stirrup-cup Richard was closeted with his councillors for some time, and John took the opportunity of showing his sister the alterations the duke was making to the castle. As the sun sank through the branches of the trees towards the bare hills of Wensleydale, Janet became better acquainted with Margaret. She was the daughter of Sir William Cropper of Skipton, and when he had been killed fighting for King Henry at Northampton, the little girl and her elder brother had been made wards of the Earl of Warwick. Eleven years later her brother had died with Warwick at Barnet, and Margaret's wardship had been transferred to the Duke of Gloucester. She had come to Middleham to wait on the duchess, and there she had met John. The duke and duchess had smiled on the match, and as a dowry Margaret had been given back her family properties.

'They were very generous,' she said, 'because my father and my brother were both attainted, and all our lands were forfeit. I can never repay the debt, however long I may serve them.'

Janet was rapidly won over by her. She was merry and witty and laughed a great deal, and it was clear why she was such a favourite with the earnest duke and duchess as well as with Janet's solemn brother.

'Frank once accused me of usurping the duties of Martin the Fool,' Margaret recalled, 'but I called him the resident troubadour in return, and he hasn't yet presented me with a cap and bells.'

That evening Janet saw what Francis Lovel had meant. With dusk the chill came back into the air, and a fire was lit in the privy chamber. It was strange to see the same tapestries, the same chests and footstools, as had furnished the room in London where Janet had called on the duke and his new wife. The chamber might have been picked up entire, complete with its occupants, and transferred by some giant hand from the narrow noisy streets of the capital to the windswept hills of Yorkshire. Frank still had his lute, and sang again, this time a French love-song, gazing soulfully into Margaret's eyes. When John in mock-jealousy carried his wife off to the other side of the room, she insisted that as a penance for his sin of envy he should sing himself. He protested, she twitted him with false modesty, and so he raised his voice in the old English round, 'Sumer is icumen in.' One by one other voices joined in, Richard and Anne as well, the duke beating time on the arm of his chair, while a great orange moon glided up one tall window.

Janet was pressed to go with the duke and duchess the next day on a visit to Lord Scrope, in his castle of Bolton on the far side of the dale. It was a dull dawn, but by the time the party had crossed the Ure and traversed the valley floor, the sun had broken through again, and sparkled on the breaking buds of the hedgerow. She found herself in the place of honour between her host and hostess, and Richard pointed out to her the landmarks they were passing. Janet had never seen him so little reserved, so nearly jovial; Anne caught the reflection of her husband's mood and glowed quietly. There was nothing extrovert about their love – none of the exuberant demonstrations of affection which were part of the king's charm – but Janet's instinct that they were made for each other had been right. They fulfilled a deep mutual need – his to protect and cherish, hers to be sheltered and defended.

She glanced back at their followers, to where Margaret was mischievously making her horse sidle away from John, who was trying to crown her with a spray of flowering blackthorn. How different they were! How different she and Edward, and her father and mother! Yet it was love, in all its varied manifestations. And in the spring day, Janet sent up a silent thanksgiving to God for so much happiness. Though passion passed, though loss and broken hearts might lie round the next corner in the climbing road, the brightness where love had been was never quite extinguished.

Feeling very much at home, Janet stayed at Middleham for nearly a week. Something of the inhabitants' attachment to the stronghold, mellowed by its lovely surroundings, infected her also, and she did not want to leave. Business, however, would be piling up, and she had to return to York en route for London. Nick Farthing was the rock on which her trade depended, but he was well-advanced in middle age, and she did not wish to burden him too far. Besides, she had had her hand on the helm for too long to be content with prolonged idleness.

And when she was installed again in the house where she had been born, she was no longer at ease as she had been before Easter. The bustle, the din, the teeming life of the Wrangwysh establishment seemed to leave her outside. In a way, she had been more a part of the Spartan yet peculiarly cultured world of Richard's court at Middleham, though there she had been a favoured guest and not a permanent resident. She was so used to the routine of her own house that little details of her father's procedure, much to her shame, began to irritate her, and Bessie's comfortably inefficient housekeeping jangled her nerves. With difficulty she restrained herself from criticising, because she was in truth a guest here as well.

Then of course she missed Edward. To be within his reach, always to live with the hope that he might walk in the door at any moment, it was how her life had been for twelve years, and even in the bosom of her long-lost family there was a lack.

There was another thing about staying in Micklegate which unexpectedly oppressed her. As she watched her nephews and nieces tumbling about her, she was acutely aware – even more acutely than when she was craving a child – that time was leaving her behind. Habitually one of the most junior in mercantile gatherings, unaccustomed to company of her own age, Janet was also remarkably healthy. The common ailments of the day had mostly passed her by, and her one troublesome pregnancy had only served to impress upon her the constant burden which undermined the youth and vitality of the majority of women. She compared the children's unhampered gambollings, once released from their swaddling bands, with the lumber movements of Bessie, who was not only very fat and short of breath, but cheerfully complained of constant pains in her legs. One day, not far ahead, age would catch up with Janet too. She thought with cold horror of the time when her limbs would no longer respond to her, when she would have to sit at home and let younger folk do the travelling and the haggling in the market.

And Edward! Men kept their vigour for years after women had retired to the chimney-corner. What would happen when she could not respond to his demands on her? Because they met infrequently, each meeting had the excitement of novelty. He had never ceased to be amazed at her stamina in love; she had never grown out of her wonder at his gaiety and his tenderness. But when she could not give herself with such ardour, would he still want her? The emptiness of the pit that lay beyond had been bridged much by the advent of Peter, but her love for Edward was still the most powerful in her life, and Peter could never supplant his father in her heart.

'Why are you sad, madame my aunt?' A small hand was placed on her knee, and Will's elder twin, Katherine, was gazing up at her with large candid eyes which were brown like her grandmother's, but with the directness of her grandfather's.

'I'm not sad.' Janet smiled down at her gratefully. 'Let's go and see if Peter is awake yet. It's time for his dinner.' And with Katherine and the inevitable Isobel trailing eagerly behind, Janet snapped out of her morbidity and went in out of the sunshine to fetch her son.

In fact, had she known it, she was the envy of her contemporaries in York. Nearing thirty though she was, she had retained a freshness which they had lost. Bridget, who was a year younger, had taken an instant dislike to her. She told Dick that she preferred not to frequent her father-in-law's house while Mistress Evershed was there, and when Dick asked with unwonted sharpness why, she said she did not approve of working women. Her husband, who was not yet completely under her sway, told her not to be stupid, and she did not mention the matter to him again. Instead, she held private hate sessions with her gossips, and declared that a fallen woman of thirty had no right to look so young and slim, and that she would doubtless pay for her sin in the next world.

The envy of a childless woman for a mother was mollified, however, when she found that, after four years of barren marriage, she was at last with child. It was a year of Wrangwysh babies. Three of Janet's sisters-in-law were pregnant: Bridget, Bessie of course, and Margaret, which was one of the reasons for her roundness at Easter. The duke had promised to stand godfather to his squire's first child.

But Janet did not really want to be involved in the birth of any more children. Like the Duchess of Gloucester, she was only interested in her own, and he was just learning to walk. For such an important step, she thought, he needed quiet and all the attention she could give him. Her father, who still read her moods very accurately, realised that she was chafing a little, and did not ask her to stay beyond the middle of May.

'A pity you can't be here for Corpus Christi,' he said, 'but I'm sure your people are needing you. Come next year for the festival.'

CHAPTER FOUR

So she set out, escorted to Micklegate Barbican by the entire family, and to Tadcaster by all the males old enough to sit a horse. The person who was most affected by the parting was Peter, who yelled and squirmed for miles of the road south.

CHAPTER FIVE

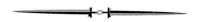

The next two years passed rapidly. Engrossed in the rearing of her son and the expansion of her business, Janet did not notice outside events very much, except where they actually impinged on her own life.

Just before Peter was two, while London was buzzing with excitement and the city was bright with men-at-arms and knights in armour, massing for the king's expedition to France, Janet suffered a severe loss. Nick Farthing, always so steadfast and reliable, took to his bed one day shivering and complaining of a headache. Three days later he was dead. Kit took over capably, but he was younger than Janet, and she could never impose in him the absolute trust that she had in Nick. He had been part of the house in Walbrook ever since the day he had appeared with the shopping and set her newcomer's mind at rest. As she listened to the words of the requiem in the church of St Stephen, she remembered the comfort he had been to her as a lonely widow, the help and support he had given her, which she could not repay. His presence still hung around the house, and it seemed impossible that his broad placid face was covered forever by a slab of stone.

That same year, her uncle Geoffrey died in the fort of Guisnes. He had been pardoned by the king after Barnet, but sent abroad to the

English outpost of Calais as part of its garrison. Probably boredom had killed him as much as the outbreak of smallpox. For old time's sake, Janet paid for two masses for his soul.

If he had lasted a few months longer, the arrival of the English invading host might have revived him. The campaign against France did not, however, have much effect on the London burgesses, though the apprentices had a field day breaking the windows in the French quarter, and a few other windows which were not French at all, in their particular version of patriotism. When Edward came back, not with victory but with a fat bribe from King Louis under his belt and a peace treaty, sentiments in the city were divided. The most belligerent of the merchants maintained that the king had betrayed the ancestors who won Crecy and Poitiers, and old Lancastrians were heard to mutter that it was not the House of York which gave England triumph at Agincourt. They publicly approved of the Duke of Gloucester, who was one of the few to stand out for continuing war instead of peace. But the more level-headed were well aware that peace with France could only be good for trade, and might lead to some curbing of the French piracy which was an intermittent menace to their shipping.

For a short while Janet was drawn into court circles, as the king gave receptions for the merchants to celebrate the treaty and to thank them for the loans they had made towards the expedition. She saw Richard Duke of Gloucester, silent and ill-at-ease as he always was at court, and John and Margaret, though their small son Richard had been left up in Yorkshire in the care of the duchess. But another small Richard was present: Edward's younger son, the Duke of York, who was of an age with Peter. Though only recently turned two, he behaved very correctly under the stern eye of his mother. As Edward had told Janet, he was a throwback to his paternal grandfather, dark and plain, but blooming with health.

After that, she did not go to court again. One of her reasons for deliberately keeping away from the palace was Elizabeth Shore, Edward's latest mistress. She knew that, as always on such occasions, Edward would not come to her for some time. She was not exactly jealous; she really did not want to be on show, praised in public, denigrated behind elegant gloved hands and passed around the current favourites. But she found it easier to ignore if she retreated into her private world and concentrated on family and business.

Shortly before Christmas, she decided to risk a less courtly appearance and accept an invitation to a feast held by The Worshipful Company of Mercers in the Hospital of St Thomas of Acon, Cheapside. Her fear of being the subject of others' gossip proved groundless; there were two far more interesting matters dominating everyone's conversation.

The first was Mistress Shore, for she was the bewitching wife of a city mercer who had charmed the king and was installed at Westminster as his chief mistress. Her husband William, they whispered, had complaisantly accepted his bribe of a pension and retired to enjoy his cuckoldry in comfort. Many other ladies had openly accepted the king's favour before, but she was the first member of the merchant class to climb to such heights. They were shocked, of course.

The second was the sad news that Isabel Duchess of Clarence had just died of childbed fever, leaving her tiny, sick son Richard unlikely to live for long. The assembled company expressed formal regret, but she meant nothing to them. Janet, secretly, felt genuine sorrow as she vividly remembered a nervous, tearful woman, frightened of discovery, frightened of her husband, but determined to help her sister.

Janet waited patiently throughout a winter without Edward. With the early spring of the new year he returned, strolling casually into her bedchamber as she tried to persuade a fretful Peter to settle down for the night. The child, seeing his father, was immediately wide awake and demanding presents. Janet looked round in surprise, and before she could say anything Edward was bending over him, putting a gingerbread into his ready hand. To the noise of Peter's munching, Janet shook her head reproachfully.

'He'll never go to sleep now.'

'Nonsense,' said the king. 'Peterkin, as soon as you've finished, you're to go to sleep.' The boy beamed at him stickily, and Edward led his mistress out of the room.

'He always obeys you,' said Janet ruefully.

'You're too gentle with him.' Edward kissed her and set her in her chair, throwing himself into his own as if he had never been away. 'He needs a man's hand now, sweet heart. He's no longer a baby. Why not let me choose a noble household where he could be trained? With his figure, he'll be splendid on a horse.'

'No, Edward. You know what I've planned for him.'

'To be a merchant as successful as his mother? Yes, I know. Then place him in a merchant's house and later on apprentice him. It's the common practice.'

'He's too young!' she cried, suddenly terrified at the prospect of her child being taken away from her. 'I've already decided what to do with him. And I'm quite capable of educating my own son.'

'Very well.' Edward placated her, but he was slightly annoyed. 'I don't mean to interfere. But he's my son too, Janet.'

But she had heard the tone of her own voice, and was ashamed of her arrogance. She went to him and knelt beside him.

'I'm sorry, my love. Forgive me. And I was so glad you had come.'

'I always do, in the end.' He smiled, and took her face in his hands. After a pause, he said 'She is quite bewitching, but she exhausts me. She's as hot as a sparrow and she hasn't a brain in her head. Or a scruple. I must be growing old, I suppose, but it's good to relax again.' Then he changed the subject, and Elizabeth Shore was not mentioned again.

She was not important to the world that Edward and Janet had built up over the years, a world founded on warmth and respect and companionship. Mistresses might come and mistresses might go, but the bond between them could not be eroded by others. It was maintained by mutual forbearance. Edward had discovered long ago that Janet would stand no meddling in her business life, and he did not even offer her advice unless she asked for it. Ever since the rescue of Anne Neville from the Vintry, Janet had carefully avoided comment on affairs of state, knowing that if the king wished to talk about them, he would.

But it was not only to prevent argument that the king's public life was taboo to them. Edward the king and Edward the man were often different people: the peace-lover had to fight, the creator had to destroy, the easy-going friend had to break promises and kill. The murder of the harmless Henry VI had first brought it home to Janet. After that there were other things, ruthless acts for which Edward alone bore the responsibility. He was an absolute ruler, and there was no Warwick now to share the burden or the blame. Though with her reason she recognised that harshness and duplicity were essential parts of kingcraft, her heart did not want to accept them as part of the Edward she loved.

So they were both silent, and while they were together the crushing of opposition, the despoilment of homes and livelihoods, ceased to exist. Of course, it was a fool's paradise. The king must affect the man. Edward's fair beauty had begun to coarsen, his fine frame was thickening, because of the indulgences he allowed himself to escape from the rigour of riding a high-spirited country. There was a certain hardness about the mouth, a sadness about the eyes, when his face was relaxed or in sleep. Whenever she woke before him and had leisure to study him, she had an almost overwhelming desire to fold him in her arms and keep him safe for ever from the world which was so marking him. At such moments, her love for him was like that for her son, and just as hopeless. For she was afraid that life would take them both from her arms, and leave her to cry for them.

So anxious was Janet not to stir up the darkness that their meetings passed sometimes with scarcely a word exchanged. They made love with a frequency and fierceness which was a release for both of them from the intolerable pressures of living. But it was not long before their sanctuary from the real world was impossible to preserve.

The rumour that shocked Janet and rocked her protected, orderly life was that George Duke of Clarence had murdered Ankarette Twynyho. The story was being told and retold in the streets of London ... a gang of ruffians in Clarence's pay had broken into her house in Somerset, carried her off to prison and stolen her jewels, money and goods. She was accused of conspiring to poison the Duchess of Clarence and her infant son, and after a mockery of a trial she was summarily hanged on the gallows.

Janet's memory of her covert meeting with the Duchess now extended to the quiet figure in the background: anxious, kind, trying to help other people, and surely very close to her mistress. What sort of monster would invent such a lie and do such a thing to her? Was this because the Duke had never forgiven her for betraying him at the time of Richard's wooing? She felt responsible, guilty. And frightened. She could hear Edward saying again, as clearly as if he were really there:

'Leave it, Janet, and don't dabble in things that don't concern you.'

She could no longer ignore the outside world because she had opened the door and invited it in. She waited with more agitation than ever before for Edward to come again. When she had the chance, she would have to ask him what had really happened and why.

She expected Edward to be angry with her, to blame her for what had happened, but he was too worried by everything to do with the Duke of Clarence to care about her small part in it.

'He's always been the troublemaker of the House of York, but he's become too dangerous for me to tolerate any longer. Ever since his return before Barnet he's been a source of agitation, spending recklessly, wilfully going against my policies, constantly complaining that his worth is being underrated.

'Isabel's death seemed to remove any lingering restraint from his behaviour. Not two weeks after she was buried, Charles of Burgundy fell in an obscure skirmish outside Nancy and George immediately began intriguing with our sister Margaret, Charles's widow. Their plan was his marriage to the heiress Mary, in direct defiance of my own designs for her future.

'We discovered the scheme before they could carry it out, but in his savage frustration he took his revenge where he could not be resisted, on a helpless servant. If it hadn't been her, it would have been someone else.

"I have tried to conciliate him. I have tried to endure his

delinquency. But now he has exceeded all bounds. I have learned that the real object of their plotting was to use the Burgundian inheritance as a stepping-stone to the English throne. In my brother's perverted mind, he still believes he should have the crown that was dangled before his dazzled eyes by Warwick nearly ten years ago.'

'What will you do?'

'He has subverted the laws of the realm and taken justice into his own hands. He is striking at the very foundation of my government, threatening a return to the anarchy of Henry's reign. I have to stop him. I will summon him to Westminster and arrest him.'

'But Edward, he's your brother! Surely you can't ...'

'I don't know, Janet. I just don't know.'

The nobility, it was said, were shocked by the king's high-handed action, but the city was rather pleased than otherwise. They had no liking for the old-fashioned robber-barons who encroached on their liberties and menaced their money-bags. The Duke of Clarence had borrowed and owed far more in London than he had spent and he had never bothered to cultivate the mercantile classes as the king had done.

But once Clarence was locked up in the Tower and powerless, there was a long pause which lengthened into months. What should be done with him? Opinions varied. If he had been anyone else, some said, there was enough evidence of treason to condemn him ten times over.

The Duke of Gloucester came down from Yorkshire, and before the gossip started to circulate Janet knew that he had come to plead for his brother. It tore at her heart to think that he still kept his blind loyalty to George, who had always resented him and done his best to ruin his private happiness. The ideal of the shining older brothers who could do no wrong clearly had a tenacious hold on his unsubtle imagination.

The atmosphere at court must be deadly, she thought: the queen and her kindred, including her son Dorset who was Edward's boon companion, implacable on one side; Richard and the Duchess of York, with representations from Margaret in Burgundy, on the other; and Edward in the middle. He still had not signed the death warrant.

Janet could only guess at his torment of mind. He came sometimes in the middle of the night; she learned during that terrible winter to leave a back door unbarred for him. And he would loom up in the darkness of her chamber, saying nothing, using her as if he hated her. And she dared not speak a word to help him.

She could not have given him advice even if he had sought it. Unlike Richard, she had no illusions about George of Clarence. When he was still a lad she had seen through his charm to the selfishness beneath. He was a living danger to England. And yet fratricide was a heinous sin damned by some of the earliest words of God. No one but Edward could finally decide his brother's fate.

There was little goodwill that Christmas for Janet in her house at Walbrook. Her son Peter, now four years old, went through a phase of refusing to do anything he was told. Several times Janet lost control and thrashed him, afterwards weeping bitterly at her own brutality. In January, Edward's younger son Richard Duke of York, also four, was betrothed with great ceremony to the five-year-old heiress Anne de Mowbray, Countess of Norfolk. He probably accepted this as his duty with good grace, thought Janet with a twinge of jealousy.

In the same month, the coldest month of the year, the formal processes of law were set in motion and early in February a bill of attainder was introduced in both Houses of Parliament. Clarence was found guilty and sentenced to death.

Loathing the gossip and speculation, Janet was afraid to step outside her door. In her most optimistic moments she convinced herself that Edward would never give the word. The king in him was very powerful, but the man was strong enough to baulk at killing his own brother. He had forgiven him so many times before.

The days after the passing of sentence lengthened. Janet was working out solutions to the impasse: George could be banished, like the persistent Lancastrian rebel Oxford, to imprisonment in Calais; he could be kept close in the Tower for a while, then released to one of his distant estates on his word of honour not to leave it; or he could be stripped of his English titles and despatched to a sinecure in Ireland where he was born.

On a grey morning in the middle of February, she ventured out to Bucklersbury for some Castile soap, and in West Cheap she came upon a group of women she knew by sight, rocking with raucous laughter. She could not help hearing what they said; their shrill voices rebounded from the eaves above them.

'A butt of Malmsey? I don't believe it!'

'It's true enough, gospel truth. I had it from the wife of one of the Tower sentries. He ought to know.'

'Did the king choose it? He always likes a joke.'

'No, no. It sounds as if the duke himself wanted it. What better way to die, eh, Joan? I dare swear my husband would go gladly to a death like that.'

'Well, if it's true, I'll lay you a pound to a penny it was the best Malmsey. No watered ale would suit his fine palate!'

As the women collapsed into another peal of laughter Janet walked on, sick nearly to the point of vomiting. Whether the scandalous tale was true or not was irrelevant. George was dead. She completed her purchase in haste and returned home to find that the house was already full of the story. She shut herself in her chamber for the rest of the day, trying to sort out her emotions. She had little grief for Clarence's end – a judicial murder sanctioned by Act of Parliament – though the snuffing out of any life at the early age of twenty-nine saddened her. It was Edward who concerned her, Edward himself and his relationship with the rest of his family. Richard would find this hard to forgive, especially as he would see it as proof of the supremacy of the queen and the Woodville clan over the king's will. Margaret of Burgundy, who had always been besotted with George, might prove irreconcilable.

And in Edward, the king took a step further away from the man. Did she hate him, or did she pity him? Could she bear the touch of a man who had given orders for the murder of his brother? She did not know. He had come to her before with blood on his hands: that of all the enemies killed and maimed in battle, and all the friends too, killed on his behalf; and he had dealt death many times in peace, to safeguard his kingdom. Why was it so much worse now, when George had been one of the most treacherous men in England? After wrestling with her thoughts for hours, she decided in the end that only one thing would tell her how she really felt: a confrontation with her lover. She went down to dine in the hall, as she did when she was not in a hurry, and missed afresh the reassuring figure of Nick at her right hand.

So she waited in suspense for Edward to come, starting at horses' hooves in the yard, leaping up at every bang on the door. It was just as it had been when she was waiting for his love-trap to close upon her when they were young, though now there was no pleasure in her anticipation. Peter, who liked to have all her attention, disapproved of her preoccupation and said so in no uncertain terms. But he was so like his father at times that it was painful to look at him.

It was only a few days before he came, unusually in the late afternoon, leaving his small train outside to wait for him. Janet was summoned from her pantry, her fingers sticky with preserves, and she hurried upstairs to the solar with her heart deafening her by its beating. Before the door she paused and quailed, then she summoned up her courage and went in. He was staring out of the oriel window, one knee up on the window-seat, still wrapped in his cloak. When he heard her enter he did not stride towards her and hug her as he normally did. He turned and stood where he was, dark against the failing light of day, his face unreadable. She too stayed where she was, pushing the door closed behind her. He was very tall and his bulk almost blotted out the window; he might have been a stranger. Janet could not speak.

For an age they confronted each other across the length of the room, challenging the love of many years to be strong enough to leap the gulf which had opened between them. His would have to be the first move. When he spoke, his voice dropped heavily into the silence.

'Richard has gone.'

'Gone?' she said tonelessly.

'He left the day after and returned to the North. He blames the queen. He has cursed her and sworn to be avenged on her.' Suddenly his voice took on not only vigour but urgency, almost fear. 'But it is not Elizabeth's fault. It's my responsibility, mine. It was for my sons' sake. For my sons, Janet.'

She did not understand what he was saying, but she understood the tone. In the same tone he had asked her to take him back after his marriage. She had not been able to resist him then; she could not now.

'It doesn't matter,' she said slowly. What did not matter she was not sure. But Edward was so much a part of her that to reject him would be like mutilating her own body. Life without him was unthinkable. He had loathed what he had done as much as she, as much as Richard; yet for some reason it had to be done. That the reason was sufficient she had to accept, as Richard would not. Because she was taking him back, she must bear a little of his guilt. Because she bore some of it, the weight on him would be less.

Somehow, without moving consciously, they were together in the middle of the room. There was no need for them to speak again.

CHAPTER SIX

I t was as well that Janet and Edward had achieved harmony, for
trouble was impending for her in another direction. Peter had
never been an easy child. Irksome in the womb, nearly killing his
mother at birth, he went on as he began. For the first year, awestruck
by the privilege of having a child, wrapped up in his beauty and the
wonder of his growth, she did not notice his bad temper, the fits of
rage and bouts of screaming, the refusing of food and waking up in
the early hours of the morning to demand it. Nan took some of the
chores off her shoulders, though even after weaning him Janet fed him
as often as she could. She had no one to compare him with.
Experienced mothers would have advised her not to pander to every
whim, to let him scream until he wore himself out and went to sleep.
But in her love and fear for him she gave him all her attention, blaming
herself if he was cross with her.

So she marvelled at the strength of his ferocity, admired the forceful
will which had each woman in the house running about for him, and
was overjoyed when Edward told her that he had a true Plantagenet
temper. And he was beautiful. The golden hair he had been born with
remained, and grew into corn-coloured curls. His skin bloomed pink
with health, his long eyelashes curved over alert blue eyes. A smile

from him was devastating – when he had his way. Sometimes, indulging her pride in him, Janet kept his cradle in the shop, and received the admiration of her customers like his attendant priestess.

He learned to walk and to talk very young – the former because she took him out of his swaddling-clothes disgracefully early. His aptitude for learning was quick; he was particularly fond of pulling things to pieces; and he would not obey anybody except his father. Since Edward was there only rarely he was a handful most of the time. Much as she disliked it, Janet was forced to use violence on him. This was one of the reasons why, as he passed three years, Edward urged her to send him away for his own good.

But she had settled on his career before his birth, and she was sure he would outgrow the awkward stage. She remembered the happiness of the house in York, where Thomas had unconventionally kept three of his five sons at home. In any case, she reasoned, it was her business that he would inherit, so why should he learn the trade from some other mercer?

At the age of four, he began to learn his letters from the priest of St Stephen Walbrook, a gentle old man whom Peter quickly discovered how to lead by the nose. Janet supplemented his lessons herself, and found that although he absorbed knowledge easily, it was gone again by the next day. The best available education would cure that defect; at the earliest possible age he was enrolled at the Mercers' School. He should live at home in Walbrook, and absorb the ways of his mother's business whenever he was not at school.

He did not like school. On his first day, roused from bed before dawn and escorted protesting all the way by Kit and Nan, he found that the schoolmaster was a different proposition from the old priest. He came home scarlet, his face smudged with tears, and when Janet tried to embrace him and sympathise he stiffened and pulled away from her.

'I'm not going there again, mother. He's a cruel man and he beat me with his stick.' Janet persisted and drew him towards her.

'It's for your own good, Peter. If you don't obey the master, you will never know your Latin.'

'I don't want to learn Latin. It's ugly. I want to play in Smithfield and shoot arrows.'

'There will be time for that too,' Janet reassured him.

'I want to do it all the time. I won't go to school again. I hate it!' He collapsed into a storm of weeping, and at last allowed his mother to comfort him.

But the next day he had to be dragged yelling into the schoolhouse and delivered into the hands of the usher. Only the promise of a new bow induced him to go without a scene on the third day.

Anxiously Janet made inquiries. The usher who was in charge of the younger boys had no particular reputation for harshness. It was only to be expected that new pupils would kick against the discipline. They always did, the master assured Janet, but it was Adam crying out in them to be corrected, and within a few weeks an obedient and godlier boy would emerge from his care. Janet recalled how Will, the most spirited of her brothers, had passed most of his childhood in whippings, from father and masters, and what a splendid independent man he had turned out to be. It was evidence that in spite of his looks Peter had inherited Wrangwysh blood, and Janet let it console her. The sooner he was beaten into shape and buckled down to his Latin grammar, the sooner he would mature into the vigorous warm-hearted child she knew he could be.

But he never submitted to his schoolmaster. Perhaps because he was tall and strong for his age, the beatings that came his way were more than a defiant seven-year-old usually endured. After a while he stopped demanding to be taken away from school. Instead he turned sullen and refused to speak to Janet about it at all. Even when she discovered fresh weals and bruises on his body he folded his lips stubbornly and would not shed tears until his mother had gone. This, said Edward when she consulted him, was a much better sign. It was an indication that Peter was growing up; learning to cope with his troubles himself instead of crying to his mother with them.

She agreed with him reluctantly at the time, because she would hate to tie Peter to her apron-strings, but afterwards the worry returned. His bottling-up of resentment, this closeness in a child who had always before been open with his feelings, was not natural in one so young. Everyone, she thought, was far too eager for little boys to be men. Though, of course, on the other hand, she might be at fault, a middle-aged mother who needed a young son to keep her own illusion of youth.

One evening, after Peter had gone to bed with scarcely a word to her, she studied herself unhappily in her looking-glass. She was thirty-six, and there were lines around her mouth. The skin was beginning to dry up on her hands and her neck. Yet her hair was still brown and thick; Edward loved to run his fingers through it; and her body was still firm and elastic. She was conscious of how florid Edward's face was becoming, the fat which was increasing his great bulk and dragging at the tone of his muscles. Had his hair not been fair, the grey in it would have been far more conspicuous.

She had worn better, there was no doubt of it; but then what burdens had she had to bear compared with his? A sheltered life in the close-knit merchant communities of York and London. None of the great decisions, involving heart and brain and gut, which he had had to take a thousand times as king. Her only suffering, apart from losing her mother and the self-inflicted separation from her family, had been on behalf of other people. She did not count Peter's birth. That had been compensated for a hundredfold by his existence. Suddenly she was ashamed of her well-preserved looks, the unshadowed grey eyes. Even if she had not cut herself off from heaven by her adultery, she would not have deserved it.

When she went to bed she did not sleep. Fretting about Peter, bothered by her comfortable life, the bed seemed enormous and cold. She longed to be able to reach out for Edward's broad shoulder, for him to turn over drowsily and envelop her in his huge warm embrace. But he was not there; probably he was carousing with Lord Hastings and Marquis Dorset, or making love to Mistress Shore. It was one of the rare occasions on which Janet wished he was married to her, a humbler and more faithful partner. When their son married, a suitable match with a wealthy family, an amiable pretty girl with a good dowry, she hoped he would emulate his mother's morals, not his father's.

In the spring of the following year, John came down to London with the Duke of Gloucester, who was conferring with the king on the conduct of renewed war with the Scots. Since they were staying for nearly a month, he brought his family with him, and they lodged with Janet in Walbrook. She was delighted to see them, glad not only because of her fondness for John and Margaret, but because their three sons would be company for the discontented Peter. Their eldest, Richard, was a year younger than Peter, but he was a lively intelligent little boy, and extended his friendship to his cousin at once. Peter responded to Richard rapidly; he had plunged into a black mood when Janet would not give him a holiday from school for the length of the visit, but he soon emerged from it and blossomed into a cheerful, normal boy.

There had never been such laughter in the house. The two boys were to be found with their heads, dark and fair, together in odd corners of the house and outbuildings, or shouting and chasing and scrapping, whenever Peter was at home. They spent best part of the first Sunday in Smithfield, under the chaperonage of Kit Cely, shooting at the butts. The final victory was disputed bloodily, but when they returned, though there was caked blood all over Richard's nose and Peter sported a black eye, they had their arms round each other's necks. Sometimes they condescended to letting five-year-old Jack, a round dimpled child just like his mother, join them, and Peter imitated Richard's patience with quiet little Robin, who was concentrating fiercely on keeping his feet.

Only one incident marred the visit. On an evening not long before the Wrangwyshes left, the adults were talking in the solar after supper about the liking which had sprung up between the two cousins.

'Why not let Peter come up to Middleham?' suggested John. 'I'm sure my lord would be pleased to receive him in his household. I noticed when we rode out to Mile End yesterday what a good seat he has on a horse. He'd make an excellent squire.' To her brother's surprise Janet reacted with annoyance.

'Peter is not going to be a knight, John; he's going to be a merchant.'

'I know,' persisted John, unaware that he was treading on dangerous ground, 'but a couple of years' polishing, living with other lads of his own age, could do him no harm.'

'He doesn't seem very happy with his present schooling,' put in Margaret gently. In her anxiety to justify herself, Janet was more vehement than she needed to be.

'Peter's a very wilful boy,' she said, 'and he isn't used to discipline yet. When he is, he'll be happy again. And I will not give him ideas above his estate. A successful mercer has no time to dance and pay compliments to ladies.'

'And a great pity that is!' exclaimed John, trying to laugh away his sister's ill humour. 'A little more grace and courtesy in the Guildhall would brighten many a drab meeting.'

'Don't be so frivolous, John,' said Margaret, laughing with him at the thought of solid burgesses performing court ceremonials, but with an eye too to Janet's distress. 'It was only a suggestion, my dear, because Peterkin and Richard have become such friends.'

'Of course.' Her sister-in-law was shamefaced. 'Forgive me, but it's something I've thought about very deeply, and I'm sure what I'm doing is for the best.'

Equanimity was restored, and even when Peter asked vociferously to go with the departing Wrangwyshes, nothing more was said.

Afterwards he retreated again into his sullen shell. As the summer passed, and he did not come to terms with the long daily grind of parsing and declining and repeating by rote, he was a constant nagging problem at the back of Janet's mind.

In the autumn, she was to travel to Flanders, partly to survey the progress of her concerns there, partly as the king's unofficial ambassador to his sister Margaret the dowager duchess. She had been in London the previous summer, on a kind of reconciliation visit, and Janet's mission was to cement the renewed friendship between George's brother and sister. The peace-offering was a richly-embroidered mantle which Edward had commissioned from Janet. She had intended to leave Peter in the care of her staff, but since he begged her frantically to take him, and cried every night for three days when she refused, she decided to let him go with her. A smattering of another language would benefit his career, and it would be good for him to see something of Flemish industry at the same time. Privately Janet acknowledged to herself that a break from Latin would also do him good.

They embarked in September, on a rare still day in a rainy autumn, and stood on deck together, watching the flat green marshes of the Thames estuary slipping past to merge behind them with the grey blur which was London. Peter, bolt upright beside his mother, was gripping the rail as if he thought his master might swoop down from the sky on the black wings of his gown and drag him back to the dark schoolroom and his horn-book. But as the river widened his grip relaxed, and he began to ask questions, first a few, rather stiffly, then more, until by the muddy Isle of Sheppey at low tide they came in an endless stream. Janet tried valiantly to keep up, enlisting grinning sailors to help with the nautical queries. Her spirits were rising into a great happiness. This was how she had always pictured her son, enquiring, eager, trusting in her.

As usual she suffered badly from seasickness when they came into open water, though the Channel was no more than choppy. But Peter bounced into her cabin and pulled her, limply protesting, up on deck to watch the moonlight on the wake of the boat, and the round moon which swayed gently above the great square sail. Under the unwinking stare of the moon and her son's big owl's eyes, she confessed that she did not know why there was a face in the moon, nor how the sailors could steer if the stars were covered by cloud.

When they docked at Sluys both were so tired that they could barely make the inn where one of Janet's agents had engaged a room for them. They slept so soundly that they did not even notice the abundance of fleas and bed-bugs. Soon after dawn Janet pressed on towards the dowager duchess's palace. It was raining, and they were soaked after a few miles, though it would at least, Peter remarked cheerfully, drown most of the fleas they had picked up at the inn. He was still communicative, enchanted by everything he saw and heard; listening raptly to the clipped Flemish tongue, staring without shame at the fat burghers and their fatter wives, pointing out to his mother the boars on the canals and the unfamiliar style of the buildings by the road. His excitement made her see it all with new eyes.

They were lodged in a convent (fewer fleas, Peter observed) close to the duchess's residence. Margaret of York did not keep them waiting long for their audience. Although she had lived in Flanders for thirteen years, her love for all things English had not left her. And the accredited messenger of her brother the king of England was particularly welcome. Janet prepared herself and Peter carefully for the occasion. The height of Burgundian court magnificence, fountainhead of European fashion for a hundred years, had passed with the death of Duke Charles but it was not yet apparent; Margaret, like all Plantagenets a devotee of beauty, had carried on her husband's reputation for extravagant pomp to the best of her ability.

Janet herself was dressed, as became her estate, with sober richness, her inevitable black gown in heavy brocade with satin trimmings. But she allowed her long-frustrated love of fine clothes full rein in the costume she had made for her son. A purple velvet cap was perched on his curls, which were gleaming with much brushing. His jerkin was sky blue velvet and his hose sheer purple silk. As a kind of secret assertion of his ancestry, she had worked a narrow border of golden broom-cods round the hem of his tunic. With his slim well-proportioned figure he looked nearer eleven than eight. As he twisted and postured in front of the tiny polished steel mirror Janet had brought with her, she thought proudly that she had scarcely ever seen a handsomer child, and for a moment, through her pride, she had misgivings about the life she had chosen for him. She suppressed them, and gave his tunic a final tug before she picked up King Edward's gift to his sister and left for the palace.

There was an opulence about the dowager duchess's court which far surpassed that at Westminster, even though Edward had brought it to a civilised elegance never before reached in England. Here the tapestries, the furniture, the costumes assaulted the eye with invention and colour. Following the page, who looked and strutted like a peacock, into Margaret's presence chamber, Janet saw that Peter was open-mouthed with wonder. But she had no need to worry about his behaviour, for as soon as Madame Evershed was announced he fell back as she had taught him and allowed her to go forward alone to make her courtesy to the duchess.

Margaret of York in her mid-thirties had not inherited much of her family's charm. She made her mark with the strength of her personality, expressed in a thin clever mouth and shrewd eyes. Of all the Duke of York's children she had made the most brilliant marriage, yet there was discontentment in her narrow face. She had given her glamorous erratic husband no children, and since his death she had been on a restless search for something to occupy and absorb her unfulfilled spirit. Janet had not met her since she was an adolescent, awed with George and Richard by the new splendour of their eldest brother's reign. Now, though she did not warm to her very much, Janet felt a certain pity for her.

The duchess was gracious, admiring the craftsmanship of the mantle and complimenting her on the other merchandise she had bought from the Evershed shop in Bruges. But just before she was dismissed, Margaret's eyes slid past her, and Janet saw a peculiar blind look of fanaticism spring into them. Then she turned back to Janet and said in a low voice, 'Will you not present your page to me?'

Startled, but somewhat gratified, Janet beckoned Peter forward, and nearly wept with pride as he approached the throne unhurriedly, and bowed to the duchess with a grace she had never trained into him. His face was flushed and his eyes very brilliant, and as Margaret leaned forward to give him her hand, a strange intimacy seemed to flash between them.

'Who is he?' the duchess asked, but she did not take her eyes from him.

'He is my son, Peter, madame,' Janet answered, trying to stifle her uneasiness.

'A fine boy. He deserves well,' murmured the duchess, and then she did look at Janet, a sharp penetrating glance which suddenly reminded Janet of Edward, when he wanted to read her thoughts. After a painfully long pause, Margaret said loudly 'He will always find a welcome in my household.'

She dismissed them, and they were escorted back to the gates. In an absorption so deep that neither noticed the rain, they returned to their room in the convent. Quite why the encounter had been so disquieting Janet could not say. Nothing that had happened would explain the sense of foreboding which was weighing her down, mollifying the pride she had felt in her son at his perfect behaviour during the audience. He did not talk about it either – a great change from the perpetual chatter of the past few days – but his eyes still held that exalted glitter, and his cheeks were still pink.

Not until she had stripped him of his finery and tucked him up in the narrow cot beside her own did she comprehend, and only then did she breath easily again. Peter's likeness to someone had been nagging at her since she first dressed him in his court clothes. She had dismissed it as a resemblance to his father, though it did not fit the elusive image in her mind. But of course, it was not Edward, it was George, the confident precocious youngster she had met at the Pastons' house in Southwark, and later at the palace reception with his elder and younger brothers. And that was whom Margaret had seen in him, the dead brother she had grown up with, her favourite brother. The mutual recognition which had passed between them had been Margaret's intuition of the kinship that he knew they shared. She had wondered if he could be a Plantagenet. That was all.

No wonder Peter was overcome. He had never seen his father in the formal atmosphere of his court. Whenever Edward came to Walbrook he was affable, relaxed, casual, his aura of kingship hidden. To be singled out for attention by a great lady he knew to be his aunt, before a glittering assembly of Burgundian dignitaries – it was enough to flush any boy's cheeks. When she was ready for bed and had risen from the prie-dieu, Janet went over to look at her son. Asleep, he had lost the air of surprising sophistication and seemed much younger, lips parted, golden fringe ruffled. Too young and too innocent for the superficial world of a courtier. No, she thought with a surge of fierceness, he shall never become one of those scheming peacocks. She smoothed the hair out of his eyes and went to bed.

The next day they left for Bruges, and though at first Peter maintained his silence, the novel countryside soon roused him to alertness again. He was vastly amused by the barges and wherries sailing apparently across flat fields, and by the profusion of windmills.

Janet's shop in Vlamingstraat was in spotless order, ready to welcome its proprietress. She found little she could fault. Peter was far more interested in exploring the town by boat and climbing up the Belfry with the senior apprentice than in inspecting the workshop and the accounts. The Flemish lad, who spoke only a few words of English, was eager to take charge of his employer's heir, who was ten years his junior and his namesake. She let them go, hoping that her son would pick up a few words of the language.

He did, with remarkable speed, and within the two weeks they spent in Flanders, while Janet supervised some alterations to the shop, he was able to understand Pieter Brouwer when he spoke slowly and simply, answer him, and also to speak a little French. Janet was pleased; she did not expect him to take much interest in the business side of things yet, but his ear for languages was a good sign. And he had clearly forgotten all about the disturbing incident at the duchess's court. When the time came, he did not want to go home. But his mother promised him that they would come back, and he accepted it with quite a good grace.

The voyage back was very rough, as they were caught in an autumn gale. To begin with Peter stayed on deck, drenched and exhilarated by the waves which washed over the little ship; then Janet staggered up to him, fearful for his life, and dragged him below, where he succumbed to sickness. Thus, green and empty, he was as relieved as she to set foot on dry land in London.

Peter went back to school without a word of protest, though he lapsed into taciturnity as his mother had feared he would. Still, he was apparently reconciled to his career, she told herself, and had returned to study refreshed by his holiday. But on the king's first visit after their homecoming, Peter was alone for a short time with his father and when he was in bed and Edward and Janet were comfortably installed by the fire, Edward said, 'Did my sister offer Peterkin a place in her household?'

'Why? Has she written to you about it?' asked Janet sharply.

'No. Peter told me.'

So he had not forgotten. Janet felt a spark of anger at his deceitfulness.

'He had no right to go to you over my head! In any case, nothing definite was said. It was simply the duchess's graciousness. She said the same to me.'

Edward nodded. He was used to her touchiness about their son's future.

'What did you tell him?' she challenged him.

'Don't attack me, sweet heart,' said Edward mildly. 'I told him that his place was with his mother, and that he should obey you in everything. I explained that all your work was to make a rich inheritance for him. He took it very well, though I think he was disappointed. The lad is learning young to control his feelings.'

Janet was relieved and smiled at her lover, grateful for his tact.

'You know how children misunderstand,' she said. 'He was overawed by the splendour of your sister's court.'

And they talked of Margaret and Flanders, and dismissed Peter from their minds.

Janet could not say definitely that her son was unhappy. He was quiet, spoke to her little about his lessons, never about the future. There were no more displays of temper, and he was more docile than he had ever been. But the companionship they had shared in Flanders was gone. Perhaps the secret ambition he had nursed and which his parents had thwarted had driven the wedge between them. Whatever the cause, Janet could not reach him. It was no doubt a natural consequence of his growing up, this growing away from her; yet it hurt her, that the child who was part of her should sometimes appear so alien.

Only in two things did she approach him. He was keen to learn French, and she taught him a little, promising him a tutor when he was older. And though with Latin he made minimal progress, still collecting beatings for his backwardness, he absorbed French quickly. The other sign of animation came at Christmas, when the boys of the Mercers' School performed a Latin tragedy by Seneca. Peter was given a small part, grudgingly, and he knew his words before any of the others, and stole his scene. Once more Janet was proud of his self-confidence, and came to the conclusion that her son was by no means dull; he merely selected where he would succeed.

She did her best to ensure that he would choose to be a good businessman by drawing him, as often as she could, into her affairs, instructing him in the technicalities of buying and selling, letting him help Agnes and Kit, showing him how she kept the accounts. He listened politely and did what she asked him, but absently, as if he were thinking of something else.

Boys, said the few people she confided in, were always like that. Wanting to go and shoot sparrows, or play foot-ball, when they should be assimilating their elders' experience with humble thanks. But it was stored up somewhere. After all, wrote her father, just defeated in a stormy mayoral election, Tom and Will had been idle inattentive boys once; now they complained to him, as Janet did, about the same faults in their own sons. Janet tried to take comfort, but she was not convinced.

One morning in April Nan, who usually packed Peter off to school, came early to her mistress's room. Janet was fastening up her hair.

'Is Peter giving you trouble, Nan?' she asked, for her servant could not really handle him.

'No, mistress, it's not that.' Nan's forehead was puckered. 'He's gone.'

'Gone early? That's unusual for him. Perhaps he had something to do before school.'

'His quills and tablets are still here. And he's taken his thick winter cloak.' It was a mild day, grey and soft with coming sunshine. Janet let her coif fall.

'Do you think he's truanting, Nan?' He had done it once before, last summer, soon after the visit of the Wrangwyshes, and had spent the day, as far as she could tell, bird-nesting in Moorfields. The whipping she had administered had hurt her, but had hurt him far more, and he promised he would not do it again, especially when he was given another beating at school.

But he would not take a warm winter cloak on a day's truancy. Nor his savings, which he kept under his bed in a little jewelled box that the king had given him. The discovery that his box was missing struck the first real chill to his mother's heart. He might possibly take some money out of it, but to take the box...

It was enough. In a suspended state of unreality, Janet went to the school, and when they denied all knowledge of him, she hastily despatched every available man and woman in different directions to enquire for him. From her associates and acquaintances there was nothing. A discharged soldier, sleeping off a night's drinking in a corner of Thames Street, swore he had seen a boy like Peter passing him wrapped in a thick cloak just before dawn. But he had been given a shilling, and for a mark he would probably have sworn to seeing the Grand Turk of Constantinople go past.

When at midday there was no news of him, and all her messengers had returned, Janet sent to the king. It was the only time she had ever appealed to him for help, and it was foolish, she knew, because Peter would undoubtedly turn up with sunset, dirty and guilty, prepared for punishment. But considering the situation rationally, as she had been doing all day, she decided on balance she was justified. So, apparently, did Edward. Though at the time he was closeted with the Portuguese ambassador, within two hours of receiving her letter a detachment of his men-at-arms was out to every gate of the city, making sure that no fair well-grown lad of eight or nine went in or out without questioning.

Yet although Janet carried on doggedly with her usual work, refusing to let herself think of how the time was passing, sunset came, and householders hung out their lamps, and the curfew tolled from St

Mary le Bow, and there was no Peter. Occupied with entertaining a rich merchant from Antwerp who was a potential client, she went to bed late and slept soundly.

She woke in the first light, and went to search her son's empty room, then to sit in the window overlooking the street, straining her eyes to the corner for every small figure that turned it. Kit Cely, coming to his mistress for orders, found her seated there two hours later, and persuaded her gently back to her duties. All day her gaze wandered eagerly to the street, and someone was on permanent sentry outside the shop. It was as if she was awaiting, with controlled excitement, the arrival of a welcome guest.

Peter did not return. With the king's precautions and her own people vigilant, Janet had done all she could; but when she dared for a moment to think about it, she knew it was too late. In that hour or so before his departure was discovered, he could have slipped through any of the gates as they opened to admit the traders from outside. He could have been well on his way, in any direction, on the bustling early morning roads, before the net was thrown out to stop him.

But he would come back. Of course he would. Janet could understand that he had found life at the Mercers' School intolerable; the first flush of spring had wakened wanderlust and he had been unable to resist it. When he had had his fill of freedom, when his money had gone and he was hungry, he would come home. And like the father of the Prodigal Janet would welcome him with open arms, and try even harder to make him content with his lot. She was almost cheerful, so sure was she that he would return. She talked composedly of 'When Peter is at home again,' and her household, far more concerned, outwardly, than their mistress, had to humour her mood.

After five blank days, Edward managed to pay her a short call. He had sent bulletins every day, generally scribbled in his own hand, and had come himself at the first opportunity. His optimism bolstered Janet's. It was a jaunt to assert his independence, he said, a striking out on his own to prove his manhood. Evidently he almost approved of the exploit, though he was annoyed at the boy's leaving his mother in such ignorance, and would see that Peter was chastised for that on his return. They could only wait, for, alas, there was little chance of tracing him, Edward warned, though he had sent his description far and wide and alerted the customs men in the ports.

'In the ports, Edward? You surely don't think he would try to leave the country?'

'No, no. I doubt if he would go as far as that. It's only a precaution.' And he left her with reassurance ringing in her ears.

Paradoxically, his very lack of concern began a change in Janet. Gradually but inexorably her confidence began to drain away. Days began to pass with horrible speed; three weeks were gone, and nothing had happened. The dread she had staved off so far, the dark imaginings which she had kept under tight hatches, began to rise in her. Visions, hastily dispelled, began to lurk on the borders of her consciousness, of Peter's body lying murdered in a ditch, of a starving boy crawling into a field to die, of Barbary pirates carrying him off for the dreadful pleasures of their rulers, of French marauders kidnapping an able-bodied little slave.

And on the night when Edward came again, to sleep with her, they broke in a tidal wave over the barriers she had built against them. First quietly, and then in an increasing flood of hysteria, she poured out her fears. With the forbearance which he could draw on in times of need Edward heard her out, holding her gently in his arms and seeking through his own strength to restore hers.

Naturally he was not himself as deeply affected by his son's loss as Janet. He had many children, legitimate and illegitimate, and the temporary disappearance of one of his bastards, attractive child though he was, could not compare with the troubles he had borne and was bearing. But he had the insight to see what it meant to the woman he had cared for steadily for twenty years, and the generosity to feel it with her.

So he said nothing, except soothing words, until, practically incoherent with sobs, she muttered, 'It would be better if I knew he was dead.'

It was time to rally her, and he said briskly 'Rubbish, Janet. As long as you hear nothing, there is every probability that he's flourishing somewhere. Would you wish Peter dead rather than give him the opportunity to find his feet and come back to you a man?'

She denied it with fresh tears, and he was able to bring her slowly to a rational state of mind.

More to comfort her than anything else he made love to her, and she fell asleep against his chest. Once in the night she woke to cry again, but he stilled her again with caresses. Realising, even through her distress, how kind he was being, she decided sleepily to behave with more dignity from then on.

And she did so. Now that she had faced the worst possibilities, and had put them into perspective with her hopes, life resumed a more natural course. Her heart still leapt into her mouth each time someone walked into the shop, but the false brightness vanished, and she no longer had to make a conscious effort to avoid thinking.

As the weeks went by, and spring turned to summer, she accustomed herself to a different future. How much she had been building her life around Peter she did not realise until he was gone. The continuation of her blood, the handing on of an inheritance, was only a tiny part of it. She had looked for a companion, an adviser, an equal, as she had been to her father in her mother's last years and after. Even in the battles of will she had waged with him, the obstinate spirit of independence pulling away from the tender ties she tried to bind him with, there had been a perverse joy. A submissive child would not have been the son of a Plantagenet and a Wrangwysh.

Most often, in those long lonely summer days, she thought of the beautiful lusty baby who had fallen asleep at her breast, and the eager little boy who had chattered about windmills in the Low Countries. And, though hope of his return never quite died, every day saw the embers nearer to ashes. Her world, which for years had revolved round two centres, resumed its orbit round the sun. Her fate was bound up with Edward; after him, nothing.

She did not see the king very often. Involved negotiations with the Emperor of Austria and Louis of France, the administration of the war with Scotland, and internal money troubles, were making him work harder than he had ever done. When he did escape to the house in Walbrook he wanted peace and civilised conversation, and Janet provided them as she always had. She could tell that the business of kingship became no easier as his years on the throne lengthened. The grind of state affairs demanded more frantic unwindings in debauchery and revelling; the toll of pleasure made him less fit to face the grind again.

Janet was sometimes tempted to ask him to curb his excesses. What had been an elegant and gracious court was becoming luxurious and overblown; the people, though they loved him, told scandalous stories against him. It was said that Elizabeth Shore shared her body between the king and his bosom friend Hastings, and that the three compared notes afterwards. The queen and her relatives were openly unpopular, though little Prince Richard and his tall beautiful sisters were cheered as their father was. But the excesses were part of the person that Edward had become, and he positively could not do without them now. As usual Janet kept silent, and loved him.

For his part, Edward did not mention Peter, or the future which had disappeared with him. They spent many hours poring over books, especially the new printed ones, which were being imported from Germany by cultured English collectors and the exclusively English editions produced at the sign of the Red Pale by Westminster Abbey. In the worlds of chivalry and philosophy between the covers, they both found stimulation and refuge.

The Scottish war was brought to a successful end by the brilliant generalship of Richard of Gloucester, who had occupied Edinburgh with impunity and forced the Scots to sue for peace. John Wrangwysh was knighted on Hutton Field at Berwick after the taking of the Scottish capital, so now Margaret Cropper, daughter and sister of knights, was the wife of another. In London, the victory was celebrated by the people in a less ceremonious way.

But at Christmas the rewarding achievement of Richard was counteracted by a shattering blow from France. Louis XI, the Spider

King who had schemed all his reign to enmesh Europe in his sticky web, broke his English alliance and made a treaty with the Austrians. Princess Elizabeth, who had been addressed as Madame La Dauphine since the age of nine, was rudely divested of her prospective husband the Dauphin, and Edward's carefully-built edifices of diplomacy crashed in ruins. Janet understood the importance to him of his French ventures: it was a personal duel with Louis, intellect against intellect, as well as a national issue. To be outwitted after so long, and when everything seemed set fair for peace and prosperity, was a terrible wound to Edward's self-respect, a violent jolt to the confidence with which he controlled England's fate.

In February she received a brief message from the king, commanding her to Windsor. Putting off a voyage to Flanders, she rode out to the castle in a drizzly mist, and was taken to a postern where Edward soon joined her. Without a word he rode off into the fog, and she followed him. The attendants, perhaps with orders to linger, dropped behind and, before they entered the forest, the mist closed around the two of them in a damp white circle. He waited for her to come up with him, and smiled at her as her mare drew alongside.

She had not seen him since Christmas, and the signs of the French disaster were in his face. The florid puffiness, the grey hair now spangled with beads of moisture beneath his cap, the cynical wryness of his mouth had become familiar. But there was a new bleakness which had not been there before. He looked as though he had given up. In her first shock of pity, Janet wanted to throw her arms round his neck and tell him that she would take care of him, but she restrained herself. A matron of thirty-eight did not behave like an impulsive girl, nor would it have helped Edward if she had.

Instead she said quietly, 'You wanted me, Edward?'

'As ever, sweet heart,' he replied, and laughed.

Relieved that he could still tease her, she said 'I always do as you ask, my lord, but it hardly seems the day to explore Windsor Forest.'

'I know.'

They rode on, past trees that loomed grey, then black out of the mist, and dissolved again behind them. They might have been the only people in a dripping noiseless world. The mist drifted aside a little, and they were in a clearing, the grass long and lush green against the brooding shapes of the trunks all round. A blackbird, startled by the trespassers, blundered across the glade, his alarm call echoing when he had already vanished.

The silence broken, Edward gestured about him. 'Was it here, I wonder?'

She did not need to ask what he meant. Her mind had been running too on that bright October day when she had been a virgin, and he had seduced her and she had not liked it.

'Places change,' she answered, shaking her head.

'And they wear better than people,' remarked Edward lightly.

'My heart is the same.'

'Is it? I don't think you were very fond of me that day. But I promised you it would be better.'

'You kept your promise. And I was so sure I hadn't pleased you.'

'Not pleased me? With that beautiful body you had kept for me?'

'A long time ago.' She shivered. He made the big bay he was riding side-step until it was alongside her roan. Then he wrapped her inside his cloak and, bound together, they stayed, while their horses dropped their heads and champed idly at the grass with a faint jingling of harness.

After a long pause, Edward said in a low voice 'No, you haven't changed. Your constancy is one of the few things that hasn't disappointed me – yours and Dickon's. I've been able to rely on you, always.'

'But was it real, Edward? Haven't we been living in a world of dreams all these years, shut safely away from anything that might hurt us?'

Edward lifted his shoulders.

'What is real? I sometimes think that the manoeuvres and double-crossings of my council chamber, the lies of diplomacy, are far less real than your solar and your bed. Perhaps it's because I never can succeed in making of England the country it could be – not in one lifetime.

Once I thought I could, but it was a dream, and the reality has fallen short. But with you, perhaps I haven't failed altogether.'

'You haven't failed at all,' she cried, 'you've pulled England out of a deep slough and made her great. The people love you.'

He smiled sadly into the mist.

'And how long will it last? My children, how will they fare?' He turned to her urgently and went on: 'I'm afraid for Ned and young Dickon. Take care of them for me, Janet.'

'How can I, Edward?' she protested, dismayed by his vehemence. 'I have no power to protect them. I couldn't even handle my own son. And why do you speak as if everything were over? You are still king, you'll reign for many years and keep the throne secure until Ned is old enough to rule without protection.'

The king sighed. 'Yes. Of course. But you mustn't blame yourself for Peterkin, my dear. He was torn between two different ways of life. There were longings bred into him which you couldn't fulfil. It's better that he should have gone before he was broken by them.'

She could not answer. What he said was true, though she had not faced it before. He pressed her closer to him, and silence fell again. The mist shifted about them, and all their clothes were sprinkled with droplets. She began to realise that she was leaning against Edward at an uncomfortable angle. Numbness was creeping up her right side. Drawing away, she shook life back into her limbs, feeling the pain of rheumatism which had grown intermittently since Peter's birth.

'Oh, I am growing old,' she laughed, but he was still looking at her gravely.

'I haven't loved you well enough,' he said slowly.

Responding in the same tone, she said 'Well enough for me, Edward.' She smiled at him, and an answering smile touched the tired eyes of the king.

PART 3
THE PRINCES

CHAPTER ONE

For once she consented to stay the night with him at Windsor, because the queen was in London, and Edward clearly needed the comfort which Janet could give him. Early the next morning she took leave of him and returned home. A few days later she left for Bruges. The transactions took four weeks, and then she travelled overland to Calais, paying several calls in Flanders on the way. Whenever she was not in a hurry, she took the short sea-passage. Even so, the ship was driven off course by strong winds, and it was April 13th before she docked in Southampton. None of the English ships was flying its pennant, and as she disembarked she saw that all the port officials were wearing black. She questioned a sailor who was lounging on the quay. He spat into the water.

'The king is dead, mistress.'

Everything went dark around her, the ground turned into a marsh in which she could not stand upright. Hands were dragging at her, voices were shouting in her ears, but they were all unreal. Vaguely now she could see faces which opened and shut their mouths, swooped closer to her and then away, white against a dim background. But she could hear nothing except an echo which grew louder and louder, filling her head with its din.

'The king is dead.'

Some other part of her was saying 'It was the rough crossing. I'm a very bad sailor. I shall be better in a moment,' and knew that Nan was near her, pale and frightened. She let them pour wine down her throat, and convey her somehow to an inn. Then there was stillness, and no-one except herself and the echo.

'The king is dead.'

She supposed later that she had asked to go home, because her surroundings changed to a swaying litter and the beating of horses' hooves. By the time she reached London, she was conscious enough of what was going on to have gathered that Edward had had a seizure during a fishing expedition at Easter, and that after a short illness he had died on 9th April. Everywhere people were vociferous in their sorrow. Many a tear-stained face there was on the road and in the city, and loud lamentations over the end of the Rose of Rouen, their king, who had known how to laugh and how to spend money, but had known too when to save and when to be severe.

And, though Janet paid no heed to them, there were misgivings expressed also about the future of England under another boy-king. Old men could remember only too well the troubled days when Henry VI had been a child, and his uncles had torn each other and the country to pieces over his head. Young Edward V, aged twelve, had been sent for from Ludlow, yet nobody knew who would rule the country in his name. The Duke of Gloucester had been named Protector in the king's will, but he was far away in Yorkshire.

The queen mother, excluded from the regency by her husband, was, on the other hand, on the spot, and Edward V was in the care of her brother Lord Rivers and her second son Sir Richard Grey. There was every indication that the Woodvilles intended to assume the government permanently; the late king's treasure, the Tower and the navy were all under their control. Since the Duke of Gloucester was unlikely to acquiesce in this arrangement, a renewal of the civil wars seemed inevitable.

The nation-shaking events which were exploding in London did not touch Janet, enclosed in the lightless misery of her loss. For the first time in her life she let business slide. Kit did the best he could, but he was distracted, not only by his mistress's unprecedented lethargy, but also by anxiety over the political situation. He was more volatile than Nick Farthing had been, and could not give his full attention to his job while the leadership of England hung in the balance.

Unlike the extremes of Janet's indifference and Kit's apprehension, many London citizens followed the comings and goings, the ups and downs, with detached interest much as they would watch the mummers in the courtyard of the White Hart in Southwark.

They wagered on the outcome of the race for London and the control of the new king – in secret, for fear of who might be standing behind them in the busy city streets. They criticised Gloucester for lingering in the North too long, until they heard rumours that the queen and her relatives deliberately kept the news of his brother's death from him. They censured him again when he set out from Middleham with a small train of mourning gentlemen, hearing requiems for his brother's soul on the way, apparently letting Lord Rivers steal a march. And, just as they were revising their bets, they were confused by the latest despatch saying that, on reaching the rendezvous at Northampton arranged with Rivers and the king, he had acted with a speed which completely turned the tables on the conspirators, gaining possession of the king's person and placing Rivers and Grey under arrest. There was no bloodshed. With the powerful support of the Duke of Buckingham, who had appeared from nowhere and offered his services to the protector, Gloucester was making for London.

When the Woodville bid for power had failed by the end of the month, London's merchants applauded the swift efficiency of the Duke of Gloucester, for they had no wish for a dynasty of the arrogant upstarts. They watched as the queen and all her younger children fled for Westminster Abbey, taking with her all the royal treasure which her brothers had not already managed to smuggle away from London. A wall had to be knocked down to get all her possessions into the sanctuary, they said. And then they crowded into the streets to cheer the young lad who was coming home to his capital to claim his kingdom, riding between his uncle and his cousin who had met no opposition on the way. Richard of Gloucester, sallow and serious as ever, acknowledged the acclamation gravely, but the eyes of most were on the young king, touchingly pale, tall and fair in blue velvet, and on Henry of Buckingham, smiling charmingly and blowing kisses to the women.

The Londoners did not know or love Richard as they had loved Edward IV, but they had rejoiced over his humbling of the proud Scots, and now they were grateful for his bloodless assumption of his rightful place, which would allow their trading to continue in peace. He might not have the glamour of his brother, they agreed, but his integrity and steadfast record promised a firm and trustworthy rule. So London's bustle returned more or less to normal, the apprentices reluctantly went back to work, and the city prepared for the coronation of Edward V.

Powers of thought and action were coming back to Janet slowly and painfully. She had not wept, and she never would. This was a sorrow too deep for mere tears. For twenty-four years she had worn mourning for a man she had not known; for the only love of her life, what outward shows could express her grief? That she had not seen him above twice a month even when he was in London, mattered not at all. That he had never been faithful to her, that she had not been more than a small part of him, mattered less. She had loved him with all her heart, and he in his way had loved her too, and needed her. The fire of his great personality, his zest for living, had enclosed her and warmed her even when he was absent, just as it had encompassed the whole country.

Then at last the heavy burden he had taken on himself alone had conquered his strength and sapped his energy, and he had succumbed to its weight. They said that he should not have died; the fit had not been fatal, and his doctors expected him to recover; he was only forty. But he had had no heart left for fighting. Louis' betrayal had knocked the last spark out of him, and he had surrendered without a struggle. If I had been here perhaps I could have given him the will, the thought nagged at her, and dully she cursed the business that had taken her from him.

There was no use in saying 'if only.' She had resigned herself to the loss of her son because there was always the faint possibility that he would come back. Edward's departure was final, and left her more alone than she had ever been. No-one could understand the vastness of the emptiness which surrounded her. When John and Margaret came south with the Lord Protector they called often to see her, yet although they were sympathetic they could offer no real comfort. It was years too late to run home to her father. They were separated now by half a lifetime. For months to come the desire for Edward's arms about her was an almost unbearable physical pain. Within a year, the two reasons for her existence had been snuffed out, and left her without a path to follow.

Drearily she began to take up the threads of her business again, rating Agnes out of her slackness and warding off a couple of creditors whom Kit had forgotten to pay. It all seemed quite pointless to her now, but the habit of a quarter of a century was hard to lose. The fact that her friend the Duke of Gloucester was ruling the country had caused her no surprise, and in her blunted state of reception, no pleasure. She knew the penalties of power too well to wish them on anybody, and though it was only proper that the most capable of Edward's servants should take over the administration, she did not think Richard would enjoy it. The cut and thrust of politics, which Edward had relished until his last years, was alien to the stern unsubtlety of Richard's moorland makeup.

The sudden execution of Lord Hastings, for conspiring against the Protector's life, did not succeed in rousing her from her torpor, though she felt a passing pang for the fatal rift between Edward's oldest friend and his most loyal brother. John, who had been with them on their headlong flight to Flanders thirteen years ago, came to her house the evening of the execution, and stared gloomily into the empty fireplace for hours before he left for the duke's house in Bishopsgate, still silent. He had not suffered before from the division of loyalties which so afflicted the Plantagenets and the Nevilles. His faith had always clung simply to Richard, and he was only beginning to realise what Janet had known years ago, that for the greater good a man in power, and his servants, must be ruthless. From her own barely-healed pain, Janet could only give her younger brother a sympathetic silence.

But his visit helped to bring home to her the self-indulgence of her grief. Outside the new green of the leaves was deepening, a new administration was taking root, and other people had their problems too. Even so, not until St Etheldreda's Day at the end of June was she shaken roughly out of the past into the present.

There had been a few rumours flying about that the Protector would take the throne for himself, but they were inevitable in a situation like this, and Janet was inclined to believe that they sprang from wishful thinking. She knew Richard too well to imagine that he would do anything so illegal, and so against the terms of his eldest brother's will. Then John called briefly and with suppressed excitement told his sister to be sure and attend the sermon by Friar Ralph Shaa at Paul's Cross the next day. The Protector and the Duke of Buckingham would be there, and it concerned the future of England.

With grave forebodings, Janet went, and found most of London there too, crammed into Paul's churchyard in a sweaty throng on a hot summer's day. And the subject of the sermon was shattering indeed. Incredulously Janet listened as Edward's children were declared bastards, the offspring of a bigamous marriage, and so debarred from the throne of England. The crowd received the tidings in stunned silence, and drifted away to digest it. Janet caught only a glimpse of Gloucester, far over on the other side of the churchyard; soberly dressed, insignificant beside the sumptuous Buckingham, as he had been beside his brothers.

Was it Buckingham's doing? Had he determined to follow in Warwick's footsteps and make a king? Had he brewed the story and palmed it off on a credulous protector? Or had Richard connived at it to give himself a good reason for reaching over his nephew's head to the temptingly-dangling crown? No. That was utterly out of character.

A devious scheme like that would never have its origin in Richard's brain. If he had had any ambition to take the throne, he would have taken it openly, by force of arms if necessary. And however much he was under Buckingham's brilliant sway, he would not have taken his word for such a tale. There was firm common sense beneath his idealism.

Then it must be true. As, with the rest of London, she pondered the thunderbolt, little things that Edward had said began to float to the surface of her mind. She remembered how insistent he had been that he was legally married to Elizabeth, and the anxiety he had displayed in his last months about his sons' future – an anxiety quite out of proportion. Above all, she recalled that final reason why he had killed George – the crime which, unlike all the others, had been unforgiveable. Had George known about the previous contract which Edward had made with Eleanor Butler, only now disclosed by the bishop who had witnessed it, which left Clarence Heir Presumptive to the throne?

That night she did not sleep, and rose the next morning with a blinding headache, but at last in certainty. Knowing the characters of Edward, George and Richard, putting together the snippets of evidence, she was sure that Edward had not been Elizabeth Woodville's legal husband, and that Richard could do nothing else but declare the children illegitimate and take the throne. Only later in the day did she realise that, for the first time, she had been thinking about Edward, recapturing his words and his face and his actions, without the world going black about her.

So his successor would not be Elizabeth Woodville's stripling, but his faithful brother Richard. Richard III. Perhaps it was because of her mourning that Janet felt no elation, but she thought not. That it was the best thing for England she had no doubt: a proven ruler, a grown man with an indisputable claim to the throne, untainted by disloyalty or doubtful legitimacy – a far safer prospect than a regency which would be only makeshift until the child-king grew up to be either grateful or ungrateful to his protector. But the honour would not sit easily on the youngest of the Duke of York's children. He had always avoided the court, because he disliked high politics. Now he was committed to a life of them. Janet did not envy him.

London, coming to the same conclusion as she about Edward's previous contract, found its convictions marching with its desires, and accepted Richard as their substitute king without commotion. He ascended the throne on his wife's name-day, the Feast of St Anne, and his coronation was set for 6th July.

But what of Edward's children? As soon as they were presented with a ruler they approved, the Woodville brood slid from Londoners' minds. The ex-queen, still in sanctuary, found herself ignored, the nine-days' wonder over, together apparently with any hope of future influence over the destiny of England. Young Edward and young Richard of York, who had been extricated from sanctuary to keep his brother company, were forgotten in their apartments in the Tower.

Mindful of what was virtually her king's last request to her, Janet went to see Lady Margaret Wrangwysh at Crosby's Place in Bishopsgate, where she was waiting on the queen. Margaret, who had also wondered what would become of the boys, promised to speak to her mistress. As a result, only a couple of days later, on Peter's birthday, she was summoned to Baynard's Castle, where the king was staying with his mother the aged Duchess of York.

Richard received her informally, sitting very upright in a small chamber, twisting a ring on the little finger of his right hand; his wife and John and Margaret were seated nearby. Although most of the court had resumed its usual gaudy clothing, in private he still wore deep mourning for his brother. It did nothing for his olive complexion, though probably the shadows under his eyes were the consequence of many sleepless nights. Richard did not age; he looked much the same as he had at seven; but there was an indefinable wearing of his face, a closing in as he grew older. Only in Yorkshire, where Janet had met him a number of times in the past ten years, did his face relax.

Nevertheless he smiled at her in greeting, and gave her a stool as soon as she had saluted Queen Anne and her relatives.

'I have arranged for you to visit my brother's sons, Mistress

Evershed,' he said without preamble. 'My wife has told me of your concern for their welfare.'

'Thank you, your grace, but I did not intend – .' Richard raised his hand.

'Don't thank me. The children are much on my mind too. It is a hard fate that has cast them from the heights down to nothing so quickly. Do what you can to comfort the boys. You know children better than I do, and you'll know what to say.' He paused, and glanced at Anne, who gave him a little smile of encouragement. He continued, almost shyly, 'Young Richard is content enough, but I haven't been able to convince his brother that I am not an enemy.'

'I understand, my lord,' put in Janet quietly. She had heard from John of the lad's hostile reception of the strange uncle he could not remember at Northampton; she could picture vividly Richard's earnest efforts to break down the chilly reserve of the twelve-year-old who had been brought up by the Woodvilles to regard the Duke of Gloucester with suspicion at the least. Lacking the easy charm of the boys' father, it was not difficult to see why he had failed.

Because she recognised that the reserved king was taking her a long way into his confidence by admitting as much, she ventured to ask him the question that had been troubling her.

'What will become of them?'

Richard frowned, but he was not annoyed. 'That question has been troubling me also ever since Bishop Stillington's revelation ten days ago. We have not determined yet. But you may be sure that they will be treated at all times as my royal brother's children.' He smiled anxiously at Janet, obviously aware that he had not satisfied her. She could see that he was not satisfied himself.

Richard bent his head over a desk and carefully selected a document which he proceeded to complete, sign and seal. She wanted to cry out 'Why did you take the throne from Edward's son?' but she bit her lip and remained silent and very still. He would not explain to her his decision to take the crown from the nephew he was pledged to serve. And yet, watching him quietly dealing with the consequences, she found it impossible to believe that he was selfishly seizing his opportunity for ultimate power. She had watched Edward as he tried to decide between the good of the state and loyalty to his family, and she was sure that this man was being torn apart by the same exceptionally difficult choice. Now that Stillington had broken his long silence, the secret could not be reburied. Richard of Gloucester had to accept the children's illegitimacy and give England a strong ruler; if he failed to act, someone else would. A young, weak king would be the spur to new rebellion, whether by Woodvilles nursing their new grudges or Lancastrians their ancient ones.

Richard handed her the completed parchment and continued: 'Here is my authority. The Constable of the Tower has been notified that you are coming. I believe you know him – he hails from Yorkshire too. Robert Brakenbury.' Janet remembered him well; his brother was a colleague of her father's. She was glad the princes were in such safe hands.

'I shall go today, if it please your grace.'

'Certainly.'

Before she left, the king had another request to make. 'We should be grateful if you would put a little of your excellent needlework towards our coronation. My Keeper of the Wardrobe, Peter Curteys, will tell you what is required.'

'I would be honoured, Sire'.

Janet had not been inside the walls of the Tower since the November day when she had waited for Richard with news of the Lady Anne, and never as far as the State Apartments. This time she had to resort to no bribery, and was escorted to the boys' chamber by the constable himself, a slow, kindly man without an enemy in the world.

The windows, facing south, were flung wide, and a cool breeze blew in from the river. Their lordships had been at the butts, Brakenbury explained, but a shower had brought them inside and now they were engrossed in a game of chess. As Janet entered, the little Duke of York had just lost his queen. Edward had removed it and was saying with a touch of patronage, 'You shouldn't have moved your knight, Dickon.'

'I know, I know. But I was sure that I could mate you in another three moves,' said the younger boy feverishly. They had been playing for over an hour, and he was growing bored.

He heard the door open, and nudged his brother, and two heads turned curiously to face the newcomer.

'My lords,' said Brakenbury, 'here is the visitor I promised you. Mistress Evershed.' Then he nodded genially at Janet and ambled away. An elderly attendant, who had been dozing in the sun, followed him.

Janet remained where she was, conscious of a critical scrutiny from the two boys. While they weighed her up, she did the same to them. The elder, lately King Edward V, was tall for his age, but looked as if he had outgrown his strength. He was pale, and his fair lashes blinked constantly over his light eyes. With straight flaxen hair and slender limbs, he was like a plant grown in a dark cupboard. She had seen the Duke of York before, but never spoken to him. As Edward had observed at his birth, he was a changeling. His dark hair was ruffled, his hazel eyes were bright, and his head was on one side: a little brown bird. Though his brother was clearly on his guard, Richard showed only frank interest in the woman who faced them.

Edward remembered his manners first, and rose to his feet, holding out his hand and saying stiffly, 'You are welcome, Mistress Evershed.' But Richard nudged him again and he flushed, biting his lip. In the novelty of seeing someone strange, he had forgotten that he was no longer a king, but only Lord Edward, whom he had once heard one of his attendants refer to in an overloud voice as the Lord Bastard. Janet had immediately understood his embarrassment, and she quickly crossed the room and knelt to kiss his hand. It was thin and rather cold.

'Did my uncle send you?' he asked suspiciously.

'He gave me permission to come. I asked him if I might.'

'Why?' piped Richard. He could tell that she was different from the ladies and gentlemen who had surrounded him at Westminster.

'It was your father's wish.' The children crossed themselves and Janet followed suit.

CHAPTER ONE

'Master Brakenbury said you were a friend of our father's,' said Edward doubtfully. He was plainly trying to work out where her loyalties lay, whether she was on his side – that is, his mother's side – or on his uncle Richard's side.

'Were you my father's mistress?' asked Richard, as though he were making a wild guess.

'Yes, I was for many years.'

'Oh.' The younger boy cocked his head on one side again and said consideringly, 'You're not at all like Mistress Shore. She used to wear bright clothes and she laughed a lot. I liked her. My mother never smiled.'

There was a hiss of indignation from Edward, and he glared furiously at his brother. Having lived away from Elizabeth Woodville for most of his life, he had been trained by her brother and her son to regard her with the reverence of worship. A word against her was almost a word against the Holy Virgin. Richard, who had been reared in close proximity to her severe beauty, was rather more clear-eyed about her. But under Edward's displeasure he hung his head, and for a moment his chirping was dampened.

In the silence, Janet knew that Edward was plucking up the courage to ask her something. She smiled to prompt him, and he said, 'Is my mother the queen safe?'

'Quite safe, my lord. In Westminster Sanctuary with your sisters.' Janet realised that she had progressed a step towards neutrality. Edward was appealing to her to confirm the truth of something he had heard from those in King Richard's camp.

'But my uncle Rivers and my brother Grey are dead, aren't they?' he went on defiantly, and his blinking increased to hide his feelings for the only two people he had ever loved.

It was true. Earl Rivers and Sir Richard Grey had been beheaded at Pomfret a few days earlier, in the presence of the Earl of Northumberland and a contingent of forces from York led by Thomas Wrangwysh and William Welles. Thomas, in writing to announce his imminent arrival in London, had told Janet the news without comment. Like Hastings' execution it was a political necessity, forced on Richard by the same circumstances that had thrust him on to the throne and his nephew off it.

But it was no good mouthing 'political necessity' at the boy before her. Political necessity, and an irregularity of birth, had snatched him away from everything and everyone he knew, from routine service and attention and deference, and shut him away from the world, disregarded, with only his little brother for company. What could she say to justify King Richard's actions, when even Richard himself, she had seen this morning, was uneasy in his conscience about them?

'Yes, my lord, they are dead,' she said gently. She felt much as she had when Peter had come home from school refusing to cry over a particularly severe beating. Yet she knew that, if she were to take Edward in her arms, he would stiffen and reject her sympathy, just as her son had. She dared say no more at present. If she tried to explain, Edward would think she was defending his uncle, and she would lose the small place in his confidence that she had hardly won.

There was another strained silence; young Richard kept glancing anxiously up at his brother as he strove for self-control. Then he put out his hand unobtrusively towards Edward's rigid arm, and Edward gripped it convulsively. It was a gesture which touched Janet and gave the elder boy enough resolution to say rather huskily 'God give them peace.'

Richard said in an audible whisper 'Ned, may Mistress Evershed sit down now?' And in his fetching her a stool, and Edward's asking her to be seated with a brave attempt at graciousness, the tension was broken.

Satisfied that his brother did not need his help any more, Richard turned his attention back to Janet. He liked this woman with the quiet face and sad eyes, and he wanted to find out all about her.

'Are you in mourning for our father?' he asked, and in answering his barrage of questions Janet relaxed. Within a few minutes, Edward too was adding tentative enquiries, and she knew that all was well. King Edward's sons would accept her.

When she left, Richard asked with his customary lack of inhibition if she was coming again. Janet said that she would if she could, and if my lord Edward was willing? Edward was still wary, but he said he would be pleased to receive Mistress Evershed again, and it was not entirely good manners which made him say so.

She wrote to the king the same evening, not expecting an answer until after his crowning. But even at so busy a time Richard did not neglect small matters. His secretary, John Kendall, a Yorkshireman like many of his intimates, was the most industrious of clerks. Within the week, she was authorised to visit 'the sons of King Edward' as often as she wished, the only stipulation being her discretion. She told no-one, not even her father, who arrived a few days later.

With Will and Young Tom his eldest grandson who were among his levies, he came to stay in Walbrook in a noisy family party. Thomas's fellow commander, William Welles, had also been a mayor of York, and was now almost one of the family himself, since Will Wrangwysh had married his kinswoman six years previously. Janet's house became a rendezvous for Yorkshiremen. Summoned by the protector when he feared he would need armed help against the Woodville faction, they reached London in time to join in the celebrations for his coronation. They were cock-a-hoop that their duke, who had worked with them and for them for so long, was raised to the highest position in the land.

Janet was kept so busy entertaining, catering and supervising, and working at the embroidery commissioned by the Royal Wardrobe, that she had no time to go to the Tower again before the coronation. The undiminished vitality of her father and Will, and the north-country heartiness of the men who blew in and out of her house, was a little repellent to her. She could not join in their rejoicing wholeheartedly. She wondered if it could be a sign of age, for although fate had cast her in a solitary role, she had always been a gregarious person by inclination. Lacking someone close to talk to, she had not realised that her craving for quiet and doing nothing was in fact a reaction to Edward's sudden death.

Her father came upon her one morning, standing irresolute in the middle of her pantry, a jar of preserve clutched in her hand and her eyes fixed on nothing. It was so unlike his generally practical daughter, that Thomas sat her down and drew out of her what was wrong. Then he carried her off to St Stephen's and stood on guard while she made her confession. The submission to Holy Church after so many years was, as he had hoped, a great relief to her and together they lit candles to St Edward for the late king's soul.

On the first Sunday in July, King Richard was crowned at Westminster. Tactfully he had sent his nephews in secrecy off to Windsor for the weekend, to hunt in the forest. So they did not hear, even at a distance, the acclaim given to their supplanter as on the day before his anointing he made the traditional journey from the Tower, through the swept and decorated and packed streets of the city, to Westminster Palace.

Among the aristocracy, it was the best-attended coronation of the century. In their relief at being spared from the perils of a minority and the rule of the nouveau-riche, Lancastrians sank their differences with Yorkists, and came to support the dedication of King Richard III to God and the good of his country. Even Lady Margaret Stanley, the mother by her first marriage of the implacably anti-Yorkist Henry Tydder, was the queen's train-bearer.

Sir John Wrangwysh had secured a good vantage-point for Janet in Old Palace Yard, so she could see the king and queen as they passed from the abbey to the great ceremonial banquet in Westminster Hall. It was a long wait; the day was hot and muggy, her feet hurt and her back and head ached with the crush and the standing. She thought back to the last crowning; to the radiant young king who had appeared like a god descending from heaven in his rich vestments, flinging the bounty of his smile and his presence over the dazzled crowd. Her knees had shaken then, her breath had stopped with her desire for him, and the exhilaration of the multitude had caught her up to hover above the ground.

But she had been very young then, only seventeen, and untouched by life. And this was quite a different kind of occasion. Edward had seized kingship with both hands, to wield it vigorously with all the youth and strength of his outgoing character. Richard lifted the mantle on to his shoulders with deep reverence, only too aware of its weight and its holiness. His face, as he passed quite close to her, was exalted and withdrawn, still under the spirit of dedication with which he had received the unction and the crown. Anne, by his side, was labouring under her coronet and robes, but she too was walking on a loftier plane. Instead of wanting to cheer, Janet was suddenly blinded with tears.

CHAPTER TWO

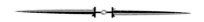

Not long after the coronation, there was an exodus from the capital. The king was setting out on a progress to the west, taking the major part of his court with him. The superfluous soldiers were dispersing to their homes, and so Janet found herself saying goodbye to five members of her family within a few days. Thomas was confident that he would be elected Lord Mayor of York for the second time next year, and made her promise to come up for his installation. Though she waved goodbye to them at Aldersgate with some regret, she also felt a wave of relief that her house would be her own again.

Just before the king and his train departed for Windsor, Margaret called on her. The ostensible reason was to tell her, with great pride, that her husband had been created an Esquire of the Body, and was thus officially one of the inner circle of the king's attendants. But her kind-hearted sister-in-law also wanted to talk about children; to hear how Janet had fared with the princes, and to boast that her own three boys, who had been brought up with Lord Edward of Middleham, were to be trained with him in his new establishment at Sheriff Hutton. The delicate lad who was now heir to the throne was to be placed under the government of his cousin the Earl of Lincoln, and as nominal Lord of the Council of the North, he would serve his apprenticeship for ruling.

'The queen says little,' confided Margaret, 'but I'm sure she misses her son very much. She worries about his health when she's not with him. They haven't been separated for so long before.'

'And you, Meg? Don't you miss your children?' Margaret shrugged and smiled.

'Why of course I do. Separation is a new thing for me as well, though I don't have the concern about their health that Anne has. Bless their hearts, I've never known sturdier children. John scolds me and says they must live away from us to grow up independent, but really he feels the same.' Her hazel eyes regarded Janet humorously. 'There is something about Middleham that makes parents indecently fond of their children.

'The king may send his brother's children up there too,' she added with characteristic irrelevance, clearly meaning Sheriff Hutton.

'But the girls are still in sanctuary,' objected Janet.

'They'll be out soon. Dame Elizabeth will tire of her solitary confinement before long. His grace is confident that she'll give in to his terms in the end. Even if her sons are out of the running, she has five marriageable daughters to play with.'

'The king will …… treat them well?'

'Really, Janet,' Margaret said severely, 'you've known him longer than I have. Surely you know that he's kind to a fault?'

Perhaps, thought Janet, he was indeed kind to a fault. Kindness was not always a useful asset for a king, however praiseworthy it might be in a subject.

The Duke of Buckingham, newly created Constable of England, clattered west at great speed with his followers a few days after the king, and Margaret was in attendance on Queen Anne as she left a week later at a more gentle pace, bound for a rendezvous in the midlands with her husband. London life resumed its rhythm as if no change of regime had taken place, and Janet found herself with an empty house and time on her hands.

But instead of the blank dreary future she had envisaged for herself, with no incentive and no direction, the king had provided her with one channel for her energies. The moment her duties as a hostess ceased, she turned her footsteps again to the Tower, half in dread, half in eagerness. She feared that in the few weeks since she first met Edward's sons, she might have lost her narrow foothold in their confidence. For some reason it was very important that they should trust her. She wanted to be their friend, perhaps just because they did not seem to have any others, or perhaps because they were part of Edward and a link with him.

They were playing hoodman-blind along the ramparts with a couple of the children of the Tower officials. Passers-by under the walls, hearing their shouts, looked up and smiled indulgently as the bright figures flashed by the crenellations. Janet was glad to see that young Edward was for once behaving like a boy instead of a deposed king.

When they joined her, breathless and rosy-faced, on the lawn of the Lieutenant's garden, her heart was in her mouth. But Richard, at least, was prepared to take up their relationship where they had left it. Edward took refuge again in the frosty dignity which sat rather pathetically on his youth, but he was not hostile as he had been last time. Asking to meet their companions, she was persuaded into hoodman-blind for a short time, until she had to cry off through short-windedness. Richard suggested that they should take Mistress Evershed to see the wild beasts, and she was conducted to the menagerie in the Lion Tower. The depressed lions and ageing bear were objects of fascinated terror for both boys, though the elder tried not to show it.

'Sometimes at night,' the younger told Janet with round eyes, 'we can hear them roaring.'

'Not that we mind,' put in Edward off-handedly.

The old ravens croaked and hobbled around the grass trailing their tattered wings, picking up the scraps put out for them by the Lieutenant's cook. The sun threw the dark blue shadow of the battlements on to the greensward, and its rays were warm on her back. Her heart was lighter than it had been for months.

But on her next visit, though the early August sun was beating down and the air was shimmering above the walls, there was no sign of the boys outside. There were more guards about than usual, and she was kept waiting in the gatehouse of the Byward Tower until Robert Brakenbury came to meet her. His usual placidity was ruffled.

'Forgive the discourtesy, mistress,' he said, 'but I should like a word in private with you before you see their lordships.'

As he led her to his private apartments, Janet's apprehension grew. He offered her a seat and a glass of wine, and took up an imposing position before the wide hearth. Janet noticed that the rushes were clogged with refuse, and the room stank. Brakenbury was a bachelor.

'You realise that we have increased security precautions since you last came,' he began heavily. She wished he would talk faster. 'They are on the king's orders, and they are the consequence of a – ah – rather alarming incident last month.'

'What has happened? Are the princes safe?'

'Yes, yes, their lordships, praise be to our Blessed Lady, are in good health and as happy as can be expected. But these extra measures are to keep them so. I'm afraid there has been an attempt on their lives.' Janet's heart lurched, but she said nothing. 'I can't give you details, of course. It's state business and a very weighty matter. But it does concern you in a small way.'

'If there's anything I can do.....' she murmured faintly. The constable came to the point, screwing up his good-natured eyes so his grey brows jutted.

'Because of their danger, the lads have had to be moved to the Garden Tower, nearer here, and much more closely confined than before. I can't let them run loose about the place as they were doing. They have to be watched, and all visitors carefully vetted by me personally – that's why you were kept waiting.

'The trouble is, of course, that the lads don't see it like that. For them, it's imprisonment, and I suspect my lord Edward is prepared for summary execution.'

'And you wish me to explain to them that you're not keeping them in, but others out?' Brakenbury nodded, smiling.

'You inherit your sharp wits from your father, Mistress Evershed.'

'I'm not sure that they will accept the truth from me, Master Brakenbury.'

'Under your correction, mistress, but I think they will. You have a stout ally in young Lord Richard, and if only my lord Edward would allow himself, he would be yours too.'

She was gratified by this outsider's confirmation of what she had hoped, but something else was worrying her.

'How long will their confinement be?' The constable made a vague gesture.

'I can't tell. Until the danger is over ....or until the king considers it safe to move them elsewhere. We are doing our best to make their lives easy.'

'I know it. You bear a great responsibility, Master Brakenbury, and nobody could bear it better.'

He waved away her compliment and took her along the ramparts to the princes' chamber.

It was a hard task he had given her. Like a frightened horse Edward shied away from explanation and sympathy alike. Richard was frightened as well, and stood squarely in front of his brother as if to protect him from an unexpected attack. She had wanted to avoid telling them directly of the assassination attempt, but she rapidly realised that it could not scare them more than their vague dread of a threat from within. So, disregarding their defensive silence, she told them gently of enemies who had hated their father, and now sought to harm them – enemies who had been kept away by the devotion of Robert Brakenbury and his men.

'And though now the enemies are taken and the danger over, he must keep a close guard over you for a while, in case anyone else tries the same thing. He's a very prudent man, and he cares very much about your safety.'

Surprisingly, it was Edward who spoke first, slowly, as if he were trying to work something out.

'Duke John of Burgundy was assassinated, wasn't he?' he said. 'They called him Jean-san-Peur, and he was a great and terrible man.'

'Yes.' Janet hastily dredged up from the recesses of her memory the old detail of foreign history.

'Only important people are assassinated, aren't they?' pursued Edward. 'Like Julius Caesar.'

'I suppose so, my lord,' Janet agreed doubtfully.

'Then we are important!' His pale eyes suddenly blazed with a life she had not seen in them before.

'But, Ned, I would rather be unimportant and stay alive,' objected his brother, who did not follow.

'Then you're a fool, Dickon,' said Edward scornfully. 'If someone thought us important enough to try to kill us, it means that one day our uncle will have to release us to take our places in the country.'

Abruptly he bottled up his strange excitement and said to Janet with dignity 'Thank you, Mistress Evershed, for telling us what has happened. We shall try to bear our confinement as noblemen should. Anyway, we're too old to play cup-and-ball and hoodman-blind, and now we may spend more time on our studies.'

Richard looked rebellious; he did not feel in the least too old for games, and the thought of someone after his blood did not comfort him in the way it did his brother. So he turned to Janet and said 'Master Brakenbury is sure the danger's over?'

'Yes, my lord. And even if weren't, he would protect you with his life.'

He seemed satisfied and by the time she left them she knew they were happier with their lot than when she came. But she was not sure about Edward. The boy clearly had implanted in him, either by heredity or training, a fair share of Woodville ambition which the life ahead of him was unlikely to fulfil, however good the king might be to his nephews.

About this time Janet first heard a rumour that the princes were dead. It came, of course, through Nan, who in middle age had not lost her relish for gossip. She brought the news to Janet from the market, her face trembling with excited indignation.

'They're saying that the boys have not been seen lately,' she said conspiratorially, 'and that perhaps the poor children have been done away with.'

Janet slammed the abacus she was using down on the table and turned on her servant with fury.

PART 3: THE PRINCESS

'"They" have no right to say anything of the sort,' she said roundly,
'and no reason, either. I've told you before, Nan, not to listen to such
poisonous tittle-tattle.'

Nan stepped back, looking wounded. 'Nay, mistress, they don't
say it's true – just that it might be.'

'Well, it isn't,' Janet said flatly. 'And I'll thank you to say the same
to anyone you hear repeating it.'

'Yes, mistress,' said Nan sulkily, and took her baskets to the kitchen,
giving Janet a queer glance as she went. No doubt she wonders how
I am so sure, thought Janet, but she knew that she would be obeyed.

The rumour, however equivocal, disturbed her. The disappearance of
the boys from daily view could quite easily have a fatal construction
placed upon it; and if the malicious tale gained ground, it would
destroy King Richard's plan to let the children slip quietly out of
people's memories, and then release them into his northern
headquarters to live a secluded, but normal, life. And she wondered,
fleetingly, if the assassination attempt had any direct link with the
rumour. She supposed that the source of both must be either diehard
Lancastrians, or the unreconciled Woodvilles. Though the killing of
their two best hopes would hardly gain the approval of their mother
the ex-queen.

The two incidents were followed at the first signs of autumn by far
more serious events. Janet continued visiting the princes in secret and
in public professed no interest in what was going on behind the locked
doors of the royal family and nobility. But she watched the movements
in the streets and kept her ear tuned to official announcements and
any rumours or gossip which came her way. She could not bring
herself to ask Nan what she'd heard in the market, but sometimes found
herself pausing on the stairs to listen to her gossiping in the kitchen.
In these ways she managed to follow what must be happening - and it
worried her.

There was discontent in the country. Richard's deputy in London,
the dour Duke of Norfolk, twice had to ride out to quell mutterings of
revolt, first in his own East Anglia, then in Kent, always a hotbed of

discontent. And in October, as well as driving storms, came unbelievable tidings: the Duke of Buckingham, King Richard's most prominent supporter, and the most showered with favours and offices, had risen in rebellion and was marching on London. The Lancastrian white hope, Henry Tydder, was expected daily to land in the West Country at the head of French troops to aid him.

It was like plunging back thirteen years into the uncertainties and alarms of Warwick's rising. The Duke of Norfolk swiftly threw the city into a state of defence. The whole of London was full of hurrying soldiers and anxious people doing nothing. Janet felt sorrow for Richard, whose open-handed generosity had been rewarded with such vicious ingratitude. It brought back painful memories of Edward and the treachery of his greatest supporter Warwick and his brother George; she could see the pattern of betrayal repeating itself for the House of York.

The king moved with his usual decisiveness. Marching rapidly from the midlands, he intercepted Buckingham's advance from Wales, but no blow was struck by the royal army. Apart from a few malcontents, it appeared that no Englishmen had joined the rebel. Tydder was frightened off the Devon coast and the king found an unexpected ally in the torrential rain and floods which scattered and destroyed Buckingham's forces. The duke fled but was captured, tried and beheaded in Salisbury at Soulmas. Richard, they said, had refused his repeated requests to see him once more face to face.

The king punished only a handful of the other ringleaders and immediately resumed his restless progress around his realm. Before the end of December he was back in London, the country quiet again, his position apparently strengthened by the abortive rebellion.

But London, noisily carrying on with its Yule festivities, was shocked to hear that on Christmas Day itself, Henry Tydder had sworn a solemn oath in Rennes Cathedral to take Elizabeth of York, King Edward's eldest daughter, to wife. What could this be but a formal declaration of his purpose to challenge Richard for the crown? Without such a marriage, he had negligible claim to the throne. And even more disturbing for Janet was the suspicion that Elizabeth Woodville, still ensconced in her refuge, had sanctioned the match. Edward must be turning in his coffin, she thought to herself.

Then there was an astonishing turnabout. The former queen's position changed from inexorable hostility to apparently trustful capitulation when in March she accepted the king's terms, unfavourable though they appeared to be to her, and released her five daughters to the court at Westminster. What was more, she wrote immediately to her eldest son, Marquis Dorset, who had fled to Tydder's shadowy court in Brittany, urging him to come back and trust himself to Richard Plantagenet.

The whole city was perplexed. The rumours about the princes' disappearance, which had revived on the news of the marriage oath, died down abruptly. Surely Elizabeth would not give her daughters, and advise her son to return, into the care of a man she suspected even remotely of having harmed young Edward and Richard?

Janet, whose friendship with the boys was strengthening slowly, understood glimmerings of the truth which hardened into conviction the next time she visited them and they met her at the door of their chamber with unusual excitement.

'Mistress Evershed! We have seen our mother!' Dickon burst out before the normal civilities had been completed. 'She came with King Richard, after dark, we were already in bed, she only stayed a short time'.

'Did she bring news for you? Or gifts?'

'Oh, she just wanted to see that we were being well looked after. I asked her when we could leave the Tower, it's so tedious here, but she just hugged us and said to be good and not be a nuisance and learn our lessons.'

Janet had a vivid picture of the strange reunion: two children in their night-shifts, stupid with sleep and bewildered in the flickering torchlight; two startled faces turned towards the door, little white ghosts in the darkness; the king standing aside, unobtrusive, his sober clothing merging into the shadows; Elizabeth, pausing for a moment on the threshold then swooping towards the boys in a rustle of rich mourning silk and velvet and clasping the two heads fiercely to her.

'When did she come?'

'It was about a week ago'.

Just before she made her peace with Richard. Janet found herself glancing at Edward, who was standing quietly with his usual dignity and not joining in the conversation. She was startled to see an understanding in his guarded look which suggested far more knowledge of what had really been happening than could be expected from a boy in such constrained circumstances.

Edward suddenly spoke. 'I hadn't seen her since I was three, and Dickon not for nearly a year. She looked more angry than pleased to see us, not with us I mean, with someone else. As if she was surprised that we were really here.'

Someone else? Buckingham and Henry Tydder, of course. They had told Elizabeth that her sons were dead, murdered by Richard. They had gained her support, persuaded from her the precious hand of her eldest daughter, for a lie. But if the princes had in truth been killed, she would have stayed on their side. So Buckingham, the new Constable of England, in those few days before he followed the king last summer, had both the reason and the opportunity; he was the failed assassin. He was condemned to death because he was a traitor, but Richard refused to see him before his execution because he knew that Buckingham had tried to murder his nephews.

Aware that she had been silent for too long, and frightened of letting Edward guess at her thoughts, she changed the subject by producing from her bag the sweetmeats that she had cooked for them. She did not dare to make promises on matters that were completely out of her hands, but she spoke optimistically of the future. Their enemies were defeated, the king and their mother had resolved their differences, their sisters were at court, perhaps soon they could travel to Sheriff Hutton and stay with their cousins John of Lincoln and Edward of Warwick. Her love of Yorkshire infected the boys who were soon too busy asking questions about it, through mouths stuffed with cake, to worry about anything else.

CHAPTER THREE

A year had passed since King Edward IV's death. Spring was once more creaming the hedgerows with green and white. And although she had believed it would never happen, Janet's spirits were reviving. Sometimes she was almost happy, especially when she was going to see Edward's sons. She had not yet completely won over young Ned; he was still a little on his guard against her. But she was growing fond of Dickon, a cheerful, outgoing child who accepted life as it came, and had accepted her too. The association would have to end when the lads were sent up to Yorkshire, but there they would be in the company of other children of their own age – including Janet's three nephews – and she knew that it would be her loss and not theirs.

She was pleased for her father, who had, as he predicted, been elected Lord Mayor. He had received the news while staying with Janet for the parliamentary session, and on impulse invited her home to York for a long holiday, to take in her fortieth birthday and Corpus Christi. For years now, in London and Bruges, her business had virtually been running itself. Her junior partner Kit, who was now installed with his wife in a part of Janet's house, was well-drilled, and she had no anxieties about leaving him. Only one small pang she had – to lose any time with the princes when it was limited anyway.

But that was foolishly sentimental, and as soon as the king and queen had departed from London for the midlands, where Richard intended to make his summer headquarters, Janet also prepared to leave. Nan tended to grumble a great deal these days, and although only a few years older than her mistress acted almost like an old woman. The prospect of home, however, overcame the aches and pains she usually developed when a journey was in question, and she helped with the arrangements with quite youthful spryness. When Janet told the boys she was going, even Ned expressed regret. She promised that if she saw her nephews, the sons of John Wrangwysh, she would tell them all about their future companions.

She rode north through a drift of blossom. The wild cherry, the crab-apple, the hawthorn were particularly prolific this year, making up with a riot of beauty for a hard winter and a late spring. The countryside was fat and prosperous: well-fed peasants drove well-fed cattle to market, and contented shepherds blew their reed pipes for the indifferent ears of their contented sheep. A peaceful land which, God willing, would long flourish under the rule of King Richard. At one of the chantries where they stopped on the way, Janet said a special prayer to the Virgin for peace.

But her prayers in the chantry at Wakefield, endowed by Edward IV in memory of the brother who was killed there, were for the soul of Edward of Middleham. On the road, the tragic tidings of the death of Richard's only son had caught up with them. He had died at his birthplace, Middleham Castle in Wensleydale, at the age of eleven, his frail body unable to wage any more his lifelong battle against ill-health. His parents had been far away at Nottingham when they heard, and after that Richard called Nottingham the Castle of his Care.

Janet shed bitter tears for Richard and Anne's loss, remembering the angelic fair baby who had sat still and smiled, while Peter crawled energetically around the chamber at Middleham and chewed the rushes. Now they were both gone. Having herself lost an only son, though not so finally as they, she could comprehend a little the agony they must have been enduring. But for the king and queen, deeply though they must feel it as human beings, it was far worse.

Not only their love and their hopes had been lavished on the delicate little boy in Yorkshire, but the future of the dynasty which Richard had founded. Anne could bear no more children; Richard would not dream of putting her aside to take a more fertile wife. The loss was irreparable.

The people of Yorkshire, which the prince had never left, shared their sovereigns' grief. In an age when the death of children was an everyday occurrence, the extinction of Edward of Middleham affected them unusually. Anything close to the heart of their duke was close to theirs too.

Up in York, Thomas told Janet of the king's solitary journey with his son's corpse, from Middleham to Sheriff Hutton. Queen Anne had been so prostrated by her bereavement that she could not face the mournful pilgrimage to lay her child to his last rest. He was buried modestly in a small white tomb, in the parish church beside the great castle which commanded Gaultree Forest. It was the place where, under the guidance of John of Lincoln, he was to have grown into a king.

'His grace,' said Thomas, who had been Richard's friend all his adult life, 'is much changed.'

It was a sad homecoming for Janet, but in a house fuller than ever of children, she could not for long remain plunged in gloom. There was a little Thomas of the fourth generation running around with the authentic Wrangwysh ring to his voice. He was the elder son of Young Tom, whose busy little wife Joan was fast taking over the management of her grandfather-in-law's household. Bessie, who had at last given up producing children, had retired to the chimney-corner, and was so vast that she moved with difficulty. Only the bright twinkle of her eyes, embedded in rolls of fat, suggested that, at forty-two, she had simply taken the easy way out.

Janet was content to sit beside her, catching up on the family news and York gossip, of which as ever Bessie was a bottomless fund. They talked woman's talk, and Janet reflected how fortunate she was to have two sisters-in-law, so different and yet both so sensible, with whom she could share her purely feminine troubles.

She heard too, in the shadow of the king's tragedy, all the details of last autumn's state visit to York by Richard, Anne, and the newly-created heir to the throne. In the splendid ceremony to install his son as Prince of Wales, Richard had given his second city, and the first of his heart, almost another coronation. Perhaps York had not touched such a peak of glory since it was the capital of a kingdom itself in the days of the Vikings. Perhaps also it had been Richard's greatest moment of glory, acclaimed with rapture by the city he had made particularly his own, with his beloved wife and son by his side.

Several times, while Janet was in Micklegate, he passed through the city, en route for his fleet at Scarborough, or for diplomatic conferences in the midlands. As Lord Mayor, Thomas Wrangwysh was responsible for his reception each time, but Janet did not see him. She let the days slip by her, not worrying, as she had on her last long visit when Peter was a baby, that time was leaving her behind. She allowed the comfortable warmth of the familiar surroundings, the affection of her family, the sweetness of the flowering spring, to lap her round, and she did not struggle to free herself. Because there was nothing to hope for in the future, she had learned to live in the present.

Her fortieth birthday came, and she watched her father take the foremost role in the Corpus Christi celebrations, important and vigorous still in his sumptuous robes. The children who bobbed and babbled about her were the offspring of the brothers she had shepherded on that faraway day, in another existence, when her mother had walked with her father behind the banner of the Trinity Guild.

This time it was hard to drag herself away from York. Nothing waited for her in London except work, and a few visits to the boys in the Tower who might already be leaving for Sheriff Hutton. She postponed her departure several times, and it was early July before she rode down the gentle slope from Micklegate Bar, ululating children racing alongside her mare, until they lost their breath and had to stand and wave instead.

There was an unpleasant shock awaiting her at the Tower of London. Not only would they not let her in, but they even refused to tell her if the boys were still there. The sentries at the outer gate knew her, and were very apologetic, but they were the king's orders, they said and could not be waived for anyone. Master Brakenbury was away, and there was no one in London she could appeal to. Her old fears for the children's safety revived, but all she could do, not wanting to trouble the king in his grief, was to write to John.

Desultorily, in the heat of summer, she carried on with her work. She had not realised, until she could not see them, how much she had been counting on the boys' company to enliven her humdrum existence. Then John answered her letter with the news that the king was coming to London next month.

Janet hoped to make a personal plea to Richard for information about his nephews. But she had no need to seek an audience. One day a week after the king's arrival, she received a royal command to attend him at Westminster Palace the following evening. It was written in terms of urgency and enjoined secrecy.

The night was still and sultry, and though the windows of Richard's closet were open, no breath of air disturbed the candle flames. He was alone, but for his secretary John Kendall, and sat behind a desk covered with orderly piles of parchments and books, shading his face with one long brown hand. Janet had her father's warning that he had changed, and Margaret had told her that the queen, stricken by her son's death, was likely to follow Prince Edward to the grave. All the same she was appalled by what she saw when he looked up to greet her.

The old-young face beneath its smooth cap of brown hair had grown haggard. And in his eyes there was the terrible fatalism that had appeared in his brother's in the last months of his life. He would soldier on; in a way his hold on life, fought for from birth, was more tenacious than Edward's had been. His sense of duty, if nothing else, would make him carry on. But although by an effort of his indomitable will he might keep the Tydder at bay and continue to rule for the good of his people, he had no power against the enemy which had taken his brothers and his son, and was taking his wife. His proud puritan character could find no escape in debauchery, as Edward had done, or in any other kind of forgetfulness. He would draw away from sympathy with horror. There was nothing Janet or anybody could do for him. He would go on, without hope.

So she waited in silence for what he would say to her.

'I have called you on a matter of very serious import,' he said. 'There has been another attempt to kill my nephews.' Janet gripped her hands tightly together in her lap, her fears confirmed. 'Two of the Tower guards were stopped just outside the children's chamber. They were put to the question and confessed to being agents of Henry Tydder.'

As if in response to the name of the adventurer over the Channel, patiently laying his dark plans, a breath of turgid air from outside made the candle flames shiver suddenly. A mutter of thunder came from far away. John Kendall emerged soft-footed from his corner and closed the windows. Richard was staring down at his hands, reverting to the nervous habit of twisting the ring on his little finger. Janet said timidly, 'Why do you tell me this, your grace?'

He raised his head with a start, and brought his mind back from its baffled contemplation of his adversary's methods.

'I had intended,' he resumed with his usual briskness, 'to send the boys up to Yorkshire last month. But this latest incident makes it unsafe to move them at all. The Tydder is no Buckingham. If he fails once in his purpose, he will try again. And not cease until he has succeeded. The Tower is the most secure fortress in the land. If he can penetrate that he can enter anywhere.'

'But what has he against the children? They're only boys, and they have no power or status.' Richard lifted his shoulders.

'The Tydder has sworn to marry their sister,' he said in a dead voice. There was no need for him to explain further. If the foreign pretender would sweep aside an act of Parliament and the will of the people to clear his illegal path to the throne, the lives of two small boys would be of no consequence, even if they did happen to be his brothers-in-law. Janet felt sick.

'What will you do?' she asked the king faintly.

'Since they are no longer secure where they are, the children must be hidden. I have decided to send them abroad for a short time, until the danger of assassination or invasion is over. That is why I have called you.' He leaned towards her over the table, frowning intently into her eyes. 'I have a task to lay on you, if you are willing, Mistress Evershed.'

She knew what he was going to say before he said it.

'I wish to place my nephews in your charge. You have a house in Bruges. They can be transferred by night to your London house, and thence down river and across the Channel. There's no need for me to elaborate. You have the wit to work out the details. You will keep them in Flanders until I send word for their return.'

'What of their mother?' she said calmly. 'I couldn't take them without her consent.'

There was no question of Janet's refusing. It might mean throwing up her business schemes, breaking obligations, leaving her homeland for an indefinite period. She did not hesitate. Only one thing troubled her.

'Why have you chosen me, my lord?' He had made Elizabeth Shore do public penance as a harlot, walking barefoot through the streets of London with a lighted taper in her hand. Janet, no less, had been King Edward's concubine.

'Because I trust you,' said Richard simply. 'Many times you have shown in small services for my family that you are a woman of integrity. And, for me, in one great service.

'The children trust you too, and will go with you without fear. Indeed,' a shadowy smile passed over his worn face, 'I think young Richard will enjoy the escapade. Also, you will not be noticed. You have crossed the Channel a number of times, once, I believe, with your son. One more journey – with two young relatives, perhaps? – will pass without comment either in London or Flanders.'

He finished speaking, and silence fell again in the room. Into the hush, the thunder rolled nearer. When Janet made no move to accept, Richard said anxiously, 'If you wish, you may have time to consider. It's a heavy responsibility for a woman.'

'I will take them.' Richard nodded, as if he had not doubted it.

'Thank you.' He signed to his secretary, who went to the inner door and disappeared into the next chamber.

Kendall returned with a tall slim woman swathed, in spite of the heat, in a full-length dark mantle. Though she was nearing fifty, time had made little impression on Dame Elizabeth Grey's beauty. Her high forehead, the envy of a generation of court hopefuls, was unlined, the rouged lips still perfectly shaped. It was no wonder that she was accused in whispers of resorting to witchcraft. But Janet remembered with sharp clarity what Edward had said to her, on the evening he came back from his wife to her.

'Her passion is possession......I have never found a spark of warmth in her.' It was easy to preserve one's beauty frozen in ice.

Across King Richard's study Edward's two women confronted each other. Because of the Rose of Rouen's carelessness, the ex-queen was now demoted to an equal standing with the merchant's daughter – a lower standing, for Janet had influence and possessions and a flourishing trade. And she was going to give her sons up to her as well. The loss of her children, Janet thought, could never hurt her as the loss of Peter hurt me; because of that lack in her, though she would never have imagined it possible to feel pity in connection with Elizabeth, Janet was sorry for her.

'I apologise for keeping you waiting, Madame,' said the king, with the meticulous courtesy he used towards people he did not like. 'Mistress Evershed has consented to take your sons Edward and Richard into her care. But only if she is assured of your compliance.'

Elizabeth turned her gaze on the other woman. Adversity had done nothing to diminish her haughtiness.

'His grace has my permission.' The words fell from her coldly. She said no more. No entreaties to look after them well, no fond last messages, no good wishes for the journey. She remained drawn up proudly, her face a beautiful mask, until the king told her she could return to the Abbey. In spite of what Edward had said about her, Janet could not believe that she cared so little about the taking away of her children. It must be that she would give no hint of her feelings in such company.

After the departure of the chill presence of the former queen, Janet felt inclined to turn to the man beside her and sigh with relief. And they did exchange a glance of complete understanding, before she remembered that she was in the king's company. John Kendall had gone to conduct Elizabeth out, and Richard was leaning on his desk. A flash of lightning penetrated the black velvet of the windows, and for a second the candles were pallid imitations of light.

'There will be a storm,' the king remarked unnecessarily. He was more at ease than he had been when she came. But he returned to business at once.

'Dame Elizabeth has sworn on a splinter of the True Cross to reveal neither your identity nor your destination. She would not have known them herself if she had not agreed to the oath,' he added drily. 'The only two others in the secret are my secretary and Master Brakenbury. Can you arrange your affairs within a fortnight, mistress?'

'It is short notice, but I shall manage it.'

They discussed the technicalities of the plan rapidly. Both being of a practical turn of mind, they wasted no time. Only an hour after her arrival, Janet was ready to leave. As Richard escorted her to the door, he drew off his little finger the ring he had been playing with.

'It will be useful to pass through Ludgate at this time of night.' He said, 'And also to show at the Tower when you collect the children. Send it back if ever you are in need.'

She took it and slipped it on the fourth finger of her right hand. It was a signet ring engraved with Richard's personal cognizance, the boar. She knelt to kiss his hand, and he said with a melancholy smile, 'I am under a great obligation to you already. Instead of repaying it, I have placed myself even further in your debt.'

'There is no debt, your grace. The honour is entirely mine,' she said sincerely.

'Godspeed, Mistress Evershed. May the Blessed Virgin watch over you.' He opened the door for her, and as she curtseyed outside, another flash of lightning silhouetted his spare figure against its livid glare.

She had reached the bridge over the Fleet Ditch before the rain began, great heavy drops which flopped on to the cobblestones out of the blackness above. Urging her placid mare on to more than her usual steady pace, she rode at a fair trot through the last stretch of ill-lit Fleet Street to Lud Gatehouse. Sheltering there with the watchmen, who were fully prepared to be coarse until she displayed the king's ring to their lanterns, the solid sheet of rain soaking the streets outside cut her off finally from the strange interview in Westminster Palace. She had taken it all so rationally, with scarcely any surprise, but now it was hard to believe it had happened at all.

It was a wild plan, quite incredible, a tale out of 'Morte d'Arthur.' That could not have been she, Janet Evershed, daughter and granddaughter of practical Yorkshire tradesmen, lending herself to a scheme of such ludicrous fantasy. The close room, the squares of blue velvet in the windows, the steady light gleaming on the panelling and throwing into relief the austere face of the king, it was like an Italian painting. Something far removed from her and from everyday life.

She would make the arrangements; she would go to the appointed meeting at the Tower postern a week from now, but she could not believe that she would be met by the constable and two small charges in concealing cloaks.

Yet it all happened with remarkable smoothness. A passage to Sluys was bespoken on a cargo ship leaving before dawn on the last day of August; the household was prepared for the visit of two of Janet's young cousins from Yorkshire; and Kit was let far enough into the secret to be persuaded to hold his tongue. He and his wife were to escort Janet and the boys to Bruges. Reluctantly Janet had decided to leave Nan behind. She was loyal, and a good servant, but she was incapable of keeping a secret. And Janet needed someone experienced in charge of her London household until Kit, and later she, returned.

Only one thing marred the ease of preparation. Since coming back from York, she had been having trouble with her health. Bouts of giddiness, sudden hot flushes had slowed her down, and she frequently had to fight against groundless depression. From her gossip with Bessie, who had just been through the phase, she knew she was passing into old age. It did not worry her. After Edward's death she was quite resigned to growing old. But it was a nuisance not to be completely fit on the brink of such an important adventure.

On the morning of the meeting at the Tower, she felt dreadful and became irritated when Nan fussed round her and tried to put her back to bed. Kit looked grave, and wondered if they could postpone anything. She brushed them away, set her jaw, and took up her work.

She was still a little wobbly when, Kit in attendance, she arrived at the appointed place half an hour after curfew. Three dark shadows, one tall, two smaller, detached themselves from the greater mass of the walls, and after a quick exchange of words, a flashing of Richard's signet ring, the two smaller figures were mounted on ponies and following her down Tower Hill towards the huddled roofs of the city.

During the next week, the boys were kept as much out of view as possible, though to allay suspicion they dined with the household once or twice in the hall. Janet had endowed them with the name of Markenfield, a gentle family of Ripon which was related to hers by marriage. As the king had predicted, young Richard took to the odd situation with relish, and Edward too was grateful for the change in scenery. It was really only exchanging one place of confinement for another, however, and both were looking forward to the journey.

Edward, resigned to a temporary eclipse in foreign parts by a letter from his mother, spoke little. Janet had the impression that he thought the whole escapade, with its darkness and assumed identities, rather beneath his dignity. To try to break down the reserve which still stood between them, and was, Janet now recognised, inherited from Elizabeth Woodville, she told the children the story of their father's escape to Flanders, fourteen years before, and his perilous return to triumph, as she had heard it from John.

'When shall we return, Mistress Evershed?' was what Edward wanted to know, and she had to give him a vague answer which did not satisfy him.

They slept in her own chamber, while she bedded down on a cot in the solar. All the doors were carefully barred and chained under her personal supervision every night, and Kit was constantly on the alert. Though the danger was remote, Janet had, in her low moments, horrible visions of the all-pervading influence of Henry Tydder piercing her security and dropping slow poisons into the children's broth.

But the only scare was very innocuous. John and Margaret turned up unexpectedly one day. The boys, who were playing their favourite game of chess in the solar while Janet served in the shop, had to be hustled into the bedchamber with their chessboard before her brother and his wife could be entertained. Janet would dearly have loved to tell them her secret. It was, as King Richard had said, a heavy responsibility for a woman, even as capable as she was, and she knew that John and Margaret wished the children as well as she did herself. But she must keep silent and behave as if the trip to Flanders was on routine business, and also get rid of them before they heard about the spurious Markenfield cousins staying with her. All the same, she felt guilty of betrayal in not being frank with two of Richard's closest friends. She embraced them with particular warmth at parting to make up for it.

In the uncertain greyness before dawn, the five travellers from Walbrook slipped down to the quay at Queenhithe. The old-fashioned ship, hardly changed in design since the Conquest, lay motionless at her moorings, sails spread to the windless air, ready for the morning tide. Not until the foaming rapids of the Bridge were left behind, and the bulk of the Tower battlements, outlined against a shell-grey sky, slid smoothly past, did Janet feel safe.

She had insisted that the boys remain below in their minute cabin, until they were well on their way down river. This had led to mute resentment and vociferous protest respectively, because they had never been on a ship before, and disliked the close reek of below decks as much as they wanted to watch what was happening. But against her quiet insistence they had not held out long. Her attitude towards them was respectful, friendly, but firm. Accustomed to obey, they accepted her as their figure of authority.

So she stood at the rail astern, mounting guard over them until there was not even a slight possibility of pursuit. The shipmaster, an old acquaintance of hers, had been told that she needed a swift passage to clinch a business deal, and they were the only passengers.

The boys emerged from the bowels of the ship a little uncertainly, not acclimatized yet to its pitching in the full rush of the outgoing tide. The sun, rising from a mist over the marshes before them, stained the water with a dull copper glow. It was the first open vista the children had seen for over a year, and for a while they stood transfixed by the vast sweep of the landscape, awesome and lonely in the first level rays of the sun.

She was reminded irresistibly of Peter, gripping the rail beside her as if his life and freedom depended on it. And briefly her thoughts went back into the old well-worn channel of wondering where he was, if he was. Well, God had taken away, and in his place at her side were two more of Edward's sons, far more illustrious than her own beloved bastard. These were only lent to her, but she knew it would be too easy to build her life again around them. The maternal love which had had so short and troubled an outlet with Peter, was ready to overflow anew towards Ned and Dickon.

Janet made a silent resolve to keep a firm check on her emotions … and clutched at the rail as the world suddenly clouded about her head, and tipped sickeningly sideways. Four strong young hands steadied her, and as the mist cleared, two pairs of eyes regarded her anxiously.

'Are you unwell, mistress?' enquired Richard. They helped her to an oily coil of rope, and then stared in amazement as their elderly guardian burst into a peal of laughter in sheer relief.

CHAPTER FOUR

Their arrival in Bruges was something of an anti-climax. Prepared in advance for the visit of their mistress with two young relatives, converted for the occasion into nephews learning the trade, Janet's Flemish household received them stolidly. Nobody except Janet felt the acute sense of danger hanging over the whole enterprise, or her relief at reaching journey's end. The boys had revelled in their first sea-voyage; Edward sprang ashore at Sluys with a good colour in his normally pale cheeks; but the prospect of penning up again which faced them in Flanders dampened their spirits a little.

As they settled in, however, Janet realised that, even if she had had cause to fear pursuit, the fears were proved groundless now. Elizabeth, who depended on King Richard's charity for her subsistence and that of her family, would keep her oath; Kendall and Brakenbury were thoroughly trustworthy.

What was more, there was no one who was likely to recognise either of her charges for what they really were. Richard had never appeared much in public; his brother had grown six inches since his entry into London as king. Even in England it would take an exceptional memory and a sharp eye to place them. It would be safe, she decided, to allow the boys a reasonable amount of freedom within a short time.

PART 3: THE PRINCESS

They were acting the roles assigned to them with fair success, though she knew that Edward did not like it. But to lend colour to their story, she gave them both instruction in business, took them with her to the cloth-market, and let them attend meetings with customers. Edward took it all with an air of condescension which made some of those around defer to him and annoyed others. When Janet was not occupying him, he would not speak to the apprentice, as Richard did in fractured English and French, but sat by himself, idly moving the chessmen on his board.

He was not content. Janet could tell that he was waiting to be recalled to England, to what he considered his rightful place of authority. He was nearly fourteen; at his age King Richard had been leading soldiers to muster, Commissioner of Array and Admiral of England, and his own father had been blooded as a commander. There was a hungry anticipation in his thin face, which Janet could not hope to satisfy with talk of clients and ells of cloth. He treated her with cordial respect, but he did not confide in her.

Only once, when they had been in Bruges two months, did he ask her casually, as he and his brother bade her goodnight, 'Is there any news from England?'

She knew what he meant, and told him there was none. The light lashes flickered over his blue eyes but he left the room without saying any more.

As time went on, Janet began to wonder herself when news would come from England. The king had been very imprecise about the conditions which would ensure their return. When Henry Tydder was dealt with – what did that mean? There was no sign of movement from Brittany. The Tydder was still preparing the ground, biding his time, watching for his moment. And as long as he was at large he would have agents abroad. She should have enjoyed the company of the boys while she had it, but always they were overshadowed by this vague impatience for something to happen.

She sent Kit and his wife back to London; Kit, ambitious to enter the Livery, did not want to kick his heels overseas for long. At Christmas, she laid on lavish celebrations for the household, but wished she was keeping it in London. The carols sounded wrong in the Flemish dialect. She had had a brief note from the king, thanking her for her services, but she had to rely on infrequent letters from Margaret and her father to keep her informed of the news from home.

It was in March, just after a comet, blazing across the night sky, had brought all the citizens of Bruges into the streets to gape, that tidings came of Queen Anne's death. Her husband had watched her helplessly, growing feebler and feebler, and in the last weeks he was even denied the consolation of giving her comfort in bed. Her consumption was infectious, and the royal doctors would not let him share her chamber. Richard, man of rigid self-control, broke down and wept at her funeral. And she was not cold in her tomb at Westminster before poisonous rumours crept abroad, insinuating that the king was hot to marry his eldest niece, the lovely Lady Elizabeth. In the midst of his new grief, Richard was forced to call a meeting of city officials, and publicly deny the scandal.

Still there was no invasion. The king moved back to his Castle of Care at Nottingham, watching and waiting. John wrote that he had taken to furious bouts of hunting, a sport he had not indulged in before. In the depths of Sherwood Forest, in the countryside where he was at home, Richard must have been trying to conquer his sense of despair that all his actions and precautions were to no purpose.

The months slipped by; it was summer again. Janet fobbed off friendly entreaties from her family to come back to England with a string of excuses. Her physical being remained in Flanders, guarding the growing boys under her care, but her thoughts were over the sea straining towards the land which lay in watchfulness.

It was almost a relief when the news ran up the coastline that the Tydder was on the move, mustering a small band of Lancastrian faithfuls, and a larger band of French prison-sweepings, for the crossing to Wales. Among the indifferent Flemings, occupied with their own struggles against the tyranny of Austria, Janet relaxed. In scheming and espionage King Richard was no match for the Welsh adventurer; in open warfare the veteran of Barnet and Tewkesbury, the victor over the Scots, held a great advantage.

Only a few days after this she received another note in John Kendall's neat script. Instructions regarding your charge, it said discreetly, would follow very shortly. And underneath, scrawled in Richard's generous hand, was a reminder that his sister of Burgundy would always receive her graciously.

Then, a long and agonising silence.

In after years Janet could never quite suppress a pang of irrational guilt that she felt nothing on the morning of Monday the twenty-second of August. No presentiment of disaster disturbed the even tenor of her working day; in the evening she gave a small supper-party to celebrate the election of her journeyman Pieter Brouwer to the Mercers' Company of Bruges.

While on a reedy plain in Leicestershire, King Richard III, the Duke of Norfolk, Sir Richard Ratcliffe, Sir Robert Brakenbury, John Kendall and her brother Sir John Wrangwysh died in battle against the invader. It was said that the Lancastrian usurper was crowned on the battlefield with the dead king's circlet by Sir William Stanley, one of the trio of noblemen who had pledged their support to Richard but then by their defection brought him defeat and death. By the time the news filtered through to the commonalty in Flanders, Henry VII was in London with his foreign army, master of a stunned and unresisting country. England was given no chance to change her mind.

Fighting against the misery which threatened at any moment to engulf her in tears, Janet went to break the news to King Richard's nephews. For a brief second she thought she caught a furtive gleam of triumph in Edward's eyes, but she must have been mistaken. His expression of sorrow sounded as fervent as his brother's.

But however he might take the death of his uncle and the fall of the Plantagenet dynasty, the crisis had come to them. Whilst mourning in her heart for the loss of so many and so much that had been fine and good, Janet Evershed began immediately to consider her future, which was now inextricably bound up with that of King Edward's sons.

Of those in the secret, only she and Elizabeth Woodville remained alive. Elizabeth would soon become the king's mother-in-law, perhaps on the climb again to heights of power. What would she do about her two dispossessed sons? It depended on who would win the trial of strength between herself and King Henry – cold ambition against cold mastery. Janet had never met Henry Tydder, but she would have backed him in any fight which was not fought with steel. Yet whoever won, Elizabeth was not likely to keep her oath.

As she had had no hesitation in taking charge of the boys a year ago, so Janet did not hesitate now. She had undertaken to protect them, and whether it was from Henry Tydder or from their mother's schemes, she would continue to protect them. A few months before, in a journey up to the northern port of Amsterdam, she had passed through Delft, a small, somnolent town girdled by a river and dominated by a leaning church tower. There had been a house for sale, and with no clear purpose in view, she had opened negotiations. Now, acting with quick decision, she sent a trusted agent to Holland and completed the purchase. They needed a bolt-hole known to nobody in England, and she had chosen Delft.

In her determination she would have been quite prepared to abandon her business at once and fly, but with her native caution she made careful arrangements, and spread the story that she was going on pilgrimage to Rome to pray for her brother's soul. She planned to leave before the end of September.

There remained only to tell the boys. It was no longer any use simply ordering them to accompany her wherever she went. Edward was close on fifteen; Richard was twelve. She had always encouraged them to speak their minds, though only Richard had taken advantage of it; their relationship was such that she would have to ask them to go with her, after explaining the circumstances. She put the interview off until it could be postponed no more: they must go in a week, and they were beginning to look askance at small upsets in the daily routine. So, nervously, Janet sent for them.

They stood before her, tall slender Ned and square sturdy Dickon. Though she disliked calling them by their Christian names, the necessary public deception had long since been carried into private.

'What's happening?' Edward began. 'Are we going back to England?'

'No, Ned. We can't go back at the moment.'

'Why not? We shall be received with honour. Our sister's going to be queen.'

'It's not safe.'

Edward tossed his head, and the silky hair swung.

'You only say that because you were one of my uncle's followers. Our mother's free now and she'll make sure that we are given our rightful places.'

'Your mother was free before. And what are your rightful places, Edward?'

He hesitated, and Richard put in helpfully, 'The brothers-in-law of the king. We shall be treated as King Edward treated my lord of Suffolk and my lord Rivers.'

'But you're not yet in that position,' pointed out Janet.

'We soon shall be,' said Edward.

'How do you know?'

'Because Henry Tydder has sworn to marry Elizabeth,' Edward said impatiently, as if explaining to a backward child. Janet was irritated by his manner of knowing everything, as she had often been before.

'He might break his oath now. There are many foreign princesses who would make him a better match.'

'Why do you attribute such base intentions to him, madame?' Edward spoke almost with venom. The reference to his dead uncle Rivers had not passed unnoticed.

'Have you forgotten already that this man tried to murder you?' she cried.

'You only have my uncle's word for that,' the elder boy said scornfully.

'And I would take King Richard's word before all the world,' she snapped. She was losing her temper. This stripling had no right to question the honour of a man like Richard Plantagenet. But she controlled herself and said as quietly as she could, 'Ned, I knew your uncle from a little boy. He never told a lie. Anyway, why else should he have taken the trouble to remove you to safety?'

Edward had his answer ready.

'To get us out of the way. In case his enemies wanted to use us as leaders against him.' And it was partly true. There was perception behind that closed young face. He was glowering at her, burning and chilly, and she, temporarily at a loss, stared back. His hostility disturbed her deeply.

Then Richard, who had been watching the duel with his bright eyes, broke in.

'Madame, where do you want to take us?' She turned to him in relief.

'I'm afraid we must go away again. However much your mother may wish to help you, Henry's intentions can't have altered. And now he's king, he has more means and more authority to carry out his intentions. I've bought a house in Holland. While everyone in Bruges thinks we're on pilgrimage, we should go to Delft, and lie low.'

'And then?' Edward asked harshly.

'I can't tell, Ned,' she burst out. 'Who knows what will have happened in a few months' time? Perhaps the English will rise against the Tydder and throw him out.' She was speaking desperately now, aware that she was making no headway. 'All that matters is that you two should be alive and free to see it.'

'No,' he said flatly.

'Ned?'

'We're not going to Delft. I won't run away. I'm old enough to face what will come, and so is Dickon. If our mother sends for us, then we'll go to her. If King Henry tries to kill us – and he won't – I can handle a sword, and I always keep this dagger under my pillow.' He produced it from beneath his tunic, a delicately-chased rondel. 'I've carried it ever since we left the Tower.' He stood straight and obstinate, the deadly weapon held loosely in his hand, and it was like facing Peter across the years. She would beat in vain with reason against his independence and self-will. She knew she was defeated.

'What do you say, Dickon?'

'I'm sorry, madame,' the lad said unhappily, 'but I must stand with my brother.'

'Very well then,' Janet said quietly. 'There's no more to be said.' She sent them away, and there were tears of frustration pricking at her eyelids.

Unable to stay indoors, she went down to the bridge over the canal which ran near her house. The willows swept the surface; swans, mirrored in the dark green water, made no ripple as they glided on their mysterious and majestic errands. She leant against the parapet, watching apathetically as the swallows flickered beneath the arches and swept up into the washed blue of the sky. They would be gone soon; instinct told them when to fly away. And she must stay.

'Oh, Edward,' she sighed to her dark reflection, 'Why did you father such wilful sons?'

The battle with the boy had exhausted her, drained her of her energy. After all the strain and tension of the past months, the waiting, the crisis, the planning, the check to her schemes made her feel old, and gross, and useless. Clay and dust, creature of earth, chained to it by her own humanity. Not a spirit of the air and light, like the birds which soared thoughtlessly over her head.

She could not take the boys to Delft against their will. By consulting them she had destroyed the last trace of any unquestioning obedience they would once have given her. And although she might reason Richard round to her way of thinking, she knew Edward well enough to be sure he would not change his mind. Yet instinct told her, as it would shortly tell the swallows, that they must not stay in Bruges. The sense of threatening danger was much stronger here than it had been before they left London.

Perhaps she was selfish. Perhaps she had fallen prey to the possessiveness which she disliked so much in Elizabeth Woodville, but she feared an obsequious emissary from the ex-queen as much as a bunch of Henry's hired assassins. She drew her breath in sharply and bit her lip. Never before had she questioned her own motives. She had been sure she was right. Even in striking out on her own initiative and preparing the hideaway in Holland, she had been confident in her mind that the spirit of King Richard was approving her action, that if she told her father he would smile and give her his blessing.

Yet now ... Young Edward had led a sheltered life, but his innocence had been tempered from birth with Woodville sophistication; maybe in this case he spoke wisdom. Elizabeth was their mother. She had acted irresponsibly in the past; she had been a menace to peace in England. But she had a right to decide the fate of her children. Janet was painfully conscious of her own fierce insistence on her authority over Peter.

Quite suddenly, she was terrified. A doubt had filtered into her complacent mind and now others flooded into the breach. Had she been right in her handling of Peter? Was she, who had lost her only son through negligence and total misreading of his character, presuming to judge another woman's treatment of hers?

What then was to be done for the best? If her judgement was so faulty – or if she had lost faith in it – who else was there to decide for her? She had cut herself off from her family again, voluntarily, at the request of a king, and there was no going back on it. Once before she had done the same thing for another king, and she had never regretted that. But where was his strong arm now? She had not leaned on Edward when she had him, though he had often offered to order her life for her. Always she had refused; she would sell her independence to no man, she had told him when they were both very young.

Now, in one afternoon, her belief in her ability to stand alone was shattered. She was only a woman. The other merchant wives who had looked in disapproval on her masculine ventures were justified. In the end, it was man who was the master, and, as in love, so in life, it was the woman's part to submit to his dominance. But Edward was the only man to whom she could ever have subdued her will, and he was gone. On top of the wave of terror, a wave of loneliness swept over her.

'Edward, my love.'

She spoke aloud, without knowing it, and she was crying helplessly. She wanted to run away from everything and lose herself in the vast warmth of his embrace. The prospect of life without him that lay ahead of her was too terrible. She could not face it.

'Madame. Mistress Evershed.'

In spite of the urgency of his voice, Richard had to touch her arm before she noticed him. The colour was draining out of the sky and a cold little breeze was rustling the willows as dusk gathered beneath them. Without bothering to dry her eyes, Janet turned listlessly to face him. Her appearance made him pause, glancing at her with concern, but his errand was important.

'There's someone to see you,' he said. 'I think you should come quickly. We've been looking everywhere for you.'

Immediately Janet's despair vanished into present fear.

'Someone from England?' she asked quickly, and Richard was relieved to see the old alertness returning to his guardian's manner.

'Yes. I think so.' Then he had to run to catch her up as she set off back to the house. Had Dame Elizabeth acted already? Was this the summons she had meant to escape?

Engrossed in such anxieties, Janet's bafflement on entering her hall was doubled. No smooth-tongued messenger in Woodville livery. No threat at all. A small, dishevelled woman coated with dust, her face stained with dirt and tears, leaning against the wall in an advanced state of exhaustion. Three half-grown boys, eyes staring fearfully out of dirty masks, pressed against her, half-protecting, half-cowering. Janet's household was grouped a little distance away, completely at a loss, and Edward stood in front, a rejected tankard of ale held awkwardly in his hand.

Janet did not know who it was. Some beggar-woman and her brood? Then why had the servants let her in, instead of giving alms and sending her on her way? She had not the boldness of a beggar.

When she saw Janet, the woman broke from her refuge by the wall and stumbled towards her, falling at her feet with a dry sob.

'Janet!'

She could not believe it, but looking down into the dulled eyes, she recognised who the woman was. Her sister-in-law Margaret. And the children clustered together behind her were Janet's nephews, the orphaned sons of Sir John Wrangwysh.

CHAPTER FOUR

For a long time Margaret said nothing coherent. It was the eldest boy, ten-year-old Richard Wrangwysh, who told Janet that they had landed at Rotterdam several weeks ago, and had been wandering ever since, trying to reach Bruges. The children, she soon discovered, were upset only by their mother's distracted condition. They were thin, but no more so than normal little boys, and they were healthily tired.

They were asleep in Edward and Richard's bed, clean and with their bellies full, and still Margaret had not spoken. Despite her exhaustion, she would not rest. Some kind of nervous compulsion kept her awake, her eyes burning with a feverish glitter which was tragically different from their former sparkle. Late in the evening, when the staff were abed, she sat with Janet in her chamber, rigid against the cushions, nursing untouched a goblet of hippocras. Edward's two sons were lounging unobtrusively on the floor behind Janet's bed, keeping very still so as not to draw attention to themselves at such an advanced hour.

Janet, who had not asked her any questions, watched Margaret narrowly, and waited. The only sound was the faint crackling of the logs in the fire, especially lit for the occasion. Some horrible revelation, they all knew, was hovering over the room. The boys were holding their breath.

'They treated him as a common felon,' Margaret said into the fire in a low distant voice. 'Naked and bloody with a halter round his neck.'

It was a voice so unlike the vivacious tones which Janet remembered, so bleak with an excess of horror and grief, that she could not help shuddering. She must be raving, Janet thought. But after another long silence, Margaret went on in the same drained monotone, and her narrative was quite coherent.

'I went to Leicester with the king's army. John and I were lodged in a house by the bridge. I watched them ride out, and everyone was cheering, but the king didn't smile. He knocked his foot against the parapet of the bridge. John waved to me as he passed under the window. That was most unlike him – to wave. I'm glad he did.

'I stayed by the window all night. There was no sound. The city might have been dead.

'Then there were soldiers coming across the bridge, and at first they

·

237

were running, and unhurt. But then they were wounded, and the horses too. And one of them was in the Duke of Norfolk's lion livery, and yelling that the duke was slain. I did not believe it. Then there were men wearing Blanc Sanglier, and they came faster and faster, and more and more, and one of them stumbled on the bridge, and fell down, and did not go on. I went to help him but he didn't move and his boar was red.

'People were starting to run from the town too, with bundles, and I asked what was happening but no one would stop to tell me. A knight came in on a horse and he was shouting that the king was dead, he had seen him cut down and all his household knights round him.

'It was a magnificent charge, they said, Richard's last chance because Northumberland and the Stanleys had betrayed him. He led his best men to find the Tydder and kill him before everything was lost. And he nearly succeeded. No one could stand before his courage or his battle-axe. He carved his way through the enemy ranks and felled the standard-bearer. His men were yelling in triumph and the Welshman was white with fear, cowering behind his bodyguard'.

The light died out of Margaret's voice and she relapsed into bleakness.

'William Stanley attacked them from the rear and they were cut off and over-whelmed. Frank said the king was crying "Treason!" as he fell.'

She stopped, and Janet pondered with fresh grief the treachery that had dogged Richard's life and finally dragged him down to death.

'I knew we should have to go when John came back, so I collected our things and waited for him. He didn't come, though I watched the bridge all day. They brought the king back instead. The Tydder was at the head of them, wearing the king's circlet on his head, and the two Stanleys beside him. He has a face like a ferret and his armour was not dinted. They had stripped the king's body and flung it over a horse, with a rope round his neck. One of his heralds was riding with him, and he was crying all the time. As they crossed the bridge, the king's head struck against the parapet. His hair was stiff with blood. I couldn't see his face.

'After that I didn't know what to do. John hadn't come back. When it was dark Frank came, he had lost his helmet and his surcoat was torn. He told me that they were all dead except him, and we must go at once. So we ran away.'

That was all. The nervous energy which had sustained her suddenly evaporated, and she surrendered to her fatigue. Her eyelids drooped and she fell back against the cushions, the goblet dropping to the floor unheeded. Held in thrall by the vision of disaster which she had seen through Margaret's eyes, for a while Janet made no move.

She thought she understood now what it was that had deranged her sister-in-law. In one day, all her safe world had collapsed in bloody ruins. The master, the husband, the friends and companions who had sheltered her throughout her adult life had been swept brutally away. And it was summed up for her in the dreadful spoliation of the man she had worshipped as her lord and benefactor. It was a vision which would long haunt Janet also, made real for her by the starkness of Margaret's description. She remembered Richard's grave smile and earnest eyes, and was appalled at the ravages which fate and the cruelty of men had inflicted on them.

Helping Margaret into her bed, she drew the curtains, certain that now she would sleep. Then she retired into the little box-like ante-room to let her drowse off in peace.

It was nearly midnight. The strain and shocks of the day weighted Janet's eyelids too with lead. She took up a piece of embroidery, and dozed over it. She woke with a start at a slight noise near the door, and Edward was hesitating on the threshold. He was uncertain and nervous, quite unlike the defiant young man who had frustrated her plans in the afternoon. In the excitement of Margaret's unexpected advent, she had forgotten the depression which had come close to paralysing her will earlier in the day. To show that she bore him no malice, she smiled at Edward, and he came forward and said firmly, 'I've been talking with Dickon, and if you think it wise, we'll go to Delft with you.' She was too tired to feel more than a mild surprise.

'Why, Ned?'

He looked at the floor, blinking furiously; he had not done that in the earlier interview.

'Perhaps you're right about Henry Tydder,' he said. 'It's better to be prudent than to court danger needlessly. From Delft we can watch and plan in secret. There must be friends of my father still who will follow me.'

A new Pretender in exile. Was that how Edward saw himself? Janet's relief at his capitulation was diluted with misgivings, but she must not look too far ahead. Her first end was achieved when she had thought it quite lost. And though she risked offending him, and startling away from her this highly-strung young animal which had just offered her his confidence, she had to ask why.

'What has happened to change your mind?' she said gently.

It seemed at first that he would not answer, but then he gazed straight at her and said, defensively, 'A man who treats his fallen enemies with such dishonour is not to be trusted.'

What an extraordinary mixture of naivety and worldly-wisdom this lad was, Janet thought. She remembered the corpses of Warwick and Montagu, flung on to the floor of St Paul's at King Edward's orders, and wondered what his son would have said about that. He had a great deal to learn if he wanted to achieve his aims. And yet Janet thanked God for his idealism, instilled in him from the age of three she supposed by Anthony Woodville, the foremost champion of chivalry at the court of Edward IV; not only because it accorded with her own beliefs, but also because, in this case, it was working for her.

But although Margaret's arrival had removed one obstacle to their flight, it had presented another. Her illness was not simply weariness and grief; it was more deep-seated than that. The confession had only temporarily eased it. The feverish strength which had brought them to Bruges was all used up, and succeeded by complete lassitude and indifference. She left Janet to look after her three boys, though she had taken fanatical care about their protection en route. And she showed no sign of recovering or of making any decision.

Janet bore it for a few days, feeling only great pity for her sister-in-law; but she and her two charges were due to leave at the end of the week. One morning she met a visiting clothier from London in the cloth-market. He said it was generally rumoured that the new king had the Earl of Warwick shut up in solitary confinement in the Tower. Warwick was the only surviving son of George and Isabel. During King Richard's reign he had lived free with the other Yorkist children at Sheriff Hutton; now, though debarred from the succession by the attainder on Clarence, he was under lock and key. It might be another of the scurrilous rumours which had fogged Richard's years on the throne; nevertheless it made Janet more uneasy and eager to be gone.

There was no change in Margaret. She had no plans for the future. Tactful questioning produced only an overwhelming terror of returning to England. It had puzzled Janet that she had not, on her flight from Bosworth, gone straight to her father-in-law in York. Now she discovered it was because Margaret's ailing imagination had magnified Henry Tydder into an omnipotent tyrant, who would not only confiscate all her family's property, but murder her children and herself, and destroy anyone who dared to shelter them. No gentle reasoning would shake her conviction.

Janet told her of the pilgrimage and suggested that perhaps if she was not well enough to stay alone, the sisters in the nearby Begijnhof of St Elizabeth would look after them all. At this Margaret broke down into weak tears. Everyone despised her, she wailed, she was a leper and everyone was rejecting her, even her own family. Her sister-in-law tried to be sympathetic, but she could not abide self-pity. Only the memory of her prostration after Edward's death restrained a sharp reply.

Apparently she was fated to ride to Delft over people's bruised feelings. There was nothing for it but to tell her the truth, and try to penetrate through her indifference with the urgency of the situation. Margaret had never shown any curiosity about the two mysterious boys living with Janet, though her sons had made thorough investigations and discovered that they had a couple of unknown cousins. Nor did she show any surprise when their identities were revealed.

'I thought I knew the elder,' was all her comment, and she gave Janet the oath of secrecy without demur.

Since it was Margaret who had originally brought her and Edward's sons together, Janet was disappointed that there was no greater reaction. She had shown such warm concern for the princes' welfare in the Tower; Janet had wanted so much to share with her and John the astonishing news that she was made their guardian. And she had hoped that the same news now would shake her from her torpor. But with no spark of interest kind, merry Margaret merely assented not to hinder their escape from possible danger.

This, Janet decided, was what shocked her most about the alteration in Margaret. She had always seemed so practical, so sensible, so well able to cope with life. Yet when tragedy struck her, she had gone to pieces, as Janet knew she would never have done herself. What would have happened, Janet speculated, if Lord Lovel had not come for her in Leicester?

Margaret and her children were removed into the care of the sister superior of the Begijns, a cultured woman Janet had supplied with an embroidered altar-cloth for her convent church some years before. She promised that, besides providing material comfort for the sick Margaret, she would try to cure her with spiritual consolation.

'Your pilgrimage now must be for your brother's widow as well as for his soul's health,' she said graciously to Janet. Margaret came out of her lassitude far enough to cling feebly to Janet and implore her not to abandon her forever. Having given her reassurance, Janet left her, a little ashamed at the relief of handing her sister-in-law over to someone else.

CHAPTER FIVE

The road to Delft was clear. Nothing ominous had happened, and the day after Margaret had been delivered to the convent, the three fugitives set out. On a sharp sunny October morning they trotted over the frosty cobbles of Bruges, through the girdling walls by the Cross Gate, and set their faces to the east. Janet had purposely chosen Rome as the place of pilgrimage, because a long journey would both confuse the scent for any pursuers, and make the time of their return uncertain. With the aid of the boys, Janet had broadcast the idea that Edward was then going back to England to sign his indentures as an apprentice, and that Richard would go with him. Edward had actually entered into the spirit of the deception at last. He had an end in view, and for that he was prepared to work.

It was a happy departure. The three of them were out on the open road after long living in a crowded town. Janet's heart lightened with each mile that separated them from Bruges; Edward looked on the move as the real beginning of his adult life; Richard was happy because the others were. There was no need to hurry, but the straight flat roads, narrowing to a meeting-point at the horizon, invited fast riding. The placid hired horses responded to the unaccustomed challenge of vigorous heels in their sides, tossed up their heads and sped forward.

PART 3: THE PRINCESS

Icy air nipped the boys' ears as their hoods fell back; for the first time ever Janet heard Edward laughing aloud.

To atone for the deceit of their intended pilgrimage, they stopped at every chantry on the road to say a Paternoster and an Ave, and in each big town Janet made an offering for her brother's soul, and for the king's and all those who had fallen with him at Bosworth. Edward parted with a gold-embroidered purse in Antwerp, and Richard told Janet later that it was for King Richard.

The devotions slowed their progress, and on the second day the fair weather broke. A curtain of fine rain swept in from the North Sea, and with water gleaming dully all round them in the dykes and rivers, and the saturated air and lowering clouds above them, it seemed that the Low Countries were sinking once more beneath the ocean. They were no longer enjoying their journey. The clinging dampness permeated their thickest clothes and filled their eyes. The exhilarating directness of the roads became a depressing eternity of sameness. Only the crossing of the great river mouths by slow lumbering ferries told them they were progressing. Day after day the rain went on; the night stop was not long enough to dry their sopping garments, and they were wet through half an hour after starting again.

But as the small town of Rotterdam detached itself from the enveloping mist, the rain let up, and there was even a glimpse of a watery disc in the sky.

'It's a good omen,' said Janet, 'To welcome us to Holland.'

The boys could only raise a rather cynical grunt of laughter.

'Is it far from here to Delft?' asked Edward, who had in general remained in better spirits than the other two in his eagerness to reach their destination.

'No. We can make it before dark if we hurry.'

'Then let's hurry,' he said, 'before it rains again. I can't believe I shall ever be really dry.'

'Ned.' Janet pushed her horse alongside the elder boy as they quickened their pace. 'There's nothing to hurry for. Delft will be just like Bruges, only smaller.'

Edward shook his head, and replied in the same low voice, 'I think there's something for me in Delft.' He spoke more intimately to Janet than he ever had before, but in the pale eyes beneath the wet plastered fringe gleamed the fanaticism which she had first seen in the Tower, two years before. For a moment a coldness more icy than the clammy damp touched Janet. Then Edward threw her a disarming smile which gave him a sudden startling likeness to his father.

'At least I shan't have to learn to sew,' he said, and digging his heels into his gelding he dashed after his brother, who was already several yards ahead. Janet laughed and followed at the more staid pace of a matron.

Richard and Edward were making a race of it, splashing through the puddles and shouting insults at each other. Both were determined to be the first to sight their new haven. Richard maintained his lead, and was weaving all over the road to prevent Edward from overtaking him. The elder boy was giving a good display of horsemanship, sidling and curvetting as best he could on a hack. With a sudden spurt he sprang for the gap between Richard's horse and the grass verge. His mount caught its hoof in a drowned pothole and stumbled violently to its knees; with ineffable grace Edward sailed out of his saddle and descended in a gentle arc into the brimming dyke.

It was impossible not to laugh. Richard, in fact, already in a state of excitement, was roaring with laughter even as he pulled up and dismounted to go to his brother's aid. When Edward's head broke surface, festooned with weed and spluttering, Janet gave way to hilarity as well. The water was only waist-deep, and with four willing hands to help, the young man struggled to his feet and, weighed down by the long sodden travelling cloak, regained comparatively dry land. His dampened pride was no proof against the hysterical laughter of his companions, and soon the watery landscape resounded to the helpless mirth of the English travellers.

But when they had christened Edward King Neptune of Holland and picked the duckweed out of his hair, Richard quenched their high spirits. Edward's horse, he discovered, had cut both knees and was limping; there would be no more racing to Delft. The boys mounted together, and led the injured gelding. Soon the sun was swallowed up and it started raining again. Edward was shivering, and Delft, instead of being just over the horizon, retreated to a long way ahead.

It was dark before they reached the town, and since the sensible Dutch inhabitants were all indoors, they wandered round the streets for some time looking for their house. Janet had been there only once before, and that in daylight. The nearby landmark of the leaning church tower, known affectionately as Oude Jan, was invisible in the wet night. They found it at last, by knocking up a disgruntled clog maker, and then there was a long delay before provender and rugs could be found for the horses, and kindling for their fire. There were no servants; no one was expecting them. Secrecy left them to fend for themselves.

The boys worked with a will, but Edward was shivering so much that he could scarcely walk straight. Janet feared he had caught an ague from his ducking after vigorous exercise. She strained every muscle to light the kitchen stove, prepare hot broth, and warm the beds. Richard, who seemed none the worse for the damp journey, helped her unobtrusively to see to his brother's comfort.

After Edward had been despatched to bed he made her sit down by the stove and mulled for her some of the ale they had brought with them. She sat and sipped it, appreciating the warmth of it drying her internally as the glow of the stove dried her externally. When Richard had been out to bathe the injured horse's knees he hung their travelling garments all round the kitchen, and came to squat beside her.

'Now I'm your squire as well as Ned's,' he said, and grinned at her. Janet was suddenly reassured. Wherever Edward's wild flights of idealism might lead him, young Dickon's feet were solidly on the ground. Edward trusted his brother and even listened to him sometimes; perhaps he would be a restraining influence in the future.

The future. It seemed pleasantly far away now. Here in Delft, at the end of the world, surrounded by phlegmatic people who moved as slowly as the cows in the flat fields, and where the only things that hurried were the windmills, she could rest from worry for a while. She surrendered herself to the sensuous heat of the stove, and the silent companionship of the child beside her. Her mind, labouring for months with vague fears and practical problems, was stilled. How pleasant it would be, she thought sleepily, to retire from business and lead a life of leisure, living on the profits she had made and growing old with dignity.

There was a gentle thump on her knee, and she saw that Richard's head, brown hair curling childishly into his neck, was lolling against it. Only a few minutes before he had been the more wide awake of the two, and now he was sound asleep. Janet roused him and they went up the spiral staircase to bed.

The rain had blown away by the morning, and Delft glimmered in a pearly autumn dawn. The old house by the canal, top-heavy with its upper stories overhanging each other, was as charming as Janet remembered it from her former visit. It was small, with only one bedroom and an attic, but Janet intended to engage only one servant, and handle the business side by herself.

Edward was not well. He rose looking exhausted and more pallid than ever, and it was evident that his soaking had given him a bad cold. He was far from strong; all last winter he had suffered from colds and coughs and agues. Though he was taller than Janet, he ate too little for his age and was very thin. In the afternoon the house was straight, but Edward's cold was worse and he complained of pains in his back. Janet was conscience-stricken for having allowed him to do any carrying in the unpacking of their baggage. She made him rest, dosed him with all the remedies and possets in her travelling herb-box, and sent him to bed early. The fact that he went with complete docility was a sad contrast to his high spirits on the road.

The following day Janet kept him in bed. His cold had turned feverish and though he did not complain again, his back was clearly hurting him. At midday she sent Richard for the chirurgeon. Fortunately he was a resourceful lad, because he spoke only elementary Flemish, and the doctor a broad Dutch patois; they managed to communicate in Latin. The chirurgeon was also the local barber, whose grammar school education had been bought for him by a rich peasant father, and who had assumed gentility.

When he finally deigned to follow the English boy, he frowned portentously at the patient, muttering knowing scraps of Latin; he tried to look exceedingly wise and succeeded in looking confused. Edward's fair complexion was unnaturally flushed, and he was beginning to sweat profusely. It was a fever, the man finally pronounced, though it was not exactly an unexpected diagnosis. He bled the boy, and ordered a fire to be lit. Janet must keep him warm, bathe him frequently, and let him sweat it out.

Richard, having acted as Latin interpreter for Janet, who spoke very little, saw the chirurgeon out, and came back to the big chamber where all three of them were sleeping. It was already growing hot, and Janet was sitting on a chest drawn up beside the bed, laving Edward's hands with cold water. The younger boy's face was puckered with anxiety.

'Is there anything I can do, madame?' he whispered, though Edward was fully conscious and turning dull eyes on his brother.

'No, my dear.' Janet was quite calm, but she had taken off her coif and her hair was coming undone.

'Can I fetch fresh water – or something for you to eat?' suggested Richard, and despite scruples about giving him too many menial tasks, she accepted his offer.

By nightfall Edward was in a raging fever. Quietly Richard had relieved Janet of most of the household tasks, and she had spent much of her time with her patient. He wanted to stay up and watch with her, or take it in turns to tend his brother. But he was tired, and nursing was a woman's job, Janet told him, not a man's. So he consented to sleep in her bed behind the screen in the corner. After a wretched night, dozing and ministering to the unconscious boy in turns, she left Richard in charge and went out shopping for essential provisions. Business matters would have to wait for a few days, until Edward was better. She had no time to look for a servant.

There was no change in his condition when she returned; Richard met her bravely, but she suspected that he had been crying. The second night, Edward began to talk in his delirium, muttering disjointedly and sometimes crying out. Day and night became timeless for Janet, and she made herself a pallet on the floor beside Edward's bed. She sent for the priest from the nearby church, just in case, and he administered extreme unction in one of the boy's lucid moments.

On the third, or it might have been the fourth night of his fever, she was woken at midnight from a few hours nap, by the watchman's cry beneath the window. She trimmed the guttering candles, made up the fire, and took her place at Edward's side, sick and lightheaded with lack of sleep. His head, suffused with blood, tossed ceaselessly from side to side, the damp hair clinging in rats' tails to his face and neck. And though most of his raving was unintelligible, his unconscious agony emerged in broken phrases ... he was boiling ... he was drowning ... he was suffocating.

'Let me out! Let me out!' came again and again with heartrending anguish. Janet sponged his burning face and prayed for him.

In a brief lull, when only his laboured breathing was audible, there was a pattering behind her and Richard appeared round the screen, a cloak huddled round his naked shoulders. He crept close to her, his eyes fixed on his brother's distorted face. Without thinking, Janet put her arm round him and drew him to her, feeling the slight trembling of the young limbs beneath their thin covering. For a moment they stared at the sick boy who had once been king of England, and Richard whispered apologetically.

'I couldn't sleep. He woke me.'

She nodded, and wiped the sweat from Edward's forehead.

'I prayed to St Edward for him,' he said a little later, 'and I said Aves until I fell asleep.'

Again, she merely nodded.

For a long time they stayed in silence, crouched together, listening to Edward's broken cries and doing the small services they could for him. Richard's eyes were very heavy and eventually he drowsed against her again. There were no pleasant dreams of retirement in Janet's mind this time as she lifted him with some difficulty and put him back to bed.

When she returned, the invalid's breathing had become stertorous. His mouth was wide open, he drew his breath in great painful gasps, and his whole frame shook with the effort of forcing air into his lungs. Janet knew that the climax was near. If Edward, with God's help, could survive the next hour, he would live.

With no sensation of hope or fear Janet resumed her vigil, bound by the dim circle of fire and candlelight to the suffering child, but powerless to help him in his lonely struggle. Outside the circle the darkness was intense, like the unknown which surrounded the brief brightness of life.

The terrible gasping grew to a crescendo, and abruptly ceased. The striving body went limp under the saturated bedclothes, the contorted features dropped into their natural fine-drawn lines. As Janet reached out to feel his heartbeat, her hand almost refused to obey her. Her fingers clung to the fetid moisture of his skin. There was surely a faint throb under the thin ribs. But that was the pulse in her own wrist. She leaned closer to him, trying to catch the sound of his peaceful breathing in a healing sleep.

No. There was nothing. Edward had lost the struggle. Sluggishly, reluctantly, Janet crossed herself and folded his hands on his breast. Then she sat on by his side, gazing blankly at the quiet form resting from its long fight, by the light of the candles which had become his funeral tapers.

Telling Richard was what brought home to her the fact that Edward was dead. She had not the heart to rouse him with such tragedy, but waited until he awoke, far later than usual, to full daylight and a fresh wind blowing through the wide open windows.

'It's cold,' he said as he sat up. 'Has the fire gone out?' Then he saw Janet's face, weary and hopeless beside him, and he asked, 'Is Edward dead?'

'Yes,' she answered, and her voice came reluctantly. Speaking the words seemed to make it true. 'He died during the night.'

Richard did not flinch, but nodded slowly, as if the news only confirmed something he already knew.

'I thought he would,' he said softly. 'May I see him?'

Janet had laid him out on fresh linen, dressed in the best suit he had with him, a wine-red tunic which she had made for him last Christmas. His face was washed and his hair combed into its old sleekness. In death all resemblance to his mother's family had vanished. He was a Plantagenet, his father's son. Richard contemplated his brother for a long time without moving. Then he said, with a touch of awe, 'He's beautiful.' And he crossed himself devoutly.

Though Janet had expected no storms of grief, Richard took the death of his brother with a quietness which amazed her. He was a child ready with affection, but he had always kept his deepest feelings to himself. In a strange way, the younger boy had watched over the elder, ready to support him, quick to defend him, the anchor, as Janet had seen in Bruges, to his high-flying fancies. His devotion had been absolute, but clear-eyed. Janet had looked upon him as an ally from the beginning; and in her preoccupation with Edward's nervous self-will, she had taken him for granted.

Only in the melancholy week of Edward's last illness had she begun to appreciate him. He had taken on the household chores and message-running without being asked; he had never complained or pestered Janet, leaving her to the woman's work of nursing. Voluntarily, he had turned himself into her servant – or, as he had put it on the night of their arrival in Delft, her squire.

The washing of clouts and the humping of logs was as much part of a squire's training as knightly exercises; somehow Richard's homely frame was less ill-fitted to them than his high birth would suggest. Perhaps, like Richard of Gloucester and John Wrangwysh, he had dreamed of riding into battle at his lord's stirrup. If the dream had died with Edward, he bore it as well as he did the greater loss.

Quite naturally, Janet consulted him about the funeral arrangements. It should be a quiet ceremony, they decided, with no unnecessary ostentation. Edward Plantagenet was buried beneath the leaning tower of the old church on his saint's day, 13th October, three weeks before his fifteenth birthday. On a marble slab over his grave, they inscribed the simple words, EDWARDUS EBORACI. Only Janet Evershed and Richard of York would ever know their significance.

The funeral banquet after the requiem mass was a modest one; they knew nobody in Delft to invite, except the deaf priest and the pompous doctor. Besides, Janet's travelling reserve of money was strained by the unexpected expense. Nevertheless, they made some friends among the neighbours with a free hand-out of honey-cakes and cheap wine, and they both felt that Edward's memory had not been insulted.

But after the dispersal of the satisfied guests, and the dismissal to her attic of the young maidservant Richard had found, they were awkwardly alone with the debris of the feast. Released from the activity of the past few days, the woman and the boy were face to face with the new gap in their lives. For over two years they had been three; now they were two. They had worked side by side, partners in the relief of Edward's soul. Now they must look beyond the present.

Janet was sitting at the head of the table, her head lowered, examining the device on King Richard's ring. For some reason she could not meet the boy's gaze, though she knew he was watching her, solemn and observant, from his stool by the hearth. At last he broke the silence.

'You mustn't blame yourself.'

She started, because he was answering the feelings of guilt she only half-acknowledged to herself. When she looked at him, there was a compassion in his face which gave it an odd maturity for a twelve-year-old.

'But I do, Dickon,' she confessed. 'There was no real danger in staying in Bruges. By running away from imaginary fears I was the cause of his illness.'

Richard shook his head.

'There's danger everywhere. It was God's will that Ned should die. Besides, he came because he wanted to. He was going to gather all the Yorkist exiles here, you know.'

'I thought that was in his mind.'

'It was going to be a crusade. In memory of our father and our uncle Richard. He wanted to make amends. That reminds me.' With an abrupt change from reflection to action, Richard sprang to his feet and ran out of the room.

Janet waited for him, immobile but curious. Before long he

clattered down the stairs and came back to her, breathless and clutching two objects. One was the dagger Edward had brought from England, with its carved horn and gilt copper grip and smooth curved upper rondel. The other was a tiny, exquisite missal, bound in purple velvet and studded with amethysts. Richard held them out to her.

'The dagger was one of the last presents our father the king sent to him at Ludlow. Our uncle Richard gave him the missal. I think he would like you to have them.' He placed them in her hands and she fingered them, feeling the contrast of the hard, textured handle and the soft cover of the prayer book. These were the gifts of two men she had loved to a boy who had hardly known them. The crackling pages of the book had not been opened.

With a constriction in her throat she said 'I can't take these, Dickon. They belong to you.'

'If they do, then I give them to you.'

'But what would I do with a weapon? I'm not as warlike as Edward.' She laughed, to dispel her inclination to cry. 'You'll have to keep that'.

Reluctantly, the lad took it back and said with a rueful smile 'Neither am I.' He threw himself on the floor at her feet in the casual way he had, idly running the triangular blade in and out of its elaborately engraved leather scabbard and watching it flash in the candlelight.

'Dickon.' She started, hesitated, dreading his answer then carrying on. 'What are you going to do?'

He raised his head and looked up at her, brown eyes serious. 'Did you see the priest talking to me before we left the church?'

'Yes?'

'He was telling me that I must comfort and support my mother in her affliction.' The mistake had been understandable. The old man was deaf, and did not speak English.

'What did you answer?'

'I promised him that I would,' said Richard quietly.

He was regarding her gravely, not pushing himself forward, waiting to be accepted. This son of King Edward could almost have been a changeling, sitting there plain and brown and solid, with nothing of her lover's animated charm in him. Yet he had been born within two months of her own Peter, his father's son all through, who had rejected her and gone his own way. God had given her Richard in his place.

Then she remembered with shame the other child that she had been afraid of loving too much. In her relief, she had forgotten that they still sat at Ned's funeral feast.

Suddenly Richard flung himself at her, exclaiming 'Don't! Please don't cry!'

She found that tears were running down her face, and in answer Richard's self-control broke down. Her arms closed round him and they clung desperately together, weeping for what they had lost and what they had found.

PART 4
THE PRETENDER

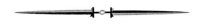

CHAPTER ONE

'The Tydder has made peace with France,' said Dickon laconically as he entered the room, throwing his thick hooded cloak on to a chest.

'Has he?' Janet put down the fabric she was embroidering with the arms of Delft for the mayor's ceremonial chair, and accepted his kiss. 'What became of his great military expedition?'

The young man perched on the edge of the table near her, swinging his foot and running his fingers through his ruffled hair.

'Oh, the army laid siege to Boulogne and King Charles gave in.'

'I suppose now the Tydder will set himself down in history as the conqueror of France,' said Janet drily. 'When your father made peace with King Louis at least he bargained from the strength of a military reputation.'

'The Flemings are very annoyed. They enjoyed stirring up trouble between the French and the English. And in Bruges they're afraid their trade will suffer.'

'Well, that doesn't affect us much now.' The previous year Janet had sold the London end of her business to her former apprentice Kit, now rising high in his livery company. 'How are Margaret and the child?'

Dickon shrugged.

'Well enough. De Gruyter is delighted to have a second son, but nothing seems to interest her very much. There's a letter for you in my saddle-bag.'

It had taken strenuous months of persuasion to alter Margaret's resolve to enter the convent permanently. Janet had reasoned and bullied, and finally provided a dowry for her sister-in-law's second marriage to a Flemish draper with a comfortable income and no children. She bore two more sons, but her spirit had died with John at Bosworth, and she merely existed, a trial to everyone who knew her.

In Delft Janet was so contented that the years seemed to fly. They had been there for seven years, and Dickon was nearly through the formal apprenticeship with her that he had entered when he was fifteen. He was invaluable to her, a diligent worker who took difficulties in his stride and showed a flair for driving a hard bargain. Most of the travelling to their headquarters in Bruges was done by him, especially in winter, while Janet remained in Holland and supplied the modest wants of the Dutch people.

She told herself sometimes that she was in danger of stagnating; but the prospect of the chimney corner which had terrified her years ago in York had ceased to be so frightening. With Dickon as her right hand, retirement looked almost inviting.

News from the outside world penetrated very slowly to Delft. With the grip of Henry Tydder on England tightening to a stranglehold, most of the news from home was depressing, and she was losing interest in it. From being for twenty-five years close to the heartbeat of English politics, Janet was marooned on a watery island where politics scarcely had any meaning. It was better than living in London, to be subjected to Henry's petty oppressions and cheeseparings, or in York, to watch the northerners wage their valiant but hopeless struggle for independence from the tyranny of London.

The north had been in a ferment ever since the York contingent arrived too late to fight for their king at Bosworth. They rose for Lambert Simnel two years later, though it was really Lord Lovel and the Earl of Lincoln they were following. But the Battle of Stoke had been a catastrophe, a brilliant gamble that failed. Lincoln was killed, Simnel humiliated out of existence, and Francis Lovel had disappeared completely. They all hoped he would appear again, gentle and smiling with his lute on his back, but he never did. The last of Richard's tight little circle from Middleham, but for the broken-hearted woman in Bruges, was gone.

The city of York fought a gallant rearguard action against the conqueror, politely blocking his unconstitutional interference with legal solidarity. The knighting of Richard York, Thomas Wrangwysh's ancient rival, after Stoke only added to the contempt of York for the Lancastrian usurper. And, still in the van of the battle, Thomas died of apoplexy after a council meeting in the Guildhall.

That was two years ago. The loss of her father had struck hard at Janet, unhappily conscious that she had never really said goodbye to him. One of his last letters had begged her again, with his usual hectoring tenderness, to come home in time for the betrothal of her goddaughter Janet, and to see the estate in the Vale of Pickering where Tom and Bessie had moved with their family. The selling of the London business a year later had broken the last link. In her heart Janet had accepted that she would never return.

What of Dickon, she sometimes wondered, for whom she had left her homeland? If he missed England, he seldom talked of it. He was the kind of person who could settle down anywhere, and not pine about the past. An easy-going young man to whom people were more important than places.

He sat on the table at his ease, apparently impervious to the chill of the large room away from the hearth. Janet was wrapped in a sheepskin cape against the draughts that seeped through the ill-fitting old casements on to her back.

'Come closer to the fire,' she invited, but he stayed where he was.

'I've been riding fast,' he said. 'I'm not cold.'

'Will it snow?'

'Yes. The snow-clouds have been chasing me all the way from Antwerp. I would never have made the journey so quickly if the wind hadn't helped me. We'll be snowed up by Christmas.'

Janet groaned and shivered at his cheerful tone, and he leaned across and grinned at her.

'Poor old lady,' he mocked. They were on far more cordial terms than most apprentices and masters; his deference to her as his senior had always been tempered by her deference to him as a nobleman. 'How is the mayor's throne progressing?' She showed him. 'It'll be the finest thing in the Town Hall,' he said. 'I have the silk for the aldermen's hoods. The quality is not as good as it should be, but London silk is hard to come by at the moment. The Dowager Duchess had just bought up all the purple in the latest shipment.' He broke off his shop talk. 'What is it?'

It still surprised her that he read her thoughts so effortlessly. The mention of Duchess Margaret had brought back to her the question that had sprung to her mind as soon as she heard about the French peace treaty.

'Is there any news of the Pretender? Surely he will have to leave France if King Charles is friends with the Tydder.'

Dickon continued to lounge, but his relaxation had vanished.

'He's in Flanders,' he said unwillingly, and he did not look at her. 'The duchess has given him a house at Termonde, and a bodyguard in Yorkist colours.'

The friendly give-and-take between them was suddenly strained, but Janet had to persist.

'Does anyone know who he is?'

'I didn't have time to listen to market place gossip,' said the young man almost sulkily. 'There are wild guesses. How can anyone know? Except him.'

'Did de Gruyter or Margaret have anything to say about him?'

'They take no interest in politics.' Clearly he did not want to talk about it. But Janet was waiting for more, and he went on grudgingly, 'de Gruyter did say that if the duchess accepted him, it was good proof that he is what he pretends to be.'

CHAPTER ONE

'What did Margaret say to that?'

'Nothing. What should she say?'

'Dickon, don't be obtuse. You know as well as I that since your mother died, Margaret is the only person on earth besides us who can be certain this man is not who he claims to be.'

'And what else can she do but keep silent?' There were traces of a scowl on his good-natured face. Then he saw a haunted look in Janet's eyes and he flushed guiltily. He slipped to his knees in front of her and took her hands. 'I am a churl,' he said contritely. 'Forgive me, madame.'

She smiled down at him sadly.

'No, no, Dickon. This concerns you more closely than anyone. You have a right to be upset, I have none. It's not me that he's impersonating.'

'They're all talking about him,' Dickon admitted. 'Flanders is full of it. He arrived from France with a train of attendants, and the duchess gave him a state reception.' He stared into the fire, biting his lip, and after a moment Janet ventured, 'Is that what worries you? That some unknown is being given the honour that belongs to you?'

Dickon shook his head emphatically.

'Let him keep his fine feathers and ceremonies. He has nothing else at present. He's living on charity; all the rest is hope and shadows.' Then he sprang to his feet, still holding Janet's hands.

'Come and see what I've brought you from Bruges.' His mood had changed abruptly back to his customary good humour. Janet yielded to his urging, and they went out together to the entrance-hall to inspect the merchandise he had unloaded from his saddle-bags. She knew she would see no further into his mind today, and she was too tactful to press him any more.

But his irritation was so uncharacteristic that it worried her, and nagged at her mind. When the mysterious young man first appeared, claiming to be Richard, Duke of York, they had talked of it, and laughed. They had expected him to be a nine days' wonder, who would posture and preen for a while, gain no credence, and disappear whence he came. It had happened before. But this one did not disappear. And Janet had noticed that, as the nine days' wonder turned into months and years, Dickon was more and more reluctant to speak of it. Jealousy was not in his nature; ambition, she had believed, was not either. Yet the unknown who had assumed his identity with growing success touched him on a raw spot. Only time would tell her what troubled him – time, and the fortunes of the Pretender.

Time was apparently on the Pretender's side. While he sat at his ease at Termonde in Flemish luxury, Western Europe stirred itself into a ferment over him. The king of France, though he had had to repudiate him publicly, was said to be still giving him covert support; Ireland was on his side; young James IV of Scotland was making eager overtures; the Emperor was reported to be interested in him. And they also said that Henry Tydder was most alarmed, and was deploying all his considerable resources to find out who the Pretender was.

Very few understood why there was such desperation in his investigations but Janet, so close to it all, was under no illusions: if the younger son of Edward IV were really still alive, the throne of England was his by Henry's own legislation. He had reinstated the legitimacy of Edward's children, but he had failed to lay his hands on the boys. Janet realised that she and Dickon should be grateful to the Pretender for attracting Henry's attention away from other searches.

What about Elizabeth Woodville? Had Henry not tried to worm the secret out of his mother-in-law before she died earlier that year? He certainly did not succeed, for if he had then she and Dickon would not be living the quiet life of merchants any more. Perhaps it was because the ex-queen's secret had been the only advantage she maintained over the new king. What dark schemes she had hatched in her beautiful, unprincipled head Janet could not know, though she had heard the strange story that Elizabeth began to intrigue with the promoters of poor young Lambert Simnel, who she knew was not one of her sons! Perhaps she was rehearsing for the return of her real sons; letting unimportant nobodies take the risks and carve a way to the English throne so that she could produce the true king like a sorcerer.

Whatever the truth was, it was certain that Henry's spies had failed him so far. Presumably driven by his failure to rather lame diplomacy, he protested to the Emperor about the honour in which the young upstart was held in his dominions.

As the furore grew, Janet found herself unable to maintain her lofty indifference to politics. She, like Henry Tydder, became anxious to find out the identity of the Pretender – for the very opposite reason. Well aware of what really happened to Edward's two sons, she wondered with increasing interest who it was that had so successfully taken in so many people. Dickon disapproved of her interest, she knew, though they rarely mentioned the subject again. She took to travelling to Bruges more frequently than she had done for years, and hoped guiltily that Dickon would not realise why.

The eldest of John and Margaret's sons had entered the service of the Dowager Duchess of Burgundy soon after their arrival in Flanders. Margaret of York was always eager to surround herself with English accents, and the recommendation of an upbringing at Middleham and Sheriff Hutton gave Sir Richard Wrangwysh an immediate entrée to her court. Whenever Janet visited her sister-in-law's big new house in Damme, she hopefully asked if her nephew were there.

Generally of course he was not, and she had to endure instead Margaret's lugubrious complaints, and her husband's unbelievably boring complacency. Margaret never smiled; Willem de Gruyter never stopped. Fortunately it was a partnership that suited them both, but it was a high price for Janet to pay for the off-chance of meeting her nephew.

Once more, as in England when Anne Neville disappeared, she had to stoop to listening to gossip. There was no Nan to help her; she had died of the sweating sickness in the same year as King Richard and young Edward had died; and no one like Nick to depend on. Thus she heard, in the market square of Bruges, some seven months after the Pretender had come to Flanders, of the Archduke Philip's reply to Henry Tydder. On behalf of his father the Emperor, he blandly disclaimed all responsibility for the Duke of York: he was being maintained by the dowager duchess, over whose actions he had no jurisdiction. The Flemings nodded over this morsel of news, savouring it with their ponderous sense of humour. Janet, who was always pleased when Henry was thwarted, smiled too, and speculated on what he would try next.

Then, returning to Bruges two months later to meet a cargo of kersey from England, she met with two strokes of good fortune. The first was that Richard Wrangwysh was at home for a week; the second was that he had joined the Pretender's train at Termonde. Dickon was luckily absent in Cambrai, discussing designs for new vestments commissioned by the bishop. Still it was with a sense of conspiracy that she invited her nephew to a tête-à-tête supper one evening.

He was elegantly dressed in a costume of black velvet and white brocade in the newest fashion, and although they were quite alone he greeted his aunt with elaborate courtesy. The manners of the court always made Janet want to laugh, especially the Burgundian court, but she managed to keep a straight face while he kissed her. His tall figure had something of the gawkiness of his father's at the same age, and the prescribed graceful flourishes sat on it a little incongruously. But the affectedness was his reaction more than anything against the rather monastic regime of Yorkshire. When they really began talking, his face fell back from its fashionable smirking into its normal dark gravity.

Sir Richard Wrangwysh was pleased to have someone to talk to. At court he was still very much a junior attendant, without noble antecedents to bolster up his reputation. His mother had lost interest in him, as she had in everything connected with her dead past; his younger brothers were also away: Jack training as a lawyer, gentle Robin at a college for novice priests. So he gladly answered the enquiries of Janet, who treated him just as she always had.

'The protocol is very tiring,' he soon found himself confiding, 'and I sometimes wonder if it's all necessary. Things were very different in England. We worked much harder, but it was not so exhausting. They don't pay much attention to military training in Flanders.'

'Not even at Termonde?'

Richard looked faintly surprised.

'No, it's just the same there.'

CHAPTER ONE

'But surely the idea is that the.....duke should invade England?'

'Oh, eventually, I suppose so,' said her nephew vaguely. 'No one speaks of it very often in practical terms.'

'What – what is he like?'

'Tall, fair, broad shouldered – a fine looking gentleman. They say he's the image of his father when he was young.'

Janet only just swallowed in time the protest that had risen to her lips. The true Duke of York was only of middle height, dark, and not in the least like his father. But Richard had not seen him before he assumed a Wrangwysh identity, and he could not know that.

'And does he behave like a prince?'

'Oh, yes! He's most regal and condescending.'

'And to you, who are English like him, he must be especially kind.'

'No, to tell the truth, madame, he has never taken much notice of me.' Richard was a little shamefaced. 'When her grace assigned me to his service she suggested that I might know him from when we were boys at King Edward's court. I told her respectfully that I had never met him because of my living in the north, and she said that at any rate we were of an age and spoke the same language.'

'And yet he showed you no favour.'

Her nephew shook his head.

'In fact,' he said, 'when I was presented he actually seemed hostile for a moment. Since then he has virtually ignored me. I can only think that he was offended by my lack of birth.'

Janet mentally raised cynical eyebrows at that, and helped him to another wing of chicken. They ate in silence for a while, and she digested the information with the meal. Made garrulous by the sympathetic listener and good food and wine, however, Richard Wrangwysh did not stay mute for long. He talked fulsomely of the privileges of living at the Court of Burgundy, and plaintively of how difficult it was to maintain oneself decently with no patrimony. Janet said she would arrange a small advance for him, and he blushed and mumbled his thanks. It was certainly a new branch of her family, Janet reflected, that could be embarrassed by the mention of money.

But her mind was running on the Pretender who looked so like

King Edward. The modest bribe, she felt, entitled her to ask another question. After steering the conversation in the right direction, she asked – and it still sounded blatant:

'Who do they say he is?'

Her nephew's frankness was veneered with several layers of polite prevarication, but his attempts to fob her off failed. He gave up and settled down to a session of backstairs gossip.

'All the servants are laying wagers,' he said. 'The chief pantler is holding the book, but I don't know when the pay-out will be. We don't have any part of that, of course,' he added hastily. 'We only talk about it.

'Most say that he's truly the Duke of York, who escaped somehow into the duchess's protection and has been lying hidden until the time was ripe. Then I heard that he was the duchess's natural son – by the Bishop of Cambrai, if you please! I suppose it's the only way they can explain her grace's inordinate interest in him. And there's a scandalous tale running round lately that he's merely the son of some petty tradesman in Tournai called Warbeck – or Osbeck.'

'But you did say - ', Janet faltered a little, not knowing quite why her throat was so tight, ' - you said he looked a Plantagenet.'

'I can't judge. He may have a look of my lord of Lincoln, who was our governor at Sheriff Hutton, but that was a long time ago. A boy's memory plays tricks. Those who know best are certain he has Plantagenet blood, even if it runs on the wrong side of the blanket. After all, there must be dozens of King Edward's bastards scattered over Europe.'

He had spoken with the worldly-wisdom of his milieu, but he immediately repented as he saw that his aunt had paled visibly.

'My dear madame, I didn't mean to offend you,' he apologised anxiously, for he had recalled Janet's relations with King Edward. 'Please take some more wine and forgive me.'

By the time he had replenished her cup, Janet was smiling at him in her normal friendly manner.

'It was nothing, Richard,' she assured him lightly. 'Just the delicate health of an ageing woman, I expect. Now sit down and stop fussing.

I'm not at all offended.' And really she had no idea what had come over her. A mad hope, leaping up suddenly at her nephew's last words, was extinguished and forgotten before she could even place what it was. Deliberately she forced her thoughts into a fresh channel.

'Have you any word from Jack in Paris?' she asked, and Richard followed her lead away from the mock-court at Termonde with some relief. He did not like to think of his healthy aunt Janet suffering from the vapours like his mother and all the tender blossoms at court.

Her curiosity, she decided, was quite satisfied. As soon as her cargo arrived, she would retreat to her refuge in Holland and resume her impartial contemplation of developments from a distance.

But the kersey did not arrive. Instead, a proclamation came from the King of England, announcing that all cargoes for the Low Countries had been impounded; Flemish merchants would be expelled from London and all trade between the two countries would cease forthwith. It was his counterstroke to Archduke Philip's refusal to repudiate the Pretender. He must have been badly frightened to cripple such a valuable economic exchange, especially as he must have foreseen the consequence. Janet lingered in Bruges, half-waiting for Dickon to return from Cambrai, half-expecting the next blow in the mercantile battle to fall at any moment.

The archduke and his council were swift to retaliate. Before many days were past, their decree was posted all over the town, and cried aloud in all the squares in English and Flemish. English merchants must wind up their business and leave the territory of the archduke as soon as possible; subjects of the Tydder king were no longer welcome in Flanders.

After hearing the decree Janet went back to her house and sat staring into space for a long time. Quite frankly, she did not know what to do. For five years she had discussed all her affairs with Dickon. She had not acted completely on her own initiative since he was old enough to be consulted. But he was away, and she was conscious that this was a problem she had to work out for herself.

Although the expulsion had been threatening for days, she had not squarely faced the fact that she and Dickon might have to leave the Netherlands. Now it had happened. Perhaps her inexplicable fascination with the Pretender had been foreshadowing just this: the casting adrift of the true Duke of York by the agency of the false one.

Where could they go? The idea of returning to England she never entertained. Rationally, of course, there was nothing to stop her setting up business again in London – or York, for that matter – with Dickon as her right hand man. No one could possibly recognise in the equable stocky twenty-year-old journeyman the bright-eyed little boy who had ridden with his father the king in royal processions, and played at hoodman-blind on the Tower battlements. But to be a subject of the man who had killed her brother, destroyed a king, and was ruling England like a usurer – that she would not even consider. It would be to betray herself, and Dickon, and the dead king.

They could go to France, or to Germany; but it was late in Janet's life to start anew, even with Dickon's help. The effort of overcoming prejudice, making contacts, winning clients, establishing a reputation, in a country where she was unknown, made her quail in imagination. Or she could retire and let Dickon do the rebuilding on his own; next year he was due to be made free in the Mercers' Mystery of Bruges – any other city would be pleased to accept such a competent and well-trained young journeyman. But that would be unfair on him, who still needed a certain amount of guidance. Besides, though Janet occasionally hankered after the quiet life of a housewife, she was well aware that it would not content her permanently until she was a good deal more senile than she felt at present.

The fact remained. As if chained to it, her thoughts constantly returned to it. They had to leave, and soon. No doubt Dickon would come back to Bruges the instant he heard the decree, but one could not break off negotiations with influential churchmen without ceremony, especially if this meant the end of the contract. By the time he arrived she must present him with a decision. As his moral guardian, and legal mistress, it was her duty.

As she faltered to a halt in her considerations, she noticed that she was rubbing her finger raw by twisting the signet ring on it. Perhaps she had caught the habit from King Richard who had given it to her. Then with the consciousness of the ring, she remembered the last letter she had received from him, written a short while before he met the Tydder at Bosworth. It lay in the next room, with his little missal, in a satinwood casket Edward had once given her.

She went into her bedchamber and took the letter out. The handwriting stood out as black and bold as the day it was written in Nottingham, the secretary's close and neat, the king's scrawling. His sister of Burgundy, the king had added, would always receive her graciously. Janet looked up at the heavy green bedhangings, embroidered with entwined Es and Js and the jennet which was her merchant's mark, not seeing them. She had never taken advantage of the king's suggestion. Almost as afraid of the duchess's ambition as she was of Elizabeth Woodville's, she had preferred to fend for herself. And when events proved that Richard's sister was tireless at stirring up trouble for the usurper, Janet thanked God for her caution.

In fact, they had never needed the kind of help Duchess Margaret could have given them – protection, money, a roof over their heads. But now things had changed. An appeal for her protection was probably the only means Janet had of remaining in Flanders. No doubt the antechambers of her residence would be crammed with Englishmen, in search of exemption from the ban through the good offices of Margaret of York. The idea of suing for royal grace contradicted all Janet's principles. With the pride of her long independence, even during the years as King Edward's mistress, Janet thoroughly disliked it.

And yet if she could bring herself to use them, she had several advantages over the common run of English merchants in the Low Countries. She knew the duchess personally: several times she had acted as envoy from Edward to his sister; she had supplied merchandise to the Burgundian court for many years. Above all, she had King Richard's ring. The cognizance of the Boar would give her an immediate entrée to the duchess's favour – and there was no need to bring Dickon into it at all.

She was roaming the room, picking things up and putting them down absently, in the restlessness of indecision. If it were for herself, she would never stoop to the course which lay so invitingly before her. She would rather starve in some alien land, she told herself dramatically, than depend on the whim of royalty for her livelihood. But it was not for herself. It was for Dickon, for the duchess's nephew, so that he should be allowed to live in peace with her.

With her! Maybe it was that old selfishness again, fearing that a removal might drive Dickon away from her. What would her father have done in like circumstances? What would Edward have advised? Clean different things, she knew. What Dickon would say she could not imagine, and could not wait to find out.

Before she came to her decision the autumn daylight had gone, and the comfortable brightness of the room's furnishings had faded to the dull colour of mud. It was past supper time, but she was not hungry. If she was to throw herself on the duchess's mercy, she must go at once, and having to beg anyone for anything always took her appetite away. A stiff-necked woman, Edward had called her playfully.

'And the older I grow, the stiffer my neck,' she said to him softly. 'All the Wrangwyshes are the same. But for the sake of your son I'll bend it a little, and even my knees, if necessary.'

Then she struck a flint to light the candles, and went down to tell her housekeeper she was leaving early in the morning.

CHAPTER TWO

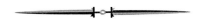

Janet was no stranger to the outer courts of the duchess's palace.
Even before she settled in the Low Countries, she had come once
or twice a year on business to her Comptroller or Keeper of the
Wardrobe. Many of her most valuable commissions came from here,
though the bills were settled rather irregularly. Yards and yards of
sumptuous velvets and satins, cloth of gold and silver tissue,
embroidered with exotic patterns and heraldic designs, had passed
through Janet's hands into those of the duchess's household. Though
the centre of government had shifted to Vienna, everyone in Flanders,
from the Dowager Duchess downwards, kept up the pretence that the
Court of Burgundy was still the brilliant focus of European culture.

But the duchess was in debt, not only to Janet Evershed, and part
of the reason was her maintenance of a separate establishment for an
extravagant young man who called himself the rightful king of England.

As Janet had anticipated, the vicinity of the palace was thronged
with Englishmen, importantly clad in their best furred robes, and trailing
retinues intended to impress. Loud English voices were raised with
the general purpose of proving that Flanders could not do without
citizens so prosperous and influential. Alone and unnoticed in her
modest black gown, Janet slipped through the milling suppliants, some

of whom had already been waiting all night, judging by the stubble which marred the proud thrust of their English jowls.

At the Comptroller's office her name was known and she was admitted, though a man looking sadly deflated was just turning away, sliding a handful of coins back into his brocaded purse. The under-comptroller received her courteously, and allowed her to wait for his superior, who appeared nearly an hour later. Janet's request for an audience with the Dowager Duchess met with a regretful but firm refusal, even when she mentioned her long business association with her and the messages she had borne from the late King Edward to her grace his sister. The duchess was much occupied, and was particularly beset at this time by many petitioners.

It was only too obvious that Janet was after the same as all the other petitioners, so she abandoned the indirect approach, and took off her finger the gold signet.

'This token was given to me by King Richard of England, whom God assoil,' she said, 'with his royal command to bring it to her grace if I was ever in need. You know the device.'

The official knew it well, and by the change in his expression Janet was sure that she had crossed the first hurdle. He showed her into his private parlour, invited her to make herself comfortable, and left her to traverse the tortuous paths of court etiquette in her favour.

She did as he asked her, and placidly munched the bread and cold mutton she had thoughtfully brought with her. If Margaret Plantagenet felt for her youngest brother an ounce of the affection she felt for her others, Janet had no cause to worry. But it was a long wait. She had inspected every inch of furnishing and embroidery in the room, and admired every corner of the Arras tapestries before a message was brought that her grace would receive Madame Evershed after she had heard Vespers.

Standing outside the doors of the duchess's presence chamber, Janet's heart was fluttering with nervousness, and her hands had gone quite cold. Ridiculous, she told herself severely. This was not even a matter of life or death. And she had had audiences – and far more than audiences – with higher than Duchess Margaret before now. It was the oppressive ceremony of life at the Burgundian court which cowed her – a kind of impersonal ritual that seemed to have been devised by an inhuman intellect.

Even the doors opened of their own accord, noiselessly swinging back to disclose the curiously immobile tableau within. It might have been an illumination from some French Book of Hours, the jewel-like colours and the stiff adoring attitudes of worshippers at the coronation of the Virgin. To walk into such a picture, and disturb such raptness, was almost sacrilegious, though the woman at the centre of the devotion was nothing more than human.

The stillness dissolved into a slight shifting and murmuring as Janet entered, and the inhabitants of the candlelit hall became individuals, posturing and rather overdressed. Approaching the duchess's dais up the long gallery she had plenty of opportunity to observe that, in spite of her finery, Margaret of York was ageing fast. The new-fangled gable headdress she wore revealed some of her sandy hair, which was flecked with pepper-and-salt. Her skin was drawing tight on her high cheekbones and long hands, as if her whole frame was drying up. But her eyes were as sharp and intelligent as ever, and there was something almost feverish in their brilliance as she turned from time to time to address a remark to the young man beside her.

He was lounging against the arm of her chair, very tall and broad-shouldered, resplendent in a dark crimson gown laced with silver, a jewelled collar round his neck. His corn-coloured hair curled smoothly on to his shoulders, framing beautiful heavy-lidded eyes and curving full lips. An almost god-like young man, though there were too many rings on his fingers. His eyes were dark blue, and held an odd expression of concentration and defiance.

Suddenly his gaze flinched and dropped away, and Janet realised that she was at the foot of the dais, and they had been staring at each other for almost the whole length of the room. Collecting herself hastily, Janet knelt before the duchess's foot, and touched her lips to the hand held out to her. On it was King Richard's boar signet, and as Janet rose Margaret drew the ring off and said, 'My brother – God give him peace – bade you come to me in distress?'

'Yes, madame. I would not have ventured to trouble your grace, but this late decree puts my future in jeopardy.'

The duchess raised her eyebrows haughtily.

'There are many more of our countrymen in the same straits. However.' She paused and leaned forward, pressing the ring into Janet's hand. 'For the sake of my royal brother's blessed memory, at least I will hear you plead your case.'

Janet rehearsed her reasons with the unvarnished eloquence she had perfected through long years of bargaining and selling. The pleading was unconscious. She could still feel the young man's eyes on her, and they were like a magnet drawing her own back to his face, from their humble resting-place somewhere below the duchess's knees. Her nerves had disappeared - the suit would succeed, because Margaret would never have seen her if she did not mean to grant it.

They were replaced by an unease far too deep for mere nervousness. She was trembling on the edge of a precipice and she did not know what lay at the bottom. The only thing she knew was that this young man, so familiar and so utterly strange, had only to reach out to touch her with a finger and she would topple over the brink. With indifference she heard the duchess's response to her speech.

'You plead well, Madame Evershed. I understand your reluctance to return to our native land. The usurper has made it fit only for serfs and sycophants to live in, and it is his vindictiveness which has placed you in your present position.' From the acid hatred in the duchess's tone, Janet guessed that vindictiveness was not confined to Welsh usurpers. She saw that Margaret had moved her left hand slightly, so it lay over that of the young man on the arm of her chair.

It was this tiny gesture of protectiveness that forced enlightenment on the stubborn ignorance she had clung to unconsciously since she first saw him. This then was the Pretender, who was so like King Edward at the same age, and behaved with true majesty of manner.

'Since you have served my family so well for many years, and since my brother the late King Richard speaks on your behalf, your petition is granted. I shall intercede with my grandson the archduke, and I have no doubt that he will graciously exempt you from this decree.'

CHAPTER TWO

Kneeling again, Janet expressed her gratitude in the well-worn phrases which came to her lips without thought. What had seemed to her on the way to the palace a matter of great importance had ceased to interest her. Dickon, for whose sake she had come, was far from her mind. She had not thought of him since she entered the room.

She was not the only one who had lost interest in the outcome of the interview. The Dowager Duchess's attention was back on her companion, and she was looking at him with such intimacy that Janet felt guilty of eavesdropping. She rose to go, and as she did so she could not help seeing the glance of veiled triumph which they exchanged.

By some means or other she returned to her house in Bruges, calling on her sister-in-law in Damme on the way to tell her of the duchess's decision. She was incapable of following any logical train of thought; she could not shake off the dreamlike conviction that the whole audience had happened before, but she shied away from trying to reach an explanation for her emotions. The Pretender's face kept appearing before her with that half-mocking, half-wary expression that tantalised and infuriated her with its resemblance to someone, yet no one.

Stabling her mare, she prayed that Dickon was back from Cambrai, so they could leave for Delft and peace of mind. In his comfortably prosaic company she could forget all about what happened yesterday. Dickon was himself, neither more nor less. She could hear sounds of movement through the half-open door of her closet, and she let out her breath in relief. Thank the Blessed Virgin he was here!

The young man with the riding-cloak drooping gracefully from his shoulders was far too tall for Dickon, and in the instant when he swung round at her entrance, she knew who he was. His hair was dishevelled, and there was agitation in every line of him, but he was Edward, and George, and Will, and her son, all at once.

He bore down on her across the little room, filling it with his movement and anxiety, and seized both her hands.

'Mother, you won't betray me, will you?'

It was something she already knew, it was no surprise, and yet the shock was threatening to push her over a precipice into a deep, endless space.

'Why should I betray you, Peter?' It seemed as if another woman spoke with complete self-possession.

Her unlooked-for calm acted upon him immediately. He dropped her hands and drew back a pace, laying on the table the cloak which had nearly slipped off in his rush.

'So you did recognise me. My aunt said you hadn't, but I told her you could dissemble like an actor. It was her idea for me to be there.'

'What did she expect me to do?' asked Janet clearly and coldly. 'Denounce you before the Burgundian court as the bastard son of King Edward and a merchant's widow?'

The young man flinched, and said, controlling himself, 'If you had shown any flicker or recognition, she could have.....'

'Refused my suit' Janet cut across his hesitation. 'And so any hue and cry I cared to raise about you would be looked on as the spite of a disappointed petitioner.' He wanted to protest, but she continued contemptuously, 'And afterwards you weren't so sure and you and your aunt decided to make sure by trying a little personal pressure on me.'

'No, no!' He sounded quite alarmed. 'She doesn't know I've come. We quarrelled about you because she said you were unimportant, but I knew you wouldn't let it rest. So I enquired secretly where you lived and came to appeal to you.'

His hands, flung out towards her in a gesture of supplication, were trembling. Janet was abruptly very weary, cold, tired; as if she really didn't care any more. She moved over to her chair and sat down, not missing as she did so his involuntary, momentary stiffening at her breach of etiquette.

'I have no rights over you, Peter. You destroyed them on the day you ran away. And it doesn't interest me, what you choose to do with your life.'

He flushed with wounded pride at her indifference, but she should not have tried to hurt him. Warmth flooded into her face too, because it was not true. The lost child, the prodigal son returned from beyond hope, troubled her still.

He took advantage of her change of mood, and came close to her again. She could smell the musk on his costly clothes as he knelt at her side, and said 'It was wrong of me to run away without telling you where I was going. But I had to go. I would have gone mad if I had stayed in London.'

'Where did you go?' Curiosity overcame every other feeling for a moment.

'Nearly to my destruction,' he said, and laughed rather self-consciously. 'I stowed away, but the sailors found me and I had to give them everything I had to save myself from slavery.'

'And then?'

'Oh, I made my way to Tournai and stayed there until I went to the duchess.' Janet had the impression that he was glossing over the less glamorous part of his adventures, but in fact he had been too exhausted by the time he reached Tournai to remember much of what happened.

'You were lucky not to starve.'

'Yes. St Peter took good care of me. A worthy couple of citizens took me in.'

'The Warbecks? Or was it Osbeck?' She was beginning to relapse into sarcasm, and he could hear it.

'I nearly died,' he said quickly and querulously. 'Katherine Warbeck nursed me devotedly, and I'm very grateful to them both.' He was trying to gain her sympathy.

'I'm glad you're grateful to someone,' she said shortly. 'And the imposture idea? Where did that come from?'

'From my aunt. She told me after she took me under her protection that it was my resemblance to the Duke of Clarence which first attracted her attention. Then later, when Lincoln and Lovel bungled the Simnel rising, she thought of using me. I, after all, had true Plantagenet blood, which that baker's boy never had.'

His slighting reference to the Earl of Lincoln and Lord Lovel, men far superior to him in birth and achievement, irritated Janet intensely.

'It's because Lambert Simnel had no royal blood that he's alive today.'

'Alive? Turning the Tydder's spit! He was a low-born gull and it's all he was fit for.'

'And you. What are you fit for?'

The scorn in her voice stung him at last out of his placating attitude, and he stood up abruptly and strode away to the window. Then he turned and threw at her, 'Better than you planned for me, at any rate! Choked in cloves of cloth, and strangled by skeins of silk, and no one but dull-as-ditchwater merchants for company. What sort of life would that have been?'

'A very good life, Peter.' She answered his rhetorical question quietly. 'Hard-working, and satisfying. And more honest than living in luxury on the charity of people on whom you have no claim.'

'It will all be repaid,' he said hastily. 'I know what they say – that I'm a cadger. But we're only biding our time until our plans are ripe, then I can repay everyone threefold, as my Father did. In November, the Emperor will receive me in Vienna. When I enjoy my own again – '

'Your own?' Janet almost shrieked at him. 'You have no more right to the throne of England than I have! Have the flattery and deference turned your head? Have you really begun to forget who you are?'

'I have more right to wear the crown than Henry Tydder,' he said defensively. 'Even you won't deny, I suppose, that I'm my father's son.'

'That is not the point, Peter, and well you know it. You're not only pretending to the English throne, but to someone else's identity as well.'

He leapt forward again in excitement.

'And my claim is certainly no worse than Richard of York's, maybe better. If I'm nothing more than King Edward's bastard, then neither was he, and I was born first.'

Was Peter right? It depended, she supposed, on whether you believed the Titulus Regius declaring Elizabeth Woodville's children to be bastards, or its repeal by the usurping King Henry. Ironically, it was the repeal of the act that had opened the door to Peter's imposture, as legitimist Yorkists might support the putative Duke of York in default of a better heir. And yet that same voiding of the act should have restored Edward's son Richard to his title and his kingdom.

Dickon came back into her mind, for the first time since she had come into her room expecting him and finding instead, incredibly, Peter. Her unassuming, reliable, quiet and contented ward was everything that this beautiful, flamboyant son of hers was not.

But Peter's placing of Richard of York in the past tense had not escaped Janet. If he believed with the rest of Europe that both the princes were dead, she was not going to disabuse him of the idea.

'But doesn't your conscience trouble you at taking so much that's not yours?'

'Oh, no one will find out, I promise you,' he said airily, his confidence all restored.

'Then, if you're not afraid of men, surely you must fear the wrath of God. You haven't deceived him.'

'It's the first time I've heard that impersonation is a mortal sin.' Standing there, with his thumbs hooked in his belt, smiling insolently down at her from his great height, he was incredibly like George of Clarence. There had been a malicious tinge to George's smile of which Edward's had always remained free.

She spoke to him softly, as she had when he had been beaten at school and would not tell her why. 'Could you not have been content to lead the life of a gentleman? Her grace would have given you everything you wanted. A country estate, a place at court, probably an heiress for you to marry. Why do you have to catch at this will-o'-the-wisp which could so easily lead you to disaster?'

'Oh mother.' He sighed impatiently, but there was a certain indulgence in his tone. 'You don't change, do you? You never did understand. Only a half-wit would disdain the rungs of a ladder which could lead so high if they were placed under his feet.' His smiled had changed, it was Edward's not George's, his expression bold and entreating. Janet sensed the power of her son's charm reaching out to her, trying to touch her.

And suddenly, vividly before her – so vividly she could have touched him – Janet saw Edward. His great frame almost blocked out the light from the oriel window. He was appealing to her not to hate him for what he had done to his brother, to go on loving him, and she was not able to resist his plea. Now Edward was asking her to do the same for her son, his son, their son; to forgive him and go on loving him too. She couldn't change his mind or prevent his journey to possible disaster, but she could pray for his soul.

'I won't betray you'. As she spoke, she forced herself to focus on the figure in front of the window, and it was Peter again. He looked surprised, confused, as if he wasn't expecting the thing he had asked for. 'Do you trust me? Or will you have to dispose of me like one of your enemies?'

'I don't want to live with you, I don't like your life, I don't like the life you plotted out for me. But yes, I suppose, I trust you, Mother.'

He stared at her for a moment, pulling himself tall again and trying to recover his confidence and arrogance. Then, catching up his cloak and throwing it round his shoulders, he turned and ran out, the elegant cloak swirling round the newel-post of the staircase. The click of his riding-boots on the wooden stairs grew fainter. The draught from the slamming door rattled the window frame. He was gone.

Janet did not know for how long she had stared at the empty doorway, but she only had the strength to sink into her chair and sit there, unmoving. She wanted to cry, but she wasn't sure there was anything to cry about.

Was this certainty worse, or better, than the endless treadmill of speculations that had obsessed her since Peter's disappearance? Then, behind all the dreadful alternatives, there had remained a glimmer of hope that he might return. Now, she had to live with the knowledge that he was never coming back to her. Then, she suffered the almost constant pain of wondering, regretting, blaming herself. Now, with surprising clarity, she could see that there was no point in recriminations – they had all been at fault and they were all victims of circumstance.

The son she had met again, by destiny or coincidence, was somehow a fulfilment of both her darkest fears and her brightest hopes. The grace and energy of the man he had become, his assurance and winning charm, had all been promised in the lovely baby and the handsome boy. She could not blame him for the single-minded ambition which he had inherited from his father – and, in a different form, from her. She suspected that Edward would have been unashamedly proud of him.

A kind of numbing calmness crept through her. Now there was

only one aspect of the future for her to resolve, and it was nothing to do with Peter.

After a while, she recovered sufficiently to face her household. They did not yet know whether they had to look for fresh employment or not. When their mistress walked into the workshop with red eyes and a skin like parchment, they immediately assumed the worst. But no, she said, with a fair approximation to her usual briskness, the visit to the Dowager Duchess had been exhausting and humiliating, but she had obtained her suit.

'As soon as Master Richard returns, we'll be leaving for Delft. I want a full account of all the work in hand, current sales and outstanding orders, on my desk by the morning.'

The journeyman and the apprentices cheered, and the housekeeper peered up the stairs from the kitchen with a broad grin across her fat sweaty face. They were so relieved that when she had gone they did not even grumble to each other about the extra work.

CHAPTER THREE

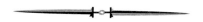

D
ickon glanced up anxiously at the sky and spurred his plodding horse into a canter. The sullen clouds were trailing the ragged hem of their skirts along the trees on the skyline, and the windmill sails were racing. It was too early in the autumn for snow, but squalls of sleet like iron filings could sweep in from the grey North Sea at any time of year. The sun never seemed to shine much here, reflected the young Englishman. Leaden skies and sheets of rain suited the expanses of waterlogged land just as fitful sunlight suited the humpy hills and winding roads in England.

Not that Dickon was homesick. His childhood in England had not been exceptionally memorable and a significant portion of it had been spent confined in sanctuary or the Tower of London. He was an adaptable person and had been perfectly content with his life in the Low Countries.

But it was not only the threatening weather which made him strain his eyes for the appearance of Bruges on the horizon. The archduke's decree expelling English traders had interrupted his smooth negotiations with the clergy of Cambrai, although they had assured him warmly that wherever Madame Evershed might go, they wished their commission to be executed as agreed. He carried in his saddlebag his own meticulous sketches of the designs for the vestments, with alterations neatly annotated. Janet would be pleased with the way he had handled it, he felt sure. Perhaps the custom might prove valuable to them in establishing a new business elsewhere.

Although he was returning with all due speed, he did not expect to be involved in any decisions about their future. In many ways he was already Janet's partner, but he observed scrupulously their mistress-apprentice contract, and was happy to leave major considerations to her unless she asked for his advice. This was an occasion when he knew she would make up her own mind. Where they went was of little importance to him.

As long as it was well away from Bruges, he admitted just to himself. He had been secretly pleased about the expulsion, because it gave him a legitimate excuse to turn his back on the problem which had been plaguing him for over a year.

He was not usually given to introspection - he had the gift of taking life as it came, and making the best of whatever did come. But the matter of the Pretender was different. That aroused his conscience and made him examine his own motives as he had never needed to before. It was not the imposter's runaway success that disturbed him, it was his professed aims that unsettled the true Richard of York. Those aims were to rescue England from the iron grip of a usurper and to restore the Plantagenet line to its rightful throne. His brother used to talk about it endlessly, after King Richard died. Dickon would listen indulgently and patiently and then, as the more practical of the two, explain the snags: they were only boys; they had no influential friends, allies or money; and their legitimacy was almost as suspect as the Tydder's. The one small consolation for Ned's death was being spared the misery of having to trail behind him in his ambitious schemes, loyal but never really wholehearted.

The trouble was that, though he had firmly declined to assume his brother's mantle at the time, he was now beginning to wonder if he had been right. He was quite open-eyed about the risks; the venture to wrest the crown from Henry Tydder was hopeless, however much loyal or moral support it might have. But perhaps he owed it to the memory of his brother, and his father and mother, to attempt it. The comfortable, well-regulated existence of a merchant-in-training began to seem too easy. None of the rest of his family had settled for obscurity and many of them had died for their rights; why should he be different?

All the solitary way to Cambrai and back again he had turned over the arguments for and against in his mind. His very pleasure in the discussions of a mercer with the civilised and cultured churchmen became a reproach. When the circular walls of Bruges came into sight, he had still reached no kind of conclusion. He was accustomed to looking at every side of a question, and there seemed to be no decisive argument to bring him down on any one side.

Nevertheless, his spirits, depressed by all the unwonted self-searching, rose at the prospect of seeing his guardian again. He resolved to put the whole affair before Janet, and ask her opinion. And no doubt she would already be packed up with a destination settled, somewhere where he could confront his dilemma without talk of the counterfeit Duke of York dinning in his ears every day.

Dickon rode over the bridge, through the huge gates of Bruges and turned left down a narrow, quiet street which led towards their house. He settled his horse in its stable himself rather than disturbing someone else and, saddlebag in hand, walked towards the front of the house. Just as he reached the door, it was suddenly flung open and a man ran out, slamming the door behind him. Dickon leapt back against the wall to avoid him, but the man stopped and stared down at him.

Dickon stared back. He had never met this person, and yet he had. It was Ned come back to life, tall, handsome, his clothes rich and fashionable, in command of the situation. Even in the sunless gloom, he had no doubt who was standing in front of him. He should have kept silent, looked the other way and waited politely for the stranger to go. It was the safe thing to do.

But for once, maybe for the first time, he did not do the sensible thing. Quietly but angrily he asked 'What are you doing here? What have you done to Mistress Evershed?'

CHAPTER THREE

'So you know who I am. And who are you to question me?'

'I am her apprentice. I live here.'

'Yes. Her apprentice.' A short pause followed. 'But I know who you really are'.

Dickon was frightened as he had not been through the fugitive years, during the travelling and the disguising and the wondering if they would be found. He saw that the man's hand was resting on his sword hilt and put his own hand under his cloak on the familiar, rough and smooth grip of the useless dagger at his side – useless because this young man, the Pretender, would have trained like Ned to be a knight, a warrior, a conqueror, while he, the younger son of a King, had not.

But no attack came. Instead, the tall figure said 'I know that you are not some obscure relative of your mistress. I have made enquiries, you see, and listened to what people say. You are her son. Born in secret and passed off as a cousin's child. If you want to look after your mother, you will forget that you ever saw me here.'

Dickon's thoughts were whirling round and he couldn't control them. The Pretender was Janet's son Peter. Now he understood her obsession with the false Duke of York, her strange concerns and questionings. This was his half-brother, his father's son. And Peter thought they were half-brothers too – but through their mother. Why did fate deal him this unfair blow – to take away his real brother and replace him with this imitation who was usurping his inheritance?

A ridiculous notion flickered through Dickon's mind - that he should offer Peter his dagger – Ned's dagger, a gift from a king to a future king. But he put the silly thought aside and, making a huge effort, spoke calmly and with apparent indifference: 'I have no reason to speak to anyone about this. It is no concern of mine, so long as you have done her no harm.'

'Give me your word.'

'I give you my word.'

Peter turned and strode away, disappearing round the corner, his cloak swinging and his soft leather boots making little noise on the cobbles. The street was silent and empty.

Dickon returned to the stables and waited there for a long time, organising his mind and trying to come to terms with the new situation. Did it change things? He stroked his horse, whispering quietly to it and wishing it could reply and advise him what to do. He would not tell Janet that he had seen her visitor, and she was unlikely to tell him that she had been visited.

When Dickon emerged from the stables, there was no sign of a major upheaval suggesting a permanent move, but some loaded boxes stood in the stable yard. Janet was in the counting-house next to the shop, taking her younger apprentice to task over some inaccuracy in the accounts. Dickon saluted her formally and stood waiting quietly until she had finished her business.

His own problems were pushed into the background as soon as he saw her. Her face was strained and she fumbled with the papers as if she were very tired, though only an eye as observant as Dickon's would have noticed it because she was covering up very well. He knew part of what had happened, but thought that there must have been more to shake her composure so profoundly.

Perhaps it was the decree and expulsion, though he had not thought that living in the Low Countries meant so much to her. Immediately he was remorseful about his eagerness to leave. He had never forgotten the time when he had found her down by the canal, on the day when Margaret Wrangwysh arrived. He had felt then a sharp pity for her defencelessness, the more so because he had always known her as the capable defender. Whereas before that incident he had only been able to take from her, he had realised in that moment that he had something to give in return. It was only a twelve-year-old's childish instinct, not properly understood, but it had shaped his attitude to her from that day to this. And if he should decide to declare himself the true Duke of York, the give-and-take of their life together would be the first thing to go. It would be to her like losing a second son.

When she had finished explaining the accounting error, she sent the Flemish lad away with the heavy ledger to put it right. As soon as they were alone, Dickon went across to her and put his arms round her. There was a weariness in the way she leant against him, and instead of letting her go he went on holding her.

CHAPTER THREE

'We're going, then?' he said. 'Where?'

'Only to Delft.' He had the impression she was trying to keep her voice steady. 'I went to the Dowager Duchess and petitioned her to stay.'

Now it was Dickon who had to hide his feelings. He was amazed that she should have done such a thing. It had never entered his head that she might resort to royal influence, so uncharacteristic was it, and he could not fathom why.

As if in answer to his unspoken question, she said 'We couldn't go back to England, Dickon.'

'No,' he agreed, though he would have been quite prepared to take his chances. But of course, it was the risk to him that she had been thinking about, and presumably for his sake she had lowered herself to begging grace of the duchess.

'Was it so humiliating, madame?' he asked sympathetically. He could see her catch at the straw he had offered her, so that she didn't have to mention the Pretender.

'Your royal aunt is not renowned for putting people at their ease. And there were many more petitioners like me.'

Dickon said lightly 'I remember the duchess visiting England when I was very young. She frightened me then, though I wouldn't have let anyone know it. She had an extraordinary capacity for making everyone around her seem small and drab. Since I was smaller than anyone else, I began with a disadvantage.'

'Yes, she has that ability still.' Janet had gratefully accepted his cooling of the atmosphere, but he was unable to suppress a sudden image of the court at Burgundy and the thought that not even Margaret of Burgundy could make Peter small and drab.

'So, by your initiative and the good graces of my aunt, we remain in Flanders!' He could see that she needed his comfort no longer and his finality meant that the subject was closed between them. He hugged her again and released her, strolling over to the table and running his finger down the outstanding orders.

'Well, Dickon, what of Cambrai?' she asked impatiently.

He looked up at her with a smile.

'The bishopric is at your feet, madame. Their lordships liked the sample you sent so well that I think they would have paid double just to keep your services.'

'Oh, come, Dickon. The designs are yours, so you deserve as much credit as my needlework. There aren't many alterations to be made?'

'No, very few, and most of them details. I'll show you the sketches presently. But we must work fast. His grace would like them for Christmas.'

Janet gave a small cry of alarm. 'Good sooth, we'll never finish them by then! Copes and mitres and stoles as well, in less than three months?'

'Epiphany would do. But they might pay us more if we deliver for Christmas.'

Continuing to grumble, Janet began to fly around the office, gathering lists and patterns and half-finished vestments. Dickon leaned on the table, watching her with an indulgent grin. The challenge had roused her and she was herself again.

They left together for Delft a few days later. Everything was as easy as usual between them, but they were both wrapped in their own thoughts and sometimes long silences fell.

Dickon had hoped that away from the centre of things everything would work out of its own accord. Janet would be able to forget that she had ever found Peter again, and perhaps a solution to his dilemma would drop from the sky over Delft, for he knew now that he could not ask Janet for her opinion.

In their mutual desire to avoid social life, their only refuge from thought was hard work and each other's quiet company. Because they could not work all the time, they went for long walks or rides when the weather was not too bad: down the River Vliet to Delftshaven, where they saw boats being loaded with merchandise and standing out in the grey water towards the invisible sea; or to Scheveningen to watch the fishermen mending their nets, impervious to the cutting wind which came straight from the North. Janet would sometimes buy some freshly-caught herrings and take them home to cook in onion.

Janet also took to going out on her own, and Dickon used these occasions to visit the old church to pray for guidance. Once, as he was going in, he met her coming out. He felt quite guilty and said lamely that going to Cambrai had reminded him how lax he had become in his devotions. She agreed with him and said so had she, but he knew she was wondering, as she crossed herself with the holy water by the door, whether he had some secret sin to confess.

By the time of Ned's year's-mind, Dickon was no longer sure whether his sin was in doing or not doing. Every year he and Janet had contrived to be in Delft to keep the anniversary of his brother's passing and always before, the requiem had been an occasion of quiet sorrow. This year, the eighth since he died, it was different.

As usual, the two of them were the solitary witnesses as the priest in the place of the old man who buried Edward reeled off the well-worn words. But the slab of white marble with its ambiguous inscription was the focus of far more passionate prayers than those in the clergy's mouths.

Dickon tried asking the spirit of his brother who had been Edward V what he wanted him to do. But hard as he tried, he could not hear any voices which might come from heaven. The only words in his head were his own, arguing on both sides, deciding nothing.

At his side there was a little slithering sound, and Dickon bent to pick up the rosary which had slipped from Janet's fingers. He supposed that she was praying for Peter's soul as well as Ned's, and squeezed her hand as he returned the string of beads. She smiled gently at him with down-turned eyes and then they both tried again to concentrate their minds on the Lachrymosa.

As Christmas approached, the pressure to finish the commission became so great that it took their minds off everything else. Dickon rode tirelessly between Holland and Flanders, carrying instructions and half-completed garments, leaving behind Janet who didn't seem to mind sitting up all night to finish a piece of embroidery. All the most intricate work she did herself, and Dickon was justifiably very proud of her when the bishop's vestments turned out to be particularly fine.

PART 4: THE PRETENDER

The arms of the See of Cambrai were interwoven subtly with Henry of Bergen's personal cognizance, on a background of gold and silver thread which gleamed like running water. There would be no doubt, when the Host was raised in the first Mass of Christmas Day, that the bishop himself was the celebrant.

The work was completed several days early and on a foggy day in Advent, Dickon set off to deliver it with a packhorse and the younger apprentice in his train. He had, of course, tried to persuade Janet to present the goods personally, but she had told him no, she did not feel like a long journey at this time of year, and anyway, the more Dickon's face was known in influential circles the better.

Dickon expected to be back well before Christmas Eve, but his journey was much slower than usual, and he began to wonder if Janet would be left on her own for Christmas. The roads were muddy and slippery and the rivers were in spate and difficult to cross, and they had to take enormous care that their precious cargo did not get wet or spoilt, or their horses injured. But they wrapped their cloaks more tightly round themselves against the wind and rain and rode on with as much speed as safety allowed.

It was worth the effort, for when they arrived and Dickon proudly displayed the vestments, the dignitaries of Cambrai were extremely delighted with them. They insisted he stay to receive the personal thanks of the bishop. The horses as well as their riders needed rest, warmth and food before their return journey, so he thanked them and stayed.

On the way back, the countryside looked even wetter than before, with strange light reflecting from large areas of water where before there had been fields and hedges. But the wind and rain had died down and the roads had drained a little, so they made better time and were optimistic about arriving before Christmas after all.

During the tedious hours sitting on his horse and watching the road for stones and landslip, Dickon returned yet again to his dilemma. The issue was becoming urgent, he realised. In August next year, on his twenty-first birthday, he would be admitted to the freedom of the Mercers' Company. After that, he would be committed to a mercantile career and it would be total irresponsibility to throw it all away. Besides, the Pretender had so much support now that the time must be short before he moved to invade England.

Yet still his mind swung between two extremes. Sometimes the giving up of his chosen life for a romantic folly – and a hopeless romantic folly at that – appeared utter madness. At other times, he could hardly bear the shame of his betrayal of his family.

In a case like this, mere points of procedure should not weigh, he was sure. Yet if he were to declare himself the true-born Duke of York, how was he going to prove it? He had none of the resemblance to his father which served the Pretender so well; no means of proving who he really was. Margaret of Burgundy had accepted as her nephew a boy with Plantagenet looks and would not recognise in Dickon, or would not choose to recognise, the smaller, darker infant from 18 years ago. He would not let Janet vouch for him, even should she offer, which was unlikely, and who would believe her? And the only other people who had known him when he was young were either dead, or, like his sisters, living under the rule of the usurper in England.

And would the betrayal of Janet, who had given up her homeland and dedicated her future to him, be a nearer and dearer treason than that of failing the kinsmen joined to him by an accident of birth?

So on one side were all the stern virtues of his upbringing as a nobleman; on the other, the sensible arguments and humane beliefs of his maturity. By the time they were winding their way round the waterways near Delft, the scales were still swaying unsteadily and the decision was not yet made.

Dickon arrived home in the early hours of Christmas morning and collided with Janet half-way up the spiral staircase, she running down, he running up. He lifted her off her feet and kissed her, then she hurried him to the kitchen and heated a pot over the revived kitchen stove by candlelight.

As he warmed himself with the hot soup, he explained about the difficulties of their journey; the satisfaction of the bishop and his chapter with their vestments; and how he bore home to Janet not only handsome payment, but a blessing from Henry of Bergen.

Dickon knew that Henry was one of the putative fathers of the Pretender, and he saw from the way Janet's expression changed that she had heard this, too. He added abruptly: 'Last month in Vienna, the Emperor acknowledged the Pretender as rightful king of England, Richard IV.'

'Yes, I know,' Janet answered quickly, so he said no more.

It was a small incident which, in the end, turned the scale and made Dickon's decision clear. On a glancing blustery day in April, they had come home from praying for the soul of King Richard's son Edward, ten years since Janet had first prayed for him in the chapel on Wakefield Bridge. There was a letter from England waiting for her, written weeks back and come by way of Calais. She heard occasionally from her family; her priest brother Robert wrote, in an exquisite hand, bewailing the decline of York; Bessie sent a screed once a year, rambling and almost illegible, with a list of all the latest arrivals.

But this was from Will, who had never been known to put pen to paper except in the way of business, and Janet hardly recognised his writing. The news was bad: his only son, a promising woolman's apprentice of sixteen, had died suddenly in January just two years after his second wife Mary had passed away.

Janet had not seen her nephew since he was a child, but she knew Will, and felt for his grief which would be the worse for being kept under control. They had often talked, in the old days when Peter was small, about the emptiness of wealth and success if there were no children to inherit them. He might marry a third time and try again, but to lose a son so nearly a man, so rich in hope, was not easily mended.

Knowing none of them, Dickon kept a tactful silence. Quite frequently these days Janet talked about various brothers and nieces and nephews that meant nothing to him, and he gave her his attention politely. But this news seemed to hit her harder than it should have done; she fell into a melancholy mood and Dickon thought it better to stay with her than go out as he had intended.

The sun, striking blindingly through the thick window-panes

CHAPTER THREE

between the racing clouds, shone starkly on her face, etching out the fine lines round her eyes and mouth. Dickon admitted to himself that lately she had begun to show her years, and from seeing her hair unbound one morning, he knew it was turning grey and white.

'There was never any lack of boys among the Wrangwyshes,' she was saying. 'The line has come down, father to son, for nigh on a hundred years. My mother bore six sons and only two daughters. But poor Will has four girls and now no son to carry on his name.'

'But your other brothers have sons,' Dickon suggested.

'Oh, yes ... yes ... but it's Will who is really my father's heir. Tom's become a landowner, John's boys are far from Yorkshire, and Dick is struggling. Father always trusted Will most.'

The sun went behind a cloud, and Janet leant forward earnestly. As the shadows played across her face, Dickon saw again the handsome, attractive woman that his father had loved for so many years.

'You must marry soon, Dickon. Your family has lost so much – we couldn't save your brother and it's on your shoulders now. I know it's the custom for men to establish themselves in the livery before taking wives, but you have no need to be bound by convention. My name is good enough. I'll help you – if you give me leave – and you shall have the house in Bruges. It's big enough for a family. For the sake of King Edward and King Richard, Dickon.'

Floundering after her in her ramblings, Dickon was suddenly in clear water. She was not just thinking of her brother's loss, and the losses of the family of York. It was herself she was speaking of, herself and the loss, though not through death, of her only son. Peter might marry, if God spared him from the dangers of his enterprise, he might raise sons, but Janet would never know them or tell them stories of their great-grandfather the Mayor of York.

And then he knew, with perfect clarity, what he had to do. His dead ancestors had no claim on him any longer. His debt to those who had given him life would be paid by giving life to their descendants, no more. He had no genius like his father, nor the total commitment to a cause that his uncle Richard had possessed and his brother Ned would have developed. He had no natural talent to rule; no ambition to be King Richard IV. The ghosts of the Plantagenets would give him small thanks for bringing their line to an end with an inglorious rebellion.

He would stay, and support Janet as he had promised to the well-meaning old priest at Ned's funeral. He would fill her house with children that she could love as her own grandsons and granddaughters.

His path was so straight before him now that he doubted whether he had ever really seriously considered the alternative. The next time he went to Confession he would burn a candle to St Edward, to placate his father and his brother; though he thought that his father, who had loved Janet and asked her to take care of his sons, would understand.

He had been silent for quite a while and he realised that Janet was staring at him with a doubtful, anxious, fixed look.

'You never cease to astonish me, Madame Evershed,' he said, mocking the unhappy expression. 'I never heard before of a woman who was eager to share the keys of her house with another.' And he went on grinning at her until the rigidity left her face and was replaced with an amused look, eyebrows raised.

'Only because I have two houses, Dickon,' she replied.

EPILOGUE

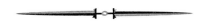

FREEDOM

They were out in the narrow stable which they shared with the retired clog-maker next door, admiring Dickon's new gelding. It was a present from Janet to mark his twenty-first birthday and his election to the Freedom. He was still scolding her for spending so much money on him.

'I have enough money to buy you a gift without depleting our capital,' she excused herself, 'and of course I embroidered the saddle cloth myself.'

'I shall have to become mayor, with a mount and a saddle so beautiful,' Dickon said sincerely. He ran his hand along the smooth flank, and the horse whinnied softly. With his arm round the animal's neck, he turned back to the woman leaning against the half-door, dark against the westering sun.

She had been happier lately, though she did not like his going away, and was reluctant to leave Delft. She approved his choice of future wife - Mary Chichestre from Cambrai, whose fearsome mother was a distant cousin of the Dukes of Norfolk and whose father was a wealthy Stapler, a committed Yorkist who preferred life in the Low

Countries to going back to Henry VII's England. She would be given a good dowry. Not, of course, that that was Dickon's reason for choosing her. He smiled to himself as he thought of her young, uncertain face with intelligent eyes and that sudden piercing smile.

But his contentment wavered as his thoughts returned again to Janet. There was a waiting about her, a hidden suspense when she looked at him, which Dickon did not understand and which troubled him.

Today he hoped it would disappear, with his attainment of the honour she had worked so hard to give him. He had taken up apprenticeship with her of his own free will, though she might still be wondering if he had had second thoughts. Of course, he said to himself, why have I been such a fool? It is her uncertainty about my real aims which is making her anxious.

'A while ago,' he said casually, 'it was in my mind to declare myself to my Aunt the Dowager Duchess.' Janet was a shadowy figure against the golden light so he could not see her expression properly, but her whole figure stiffened. She said nothing.

'I decided not to.'

'Why, Dickon?'

'Because I couldn't see any way of proving who I was.' His tone was light, but his face said all the things that his words did not.

Janet just nodded. But he could see her dark outline becoming taller and softer, the tension flowing away, and he was sure that she was smiling. They went in together, arm in arm, to dress for his celebration supper.

- The End -

SONS OF YORK

EDITORS' NOTE

This book is the second volume of 'Sprigs of Broom'. Chronologically, it starts at about the same time as The White Queen of Middleham – when Yorkist fortunes were in the ascendant - but continues on past the death of Anne Neville to the Battle of Bosworth and the dramatic events that followed. Lesley Nickell actually wrote Sons of York first, fascinated by the character of Edward IV and the continuing mystery of what happened to his sons, the 'Princes in the Tower'. It was while researching for this that she also found herself drawn to the enigmatic characters of Richard III and his wife.

Lesley died before the publication of this and the third volume, Perkin. As Sons of York was originally written as a stand-alone historical novel, it was necessary to edit it for consistency as part of this trilogy. We wish she could have edited it herself, but we hope that she approves of what we have done.

She did not write a historical note for Sons of York, but her note published at the back of The White Queen of Middleham is very relevant to this story as well. As she explained there, Janet was her own creation, but the central figure of this book is surrounded by real historical figures involved in real historical events. She fits in like a missing piece in a jigsaw. Janet Evershed might not have existed; and yet we sometimes wonder if one day, as we admire some richly-embroidered bedhangings in a stately home, we will suddenly notice entwined Es and Js.

Rosalind Winter, Chipping Campden, Gloucestershire
Tricia Callow, Minchinhampton, Gloucestershire
August 2015

ND - #0462 - 270225 - C0 - 203/127/25 - PB - 9781861514608 - Matt Lamination